The final book in The Boy

THOUGHT BOYBANDS WERE
ALL MURDERED ... THEY'RE

NOT

HOW TO MURDER
A BOYBAND

JASON ROCHE

CRANTHORPE
MILLNER

First published by Cranthorpe Millner Publishers (2022)

ISBN 978-1-80378-098-6 (Paperback)

www.cranthorpemillner.com

Cranthorpe Millner Publishers

For my sister,

Leanne VI

*Chapter 1*

Let's get straight to the point. Boybands have changed. I mean not in what they wear or the music they produce but in their spiritual significance to this generation. Is it really time for a comeback? Or a Nutribullet blend of haphazard 'talent'? Am I back and is there a Big Fat Arse blocking the path … no, he's dead and buried. And rest assured there will be no Shyamalan twist at the end where I turn out to be a reincarnated Paton or his illegitimate daughter (oh by the way I'm a woman). But Boybands have changed. They've cleaned up to the point where they are likeable; they're relevant and their tunes are half decent. Cue villainous chuckle. But it is difficult to absolutely abhor them like Paton did; like Paton's generation did. The past naff quota has been replaced either with elderly dignity or fresh disadvantaged background dun-good sympathy: 'They're nice lads!'

So what I'm about to tell you will come across ever the more shocking, ever the more trend-busting, ever the more deeeeeeep. What is the actual formula to NOT Murder a Boyband? I studied the life, times, work, woes and deeds of Paton Stipps and his inadvertent protégés to understand how an ordinary person goes from humdrum to murdering a Boyband according to each of their infamous traits.

I'm dating one. He made me tea and a healthy breakfast this morning – quinoa with blackberries, papaya and sweet avocado. Not overdone but with a flower laid beside the dish; a relevant flower. Just nice. And wholesome. They don't do the things they used to do, don't try get away with the things they used to. At their core they are performers, not musicians but entertainers destined to fulfil both an empty aging has-been generation and a clueless, naïve 'we know better than all of you by the age of twelve' generation. The breakfast is good. We're not messing with the natural health regime at this stage. The life of a celebrity Boybander still has limits: if the paps snap a pic of either me or him with an unsightly roll undershirt peeping it impacts attention, likes, follows, favourites and most of all sales.

I'm up, not so reluctantly now that the breakfast is consumed (he followed up with an almond milk espresso), showered, spotless and off to work. Well, it's not really work, it's a pastime hobby passion that luckily pays the bills and some. And I won't lie – it has all changed since I became affiliated to the Boyband but then let me compound the non-lying and be honest by saying that it hasn't changed me or the roles I'm accepting. The theatre is too often misunderstood and the natural springboard for English-accented thespians to high-budget American television or the

Superhero conglomerate machine that is really twenty years too late. And the offers are eyewatering but prancing around in a nipple hugging painted on suit shooting arrows so a male Superhero gets all the 'classic dude' one-liners is hardly the route that years of acting school bludgeoned me towards. Plus let's be candid about money … more of it just means more hassle in looking after it and making sure someone else isn't about to relieve you of it like extracting a sneeze with cat fur. Sufficient is as the word states: sufficient. No more required. Enough to be happy on and not worry about the next breakfast quinoa with blackberries, papaya and sweet avocado.

So of course yours and every obsessed fan's mind will tumble past the gutter, directly down the descending bowling alley, through the depths of depravity, into Satan's mouth and burst out his arsehole into the 'it' gutter, so I'll answer it now – no we haven't and there is no talk of it on the horizon, just past the horizon or on the next horizon once the journey across the plains between the two horizons is complete. Fucking is a bit gross for one and for two it will not only jeopardise his career but mine, all that sordid kiss and tell malarkey splattered all over the tabloids or from the mouths of the peripheral hanger-oners. It not all about the base, Meghan.

I mean I do have friends who do and jeepers do they tell but it comes as part of them, like a person who smells funny will always smell funny and folk just come to accept this rather than judge: acclimating to a girl who is comfortable being at the end of multiple ends. This is probably a good

3

time to tell you about my circle of friends: there are seven of them plus me which probably makes you go, "But there are always three or five but never seven; it doesn't make sense because loyalty and strength of relationship doesn't exist in such a group – you're just acquaintances really aren't you?" But no. We're tight. So tight that even if I was to kiss and tell them it would be safer than a sworn affidavit in front of a high court judge with a man with no tongue.

Friendships that go beyond friendship are not bound by what you believe you have in common or honesty or selflessness or spiritual connection or anything you formed on a last season social media platform (in fact all social media is now last season) but rather a common purpose and a sense of shared travail; a bind perhaps stronger than familial: conjoined twins so that there are no metaphorical ropes between you but actual skin where the only way to separate is to actually tear, cut or scythe flesh. An image a bit too Sky Horror for this time of the morning, sorry, but hey what the fuck is a girl to do when showing some real love for her sister. Or sisters more precisely. Seven hairless (bar one), hapless (bar three), hopeful, harmful, hedonistic (bar four), healthy (bar two) heroines.

All of whom are dating a Boyband.

# Chapter 2

# DANIELLE

Danielle had a weight problem when I met her. She knew she did and didn't really care because she was so stunning on the outside and in; it didn't really make a dandelion flake of a difference that she was carrying a few extra pounds. But we did meet at the gym which meant I got suckered early on into protein shakes, fasted cardio and thermal fat burners. I would partake in a supportive sister role rather than believing they actually did anything. Plus I eat like a demon horse so anyone coming between me and a million flavours of curry, Doritos and Domino's risks literally losing a limb or eight. Once Danielle stripped the weight off she was left with the most perfectly formed pair of breasts meaning her inner beauty got bridesmaided into second place with most of the salivating, grinning, sappy, flappy male population (of the gym-goer subspecies because they are traditionally the classic ugly headed narcissists that loiter next to sweat encrusted machines jutting out in every direction like futuristic oversized metal pinecones) forming a disorderly queue to ogle from afar and aclose while using every ounce of vein-distending effort to show those puppies that when they pump ... this shit gets real. She needed some advice on how to handle this unwavering attention and that is most likely when our sisterhood became something more: an outer shell to deflect the menfolk. So I suppose you will ask when she started dating Gerson from the Boyband Xtreme Believe but I will, of course, get to that just as the ball in a pinball machine will at some point be swallowed down the middle channel as the two levers quack helplessly astride.

Okay I lied: I'll get to it now. Gerson (pronounced Jerson) is barely legal; not helped by rosy swollen cheeks, a milky glass complexion and perfectly circular eyes that seem to only blink perfectly on cue. A few months ago in a trendy coffee retreat off Landor Road, an old (granted confused and probably a few kings and queens short of a full deck) lady mistook him for an actual genuine baby. She grabbed his cheeks, gurgled at him and even tried to pick him up to cradle. It was public so he didn't freak out – the opposite – he blushed, the paps swept in and the next day he was even more of a darling. A modern-day male baby Spice Boy.

What makes it all the more intriguing and odd and I suppose current (Google teens and mums and the teens are actually boys getting ragdolled in the air from orifice to mound) is that he models his behind-the-scenes misdeeds on Christian Grey; claims to have read all the books. Danielle, after much coercion, claims sometimes from the sheer anticipation in the lead up he passes out, wets himself and ends up screaming mum-related obscenities in his sleep for the remainder of the night.

We all have a strict osculate and delineate policy in that when we kiss we tell each other and only each other. Not the Ya-Ya Sisterhood but close. I won't confess too early that we have a Boyband performance chart (mine as n/a to the disgust of most) but here's me getting all explicit and giddy and declarative. Actually Danielle says they haven't either. When he was passed out once she whipped him just to see if he would wake and he didn't so she did some other stuff to him that I suppose he imagines Christian Greying on her. If he knew how. Training wheels first perhaps?

*Chapter 3*

# TABBY CAT

Abigail or Tabby Cat keeps us all fed. She's the mother figure always making sure our laces are tied or hair's the right way or we're not showing too much flesh. If there was a world contest of plus size stunningness Tabby would be atop the podium, large smile bat signal beaming out across the room (instantly won over), large swaying heavenly bosoms discreetly tucked into a Rigby and Peller double G Cup, welcoming all other losers as winners. And her Boybander of choice is too a plus size, the big boy of the group, always generating clutches, hugs and shoulder squeezes. Larger blokes always get touched! Like some safety net for over tactile peripherals to show they accept their largeness. If someone ever touched a skinny fella there would probably be an unnecessary incident but hugging a big boned Boybander is blatantly benign and copacetic. But there is a side to Barton we never saw coming: on a night out a clubber overheard me calling Abigail Tabby Cat to which he couldn't resist "More like Tubby Pussy" so Barton ran at the man. No, more than just ran at him. Without stopping. So that nineteen stone of Boyband sent twelve stone of annoying across a lane of trafficking cars and directly into a Domino's scooter probably going 10mph over the limit. It was deftly kept out of the press with a donation and a 'non-official' apology.

I digress. Tabby Cat just knows what we like. Not only our inner stomach cravings but just about everything. Once she bought each and every one of us the perfect doughnut and pashmina combo. It was literally perfect: each flavour and colour so respectively aligned if we had tried to improve at a donut and pashmina conference we couldn't have. Mine was hazelnut maple and peach, btw.

I don't think it is right to highlight anyone's shortcomings, let alone one of my closest girlfriends, but Tabby has a problem with balance. Not a problem, say on the freak occasion she might find herself on a crossbeam, wiggling her stuck out bottom and her bent knees take the strain before a packed Olympic auditorium. No, she just crumples. In a heap. Regularly. Unprompted. Falls over a lot. As though her world either suddenly stops spinning, an old fashioned wooden top toppling over in exhaustion, or starts spinning, an almost instantaneous whirl, whipping her eyes into a kaleidoscopic mess and sending her floorwards. At first we thought she might be faking it but after countless ENT specialist visits we started to accept the phenomenon known as Tabby's Falls. Which is perhaps why her nineteen stone safety pillar serves as such a suitable suitor.

Their relationship can get a bit, well … juvenile,

sometimes. When some small event occurs that might raise a hackle or seven, the reaction becomes the big sulk standoff at Clapham Common Creek. A year or so previously Barton was (perhaps or perhaps not) flirting with one of the backing dancers; not quite sexting, more like foreplexting. It is a bit of a barrage for these poor celebrity Boybands; take Likely L: Barton's newly formed Boyband of trendy misfits. With anything new and shiny and on a stage gyrating with more clothes off than on, distracted to impress, invariably each pelvic dance thrust will red dot a Boybander from a stage away, the snipers' targets infecting each of them like the measles. One such active shooter, Desireé from the block, managed to contaminate her contact details into Barton's phone we believe and initiated an ostensibly innocuous chat about how they both had strong central African lineage, Togo in fact. Family roots moved to physical attributes to a connection of sorts to suggestion that was somewhere between a blue room and Dawson's Creek. He was relatively open about it with Tabby too until Desireé sent her a how-to instructional video with an iPhone cable and a baby marrow. Despite Barton's pleas of innocence and harmlessness, Tabby Cat went AWOL sulk. She just would not speak to him, at all. Which seemed to in turn spark Barton's refusal to speak to her. Days, weeks, who knew how long. All we knew was neither was going to relent, to break the deadlock to forgive and forget.

So Task Team Fox Force Eight would need to slide down the pole into action, engineering a chance meeting which would permit neither to swallow and restore normal order without so much as a soupcon of humility. And it worked too, mostly short term and with the status quo remaining: "It was his / her fault." During these arms folded, unrelenting episodes, Tabby would sometimes realign with her lesbian and gay friends, usually in an overt display of solidarity such as a protest, march or demonstration. She'd go into full support mode, donning the rainbow colours fist aloft at the current injustice spawning outrage in the LGBTQX community. Barton would later joke that these allegiances never really bore fruit for him, the incessant ménage a trois hints dropped like wrapped Rolos at the feet of Gretel's witch.

"I'm not gay," she'd proclaim to him. "I just stand in solidarity with my sisters and brothers." And the more they stood off each other the more she'd shove this down his throat, never dangling any carrot of any sort yet leaving him acutely aware there was this other proud fibre to her being. When Barton hired an overtly camp assistant this further aggravated the standoffs, allowing each of the LGBTQX Tontos to whisper so many sweet relationship deaths into the respective Lone ears, that the union very nearly went into spiritual descent freefall before it had really had a proper chance to dig its nails in.

We had to hold on. This was part of the master plan. As soon as you make a Boybander feel as though you are the lucky one to be in this relationship, you've lost. Plus the type of Boybander with this entitled attitude (and there are some) were exactly not the types we were after. To create this relationship masterclass there had to be a depth, a substance to the Boybands, willing to feel and love and only sometimes use celebrity for ill-gotten gains. These gains would fall outside the relationship and, by gawd, we had some horrible false starts.

*Chapter 4*

# DEBZ

This is as good a time as any to introduce Debz (and it must be a z to remind us of her blatant unconventionality) who has seven children. And here's the X-Files bit: by seven different fathers. So if your immediate reaction is slut or whore, close the book – push your glasses back up your nose and go be judgmental somewhere else, like Twitter. Debz is just one of those freakishly unluckily women (or lucky as she would put it and I have to say those kids are not only beautiful but immaculately behaved as though they all inherited Debz's accommodating spirit) where the perfect storm of conception erupted each time in her womb. And they're all boys. What the actual chauvinistic fark, ladies and gentlemen; if I didn't know and love her like a sister I would slice her to check if her blood was green. But her blood is warm, so hot that the fear is some overly good-looking gent swings a glance her way from afar and bam she's hunched over the loo in the throes of morning sickness mayhem. We sit and wait anxiously for number eight.

Debz's first conception was almost immaculate. Perfect partner: love of her life. Both virgins. Special. When she fell not a hint of regret, then a car crash on the way home, a drunk teenager returning from a Boyband concert, teeny foetus and mother barely intact with doting-father-to-be no more, his body contorted into a scarring image forever, yet not a drop of blood to be seen. Her second child was done under strict prevention controls just after Magnus was born: coil, pill, triple thick, double strength condom and even the grand finale elsewhere. But as though her ovary was cruelly magnetised a lone resilient swimmer magically made a magnificent male monster, all 9 pounds of him!

Three and four were two brothers, both solid relationships again with decent preventative controls. The latter wasn't much of a physical specimen which meant they hardly ever, well, did it; only once of any real consequence making Lionel a rather significant consequence of his own. A sickly child requiring more care that Debz was able to spare. Five, six and seven were almost accurately equidistant between one another, eighteen months per boy, just enough time for the fathers to either return to service and die, run off at the first sight of meconium or decide that an existing wife and three privately schooled children was just about as much as the emerging markets fund could handle. For each, Debz had lamented, the nine-month lead up's consideration flipped to tactless diametric, as though the newborn's presence was a crowd setback that couldn't be remedied, Debz oft the obsessive singular consumption most men were not willing to share. But for the collective post-birth twenty-seven months of loneliness and rejection, Debz felt content in falling back on the loving faces of Luther, Sean and Timothy.

It was quite a headline when it broke: 'Boyband star dates mum of 7!' but Sexton wasn't really like the others. We'd heard stories; everyone knew the stories through the tabloids as Golden Tickle had been around longer than most modern Boybands and fell faintly foul of that hedonistic era where woman were throwaway conquests and designer drugs attempted to compete with the real rockers; not the full car crash but just nicking the bumper rendering the vehicle still driveable but damaged not beyond repair. Sexton had mainly watched from afar, sometimes the consoling sponge for girls hoofed out of trailers on tour or expensive hotel rooms. He'd spend hours with each of them, gazing upon their mottled faces peeking beneath the smudged makeup and blotched clutch points on the neck. He'd been the one concerned with the emotional hangover and equally concerned with the band's dwindling reputation and flagging sales. The youth of today wanted more wholesome. So when two of Golden Tickle found Jesus, one was replaced with a transgender dancer after a failed suicide, and one overdosed in a tattoo parlour, Sexton ran out of counselling candidates. Which made him happy, he supposed, and also impotent.

Debz's multi-daddy rugrats had been the distinguishing appeal for Sexton, a natural to the step-manor born, equally adept across the pre-teen and toddler ranges and everything betwixt. With Debz's life straddled between always gagging for it and circumstantial 'it felt right … repeatedly' mantra there was natural tension and Debz had confessed she felt the impotence was a direct result of her perceived promiscuity. She knew how to do stuff, way more stuff than Sexton had ever seen, heard or wiped away from a groupie's face and this forced his paternal instincts up and his manhood down. Poor sod, but like that guy from CSI Miami, "He's good with kids."

As an unwritten, unspoken about relationship clause Debz had uninhibited reign to get whatever she desired done to her by whomever she desired. This meant that Sexton was always there for the ubiquitous post event guilt, shame and clean up: Debz had become Golden Tickle's failed groupies from the past. Sexton was even cheap babysitting while Debz went frolicking, but I do Debz a malicious disservice because as I went to painstaking book-closing lengths to assert, she ain't no harlot. Almost a condition predicated on a connection. She would never just hook up with a random stranger but rather strangers would present themselves and they would genuinely strike a mutual chord, the unsuspecting male falling more deeply in love after that one fleeting, intrusive jiffy than they could imagine. Debz, now satisfied that the condition was scratched, would run back to Sexton, her one night stand dick dangling from side to side as she strode home. He'd bathe her, sing to her and tuck her into his bed – all the while having put seven kids to bed with a healthy dinner, menagerie of stories and five flavours of warmed milk.

They'd tried. Really tried. But futile shots at coaxing the shy snail out of the distorted yet uncannily lifelike shell became inversely proportionate to the strength of their bond. Debz just had to have it. Repeatedly. She knew and we knew it would happen soon under the most extreme circumstances. And it would be special. So special that she felt Sexton's treat would end up being a treat for the fans, tabloids, other band members and Boybands in general. No, she wasn't planning to fuck him to death, just give it as solid a go as possible, leaving him splattered stuck to the ceiling, his eyes nodding in lustful belief. This one act, when it came, would mean another and another. She was convinced if she could open Sexton up in this way he'd veritably never want to take it out of her. Glued together in sinless hankering so that maybe, just maybe, an eighth would be on the cards. Just in case she got tired of the other seven.

*Chapter 5*

# Jemima

Accomplished consumption, yet the consumption was not something normal, something typical. Not a trophy in sight, either of a male or adulation nature. She just did stuff quicker and more efficiently than most which meant she acquired other stuff even more quickly; and when she tired of those intangible ornaments there were new conquests to seek out, new lands to colonise and new Ps to outdo, not only the Qs but more importantly the Ls.

Jemima had learned to walk before most babies were standing up, rolling over even. She hadn't necessarily excelled academically at a young age yet she had always understood that being near the top of the class afforded a certain level of privilege and respect the 'mid-tablers' would never know. The eyes, of a golden disposition with speckles of blue silver equally dispersed across the surface – shimmering coins in a wishing water feature fountain, always remained on the prize yet this prize went beyond fortunes.

When she was within touching distance of becoming a teen, Jemima had 'borrowed' a hundred pounds from her stepfather, claiming the money would be funding a class project that would not only be returned within the week but was for a good cause. With the money and a significant amount of juvenile fraud she'd signed up for an online trading account and started dabbling. By the end of the first day she was down over eighty pounds, further strengthening her resolve and focus to pore over the last five years of financial statements, market events and news stories enmeshing the firms she was either backing or shorting. By the second day she was bust and, without wanting to admit defeat just yet, began siphoning funds from said stepfather's account until her margin calls were safe. Now this is not when a miracle bit of luck akin to Marvel-like power puts her on a rich-list overnight. She toiled; hard and thorough, learning not to trade the politics and find investments where others feared to look. All that Buffet bullshit of true blue chips, she'd tell herself, was why he only got rich after his hair turned grey and he'd consumed enough Mickey Ds to actually keep the stock afloat single-handedly. She only passed the hundred break-even point after six months yet the symbolism was enough for her to kick on with confidence and take more risk as the invested capital began shifting from stolen familial funds to her own blood, sweat and tears profit. When I met her the silver sparkles in her eyes would literally light up when she achieved, silver stars in the golden murk completely extinguished when I lifted her out of the gutter.

When she eventually did think about closing the online

share account, she'd made enough to fund her full senior tenure at private school, buy her stepparents cars suited to their personalities and all perfectly to coincide with the usually troublesome period of getting one's period. But this awkwardly iconic moment in any woman's existence, usually etched into memory to be passed down to daughters in the next generation, was not the reason she forgot about closing the account, blissfully unaware that it crashed during the credit crisis then made record profits having been invested in toxic and highly leveraged credit default obligations, but rather another conquest. So, Jemima, not a believer in luck of any form, had put some of the account's magnificence down to good fortune but also to her conscious theory that any financial market, if left alone by liquidity doomsayers (in other words greedy shareholders or corporates so desperate to impress with short-term gains on the balance sheet) and nonsensical government intervention, would right itself if the fundamental investing logic, no matter how convoluted, was sound. This sound investing funded her next exploit, Lego blocks continually smashed down by a less capable younger sibling, until the tower was too magnificent to not applaud.

I met Jemima when her biggest tower fell over, smashing her into a million colourful pieces with the vast majority of those around her pointing and laughing. Her first ever failure to acquire the pieces for one more go would prove that the next tower we built together would be stronger. And not made out of Lego.

# Chapter 6

# GWYNNE

Everyone loved Gwynneth. She had this way about her, a magnetism that men and women and children were drawn to, hostages in their own pleasant dreams. When a woman smiles that is simplistically touted as what people are drawn to; or the glint in the eye when smiling, that cartoon reflection shimmer telling the onlooker (or looker on) that this is the person I want to be near, hear, smile at, hold and just have some of that fairy dream dust sprinkled on me. So here's the shocker; the misnomer; the control; the contract; the illogical.

Gwynne never smiled.

Her face wasn't sulky or unpleasant or sad. She just never curled the sides of her mouth up in natural or preconditioned societal habit to reveal teeth, teeth tips, crow's feet or anything. Yet people flocked. When I met her she was a kickboxing instructor filling dojos wherever she went, technically sound with sufficient ambidexterity to tame even the most exuberant pretenders, those assassin eyes and immobilised mouth giving students that sense that they knew exactly where they stood with Gwynne.

There was this one time – and I only heard this as our paths were yet to criss-cross – a promising student got a bit too exuberant and struck her flush in the mouth, splitting her lip. There was a gasp at the dojo, most apparently fearing she would swing round in rage and finish him off, splatting the protégé rat, the class eager to see what kickboxing really could do when confronted with wanton aggression. But instead – or most people assumed this – she began to (appeared to, just the one side curling like a burnt corner of paper) actually smile. Gwynne would claim to me later that it was just the angle of the blood and her reaction to first tasting her own blood. "They'd call me a vampire if I'd enjoyed it anymore," she'd joked without smiling. But she did enjoy it. A lot. The sensation of wanting retribution, albeit petty as the poor sod lost all defensive training, rolling into an armadillo apology ball while Gwynne found herself.

I'm meeting Gwynne once she has finished with Damien at the gym. They really are atomically cute when they train together, spotting each other and replacing the other's weights like any good gym citizen should do. A members-only gym, those exclusive private ones with waiters or 'spotters', as this gym calls them to support the quirky marketing, serving protein shakes and energy boosts in various flavours, varieties, serving sizes and consistencies. They're not sexist either as this is not the noughties, both male and female spotters not only ferrying healthy sustenance back and forth but also offering the odd training tip, workout routine or handy lifting hint, all being fully qualified personal trainers. Their attire is also not gimmicky – again not the noughties! No oiled torsos with hotpants, suspenders and bowties; no gym bunny wear plastered onto impossible curves for the adoring male patrons, even if mostly celebrity Boyband-types who mostly keep to themselves. They're dressed in that classic fitted corporate gym t-shirt and shorts short enough to embody not missing leg day and long enough to avoid being cast in an eighties beach cop series.

When Damien and Gwynne started training together she was far the stronger. Damien, originally the sweet pudgy one on the side of the Boyo videos (don't ask but the manager and three of the boys claim to be from the valleys, although their accents drift into more of a Souff Landon thang every time their dialect coach is catching a breather on an island somewhere), acceded Gwynne's transposed rumination that being the passive coattail crown bearer was not sustainable or particularly healthy, not only for the multitude of organ, artery, skin, bones, cells, functions reasons but the good old-fashioned self-esteem. And the intention was never to show the others up or go solo or hog the limelight – remember this is NOT a Boyband from the murdering era – just to become a better version of oneself spiritually and for the fans. And body transformations, once all the rage, now needed a twist in the media and what better headline than *My Girlfriend Gave Me My Abs ... and I Love Her For It!*

An incredibly difficult start, middle and end was how Gwynne described it. During the early part I spotted her trying to show Damien what a weighted tricep dip looked like and, after retrieving him from the crumpled chain, weight mess beneath the dip station on numerous occasions, each one with a dollop more reassurance, I was convinced there was smoke coming out of her ears. She took herself off that day and, of course, that is the day someone destroyed the masseuse table in the carpeted ladies changing room, but that would never have been Gwynne because I taught her to hate violence. And it wasn't because Damien didn't try; my gawd even if only to impress Gwynne with his never say die attitude to diet, weights and HIIT, he just never transformed; or transformed at a rate slower than any human on the planet and in different ways to anyone on the planet. Gwynne was initially convinced someone was injecting lard into his cells at night and even took to placing GoPros at every conceivable angle in the kitchen to make sure disorientated Damien wasn't midnight feasting or sleep feasting in subconscious desperation.

When the first six months of training regimes didn't work she adopted other tactics. Not only would his body just not alter, but none of his vital signs improved either. His technique with the training also didn't get any better, he just tried harder, like a man with no legs crawling more frantically when told to get up and walk. Gwynne never used the words 'lost cause' but her smileless face on a few occasions almost gave away that not only was the bottom of the barrel indented but that all her nails were decimated in the process. This was a great test for her and she knew why. Like we'd spoken about when I met her, "The best control leads to the best control." Though my gauntlet thrown down with all my girlfriends has always been, "Be yourself and don't forget who you are, but only be better at the right time and for the right reason."

Of course platitudes wear thin. Especially in this time of excess social media feel good quotes which you absolutely have to pass onto a million friends just to show each of them your good nature and how much you really care. About them. About your friendship. Which is why we all have a strict rule in the circle: no feel-good quotes, emojis, dancing Winnie-the-Poohs or similar between any of us, forwarded by our followers and especially not deemed cute, lovable or 'just right' by our lovable Boybanders.

Sorry, back to Damien's uncrackable body dysmorphic swap, how did he get so damn fine and where did the puppy fat toddle off to? Well, Gwynne first had to show him exactly what he looked like beneath all his fur, so she waxed him. Herself. Was the wax too hot? Probably, but in Gwynne's defence to extract that amount of thick Brillo hair from just about every surface, cranny, fissure, nook and folded away nether region, she had to get it sickly warm, piping hot like a toffee stew ready to take hold and never let go. And of course for all of you who stay well-versed in historic affairs, no this was not a homage to Brady the Body or whatever the fuck the press decided to tag him with to demean his legacy, dance moves and community spirit. This was simply Gwynne showing off her strength skills and verve for pugnacious action. We watched the video. We're not cruel but oh so difficult not to laugh at his expression change and little

25

bloated, red, obeying face, nodding at her functional dexterity, while tears rolled down his cheeks. When she was finished he literally looked like Piglet, or like Piglet had one stormy evening got lost in the Hundred Acre Wood and run through a billion thrashing branches, brambles and thorns to whip him pinker than pink. He seemed to grow a snout too as though with each fervent tug across his vision his nose rounded and his nostrils flared, ready for a post gym trough nuzzle. This is a tad cruel but us girls love a giggle as long as no one is truly emotionally scarred in the process. Gwynne didn't even crack a smirk.

He was better off because now he could see all his flaws and the parts of his bod where fat clung to the hardest. Gwynne wouldn't fall into the old trap of targeting these portly problem parcels as she knew fat didn't discern, it was just programmed to find a suitable place based on great granddaddy and his pulpy forefathers. We never knew Damien's father, who could have been the custodian of this obdurate recessive gene, or we had to assume this might have skipped a generation or come from the mother, but let's blame the paternal line first. So how did Gwynne achieve the impossible? She made him angry. Angry with his physique; angry with his apathy; angry with his genetics; angry with his pinkness. So angry that he once hit Gwynne. She said it was fine and largely an accident so we ignored it and went merrily on as Damien did improve, dogmatically trying to copy Gwynne's near perfect explosive gym technique and eating so 'sensibly' he actually fired his personal chef and began cooking his own dishes so as to avoid any rogue or unearned carbs creeping into the menu.   He started cooking for Gwynne too, who would pop into mine on the way home after a dinner for some takeaway curry and beer, top and tailing on the sofa eating on our laps while the indie rock assumed nothing in the background.   Five, six missed calls in she'd call him back and soothe him to sleep, his day's goal unattainable without her solace and creamy voice.   They were a nice couple; they'd become a nice couple.

*Chapter 7*

# MAGGIE

"I absolutely have to have it," I'd said to Maggie almost as a test. Checking in on the willpower.

"You might want it but do you actually need it?" she'd responded, a programmatic knee-jerk even though she'd not seen the item.

I knew it was her colour, her fabric, her size, her style, her brand, her thang. You'd accuse me of planting it there? Right there?? At that exact moment on Carnaby Street with the light angling in to catch it just right, shimmering the sheen and making it glow to the potential wearer, whispershouting, "You damn well absofuckinglutely have to have me, buy me, hold me, be me, touch me, fornicate in me!"

I knew she'd eventually look up, the solid green in her eyes coming out to play beneath the dark protective eyelashes, the only barrier between Maggie and having to have the garment. It was slow, the bringing into focus as the pace slowed and she dropped her flat white flat bang onto the pavement, bouncing once and performing one-and-a-half cartwheels before being punted further away by a fellow incessant shopper. You know those films (normally pirate) where the eponymous bad guy finds the chest of gold and opens it allowing the ruddiness to bathe his face with us the viewer, although willing it, unable to see the loot. Well this garment shone on Maggie's face, burnt it even, the pupil bleeding large to encroach on the green's space and take over. It was going to be hers. Maybe not that day but someday.

Then the pull back. Waking from a too real dream, literally yanked from the comingle of a loving embrace, leaving the lover gasping, reaching, screaming for you. To come back. But you don't. You soar back to reality. The training couldn't be this effective. Could it? And no disappointment either, no resignation, no regret; just a firm acknowledgement of place, purpose, company and destiny.

"I'll buy you another coffee," I'd said linking my arm through hers and onward marching to retrieve the old cup, put it in the correct recyclable receptacle and continue. Shades back on just in case the tabloids were back on the scent.

Maggie's nickname had been 'Silver'. Many, including her immediate family, had speculated why, then let it go as her hair, originally straighter than Hawkeye's crossbow shot (it would have been Robin Hood's arrow but you know we are actively seeking to dispel the old stories here) and a lighter shade of beige had begun to turn a silver sheen. It was gradual but unmistakable so by the time she was in her late teens, most thought she consistently had it dyed silver at the salon as the colour was too rich for premature grey and too stunning for cheap bottle dyes. Which led to the next phase of the speculative origins of the nickname and what every teenage girl would have sought in her senior school had they the funds: regular, professional, fabulous grooming. So how did Maggie consistently and effortlessly fund 'that look'? Well, it had to be through troy ounce loads and bags of silver (and access to a secret hair aficionado at some tucked away boutique up the road in Crouch End, as her friends had sent reconnaissance missions everywhere to determine the truth) hoarded away for those rainy hair days when everything should go surprised Einstein splatter pattern frizz, for immaculate was always an impossible teenage ideal.

The truth was far simpler, far less intricate and far more psychologically detrimental. For as exotic and stunning as we all thought Maggie was and is, it was always a curiosity venture rather than adulation from her acquaintances. Maggie always looked at them and wanted their hair, their vanity, their collectiveness. She'd explored most of the sports at a young age and always just been short of the best. She was top of the class right until the final end of school academic awards when an outsider shipped from Durban had joined the school and scooped cum laude at the finishing post. Maggie had taken second place, just like in the backstroke, gymnastics, cricket, ballet and narrowly losing out copping the affections of the hottest boy in school to another usurper fresh on the scene. When she'd applied to university she got her second choice and when entering the job market played second fiddle to a more ambitious, better prospect in the law firm. She was not the favourite sibling with either parent either; divorced, they'd subtly showered real affection on her younger sister who they just seemed to connect with more. And she was anything but oblivious to this.

Hers was always the Silver Medal. Just coming second; faintly losing even when everything was in her favour. Whatever she wanted (whatever she really, passionately, sickeningly, wholeheartedly wanted) had, like that stray M&M slap bang in the geometric centre, under the sofa, always been just out of reach, her fingertips tickling the prize ever so often making her want it more. So much more. Which is where I come in perhaps. I want her to have what she wants; everything she wants. I just might require a bit more self-control and restraint in the first instance: diminishing the apparent desire first.

Then taking what is rightly yours.

Oh wow let me apologise as this is getting heavier than when Jon Snow bent the knee thus renouncing all claims to both the North and (I suspect) the Iron Throne. These are the thoughts distracting me from Kit's anxious nobility as I warm my feet between the inner thighs of the most considerate BIB (Boyfriend In Boyband) around. He's watching raptly as I crunch popcorn next to his ear, perhaps not fully comprehending his Starks from his Targaryens or his Boltons from his Glovers, but he is so cute when he watches it and pretends to know what I'm talking about when I explain it later on. He's close to Maggie's chap, Digby, too as they were in the same Boyband before each of their Boybands rose to stardom respectively. They used to harmonise together in front of the mirror I'm told, both holding their collector's item Harry Potter wands, a source of much playful derision. What wasn't so playful was the purchase of this thing in front of us, this beast of an Ultra HD technological, viewing experience wonder that had to be 85 inches. Digby's was 65 inches. We'd hoped that the days of measuring and comparing a boy's length were further behind us than wolf whistles and the ubiquitous cinematic secretary fawning all over the male boss, but somehow the phallic dicker meant we were out with the appendage and in with the pixels. We tried to let them be but literally Digby just couldn't let it go, and, after one low cal beer too many, there was a cricket bat meets wide screen incident which almost saw the boys come to blows (they say it about brothers don't they, the closer they are the more bellicose the spats) while Maggie and I chortled from the side-line, swilling expensive (now fashionable again) chardonnay and tutting, "Just don't stare down at the urinal any longer, boys."

They made up of course in the way they always seem to nowadays, through their prayer groups and girlfriends. If we could get on like we do then they could too. They both had a colourful history, as did we, albeit markedly different. There would always be that 'look' though, whenever they were around; that look at the new hundred-and-fifteen-inch replacement TV and, not that it existed as Diggers could easily afford one, but that my man had got to it first, set it up and claimed all the plaudits when everyone popped around for a modest shindig and intimate soirée. Maggie had told me during the last one, celebrating the restoration of the band's charity to support rare snow leopards, she'd spent most of the night in the guest suite toilet consoling Digby about just never being good enough. He'd been staring at the Victorian bath muttering, "Everything I want he has, even the bath!" with Maggie nodding in agreement.

So as gaudy a topic as sex is I believe Maggie even convinced him he wanted me! What a good girl, even if a bit of a stirrer. That destabilising creaking of the 'bros before hoes' furniture wouldn't be necessary if we and our merry band of Boybanders did wholly embrace the #MeToo generation, but we had to acknowledge there would be this male bond: there always has and always will be. And the bond is strongest at the early informative post puberty years which meant ours, more likely strengthened in the later post child years, had to be stronger than theirs from the outset. And Maggie was at the centre of ensuring that their need for male Boyband coagulation would look over longingly at our union, void of any seam, scar or join. A complete single organism, the belle of the ball, ringing in the ears of all those who chose to stare up the chapel tower and listen. And those who chose not to. Cowering under their beds and in closets with the clang-band-dang-ding-donging echoing into every monster's eyes.

*Chapter 8*

# Renea

"Coffee?  In the park?  Sun on the face?  Jogger boy torso to gawk at?"

"Nah."

"Shopping?  No sales at the moment which means no crowds?"

"Can't be bothered."

"Online shopping!  At your house?  I'll come to you?"

"Can't be arsed."

"I'll bring something!  Something for your pretty fella?"

"Cannot be arseholed."

"Why?"

"Too much effort."

"I'm coming over anyway."

"Does the kettle operate remotely nowadays?"

Renea.  We really do love her in spite of coercive tactics to interact.  Uncle is our pet name for her, I believe after

Uncle Fester, of Addams Family notoriety, and not because she's bald, square-bodied, pale, racoon eyed or wears black (although that is, like Japanese knotweed, the predominant colour in every drawer, wardrobe, linen basket [as if!], bathroom floor, room corner, lamp shade, chair and space). It could be down to her familiar loyalty which is unquestionable or something else ... let's leave the latter for when you know Uncle a bit better. Visiting her is an exercise in avoiding tetanus. There are messy friends who bathe and wash loads, the friends we all laugh at because they're haphazard in locating anything beyond what is attached to their person but they're clean, floral scented, shiny, smooth skinned she-beings that everyone wants to get a whiff of just to feel better about themselves.

Here's the thing with Renea: she had a theory some years back that we laughed at, endured, viewed with some circumspection at its validity then truly came to believe in. She stopped washing. Any part of her. She stopped shaving. Any part of her. When it started we knew it was just laziness and, normally after a big night out, we'd hold her down and pressure wash her with the handheld in the shower; she'd wake up none the wiser smelling sweeter to us and probably grateful the effort of washing had been involuntarily outsourced. But keeping up washing another human being, albeit one of your best friends, wears thin. And, of course, where is the sense in forcing someone to be something they're not?

In the lead up to 'Lesbian Prison Hose Wash' Uncle would acquire a ripe scent, musky and strong enough to hold onto you, grab your shoulders, shake you a bit and backhand you across the face like one of those overbearing beard balms all the ironic beardies lace into their hairy appendages with capitalist gay abandon. This ripe scent would exponentialise when no hair maintenance had taken place, turning ripe into decaying, ready for the fruit recycling tub. This was a difficult phase even for Kieron who claimed to love Renea's rustic vibe, being a self-proclaimed ethno bongo feminist himself (which we all found to be bullshit when a video of his haphazard manscaping attempts went super viral). But then something incredible happened, like Jim Morrison might have belted out before I was even conceived. She broke on through to the other side. And it wasn't gradual either, the decay regressing into tolerable ripe into pleasant; no way. An instant, lightning speed flicked switch, the bulb exploding all over our heads showering glass down to embed in our perfectly conditioned partings.

She suddenly smelled amazing. And not amazing like masking something fetid with something heady amazing, but uniquely amazing. Spicy, hot, powerful, alluring amazing. Stimulating even, an aphrodisiac making her skin softer, her black attire deeper, her eyes more pronounced and her being sensuous. Her face was a picture too because none of us really believed she'd known this would be the pheromonal outcome; she was basically just too darn stubborn and lazy to care about any form of bodily maintenance and this resultant hatching from the stench cocoon was quite simply 'luck'. She'd nodded in self-congratulatory approval, more relieved than anything at the prospect of never lifting a finger again.

And of course being girls and friends and sisters we had to look, um, down there; to see what one really looked like without grooming, Boyband requests, Sharon the master Brazilian / Hollywood magician on Upper Street, plucking, waxing, lasering or any other form of extrication.

Truly magnificent was all we could muster, the sheer volume and force of a pronounced bush, never ever constrained by any pants, boyshorts or G-strings, louder and prouder than a red raw fresh tattoo. We all tried it for a bit too, until it became too itchy or unmanageable. Scant few requests to change either, likely through training or fear or more likely lack of access which is part of our sacred vow. Looking without touching is about as close as you can get to the opposite sex or the same sex as you truly appreciate this formed organism and being in front of you. Absence of touching or gratification certainly does make the heart stronger than a rock floating around in space waiting for the opportune moment to slam into our blue and wipe out all undeserving living species. No not Boybands, that's just silly and too retro. Plus they're not deserving anymore. They're decent, setting a fantastic example for the youth and never using their celebrity to abuse anything.

Well everyone is allowed an itsy bitsy slip-up every now and again right? Take Kieron for example, he really is deserving of someone as special as Renea, if not only for his unshaven porcelain doll baby good looks and pink pouty lips that would send most teenage girls' hearts into a pumping bloody spinning mess. He was pretty cut up about the whole incident too, so lucky Uncle was there to console him and support him through this. He was tasked with feeding his nana's cat every week or so while she went on a cruise, which he paid for, the kind soul that he is. The first few weeks were no problem and he even bonded with the little grey and gold feline, whose name was Rex if my memory doesn't desert me. After a while either he just forgot or couldn't be bothered, failing to visit the premises without even a tour or promotional stint to blame. Rex got tangled in a wine rack piece of modern art Kieron had given his nana, breaking his front paws and starving to death, unable to move or find food. To brand matters worse Kieron forgot the designated slot for picking his nana up at the airport, forcing her to take a cab home after several attempts to call his mobile. Renea said she thought he had looked at the phone ringing and just didn't pick up. On the way home a mile long pile up saw the chatty black cabby stare into the rear-view a few lingering seconds too long, the head-on throwing Nana through the front windscreen and onto the pile of cars that would take a full day to clear.

He was distraught and this is probably when he started smoking weed which further killed any aspirations or desires. He stopped trying to write music for the band, even though they'd never used any of his previous material with the hired song writers claiming to 'incorporate' some of his 'interesting' ideas. Uncle began smoking with him which she decided was not a good idea: even a girl with absolutely no desire to do anything has a limit on how little she would or could do. Weed as the ultimate 'get shit done' killer was something she knew Kieron wouldn't give up and that would, at some point, impact the Boyband such that either he'd get kicked out or he'd have to go through a Boyband version of cold turkey to kill the breakfast, lunch and dinner smoking habit to get high. She'd stand by him in this period, not quite reminding him that his apathy killed his nan (and her cat) but that her petition to do nothing would serve as the defining presence of their relationship. She'd hold him in this pattern like we discussed. Perhaps his regression came too suddenly, too unexpectedly for what we were prophesising. An event like that is terrible and sad but like any dark fate has to be used for good. Not used against anyone as that is not the moral of this tale but used as a sobering souvenir of what happens when you can't be bothered, when your loved ones are put behind Instagram, blowjobs and fame. Forgiveness is the left fork in the road, and holding onto Renea as tight as his doped-up hands could manage became Kieron's one true solace.

That and her smell natch because let me tell you, from the eau de Uncle initial take me now pong, an evolution of rum, sage, sandalwood, damson, shark fin and whitebait would evolve and bequeath us with a scented adventure underpinned by shoulder shrugs, head shakes and bass mouth can't be doing that nows. When it came time to be bothered, to shake the rust, to kick the duvet off, to squash the joint in her fist and mic drop that apathetic poison to the ground like dust, she'd be there.

"Uncle Fester at the ready?"

"Maybe."

*Chapter 9*

# Danielle

"Gerson's accused you of being a biter?" I bellowed a little too loudly over coffee. We both blushed as the table of posh travellers next to us oversipped their coffee so the cute Nordic-looking one with (possibly) intentional highlights in his beard fakechoked. Attention grabbed. Danielle noticed this.

"So we can't look or touch now?" I say, faintly indignant yet not failing to notice a stud in his tongue. Attention decimated.

"Doesn't that come later? Like after you've gotten to know a person? That's what you taught us," says Danielle signalling for a top-up of chai tea, the beautiful shaven headed waitress trotting over with a colourful teapot. "And not that kind of biting anyway; we're not there yet."

Every fortnight on a Wednesday we do this, Danielle and me. Not ideal but some recurring conditions need ointment or they will reappear, fester like a mountainous pussy motherfucker and take over one's being like leprosy is imagined by my generation who never saw the original Papillon, only the new one with that gassed up blonde found in a shoe store in Newcastle for Biker Grove and Freddie Mercury hiding funds up his ass.

Back at Danielle's it is already loaded in the freezer. One tub of every single known flavour of Ben & Jerry's (product placement moment not only for my TikTok but also Gerson, a proud ambassador for Vermont's finest ice cream from those lovable stoner hippies who did or did not sell out to Unilever) without dilution the greatest ice cream of a generation. Sometimes we start with the best first (has to be Vermonster or Wholly Couch) ...

"We Sofa So Good Together."

"Ha," feigns Danielle.

"I couldn't resist."

... sometimes random, blindfolded choice and sometimes bottom up. Of course there just has to be a good film, red wine and foot massages to accompany the feast. It gets a bit messy later because, well, although I'm a bit of a lightweight, stopping after three tubs, Danielle has no off switch. She pulls off eating in such a ladylike manner too, no nature programme starving on the savannah and devouring a rogue baby warthog to keep Mr Nature Death at bay. Oh no. She nibbles. Impossible to nibble ice cream, you say? Well pop around on the next 'Bulimic Wednesday' and you'll witness this feat of true tantalising consumption. But she speeds up as she goes and it always comes to rest, whatever the opposite of a delicate feather smile-arcing into a sombre parking space in the middle of a pillow is, in the exact same spot; the same out-come-da-flavas. Whereas most girlfriends hold their hapless friend's hair back after too many flaming sambucas, I'm there for Danielle after too many Blondie Brownies. It's not pleasant either because of the amount she consumes over the period, dynamic ingestion coalesced with cold cream meets warm stomach juices, the resultant flow powerful, multi-layered, coarse (she fails to chew any of the fillings towards the end) and rodeo violent. She cries too because she knows this is not who she wants to regress back to on a more than fortnightly basis.

When I first found her she was that girl who would pop off to the boutique donut shop near London Bridge and name all her filmy bae girlfriends she was buying for when selecting the heaped, calorific, sickly colourful, unnecessarily branded, topped, chocolated, deep fried dough with a hole.

"One for Amanda, Beatrice, Candice and Demi. And Emily, Frieda, Gail and Heather," translated for not only the store clerk but everyone else in the store as: "One for Danielle, Danielle, Danielle and Dani. And Danielle, Danielle, Danielle, Danielle and Dani." And throughout her early twenties fortified with an astrophysical race car of a metabolism and an unnaturally long middle finger she was able to resemble a normal figure, curves in almost all the right places and a pouted mouth born from the depths of a fashion magazine cover "more suited for smiling than scoffing," many a friend had instructed. But then the halt and the self-destructive spiral of realising that too much eating meant no more defined, pouty lips now swallowed whole by her drooping pear cheeks or semblance of curve, a square fat lass the end and enduring result. So we had to change, to alter that pattern of gourmandising because, unlike the bullshit fitness mags that tell you about how only unhappy people overeat, many well-balanced, completely content, well-adjusted folk who just fucking love the taste of food do too. It was about changing the off switch, ensuring that the path from first morsel to end was the filling of a container rather than pouring more fuel on a raging fire. And it worked but not without any sacrifice.

She's heaving a bucket of Netflix & Chilll'd as we speak. Oh lawd it didn't look that way going in! In those days she was a MASSIVE Boyband fan too, unable to control herself at concerts and with not an inch of wall to boast about what with the poster upon poster upon magazine article upon collage, spunked all over her room walls like a teenage girl's wet dream. She knew every single one of their names in those days too, middle names, pet's names, favourite ice cream flavours, girlfriends, hospitals they were born in, stylist's names and so on. Early exercises were positioning her away from being a groupie stalker and getting her to be an actual candiDATE (yes, a possible Boyband date or viable for more than a backstage suck off). Danielle could possibly have been the biggest challenge and not because beneath it all there wasn't an immaculate butterfly waiting to emerge but because she really didn't blame the Boybands for anything. And inserting her at the right place, for the right Boyband, with the right Boybander was a – for lack of a better word – clusterfuck. This isn't 2001 where magazines were still read and competitions entered with big titted E-listers who might or might not coincidentally know a Boyband who fuck around with underage girls. They are protected by people who know that Boyband knives butter their hardworking bread, that any slipup (underage or not) results in image damage, lawsuits and most importantly, sales dips.

The most boring element, as I've come to discover, is everything is conscious. Even the slipups: they are put there to darken the band's image or draw attention after a dry spell, which means all of them are either so tame you fall asleep whilst scrolling up for 15 seconds or categorically know the news is contrived. Almost like when bands ruled the airways the abhorrent behaviour was normal, acceptable, even commonplace; so much so that the competition to get to the next rung of debauchery was the unwritten call to arms for all touring band members. Now the exact opposite exists, each Boyband is so set in saccharine sweetness that any fulfilling of prophesies means that the noble, everyboy image is further strengthened by acts of decency, consideration and PR likeability.

But lest we forget, they are Boybands. Which means not all the same rules apply.

Danielle is asleep now, collapsed face down into my lap, her teeth brushed and backbone protruding from her light pink pyjama top. I'll stay with her tonight; it was a more than unusually traumatic binge. My phone buzzes and it's that Swede from the coffee shop. I'm bored so respond with

"Fuck off until you lose the stud." He comes back with the bipolar laughing, crying emoji. Like everything in this world is hysterically funny, so funny that you spout tears from your ducts. I mean how many times have you actually cried laughing? Had tears dribble and perhaps a squeak of wee if it was a sudden onslaught of humour? A few, yes, but not the billion approval responses to show your acquaintance you found their post, comment or picture liquid droll. Then a missed call from Gerson on Danielle's phone and he knows she's with me so he tries mine, a WhatsApp message though.

"She's fine but I think I want to devour your manhood," I respond. A long silence with *Gerson is typing* appearing then disappearing, his uncertainty in response hysterical … cue laughing crying emoji? Oh yes, a hackneyed trajectory of blether it can only be one direction. On bletcherous trend and with enough faltering to tell me we have these boys so tightly wound around our little fingers it is almost a shame doing what we're going to do. I respond with a quizzical emoji, suggestive almost and the purple eggplant and a sweaty face. This time the silence is longer. I slide down Danielle's pyjama bottoms and take a photo of her tidy butthole and the alluring carriage of lady parts nestled beneath like a static, perfectly formed, Mexican hammock. "Recognise this?" is the accompanying caption, trailed by the most highly underrated, underused emoji of all time: hunger.

"Next time you see it she'll want you to devour it, literally eat it out until there's nothing left. Can you do that for her? Are you hungry?"

Salivating, agreeable emojis in response. This is too

priceless but I'm getting bored and tired with Danielle's weight pressing down on me so I respond with the only shutdown emoji I can think of … crying laughing face. I get one in return.

*Chapter 10*

# WILLOW

Here's the clanger: Willow's a boy; a Boyband boy. He has wept over Willows and, in fact, chained his genitals to one while drinking earth infused soya lattes from an expensive recyclable cup. He is Jemima's other half; her missus she calls him, making the capitalist juggernaut of Jemima's raison d'être nicely incongruous to Willow's save the planet ethos. They met during the tree incident, Jemima sent in person by her Law Firm (transient, once her name was on the building she got bored and sold her partnership) to not only negotiate the Boyband surrender but splash the Law Firm's name all over the adoring reporters with her quite remarkable amalgam of intellect and attractiveness. Willow was smitten at first glance but Jemima was not, as she watched him try to untangle his bits from a chain precariously looped between his legs and conjoined with the rest of the band.

You see publicity stunts fell so out of fashion that when Boyband We Eez Da Treez did start standing up for mother

47

nature in public it was acceptable because it was on brand with their image. The boys did genuinely care about the planet but luckily were guided more than that moronic one who compared nine eleven to dolphin cruelty; as I broken record-ed at your asses for too long: Boybands have evolved. We Eez Da Treez were careful with covering up their back stories too – not one had ever heard of greenhouse gases, carbon emissions, sustainability, biogas or anaerobic digestion with one member's father even working for the largest industrial chemical manufacturer in the country but they had 'that' look. That earthy, caring, bangled, mottled facial hair collective persona that screams, "When I'm gyrating on stage I'm punishing the planet bashing corporates!"

Willow attended a private school and actually joined a Boyband that attempted to use the posh niche as a selling feature: they all wore blue blazers and rapped with lyrics like "Oh My Word, Haven't you Heard" and "If I'm making it, then mummy and daddy ain't fakin it" and so on. Pre any hint of dirty skin, ink or otherwise, he was clean-cut, slicked to the side hair and a caddish twinkly reserved for the wannabe elite. One summer too many in San Tropez saw him return brown, grubby, furry yet still twinkly eyed as though those eyes were able to infiltrate from the gunge and into the hearts of environmentally savvy teenagers the world over. Lyrics such as "If you're thinking of you, think of Yew!" and "The world in so much hurt, think I'll recycle my shirt" became commonplace with some of We Eez Da Treez's increasingly snappy songs, these tunes faring a whole lot better because the expulsion of teenage allowance sat more palatable as a worthy cause than giving Drake another celebrity to piss off.

Touring on large commercial aeroplanes and petrol masticating buses had to become obsolete which meant Treez would have to think of a way to travel without disappointing fans in faraway lands or pissing off promoters or schedule managers. They didn't. They managed to turn the spotlight on other Boybands' continent galivanting and issued shaming stay away hashtags whilst they travelled incognito. When challenged they'd produce a sequence of made-up travel blogs using local boats, hiking and electric cab firms. When a tabloid exposed this as a lie they didn't deny it but didn't admit it either, dragging the spotlight elsewhere but teaming with fallen Anglo-African cricketer Kevin Pietersen to splatter gorno pictures of mutilated black rhinos all over social media. And this is where the union with Jemima became an oh so beneficial one.

Jemima's knack for sniffing out and monetising an opportunity combined with the variety of Treez and Willow's ecoexploits meant that her intellectual fatigue was never attained with variety so rich and ludicrous; she kept coming back for more. That and our higher purpose. Turning grandiose act of brazen corporate (not quite Fight Club but …) espionage into record sales became her hobby and proving exactly how much the image improved their worth became her worth. And with Willow's level of semi-intellect, himself (and those eyes) and his frontman status entrenched him as the tightest tree hugger of the Boyband.

This allowed Jemima to work her magic until every do-good single was top of the charts and three in every four posters of recycled toilet paper sold was stinking out a teenage room all over the United Kingdom, with Willow pointing to his tattoo of a peace sign giving the finger to a fracking operation appearing just above his pubes.

The tabloids would speculate that theirs was a relationship of convenience: corporate bitch snares Eco Boyband Warrior, but really he was, like one of those adoring baby seals before its fate is sealed with a hakapik, smitten. So much so that he would be seen in public buying a Starbucks without a reusable cup if she asked him; he'd hail a black cab to see her and put his non-dolphin friendly tuna tins in the wrong bin if she asked. And she always did ask, under the pretence of daring him to give her a conundrum she couldn't turn into Sterling while secretly ensuring she knew the real truth about his Warrior status, namely that he'd retreat if she was behind the battle lines waiting in an alluring pose.

The concept of denying for further infatuated devotion was nothing new; for God's sake married women had been practising this custom for eons, swatting away the proverbial arm in the morning marital bed, but these were celebrities we were dealing with so there had to be small elements of, well, payout. And we couldn't feel like whores doing it either which meant it had to be a) somehow enjoyable and b) dishevelled into the dedication. Jemima achieved this largely through humiliation, making Willow pleasure himself at the sight of her and her balance sheet. She'd help him out every now and again of course but watching his little faux eco face change every time, she told me, gave her more than an orgasmic donkey kick in the crotch. She'd lay herself out in lingerie and surround herself with singles charts, sales figures, news articles and PR stunts engineered by her and make him thank her by adding his earthy, organic flavoured man juice to each and every success story. Until he had nothing left, once requiring hospital treatment to replace the lost fluids and get his heart rate down to whatever the fuck normal felt like after ejaculating sixty-eight times. With the black also came the red: success was expelled onto the floor but failure had consequences too. When Willow had made the wrong statement during an anti-Trump speech at a concert, focussing the crowd's vitriol on Trump's megalomaniac traits rather than his specific climate change policy, she'd had to show him the error of his ways. He loved it though; couldn't get enough of it really.

Jemima's delivery of all this congratulatory retribution was administered in such a functional, step-by-step, transactional manner that you would have been forgiven for thinking that she was hired as some leather-clad dominatrix to deliver the sentence. Well she was and she wasn't: was paid, and handsomely at that, taking an unfair share of Treez's profits and making Willow fund our ventures in an ironic twist; and wasn't, in that the act itself didn't get him off running sharply athwart impressing her. Of all the conscious coupling heroics this has by far been my easiest. With Jemima's stint as a criminologist, a profiler stretching as far into MI6 as anyone her age, the algorithm between what a reformed Eco Boybander wanted from life and what she had achieved and brought to the gluten free table told her this was a slam dunk. And it was but like every fairy-tale there is that wobble in an aerobics class, that lone speedbump in the middle of fucking nowhere, the statistical anomaly in the algorithm. It would be Jemima's thirst for attainment in a male-dominated world that would almost prove her undoing. We were unbelievably strict when we crafted the Ten Uncommandments too, number six: Thou Shalt Not Have Any Other Relations When Coupling With a Boybander. The attention she would inevitably receive at being the alpha female in business was always going to be intense but we let the covenant down on this one by not managing correctly. It meant we had to do something extreme and this would prove implausibly valuable at a point down the line: a forced hand leads to the shocking realisation that to actually take a human life was a bit more than watching the Saw films. Plus it was more Thelma and Louise, the way we positioned the story with Jemima, for the first time in like forever, supported to a conclusion rather than making it happen on her lonesome. True friends do that sort of shit for their sisters. This I promise you. Involving Willow though, was the first chink that would lie in wait, pounce and fuck us all up. Jemima persuaded him he had the stomach for it and that his dedication had no boundaries. But apparently it did. Which was luck I suppose in that it meant we knew where he ended and we began. Men just really are a bit pathetic really: no will, no follow-through, no balls.

*Chapter 11*

# MAGGIE & DIGBY

Calling a partner a boyfriend (supposing he is a boy) is a necessary evil. We found that referring to our merry band of Boyband appendages as 'partners' just became too wanky, and not current enough. 'My Man' betrayed where they were really from: a Boyband, not a Manband. Actually when any of them did become too manly they'd be de-maned, in barefaced contrast to how Robert Redford scarified his oil painting looks to take on more hard men roles. Mostly laser hair removal (from just about everywhere as the norm) but specifically as instructed by the publicists: knuckles, forearms, necks, underarms and clavicle (for those pesky jazz hands hairs that would arrive unannounced even from a round neck t-shirt). They'd also have various other youthful procedures, the likes of which we are all bored to death with from advertisements: skin peels, tucks here and there, nose reshaping, lipo, skin blemish removal, mole extraction, permanent eyeliner tattoo, micropigmentation and transplants for the thinning hair and even butt lifts for the Boybands unable to stick to the gym routine.

Digby was one who had to have it all; all the procedures, top to tail until he was just about bloody perfect. Maggie was a handholding, nodding, supportive rock as you would imagine. For some reason, though, whenever Digby went for or would have a youthfully improving procedure, something would go slightly wrong either scuppering his intention or leaving a result somewhat departed from the desired. For example when he started thinning at the temples and, gazing at some of DeliverU2Me's quaffed manes beside him feather dusting foreheads whilst hip thrusting on the stage, he decided he had to up his game, or more specifically his follicle count. And no one is stupid enough to consider Wayne Rooney carrots in the earth style transplants; well Digby was but auspiciously Maggie was on hand to show him enough celebrity horror stories to talk him off the surgical ledge. Her argument was pretty darn solid: no matter how much money they had no one's ever looked natural. And a chance encounter with a tall farmer conditioned by habit to extracting his crop might prove fatal. Plus although she knew vanity for this lot was mostly folly and transient, an act of this blatant mortification at this stage would change their popularity hence change where we were heading. Embedding was the current intention and as number eight stated: Thou Shall Not Intentionally Disfigure a Boybander Until The Time Is Perfect.

With Digby on the balding ropes he did consider just clipping it all off and enjoying being big bad bald different but his constant longing looks at the combs and hair products in the backstage dressing rooms briskly set him on his path; grease lightning for headlong locks. A friend of Maggie's was a ground-breaking tattoo artist who'd got sick of inking bikers, lesbians and private school girls so had adapted the parlour into a micropigmentation clinic where she could meet a more diverse set of folk and use her Gandalf-like skills to pigment scalps with tiny dots. The results were truly staggering and in the lead up, Digby's excitement was barely controllable.

"I'll be back to my full quota," he'd skip and sing at the bottom of the bed while Maggie pretended to read a novel, her green eyes zip-zapping across the page a little too forcefully to be absorbing words. Digby was just too febrile to notice though. So what happened next could have been construed as Maggie's fault but it wasn't really … really … am I convincing you yet? She'd booked a slot at the original parlour after Digby had spoken to the artist and mentioned she was moving premises to adapt to a more professional set of customers rather than anyone with a ring in their nipple, clit or sack. This move was an overlapped work in progress which meant she was completing some existing clients at the old tattoo venue and starting some new clients at the clinic venue. Digby happened into the parlour the day the transfer completed and her primary tattoo rival from two decades' worth of crossing needles had taken residence. Well, assuming her identity, the rival set about Digby's head, the equivalent of gang retribution.

Digby didn't notice it either as it was subtle, well 'they'

were subtle as there was more than one thing. Not only had she tattooed a large cock on his crown but skilfully provided a set of balls which, when viewed from the back, side or front, exhibited the same effect. To achieve this she'd had to place the hairline lower than was anatomically possible, halving Digby's forehead length and giving enough fodder for the tabloids to label him Dickhead for the foreseeable future. Digby though, delighted to have a set of new follicles, irrespective of location and genital design, was overjoyed at being 'back', that is until another Boybander did actually go bald, so Digby wanted that too.

Digby's mother had been Eastern European which meant her name betrayed her roots. He'd had the misfortune of multiple stepfathers as his mother's slow decline into accepting that this was as good as it got meant each split was better than the last. Diggers would look with some despair at seemingly normal and together families, playing in the park, pushing swings, buying ice creams. His mother sometimes spoke of his father with some adulation yet a discernible despair at either having not made it work or something else, Digby gleaned. She'd run out of steam, as though her effort to love this man and produce a son extracted the last piece of energy and decency inside her with the string of unsuitable suitors further eroding her will to continue. Her looks departed too quickly as well, never skilled enough in the workforce to commend any high standard of living and, post childbirth, acquiring that weathered leathered look that no one seemed to sit up any longer. Digby could see she'd been stunning as a younger woman yet looked longingly at the other mothers whose mani-pedi and park bootcamp routines kept them shining brighter than his mother.

As a teen Digby was locked up for stealing from his friends. Never having enough and always wanting more he'd got into a bad habit of just lifting what he felt he deserved and dropping it into his pocket, a home invading pickpocket who'd been invited in. His dipping in between normal lower income society and juvenile offender facilities meant he got into a gang early; not a crazy ass heroin blade thrusting one, just a gang that smoked, dealt a bit and carried knives as a symbol of being a gang rather than any real intention to slice and dice a rival. They called themselves DeliverU2Me which when written in gang colours and graffiti style sounded and looked more hardcore than the Boyband they would become. Once the notoriety was achieved through discovering they could sort-of sing and entering a reality show, they had to stick with the name.

'Underprivileged street gang wins reality singing competition, tells fans, "Boybands sure beats hustling",' would ring true when legions of fans started calling them East 2017. As songs sold and the gang life edged further away there would need to be acts to maintain the band's street cred as their core following were the confused youths caught between Grime, Hip Hop and ballad Boybands. Rap would rough-hew a large cornerstone of many of the tunes, as with most modern Boybands, and when they tried to introduce some rock riffs those songs would chart so low they'd revert even more heavy-handedly to blatant gangsta rap without forgetting to gaze lovingly into the camera. One of the carefully crafted stories was to put a Boybander into two rival gangs, Digby being one of them, then take credit for engineering a ceasefire (or 'ceaseshank', as they called it) getting the gang lords to shake hands at a press conference and quote some bogus crime stat reductions in the area. Touted the 'Clinton Boyband', bringing 'Peace in Da Middle Ease!'

Digby, of course, felt his fellow fake broker Stubzy had more airtime, credit and kudos out of the event, his face soaking Maggie's lap as her green eyes softly, lazily bore down on him, caught in a pity annoyance crossfire of sorts. This helped Maggie know Digby did not have what she wanted; well he was part of something she wanted but we'd worked on moving away from wanting something that would merely momentarily alleviate the itch as opposed to eradicating it completely. Digby's state of complete inadequacy and unfulfilled paranoia was initially the kindred spirit she'd always longed for, then a galling put-off as she realised they were never really alike. What she wanted was different from what he would never attain: chasing an imaginary rabbit, someone else's rabbit, in the darkness of space, grappling and lunging into blackholes of nothingness for eternity.

They'd met on one of those days that wishes it was another day, I believe a windy Tuesday wishing it were a sunny Saturday.

# Chapter 12

"I want this experience to be perfect; beyond perfect: magnificent. Excessively and extremely magnificent; what's a word beyond magnificent?"

"There is no stone we will leave unturned. The most customised experience on the market is a phrase that not only do we live, but die for; if you know what I mean?"

Both chuckle: beyond urbane but below clutch your tummy, sweaty, head-pulsing chortling. A knowing chuckle, each confident in what each is bringing to the BBQ.

"As many are celebrities, we need to keep this heavily under wraps. We might be breaking a few rules too. And complete and utter privacy, is that going to be a problem?" I fiddle with my hair (can't resist).

"Discretion not only comes before valour in our book but before paparazzo, kiss-and-tells, tabloids, partridges and just about everything else that might get in the way of your experience; or let's call them experiences."

"You're quite funny. Does that come with the job?" I release the hair so the curl bobbles like a dropped testicle.

Phone buzzes (ignored).

"At these prices I'll be anything: funny, scary, professional but above all else accommodating. Would you like to go through the specifications? You've already chosen the location: a gothic horror film was actually exclusively shot at the Berkshire manor house you handpicked. While shooting, there were a few inexplicable happenings by the way."

"Now you're not being funny. That's moving into sales territory."

"This is actually a property we've been trying to procure as one of our listed venues for some time. In fact in a complete departure from sales when you selected it we hadn't secured the right to use it; we were close but there were risks. You know about the secret passages and dungeons but there is also a marsh that selectively appears out the back of the house depending on where the moon is. We've tried to find it on numerous occasions but have only been successful during a full moon."

"Spooky."

"Especially as you have it booked on a full moon. Not planning to dispose of any Boyband bodies are we?"

More chuckling.

*Chapter 13*

# BRIEF INTERLUDE

An interlude is described as 'an intervening period of time' or 'a thing occurring or done during an interval'. There is no mention of apology or memory loss or conscious shelving into the depths of anxiety ridden subconsciousness but it's worth apologising especially as this is one of those Boyband tales where undoubtedly you, the reader extraordinaire, is more keen to see how the characters self-destruct or redeem or emerge stronger than originally hinted at. But an apology is right here in front of you (SORRY) because no, Sexton doesn't wank himself to death and Kieron doesn't smoke himself to death but instead I wake up, pants around my ankles at a Boyband concert, scarcely remembering if I checked that no one spiked my drink and making God damn sure not to make the rookie mistake of accepting a drink from a Boybander.

Like today these types of things come busting out of the closet as shameful badges of honour where others around you applaud rather than skulk away as in the past. People actively seek out people strong enough to admit something – hugging an AIDS sufferer: so on trend. But not this cowgirl.

Berating yourself for knowing better doesn't ease the pain; doesn't make it go away. Not knowing what really happened, if anything, makes the teacup shatter with the lightning spiking your eyeball, the coated eyelash thorning your insides even after removal.

It is your fault; it is my fault. Not the naivety because that had already been pounded out of me like the dregs of an old-fashioned glass ketchup bottle, coating the lower rim in perpetual hibernation. Which means does that one moment lead to all this? This planning? This risk? Come on! We are a bit more evolved than all that. We are generation Nolan-film rather than Scott (pre-existential-parasite really rather Sigourney-in-her-pants-Scott).

It's not an itch, a statement or a quest although it might develop into that when writing the dreaded synopsis: gawd those literary monkeys do love a pigeonhole! It's not a calling, a belief, a desire.

It's hope. It is love. And it is thorough.

How does that eighties song go: We Don't Need Another Hero? Damn straight but we do need to know the way home.

## Chapter 14

# DEBZ & DIGBY

Debz vividly remembered conceiving each one of her seven children. And not the act itself but the moment of conception, the taste in the air, the density of her saliva, the position of her pelvis, toes and arch of her back. She'd describe it to me as – you know when you have a splinter and that crisp extraction you'd feel upon its removal? The intense opposite with the fait accompli of the wiggling tailed sperm headbutting relentless into the egg, magnetised into fulfilling a life as tough as Debz's eggs were, bullseyes that couldn't be missed. Even when she'd been on the pill and rubbered up for extra protection (round about after number five); even when she'd kindly requested the gentleman (or not so gentle man they'd become when writhing around on / in / around Debz's body) complete on her breasts, face, butt cheek or just on himself if the angle wasn't conducive to an abnormally normal porno money shot finish. No matter what prevention, precaution or premature avoidance, she'd fall. Hard. Pregnant. One time she even swears she fell asleep on said gentleman's shoulder and woke up with a baby. She felt it though, which either screams deep seated psychological daddy security issues for Debz or Rohipnol. As an aside, we actually figured out it was the latter, not only because Debz has an inner soul beauty which actually peers above her sexuality but because we found this baby daddy to be a repeat offender so we used him as a type of guinea pig early on: good old-fashioned blackmail. So not only does a banking salary put a lot of food in a lot of Debz's offsprings' mouths but it affords us a bit more luxury in our quests. We stay not as desperate as might shift the balance of power Boyband way and he gets to stay out of jail for late night city rapes in his loft apartment. There have to be some culprits who support gripping other culprits by those iconic pickled egg-like sacked pairs which seem to, for some fucking ungodly reason (why perhaps God is perceived as a male), denote bravery, power and fortitude. Whereas our magical genitals really just denote weakness, cowardice and humiliation. Pisses me right off. Let's rather hear lines like "Grow a pair of labia" or "Woman up, why are you being such a penis?"

When we started there was some concern over Debz as a candidate and not only because of her virility. Looking after seven bambinos while harvesting a maniacal plan (cue evil villainous laugh the likes of which the world ain't never seen bitch) that literally required full time devotion, attention and extreme role-playing complete with media scrutiny would at least be distracting and at most be derailing. But collapsing back into Debz's character arms – she's quietly tough with a calm yet determined soul. Her interaction with Digby would prove this. And of course our mini pre-quest quest, affectionately entitled Seven Bribes for Seven Brothers which would not only give us a deeper peer through the wormhole view into the male psyche but allow us to make mistakes while the group was growing, assess the missing girls required for the job and further enforce how each and every spittle of male behaviour had been spawned by Boybands, either in direct adulation or the complete antithesis of behaving in the opposite manner to prove the ultimate modern point: I'm cool because I hate Boybands. Well I'm cool because I date Boybands. And we're super cool because we extirpate Boybands. Spoiler alert.

It seems to be about making your intentions clear without admitting what your intentions really were. If the male subject was fully to comprehend what your intentions were you would lose some of the fear and most of the surprise. If they were left instead with a wonder of self-blame for bringing this affliction upon themselves and a sense that you were trying to help the unavoidable rather than twist the rope until their little beardy faces turned blue-purple-yellow (one extra there George RR), they were more susceptible to accommodate. Which in essence meant there was no real need for a bad cop: the male target himself could invariably become his own worst cop which, I suppose, is made significantly easier when you are metaphorically holding his eyelids open with toothpicks and shining an industrially powered bulb onto his transgressions, thus paving an 'only option' path towards the form of redemption where his misdemeanour would lessen, be hidden or forgotten long enough for said male to win back his soul. This, of course, was Debz's Phase A with our collective Phase B for Boyband utilising these techniques with the deftest sprinkle of random insanity to not only keep it interesting but keep it surreal and, by random insanity, I mean that of a Boybander. Like one of Gwynneth's Phase A tasks as a kickboxing instructress, supported spectacularly by her deadpan demeanour: when no one is paying attention find the most aggressive male in the group and backhand him across the face, then continue as normal. Worked a treat: he thought he'd imagined it, the back of the hand conscious to leave less evidence than a full-frontal palm slap, and Gwynne carried on her business as though nothing in the world had deviated in the minutes prior to his awakening. She did mention that, although she's not a smiler, one almost did creep in at his initial cheek touching moment being DPed inclusive of incredulity and shame.

So perhaps a Phase A example relevant to Debz. Child number three I believe, a little boy she called Nate, was conceived on camera and posted for the world to witness. Debz had been unaware Liam had hidden a camera in the room whilst he furiously went about his business, moving the angle of attack from one side of the room to another to maximise Debz's screentime. So over a period after the video was doing the rounds we managed to find an eerily similar porn video doing the rounds on some deviant, bordering illegal websites and casually leaked to Liam that his video was now enabling paedos and had been picked up by the special branch of MI5 investigating the source of these types of footage. We then again leaked that many young innocent revenge porn dudes had in fact gone to jail even when the videos were not of an illegal nature. And we know from countless American films how the prison system lurves paedophiles. Let simmer on the hob for some time as patience is the most undervalued trait known to women. Then the way out; Liam's redemption. We shot a confession video of Debz explaining she was of consenting age but with enough regret and coercion to suggest that something untoward had actually transpired; mix in the resultant Nate and the emotion would prove Liam putty in our hands from now on. We'd obviously not distribute the video under the guise of protecting Debz and Nate's anonymity but keep it in reserve as the rod for Liam's back, benefitting all future starlets in Liam's bed and allowing us unfettered access to control Liam's treatment of women and general approach to consented respect. For the haters spouting selfishness, see … not everything is born out of gender hatred or sheriff vigilantism. Greater good, so often a by-product, arching its back over the tape to finish first. A completely different scenario if Debz had planted the camera herself. But she didn't so it was a retribution reaction but not something we could perfectly wait for with the Boybands. You have to entrap a wee bit if you want to make a wee bit of damage, I mean, difference.

Debz had asked Maggie for a lift to see one of her sons and Maggie couldn't so volunteered Digby. The two had met before without incident but, in a crowded room of ostentatiously coloured cocktails, highly poised waitresses and dim lighting, you wouldn't expect a match made in Boyband heaven to be processed immediately. Plus if you take a woman who accidentally possesses sexual pheromones and place her in front of a man jaundiced by just about everything not his, the combination would be lethally exploitative. Was Digby our first bunny? Maybe, but perhaps it was just so much darn fun for Debz (and Maggie) they couldn't resist. Like a speckled black banana, he was overly ripe and ruining the fruit bowl for the rest of us.

Debz didn't need to dress like a tart to exude sexuality. She just sprayed it everywhere, lifted tail out the back like a lion on a nature programme, whether she wore joggers or jeans, tight top or gilet, socks or shoes. If you were forced to categorise her look it would likely be Girl Next Door but not like those Only Fans North England lasses who expose their gigantic real tits, slightly fat arses whilst maintaining their 'dignified' connections with the thousands of losers who really believe an email response from a softporn starlet is tantamount to a 'relationship'. No, with her slightly upturned nose, crisp packet wonky teeth, ridiculous body proportions and a demure expression screaming *mount me when you get the chance*, Debz was the unique Girl Next Door that no boy had ever lived next door to yet wished they had. She would hold a boy's stare long enough for him to image them both covered in oil and enveloped between her thighs; he'd will her eyes closed because of him and only him as though this was the fuck that would fuck the inviting expression off her face. While she sat beside Digby in that car, the windows slightly ajar for some air carelessly blowing her brown-blonde hair across that unfastened mouth, he couldn't help but be transfixed. And it wasn't only the mouth, the expectant expressing – as he cast his eyes down he wanted the propped-up breasts lounging below his cheek; he wanted the double bracketed strong quads duressing against the denim. A pedestrian crossing leapt unexpectedly out at him, a young boy's rugby ball bobbling across his eyeline as he swerved to miss the ball, his mind staring up at a naked Debz, seeing her mouth and upper lip warmly embraced between her sensations. Still the expression and even the near death of a pedestrian's rugby ball couldn't snap him from wanting her more than just about anything he'd ever wanted in his life. But these were modern Boyband times when tedium and manners should supposedly trump getting whatever the fuck you wanted with a straw and a mirror whenever the fuck you wanted. But it would be that easy – pull over and take her. But that might not be enough – he wanted to own every part of her, every pore on her body, every sweat duct and every light golden microscopic hair on her otherwise smooth skin.

Debz felt awful about the married guy, as we all did, because at his core he was a decent fellow, perhaps bound and bullied by modern monogamous convention and entering what the pundits would term a midlife crisis just before the size of the wallet couldn't make up for the lack of abs. But this was a modern midlife crisis in that he eventually came clean and tried to involve the wife who, having laid eyes on Debz, finally understood. It made them stronger and more accepting of who the other was, channelling an understanding that one person ticking every friggin' box on the planet was just plain untenable. Like getting a plumber to repair your ACL. And our upshot was spectacularly beneficial too: we learned that to shit all over someone's life for breaking an imposed societal norm was just plain wrong and that every situation had to have a positive outcome for said individual, community or society at large while ensuring we had the tools for the next fem fatal mission. Michel was his name and he loved the idea of loving his wife like he wanted Debz, so it wasn't merely about sex but it did result in (drum roll) another bouncing baby boy filled like a container with creamy skin, puffy cheeks and Debz's open mouth. Kit spends time between biological parents, who both adore him, with Michel's wife the most adoring of the trio. As though Kit represented some form of external questionnaire to fill out and prove love could transcend through someone you loved to a being you had no initial control or love for but which was made with some form of love. Woah, sounds like a cross between a care home commercial and a clunky Freudian interpretation. To bring it back to real, Michel never actually asked for the date finger as he knew it was Debz's inaugural finger in the road never travelled that could never be replaced. And would never need to be replaced because missionary plus Kit plus climbing atop an understanding platform reserved for very few married couples was where Michel was and wanted to remain.

Back to the car journey, Digby's hands steady on the wheel while his mind masturbates him into a frenzy. He is literally frothing at the mouth, anus and eyeball as he contains his unabated lust for his passenger. And we knew this behaviour was rife in a celebrity Boybander of any decryption but we never knew how far Debz's powers could push a man to betray not only his existing relationship but the public's saccharine perception. He'd hold. He'd hold? Flash forward to Digby hunched over trying to tease out his limp prick, his Brazzers subscription racked up miles whirring like a black and red numbered electricity meter at night-time in an insomniac's home. Fuck sakes he'd think; if a mental erection could culminate in physical form, his would be one of those giant vascular light red pulsating anime cocks, swollen with ink and ready to mow down the balance of the page. But here, back with Maggie, he just couldn't arouse a single iota of blood to enter and drag droopy snoopy from the protesting dead back to the functional life. Thinking back to Maggie would help and it did. Cue tissues as Boybands clean up their self-inflicted messes nowadays and a Fear Factor bucket load of shame for not only thinking about Debz every moment since what actually happened in the car but for betraying Maggie and, most significantly, losing control such that he had to actually admit … he was a wanker.

There's a t-shirt here somewhere … [Insert our band name here which of course we don't really have]: Making wankers out of Boybanders everywhere or [Women of the World]: Revealing the true wankathon hidden in all our modern Boybanders, no matter how sweet they appear or [Girls]: your Boybander is a wanker and will likely stray once you have served your purpose, use or allowed him into your person.

So what did actually happen in the car?  Debz blushes and laughs.  From her hospital bed.

## Chapter 15

# TaBBY

Tabby was nursing a grazed cheek, sandpaper appearance like she'd been dragged down the road behind a monster truck. Appearances can be deceiving and with Barton's heft now accompanying her every move, spitting sideways glances from perhaps similarly abused marching shoppers put Barton on a tsunami to Raising Fists on Women Camp. He'd hold her arms tightly enough to let everyone know he cared for her but not too tightly as though he was frog marching a procession advertisement of couples' bliss. A few diehard fans would stop and ask for his autograph but not as many as in the past, as he'd acquired a few more pounds and with it a strange dose of skin rash. It wasn't us; well … might have been. Indirectly.

He was juicing too. And not Generation Iron doped up on enough testosterone to grow another ball sack juicing but juicing like he'd given up masticating. And he believed it was working. With the onset of the rash, shiny pink with angry red and white spots littered from brow to chin dimple, he'd received that medical advice we all live with every day … no fucking clue. Once the big bad ass conditions are excluded the UK medical fraternity goes into shrugs, refusing to answer direct questions and a litany of tests for minor conditions which really do amount to zap squat (note the juice and squat connection … one more rep bro!). So Barton took to Sir Google and found an Aussie with a similar condition and similar weight issues who basically went from a few dozen snags on the barbie to blending just fruit and veg for the rest of his life and sending his jaw muscles into hibernation. That's when Tabby fell: when Barton proved he could stay on this diet for a month. And as we know, when Tabby falls, she hits the ground or wall or earth with furious ferocious force. Like a black out without the black or out.

An enduringly positive element about their relationship was Barton's ability to lift her after any fall, as easy as scooping sand into a bucket. During their tenure as plus size Boybander and strife he'd dropped her once and this, she claimed, was purposeful after another stand-off fight where either budging to the other's doctrine was about as likely as either of the 2020 US Presidential candidates surviving until the next virus. Tabby had also given the juicing diet a whirl only to cataclysmically spin off her axes when we found her face down in a Domino's Pepperoni Passion and extra chicken kickers coma on the lounge floor.

When we quizzed Tabby on their sex life, something we tried to avoid as much was collateral damage and this role play could have negative effects in the longer term, she was cagy which told us something had happened but nothing of any great worth. Worth for Tabby that is. It emerged that the inverse proportion between Barton's arch of his gut and the length of his wanger meant he couldn't actually get it in. Straining and contorting had pushed the tip in but a fraction – a busybody shopper checking the equivalent filling of an M&S sandwich at the apex – but by then Tabby's (let's call it) entry criteria had sufficiently dried up to make it a complete no slide zone. And Barton liked to eat, so let's just say he ate then likely finished himself off next to a burrito and maple syrup donut during the pre-juicing era. And with the onset of the rash not only had Barton not felt at all like any kind of intimacy but Tabby had got it into her head she'd throw up if she looked at it too long. She feigned woman issues as it was a fine line between ostracising one's Boybander partner and getting to relationship-ending territory where there was nothing left to fight for. Bizarrely with this Generation Boy they actually grew more attached as the couple moved closer to the precipice, as though the combination of mummy issues, celebrity scrutiny and months of conscious coupling created a void that had been permanently filled with any hint of other girl permanence, sending wedding bells ringing through their little boy heads. And this was something to be avoided. Perhaps not in all cases.

Tabby had thrown up once on Barton when he showed her his back: mottled between the grey-black hairs hiding in folds along the fault lines of his fatty delts, she'd noted how the rash crusted meaning the lid of most of the segments was raised to reveal firstly what she could imagine was yellow-grey pus and secondly when he moved his shoulder a tiny volcano fissure of orange-red blood. When she told us during a gathering complete with sappy violent romcom, lentil crisps and fluffy slippers we'd all been holding our guts, Jemima actually gagging at the visceral rendition. He asked her to wipe his back after his spontaneous deposit, so she locked herself in the downstairs toilet in protest. Cue stand-off number one mazillion-and-one: she slept in the downstairs loo overtly refusing whilst propping her head on the loo roll holder and Barton, in similar obdurate mode, refused to wash it off until she came out to help. Ah gawd she recalled the sound of that shower cranking up the next day due to a rehearsal that couldn't be missed was like sweet harmonic massing music to an ear all crumpled from a night on the loo holder.

# Chapter 16

# PaRTY

Sometimes you do things because you have to; sometimes for money, sometimes for love. Sometimes though, it's because you just plain God damn enjoy the stuff. You wallow in what you actually enjoy doing: an American Beauty moment but replacing roses with say chocolate or warm velvet on a cold winter evening. When you are fortunate enough to know exactly what you like doing it becomes easier to justify, especially in this world where our generation has that luxurious middle-class sensibility of chasing dreams in opposition to survivalist chasing coin. But when you reach that edge, dangling over while someone close enough to you holds you by a thread, the precipice precedes boredom and tedium eradication. You're bored plus he's boring so you change him for the greater good and scratch your boredom but not until it becomes a Barton rash.

We all arrived at the party separately. And not because it would otherwise be a giveaway but because at its core all us girls were our own individuals. The Armageddon walk to save the planet from a meteor with Bruce and Ben while lilting Liv wept back on earth for new squeeze and daddy (less so unfortunately though) was not to be reproduced in even higher slow-mo FPS, us bitches the all-conquering front cover. Nope. And no glamorous sequins or bikinis or anything. Upon arrival no blow, no sick mansion, no dope soundtrack ... where was the fun nowadays? Would we have to bring it ... again?

When I arrived, a few people mingled outdoors and in, while the Jacuzzi bubbles bubbled invitingly yet lonesomely in vain. Taking a plunge would involve some form of nudity which was perhaps exploitation. Note to self – we'd have to crack that ostrich egg a bit later. Of the milling Millies there wasn't one with a boob job or fat stuck to the window lips or an Orangina complexion. Just normal support staff for the bands of boy and some close friends and family. A sudden panic came over me – was this a trap? A show for all those in proximity to relax their guard only for a troop of circus freaks to burst from the Jacuzzi bubbles clad in chainsaws, amputeed midgets, free drugs and unpronounceable STDs. It was what the party needed. There wasn't even a single person snogging or boy putting his hand where it shouldn't be. No protest scream to be ignored from the top room while the savages repeatedly entered the same gate. Sexton and Damien were playing on their phones opposite one another.

Breathing in the clean air was another slap in the face, not even a hint of weed tantalisingly sweet to offset Himalayan Jasmine and Grass Root air scent. The study was dimly lit with some of the boys, Willow and Gerson perhaps, watching a screen. Was this the moment it all changed, the flicker of debauched pornography of doe eyed West Coast wannabees staring up at a banana bunch of cocks? Strictly. On the TV. Shit you I do not.

Was this the prior behaviour redemption or the new excuse?

Kieron, Barton and Digby are upstairs sitting in one of the rooms. Kieron sees me and hides his vape. The other two continue debating the campaign to position Boybands as Manbands in mainstream media.

"Boybands are a dying if not dead construct," I hear Barton spout.

"But if we don't keep trying to reinvent the Boyband genre then we're letting down a new generation of adoring fans," says Digby, furrowed brow the main course. Oh how we cannot wait for pudding.

"We're men now and so is our music."

"Can we not live that ideal without an actual campaign? Too overt."

"Well like any campaign it won't be visible; we're behind it but we will be the beneficiaries."

"What type of music would characterise Manbands?"

"Adult male music appealing to teenage girls for thoroughly wholesome ideals, posters, cutting and old man crushes. The paedo's handbook," I hear my brain scream at them. Where are my girls? Further down the corridor a room with multiple double beds throbs. Throbs from a sense of anticipation but also music from the liveliest room in the house. They're all there: Dannielle snacking on a fingernail; Jemima closing a position on her trading app; Tabby refusing to budge over on the bed for Gwynneth, who pushes her back, cheeks reddening; Maggie watching Debz talking, looking up and down her body with her legs straight in the air, wiggling her toes, and Renea slumped asleep in a leather chair.

"We have been waiting for you." In unison.

"Why?"

"Thought you might be able to shock this party back from flatlining," says Gwynne.

"We have the haunted house excursion for that, don't we?"

"Well if this is sufficiently comatosed we have no foundation to begin the craziness. A skeleton jumping out of the closet will be about as exciting as it gets," says Debz.

"I take your point. So what we need is a collective generation of uncharacteristic behaviour. There are many other Boybanders about. Is that sort of mischief too base for us? What gets these boys going? It used to be sex, the promise of taboo sex, celebrity, drugs and power; now it's mindfulness, solidity of relationship, likes on Twitter, appearances on terrestrial TV and documentary deals. We need to pretend to tap into these contrived desires to bring out the real base ones then shame them for digressing. While maintaining our dignity."

"Feels like we're accelerating," says Jemima.

"Some of the relationships are creaking. And finding each's Achilles doesn't always lead to the self-implosion we're hoping for. If we don't coordinate the fall then there is no statement. And I know some of you have genuine feelings so let's go back to where it started. Go back to the why and worry about the how later. We know what happened with their mothers and yes, we know the offspring don't answer for the sins of the parent, but each would have been predestined to male domination through celebrity innateness. True modern feminism is not merely about equality and dragging the misogynistic dinosaurs into line but about holding the women accountable. The mothers. Honouring each by severing the most sacred connection of all: the umbilical cord."

Laughter interrupts from another room: old fashioned laughing at laughter, not collegiate Boyband laughter. Willow appears at the door, anxious with concern.

"We have a situation developing," he stammers. As though he's calling in the cavalry. As we gather and strut towards the noise he explains.

"One of Kieron's old school friends arrived and sort of pushed his way in uninvited. He has a dog, one of those Pitbull fighting dogs which he's using in the wrong manner."

In the room most of the Boybanders are either aloft or trying to get higher than the dog with the chain collar. It looks like it's having fun and we're probably tempted to let it fill its doggie paw boots but we have to keep up alpha appearances and this just looks too good a situation to pass up. Talk ensues and we're told we're whores and bitches and money grabbers so Gwynne benignly grabs Jamal in a headlock while we all carefully shuttle the dog into the bathroom. It is not the poor animal's fault but it will have to be put down once we've called the police and likely Jamal will need to be put down too. Glancing at Gwynne enquiring as to the tightness of her grip, she shakes her head with enough uncertainty to retain hope that he might die.

Like I said just for the fun of it sometimes.

With the problem so swiftly dealt with we're bored again.

## *Chapter 17*

# Me

There's a groan at the back of the audience. Or a resignation. Whittering on about everyone else's Boyband conquests has left us balls deep into this tale without so much as even a sniff, flick, flutter or butt cheek wiggle of my man … erm … boy. Well, this is where there could be the proverbial fly in the ointment: he's a good guy. I wouldn't go as far to say perfect because that's an absolute ideal so misused in romcoms that Matthew McConaughey (pre-Queer Eye for the Actual HIV-inseminating Wife Murdering Dallas Buying Queer Guy slash Interstellar and during the Lance Armstrong jogging shirtless bromance phase) likely had the word as his ring tone. Plus perfect is imperfect if you know what I mean: if a human being was practically perfect in every way, literally supercalmfragrantlistenerfreeofhaletosis, they'd be imperfect. It is undoubtedly our flaws that make us perfect; we are no longer idolising blinding teeth American news presenters with flawless skin, all blonder than a golden retriever; now we embrace blind presenters and ones with funny shaped heads and accents. That slightly wonky eye, snaggle tooth, downward pointing nipple or unsightly mole makes us imperfect which makes us imperfect which doesn't make us perfect because ... well ... what you just read.

Kelly doesn't even look like a Boybander. His publicist and stylist and manager all tried to get him to and, even with some choice layered all-the-rage-again nineties layers or thrown together bling or eyeliner, he couldn't look Boybandery. He has stubble for one and pretty darn sexy stubble, probably from when he was about fourteen as it looks settled, embedded and somehow permanent. He'll shave in the morning and bam, like a miracle grow cartoon hedge, it's there, dark brown spikes jostling all over his face, a sexy coat of facial paint. And he's not pushy: he's never put undue pressure on me to do anything which has meant I've kept my Boyband virginity intact. Even when leathered, pissed or buzzing after a gig, he'd not laid a hand where it shouldn't be or held my hand where it certainly shouldn't be. And this has resulted in certain relationship calm befitting of old married couples; whereas most twenty-somethings are going at it like rabbits on steroids, we're more of a "When is the next series of Ozark coming out?" pair. Initially, I picked him for this very reason, aware he was an avid reader and supporter of local bookstores, accidentally running into him in the Muswell Hill bookstore whilst browsing the James Joyce section, another noted favourite of his. There can't be many Boybands who can read, let alone read Joyce, I remember thinking. Perhaps his Irish roots dragged him towards *Ulysses* which I had to know backwards to be credible.

We'd had a coffee that day, me pretending not to know of his minor celebrity and him equally taken by the friendly, blasé, intellectual demeanour. Our second meeting had to wait even when he did get quite insistent but eventually coffee became coffee and a muffin became him trying to impress me with grandiose gestures on balloons and helicopters to romantic dinners at little known best-kept-secret restaurants which then fell into relationship territory. Kelly was difficult to read after that though, almost as though this goal of me on his arm meant he could retract emotionally, spoiling me as a substitute for emotional vulnerability.

"I just don't have issues," he'd say. "Sorry about that."

But the balanced star needed a balanced girlfriend and we worked well together, what with all my secrets. It also allowed me to focus on the other girls as this was underway during the bookstore phase. I suppose at its core being close to perfect would always help any woman seeking the attention of a Boybander, as that initial attraction had to spark but it had to be subtle with each having a kind a beauty that would attract the designated fellow. Even with the celebrity Beauty and the Beast trend, everyone had to be stunning, the entry criteria as important as the emotional hurt suffered in the past.

Kelly was straightlaced, so much so that it became fun taunting him. I'd ask him if he wanted to watch porn and he'd reel back in disgust; I'd purposefully walk in on him doing a number 2 and he'd stagger to the door arse distended, pants around the ankles to shut my chortles and feigned apologies out, my intrusive glances in direct opposition to his "Don't look at me!" crouching hunchback deportment. When he finished up he'd shower immediately after said invasions in egregious solitude, as though getting off the throne prior to the wiping extravaganza meant he had soiled his character and routine sufficiently to warrant an overly hot water and hand sanitised shower. He was also a neat and hygienic freak which also meant more fun: leaving dirty girly G-strings strewn around the floor, facing upwards, would send him into frenzied clean up and, yes … you guessed it … shower. Touching his hands was also a big no-no, in bed grabbing his palm he'd get up to wash with Dove soap and turn over in faint protest. There had to be a level of caution here though, as the girls told me, leaving a cute, healthy, sinking turd in the loo as an unearthing gift for Kelly in the morning would push him into the realms of 'disgusted by' rather than mildly annoyed and blaming himself for his obsessive shortcomings.

When we're together there is something magical though. Like Bonnie and Clyde and Malcolm in the Middle with me representing both Bonnie and Clyde. What the press term our 'adoring gazes' are often just the sharing of an internal joke or something that has tickled the funny bones. A few snaps in various publications had that blue to green umbilical cord, making us 'solid' and the 'most desirable couple of the year'. We're not overtly affectionate in public either, more bro and sis rather than puppy Tom bounding from Oprah's sofa to Joey's tower over bosom. The glance and eyes magnetising always better than being held in one another's temporary arms. And we don't look at anyone else like that, Kelly because he probably does truly love me and me because his species is the origin of all that I hold dear and this eyeball planets colliding allows me to refocus efforts in the direction they should be.

It might be difficult though. And if I'm the hypocrite who reneges at the moment of truth, I'd not be saving lives much longer. But I will confess as my one and only secret away from the girls, that I am struggling to see how this will end for Kelly. He'll either have to do something so uncharacteristically bad or I'll have to make him do something so uncharacteristically bad or I'm going to have to follow through with generational sins, biting the self-proclaimed bullet so hard I either chip a tooth or choke on the metal.

*Chapter 18*

# Damien

With enough supportive coercion to sink a freight liner Gwynne ensured Damien achieved some level of body contentment. The 'energy' in his workouts rivalled Ronnie Coleman, the plush gym surroundings betraying the grimy, rusty real gym The King would have trained in, but he did start seeing genuine results, first with the chub layer removal then with muscle density more impressive than his wildest dreams. Gwynne got into a satisfying yet mildly irritating for other gym goers habit of slapping Damien in the face before each forced set or final rep. She'd, of course, do this without even a mouse tail flicker of a smile which meant Damien had no choice but to grab the weight, take it seriously and heave. A strange side effect of all this huffing and pumping was that Damien got very vascular, as though each path from and to the heart required a bigger runway to strut on. He developed two side temporal squiggles which Gwynne affectionately named his 'gym horns'.

In line with the usual genetic confusion that blights all parents: 'little Jonny looks nothing like either of us, and behaves nothing like either of us' it might be worth mentioning that his mother was a supermodel serial killer. That's not a combination of phrases one is likely to hear often or any time again soon, but Nell was what you might call genetically gifted physically and genetically indurate mentally. Experts debated on countless crime shows as to whether her penchant for gruesome murder was born from being so ridiculously accomplished at everything without ever trying that the tedium of existence led her to explore other thrills, or whether she found genuine pleasure from snuffing out lives. Damien had always idolised her, maintaining her killing spree was more Dexterous than Mansonous in that she went after bad people and those more deserving of being in extended periods of pain. And sex was always her lure for the hapless victims, all male, the snare easier than catching a handful of worms in a bucket. Nell's theory was that men were inherently weak when it came to sex and this weakness needed to be eradicated. Her spree had been unbelievably impressive, initial suspicions quelled by her appearance: why would someone who looked like THAT need to do something as grotesque as removing a fat lawyer's genitals and stuff them in his greedy partner's mouth, the two slumped side by side in an expensive serial fuck pad apartment owned by the law firm. And she was extremely careful with the DNA too, having a brain to match the face and body plus being a CSI addict in those early days before it got shit.

Damien had kept a picture of the two of them from when he was a young boy, now dogeared from carrying it around and faded with time but even at an ungainly angle, Nell leaning over him in a sandpit, her beauteous limb length, curves and defined facial features were undeniable. A shiny natural blonde, the colour never evaporated; a picture emerged from her maximum-security prison and still the hair shone, the eyes sparkled and the body mesmerised. Stories had surfaced from the prison of some of the butcher ring-leader inmates being brutally ended in shower cubicles and cells with suspicions pointing Nell's way. Sworn testimonies from accommodated guards and evidence mysteriously tainted while held in the prison smacked of – to those who knew her anyway – Nell jumping with both feet back into her old ways; her old new ways perhaps. Reformation only works if the environment doesn't force the monster out as a survivalist.

Gwynne knew the aspiration to be a better version of one's self on the outside for Damien was driven by his mother. He'd never really been good enough for her even after placing second in a national singing and dancing competition. He'd never known his father; had only been told stories by his mother of how, if Damien was the apple, then his dad was a pear tree. Damien's arrival had initially been a happy time for Nell when in commune with other single mothers but when it became apparent that his little piggy eyes and chubby knees were a permanent fixture, Nell lost interest in raising an average baby. That's when her killing accelerated, got more extreme and invariably more sloppy. When she was caught she blamed Damien for the ultimate discovery and treated his adoring shortcomings as the reason for her fall from grace. In this classic world we live in, when she was arrested and released on bail, she shot a supermodel spread for Gucci entitled *Superkill*, setting a new fee record for print media, spawning a set of photos now more iconic by the day.

Whilst in prison, Nell signed a lucrative book detail, a 'How To' on gruesome male murders. Unlike OJ it wasn't 'if I did it' but 'how I did it' with exhaustive detail, not only showcasing Nell's unbelievable patience in planning, prepping, exterminating and disposing of but her medical-quality level of anatomical sagacity. For example, stripping meat to dispose of the meat and bones separately is a big no-no, as is the idea of watching a person's soul leave their body when life escapes. It wasn't a computer game, she'd stated, just a quick, noneventful, unimaginative slumping. She'd spent extensive time with victims, both pre- and post-mortem, genuinely empathetic to some unknown development and being woman enough to set her captives free if they showed a level of empathy in return and, more importantly, a repentant disposition. That was, of course, if the chance of discovery was less than zero only.

Damien had tried to visit her in prison and she'd accepted the odd visit only to stand him up or completely ignore him. On the visits they did interact she could barely look at him, clearly unimpressed by his dress sense or latest hair style or threaded eyebrows or man tan. In prison she'd had enough clout to start an underground Twitter account posting videos of prison goings on and Damien had followed her, which meant all his Boyband followers followed suit in turn. This so repulsed Nell she posted a series of unflattering teenage pics of Damien and asked him and his teenage girl followers to follow somewhere else. With Damien's recently acquired body and aesthetic confidence, he plotted to get into 'sick shape' then bust her out of prison, the 'only retribution available to him'. Gwynne had talked him off the aiding and abetting plank yet did use Nell as a form of motivation to get Damien into that 'sick shape'. And he had been sick; so sick it almost landed him in hospital. Without Gwynne knowing he'd bought some diuretics on the black market to remove water from his cells after hearing that this is what bodybuilders did around competition time. What the salesman failed to add was that a few of said bodybuilders had died on stage and, after a monumental headache, Damien had passed out in the changing room at Westfield. A stiff gallon of water and medical care later he was better but suffered the unsmiling assassination from Gwynne which set back his prison reveal by some months.

"You have to look natural," Gwynne had told him after an ejaculation of apologies and second coming of 'never again' rhetoric. "You can't look like a tangerine with swollen traps carrying surfboards with an additional one stuck up your arse. It has to be seamless, like you're not trying. Unremarkable grey shirt but snug enough to show your pecs; jeans that actually fit; smell good." She'd been concerned that the new image might set him away from the Boyband path onto one of credible cool so persuaded him really that this was a one-off mummy-impressing play and, besides, she knew her stranglehold over his actions, self-image, diet, choices and freedom was so tightly held that if she needed to exercise some follow-on outlandish request to drag him back to Boybandom, then this could happen easier than flicking him squarely on the forehead while completing a lateral row.

She was more progressed on Control than any of the others at this stage. Meaning either she was really good, the others needed a friendly competitive reminder to catch up, this influence was always seasonal or some would require the levers to be more sophisticated: not your basic arm around the shoulder versus hairdryer bullying but more of a subtle confusion meets historic familiar level meets sexual repression meets modern celebrity constraints gig.

But taking nothing away from Gwynneth. She was a forceful and steaming magician.

*Chapter 19*

# Renea

You know that feeling when your statement or rationale backfires to the extent that the egg on your face congeals, rancifies and runs down your head into your eyes, around your nose and collects in your gob? You actually taste the irony and not like 'I can taste your fear' late night crappy TV but actual taste where you can vividly describe the notes, flavours and ingredients. When what you had intended becomes the hindering factor. Well, all hands to the pump to avoid this burgeoning situation with Renea and Kieron …

"That's what JT did?" says Kieron.

"Who the fuck is JT?" says Renea.

"Justin Timberlake."

"What! Are you like fifty years old! Who is he nowadays?"

"Fair point."

"You won't even argue it?"

"It doesn't seem worth it."

"To argue at all or this point alone?"

"Do we have to do this now?"

"We don't do this ever. You just back down no matter what. You're too lazy to argue your point or just can't be bothered. Same diffs either way."

Kieron takes a long slow breath as though toking on a short-awaited joint of good herbal quality and consistency.

"I just don't feel having a naked girl in the lyrics sends a strong enough message."

"Now that's a fair point," Renea says realising she's falling into her own trap. "See what I did there," she continues. "I let you off the hook because I couldn't be arsed to argue or because I genuinely agree with your point. There is no real distinction with us anymore."

"You could be right."

"I don't know where you stand."

"Shall we light one?"

"No. Maybe."

"Let's light one?"

"What did your buddy JT – copying Jay-Z to become his hundredth problem by the way – do or say or sing?"

"He wanted her, or you the young girl song listener or buyer, nekid by the end of this song. It just seems impractical – why not just say he wants to take her clothes off because the song is so sexy?"

"Doesn't quite have the succinct elegance of the line?"

"Perhaps you are right."

"Perhaps I'm not right. Perhaps you should push the lyrics you want into the band as hard as you can."

"My lyrics are all just naked chick lyrics but I don't think the boys want anything saucy or controversial. Fucks with our image."

"Would your mother have cared about offending a few boys? She went a bit further on the offence chart."

"You're right and she did but I just don't like to rock – or pop the boat too much nowadays. I can barely pick my eyelids up here. Have you fed the animals?"

"No, have you?

"No. Don't think so. Might have. Where is the lighter?"

Uncle was just fucking with Kieron as they'd banned pets after the Nana/cat debacle. Kieron's apathy, although perfectly on script, was beginning to wear a bit thin on Renea and not because he was any more or less empathetic than her but because he had no distinct character left, drained of opinions or harmless debate. This might be as good a time as any to provide a hint more colour on Uncle and the origins of Renea's nickname. It was a closely guarded secret which you would imagine would be wholeheartedly accepted in this overly tolerant society, embraced even. But because the origins were in real human strife plus she'd kept it hidden for so long plus plus when I found her and we wrestled off the canvas together it became the ultimate symbol to dispose of a penis. Inverse proportionality when revealed. A swap for a swap.

Henry Cavill, previously 'fat Cavill' at school and every care home incumbent's dream boat of the month took on an iconic eighties' adaptation called The Man from U.N.C.L.E. with Guy (then just free from Madge I think) (I think I'm still a gangsta) Ritchie. The film was overtly average and the TV show likely the same but we all agreed the phrase was iconic and we didn't know why; not due to production quality, uniqueness of theme or anything. It just sounded snappy. So in the ultimate act of uncharacteristic proactiveness, Renea had decided to cut it off; well, have it removed. She'd changed from a man to a woman, hence was a man. It had been a big post traumatic teen years decision, a litany of unpleasant, soiled concord with men meaning she didn't want to be one any longer. Kieron had no clue of course as removing said apparatus was significantly easier than the other way around: growing it on your back or forearms only to have the dastardly thing attached with that skin at a low success rate, a success rate at least one of the Boybanders would likely be experiencing if all went according to plan. The reaction, though, was going to be monumental because deep below the haze of failed assertion was a deep-seated homophobia. This we knew. A lack of scarring, the healing powers of our superhuman Uncle granola ethno-bongo champion and an acute awareness of how to shut down publicity rumours in this space meant Renea had operated free as a female bird for some years now, embracing her new body by letting it be truly woman (we've covered the lack of woman scaping and general carefree hygiene approach) almost as though she was test driving a new car. Her lady car complete with all (and none of) the trimmings.

*Chapter 20*

# THE BEGINNING

Covid. Sick to the teeth of hearing the word. It's something that not only created a level of human suffering the world might never have seen but created a deterred inconvenience for us on so many levels. The Boyband generation and followers tended to adopt a blasé devil may care attitude which enflamed our circle when Jemima lost her grandfather to Covid. We all took the necessary precautions and followed guidelines which rendered many of the meticulously planned exploits either null and void or null until further notice. It made us rethink the intention and outcome of the haunted mansion group activity.

Over a few bottles of an exclusive Syrah reserve batch around mine on a chilly pre-Spring evening while the majority of the boys were banding as boys in bands do (pre-Covid) we meticulously (I say meticulously but I mean pissed as eight hens in a tumble-dryer) mapped out two levels of haunted activity. It really wasn't that hard especially when you sprinkle an overly healthy dosage of intellect, creativity and independence possessed by all my girls. The first level was to pique the interest and tap into the fetish fantasy of each, pushing the boundary under the cover of horror gimmick darkness. The second was fatal. Initially we'd hoped to do a two-prong visit using the first to lull the boys into the idea that this place was edgy yet inherently safe. The second visit would be the statement but this required some planning, especially the cover-up. So the trial run, now dented by Covid, still had those initial designs, scribbled by each of the girls while the wine sloshed and the Florentines were damaged. Some of the drawings still had remnants of spilt wine, the odd choccy smear and a general pong of chick power.

Danielle would immerse herself in a huge old Victorian bath full of peanut M&Ms, deeper than it was wide. The surprise moment would be followed by pinning Gerson in the bath whilst a huge pipe flooded more M&Ms into the bath. In the panic he might or might not drown in actual chocolate, but hard M&Ms wouldn't necessarily do the trick so the heat in the room and attached to the bath would need to be ramped up sufficiently to create this reality. If it was too hot and he got scolded so be it: another scream amongst the house not amiss in any way.

Uncle's suggestion was somewhat more genuine horror film rather than a darker Willy Wonka. She'd lived in the country and noted how, when summer became autumn, the lazy flies would invade the house with a slovenly buzz that betrayed the survival instinct of their species. They were always the blue-green big ones, splattered such that cleaning up required two pieces of Bounty and water to wipe the yellow-brown entrails off the wall. So Uncle would lure Kieron into a darkened room, clad in fake spider webs for associative atmosphere. She'd have to get him to stand in a certain spot, an X, not difficult as he'd just do what he was told. That or she could place a joint on a table in the right area. Above him would be a huge Boyband swatter which would come down – bamn! Flattening the lazy fly. Oh too much for Debz literally kicking her legs in the air in hilarity. The design of a big human swatter would be bespoke and the mechanism's force would need to be adapted for round two: stunned then flattened.

Debz always had a thing for clowns so part of her cathartic treatment was to make it sexy. That night, let's say five bottles in, we watched a trailer called Wrinkles the Clown, a seemingly real docuhorror; needless to say Debz was enveloped in my armpit screaming hysterically while the group made circus giggle noises. So her idea was to clad some exceedingly attractive prostitutes, one of which would be her, into sexy clown costumes and ascend on Sexton. He couldn't resist, could he? Especially with consent from Debz. Like the heavens opened and hailed scantily clad sexy clowns on an unsuspecting Boybander. Debz knew, of course, that if her coulrophobia was say an understated platinum necklace, Sexton's was West Coast rapper bling, clumps of gold chains pulling the wearer's neck to the earth, bowing from bling weight. And she also knew that when extremely nervous he would sometimes ejaculate, so coupling fear with sex and a brief to not stop until he'd fulfilled all his potential could becum well ... quite hilarious.

Jemima started by just drawing a dollar sign then getting stuck. With her sophisticated brain she was working around a concept, toying with how to make hers cleverer that anyone else's. She knew the horror motif was the cover so didn't necessarily have to stick to that, perhaps specifically with the reveal rather than the build-up. She had to tap into some things that Willow wanted more than anything, expose his ecowarrior hypocrisy if it existed and exchange it for good old fashioned based insatiability. So Jemima went biblical on us: Proverbs 23:5 says 'Cast but a glance at riches, and they are gone, for they will surely sprout wings and fly off to the sky like an eagle'. A good job or business and its steady earnings can be here today and gone tomorrow. Be rich in good deeds. Willow would be treated like Mammon and the personification of any sermon on the mount evil had to be exorcised accordingly. No not self-flagellation or anything of a later era just pure exorcism which implied some level or redemption, which of course there could be none. The physical disfigured form on the demon Mammon could remain with Willow but this would hamper the Boyband career so perhaps emotional for round one followed by ... well ... you get the drift. Hugging a tree while it crushes your Christian soul and you accept your failings for wanting all of the overly evolved trappings of being a good social citizen was the kind of babble we had to decipher from Jemima. There was even mention of making him really embrace Black Lives Matter by actually making him become black ...

permanently to live the struggle and disregard all privilege that came with being white but this was round about bottle number twelve so we just figured we'd leave it to Jemima whose calculating brain was literally spouting smoke from her ears.

Digression time bitches! That's what someone hollered when the night got ripe and the bottle clinking of empty vessels because louder yet less intrusive. We took selfies. It had to be an actual selfie even though it would have been easier to take of each other but the angle had to seem real; authentic: the worm had to actually dangle in perceived agony on the hook rather than hang dick limp in resignation. And we were careful; well, careful as girls are when brewing plots and sipping wide rimmed glasses and exercising one's God-given female right to have collective fun. Together is just way more fun. So the selfies were anonymous to anyone not familiar with the biblical proportions of our all female cast; we can't have these things leaking and recognisable what with all this minor celebrity status and all. Now comes the really fun bit … we swapped phones prior and made sure to leave out any majorly iconic and distinct traits (read Renea's bush, Gwynne's knees, Danielle's cleavage and Debz's well … everything in focus). So it took time to get the right one but all at once like an inviting selfie tide worming into Boyband hearts the world over, we sent. Then stood still. Then laughed. Hard.

Each believed it was said girlfriend's parts. Without question. Further confirming that to them we are literally just pieces of toned, tanned, well-formed flesh. Sending a brain

pic might be just too graphic, and too painful! Digby
received Renea's butt, immediately asking for more. Damien
got a warm snap of Maggie's furrowed brow and responded
with an angry then salivating emoji. Sexton got Gwynne's
back and smidgeon of side boob with no response
forthcoming until much later with what looked like a bashful
gay GIF. Barton got Debz's feet as every snap which
preceded we decided would be reserved for Digby at a later
date and likely to stop pulses, and he responded with "Shall
I show you mine?" Tabby was so desperate to instantly
respond "No" so we had to wrestle the phone free while she
kicked and screamed. Willow got the top of Tabby's pubic
hair, a hint squinting above the screen like one of those long-
nosed caricatures we used to draw peering over a wall as kids;
he responded with "More please!" and a downward facing
arrow likely to signify lower down bitch. Gerson got
Jemima's mouth, close up and seductively open, who
immediately responded with a litany of food emojis across
the page: a meat-eating junk foodie's wet dream. And finally
Kieron received Dannielle's butt hole without a response. I
said finally because that completed the seven circle so I was
permitted to just send Kelly my pursed lips which we debated
showed a kiss versus straining on the toilet.

The way to a Boybander's heart.

Oh and by the way girls do watch porn together. We don't
do it for the same reason as men, literally to hunch over and
yank and yank until the ever-avoidable Oh-MG he looks like
such a pathetic dickhead ejaculating; it's more comedic than
orgasmic, more judgemental than a learning manual, more

cinematic than habitual. And if there is one thing we could just put out there from the outset to all porn producers, wannabes and aspirational performers: please get rid of the ugliness. Girls care about faces; nice, sweet, handsome faces. For one it reduces the pain of seeing the contorted O-face. And of course we note some have the bodies and the cock size and the load volume but puhlease, just a few men we actually like to look at having sex.

Back to the haunted mansion pre-cauldron cauldron. Renea took a boatload of coercion to get going again plus a shipload of supportive ideas plus a planetload of gore as not many of the girls liked Kieron much. The settled consensus was glue him to the sofa. This would involve getting him naked first as we needed actual skin to superglue against the sofa. The darkened haunted room would need to be fitted with one of those turbine spinners used at fairground attractions, then we'd spin him, to a degree out of curiosity, to see if the glue or his skin held long enough, the law of separation physics pulling him off the sofa crash test dummying him into an opposing wall. 'Spinning him off his lazy glued to the sofa arse' was the less than snappy working title. Uncle seemed more content with the swatter motif, a phase two glued target easy to aim at, the fly stuck to the sticky fly paper sofa, forced to admit distress.

Is it fair to slow things down for a moment? Create some detail rather than this haze. One would think we've smoked or injected or ingested or tripped on something; well we have tripped, Tabby anyway, running into the footrest full pelt (thankfully not carrying any nachos, expectant bottles of pungent wine, homemade guac, lentil and walnut loaf or heavy-on-the-gin punch that had become the night) sending her arms aloft like one of those car dealership catch-your-attention displays and landing face first, nose squished on the base of the sofa and cheek becoming intimately acquainted with the carpet. The lounge is big enough to accommodate this pause moment like in those films when everything freezes and the narrator or protagonist (sometimes antagonist but that's edgier fodder) takes a stroll through the expressionless faces and held poses. That's where I feel I am, high on female camaraderie and plain awesomeness, strolling through the den of estrogenic iniquity while minute, important facets bombard my observative and heightened awareness state.

Starting with Gwynne's one stitch scar hidden in her eyebrow, a story not wanting to peep through, rendered to the 'only kickboxing' pile when intruded upon but really a horrible uncle when memory became tangible. Danielle's perfectly vertical dent on the front of her nose, a magician and me the only real spotters of this after countless applications of Bio-Oil and her surrounding exquisite features detracting from said blemish, another magician's trick; put there by a baked ex-boyfriend holding her head face down into a bowl of scalding beef chilli yelling "Devour the trough piggy, eat that slop!" The dent from a crack in the dish entrenching so hard from his palm pressing the back of her neck, it never really left her both physically and emotionally. Debz is sitting on my lone green chair just to the left of the soundbar, her hip at a slight angle. She looks resplendent as ever but I know she cannot sit perfectly upright from when she was gangraped, damaging both her hips when the concrete barrier beneath her broke bits of bone off as each man took his uninvited turn. Jemima flinches every time someone gets her a drink; unconscious yet acutely conscious of the consequences. Someone gets up to make the next round, even though it's just us girls, and she's up, quick as a flash to help out; a top up for Jemima and her eyes pierce across the room followed by her head then an internal admonishing so the head snaps back. During the high-flying banking days Jemima, along with a male colleague, had been told they were both up for promotion. Said colleague had persuaded her to go for a drink to celebrate only to feign insecurity, self-loathing and seek a shoulder to cry on. Jemima, off her guard, began feeling worse for wear once the Rohypnol he'd slipped in her drink began to take effect. After the evening's date rape, the next day she'd been hospitalised, too ill to go to work, allowing Boyband loving slick to sail through the assessment interviews and nab said promotion. Renea's perpetual bacterial-looking squiggly veins in the corner of her eye, three grouped close enough to make out, but always there, a product of a 'let's beat the gay out of him' boarding school call to arms. The scar on the back of Maggie's neck and the scar on the back of Tabby's neck: one perfectly horizontal, one vertical, making them a collective plus or perhaps a cross. These are the details we never see but can see when wondering around the frozen room, feeling everyone's pain, feeling everyone's past.

Cheeks sodden – and they're all hugging me and I'm oh

no this is not about me. Have to lighten the mood – some retro rock or karaoke. Should try get back to the fun, the exploits, the dark twisty adventures. Maggie's idea for Digby, neatly illustrated, started with him immersed in a bath of mild bleach, and by mild she explained would merely make him paler not burn his skin off, the words 'Invidia' scrawled next to what looked like a red apple or a breast. He would then be told the only way to remove the dry itching sensation from the bleach was to fork his tongue and catch the apple; there might have been some heroine involved too, just to create the illogical sense of solution urgency. Tabby's was more physically dimensional and endurance based: Barton would need to test how many times his bulk could fall from a higher ground until either something broke or he gave in and conceded. He'd be on a ledge and pushed off, hopefully not landing too awkwardly, then again from a slightly higher point and landing at a slightly weirder angle and so on until well … laughter? Slapping the ground in MMA UFC fashion? An actual white bloody towel thrown into the ring?

A few of the girls have gone, passed out in a euphoric boozy haze having been taskmastered to hand in the drawings or at least give some semblance of explanation prior to blackout. There is a moon out tonight, somewhere between full and three-quarters, mesmerising in its incompleteness and blinding in its radiance. We're howling at it right now! Well why not? Gwynneth rouses long enough to explain that hers needs to be the most violent, sadistic and energetic of them all. There are unhappy faces everywhere on her drawing with weights pinning Damien down and a feather to tickle his nose while under the plates.  There is also a bed of roses apparently to calm him down before the next barrage of taunting: an Ann Summers intrusive device I was too scared to ask the destination for, white gloves with little bits of coarse concrete glued on and a number of punching bags adorned with Mad Max paraphernalia such as spikes, weapons and other punching slash kicking obstacles.

Spent.  The lot of us.  All lying on the carpet facing the ceiling, chests heaving in exhaustion, almost post coital.  Without a word needing to be said our faces turn in unison, planting a kiss on the woman beside us – not a reassuring kiss but one locking a forever bond and throwing away the key.  That is until one of use retrieved the key a few short days later, unlocked the bond and gave the Boyband the ever so slightest mouse-fat-whiff of foul play.  Careless perhaps, negligent most certainly.  The person in question would perhaps be the saving grace but this was a clean-up job beyond mere mortals.  We might be forced into adopting a Boyband into the group, thereby nullifying much of the moral superiority we thought we could wield like a noble sword.

Leaving the Discovery Channel on should only happen when there are no Boybands in the room.  For heaven's sake there could be elephants mating and how would that impression ever be explained?  Ruining the act for a generation, instantly inadequate and insignificant in equal measure so that the cow's disinterested dam wall breaking conception moment is forever etched into those depths of recalls that only surface at the most inopportune moments.

## Chapter 21

# jemima & WILLOW

There's cake with all the trimmings: carrot, cheese, chocolate, salted caramel, brownie, pear, tree. Using the word 'there's' is key as it implies singular: one cake, sickly sweet from over combining flavours leaving you hunched over like the hen at her own party, spewing into a bin. All those cakes on their own, magnificent but together a spewy, concoctory mess-up. Then there's eating your cake, after the spew and again and again until the cycle of raise eyebrow, smile, open mouth, masticate, swallow, ingest, let some dribble into intestinal tract while the rest trampettes back up the gullet, shouting I'm FREE out the mouth then starting all over again. Repeat. Until too tired to ever do both at once.

We'd had this discussion with Jem at the outset as it was always clear she wanted more. More cake and more eating. Although she understood the collective success, pairing with any Boybander was going to leave a few itches untended to and a few pimples unpopped; being paired with Willow perhaps understandably a cake-size boil requiring lancing with a pitchfork.  With Willow's anti-capitalist capitalism, Jemima's pretence of caring not to care that greenbacks trumped humpbacks wore thin, not immediately but over time.  And belief played a part in our destruction too, a belief that she was in such control of everything at her feet that sprinkling a few more cake crumbs into the mix would keep the camel's back intact.  Willow would surprise us all, not only with his determination that he was right but with a ravenous accumulation hunger that would vindicate the decision to pair the two of them.  But to be clear – it did happen by accident and, as with most human dramas, manifested itself in the old-fashioned way: flesh.

How it started was innocent enough and locationally normal enough.  Jemima had been working for a boutique hedge fund shooting the lights out (never from the hip) and impressing such that her name was growing.  So much so that one of the hedge fund owners decided to take her under his wing and teach her how to make the sick cash yet keep the customer happy.  They were going to buy up all the toxic structured derivatives from failed trades in the crunch, monetise each and carve up in structures that negated the credit risk by having good names in the fund and approved accounting practices which would blur the time value of when the options would be exercised.  As much as Jemima was impressing, she was by nature never impressed by anybody else, which is why Thanos (his nickname for not so obvious reasons, namely a shortening of Athanasios, his Greek 'first civilised people' heritage not only stamped all over his name) managed the impossible at the worst time. To say she was allured by his brain, brawn, swagger, smile and wealth was an understatement; for Jemima, Thanos not only possessed six infinity stones in his hand, but two beautifully bejewelled stones of his own making between his legs. He never came onto her either which was a bit un-Greek-like she felt, so when they actually did start doing it, it was her who acquired him and her current Boyband dating situation seemed to detract from where she should be heading with her life. Thanos was initially unaware then mildly amused by this coupling, so Jemima felt she needed to explain her motivation so as to justify why someone like her would need to consciously couple with someone so entrenched in the Waitrose vegan aisle that if his name was any less earthy he might avoid being an actual cartoon character. But as we found out the hard way, involving a man such as Thanos has its drawbacks, notably that he would want a piece of the action both emotionally and financially, yet we'd been clear that this was a Girls Only Flying School. It was leaning towards us breaking that rule by picking Willow to pacify or Thanos to appease, but perhaps in the end it was the name and the enduring image of his purple bulk decimating the indestructible shield that swayed us ... Thanos could not be appeased.

It would happen through the bloody media, our conquest suffering further from more unwanted prying tabloids. Jemima had gone to an exclusive award evening with Thanos and there had been a few paps littered about. At the exact moment he held her gloved hand and kissed her cheek she'd been snapped and plastered on the fifth page with the caption 'Boyband's tree hugged at Hedge Fund Gala Event'. Now Willow would not normally buy the paper but ladies and gentlemen this is not one of those stories or movies where Jemima could buy up all the papers from the stall and save the information thrusting its way into the public's psyche. This is twenty times two and, when electronic media spills a story, it radiates and burns, acid bubble gnawing through everything and anything on its way to Willow's furrowed brow, down his face Ark Raiders style and beneath, his T made from cotton rich salvaged nappies furling in abandoned despair. Initially easy to deny, Willow had been through Jemima's stuff without her knowing – deviously uncharacteristically determined – and not only found some rather racy messages but the beginnings of our profiling documents on the Boybands. Jemima had been instructed to destroy and, inexplicably negligent and defiant, she'd spouted she just couldn't completely eradicate the quality of the detail in the work. The manifestation of the accusation was initially that Willow wanted to watch Jemima and Thanos in the act, a masochistic voyeurism Jemima was worried she had created. When she refused on multiple occasions, Willow then settled on setting up an in-absentia video camera and watching post capture, only for Jemima to attempt to go one better and download some lookalike porn. Willow was smart enough to know that a man like Thanos would not get 'Muthafukka bro' tattooed on his bicep and whiffed a rat. This gave Jemima another opportunity to deny which only fuelled Willow's forensic delving into the profiling document he had on his mother and newly discovered twin brother Barton.

A cloud of actual shit gathering getting ready to rain. People talk about a shit storm, whereas those who've actually experienced one for real know that it's not the storm the counts but the clean up afterwards; imagine a world wet with shit. We knew about the twin delivery and we knew about the cover up and we knew exactly why. How we knew was not so important but why we knew and what we planned to do with the intel would send Willow to the top of the Boyband danger chart and get each one of us loaded with ammunition, a mercurial counterattack collusion and the smarts to work out the algorithmic probability of discovery.

There was always the holding a gun to the tree's head someone in the group, which only served to further amplify the direness of the situation. Once the eco-caring front had been scratchcarded off to reveal the lack of dollar signs below, Willow was likely more conniving, calculating and capitalist than us cretins gave him credit for. Well, we did know that removing the veneer would reveal something of an avaricious disposition, but heck, this Boybander went penetrating through the thin veneer of recycled toilet paper into the heart of self-gratifying darkness. It was Bryan K 2.0 with fellow Boybanders flung under the bus like light trash disposal. Not quite solo career (just yet) but spotting the potential of a semi-criminal female relationship ring became a stick to use, not only against the establishment but everything not serving Willow. With the discovery of his brother though, he was more vigilant, allowing the sentiment to wane away before any approach.  He didn't know if Barton knew and wanted to know more about his mother, a badass pioneer named Margot.  Disappointment set in early, he remembered, before being shipped off to boarding school. He never knew what became of his father, something that would haunt him as memories of his brother began to infiltrate his memory but with enough wariness to glean that he might have recently put them there.  What might have actually happened (and details are sketchy here) is that Margot – all conquering Margot – either lost faith in her destiny or lost faith in her sons.  Disappointment as a parent manifested in different ways for mothers and fathers; fathers always seemed to believe the self-actualised sparkle would somehow emerge even if there had been little evidence in the lead up: the kid would come good, somehow, in his own way. Mothers though, once the idea of a loser child is planted, it can only grow never going backwards.  Margot would try chop down this tree but it would only emerge stronger and more resilient than before, twigs becoming branches, leaves becoming giant Amazonian ferns and so on.  She couldn't understand it either – with such off the charts genetics, she'd produced a big boned bruiser that looked like the cross between a squashed cabbage and a rusty turd and a delicate soul so obsessed with saving ants and flies and spiders and mosquitoes, she wondered where the Alpha from the biological dad had disappeared to.  Likely she'd fucked it out of him but she had no time to rectify.

With so many rumours about her, Margot disappeared, leaving enough money to keep the boys educated and enough distant family members on both sides to step in and babysit during holidays and half-terms, al la middle-class England aunties and uncles substituting for redneck trailer park relatives who were a bit too close to the gene pool for comfort. It got to a point where she couldn't look at either of the boys: the physical representation of her failed genetic experiment. DNA tests followed which coincided with her disappearance so she was never privy to the results but we were, having broken into the facility via Debz's brand of coercive persuasion: a welcome handjob for the security guard. The discovery was somewhat startling in that we could see a connection the biological father, Douglas Perfors was his name, but just the one … the Boybanders-to-be had different dads. This might have been the final push from the perfection ledge for Margot: allowing substandard sets of sperm to sneak past Doug's was unforgivable. Perhaps she knew or she knew she'd altered Doug's sperm to the point where it was useless, not quite blanks in a gun but putting a bullet in the chamber and firing only to leave the recipient in hospital not on a cold slab, cream coloured and fake plastic peaceful.

Willow had his gun loaded which put us all in danger. The uncertainty of how he planned to use that gun created the first of its kind hump in the road we'd have to navigate. Jemima took the slip up personally as a failure which spurred her into resolution mode and, as we were acutely aware, a determined Jemima does not leave any stone unturned, in fact, all the stones in the Boyband neighbourhood knew their time was up, cowering in anticipation of imminent flipped disposal, little upturned stone turtles dead all over the shore.

# Chapter 22

# GWYNNe

Welcome distractions that do contribute towards existential progress are simply the best, not better than all the rest so let's call them simply one of the best, better than most of the rest. Gwynneth and Damien's celebrity status began to grow, concentrating in health, fitness and general human vanity. With Damien's Twitter and Insta becoming more intermittent fasting, ketosis and kale up your butt than dreamy lyrics, tour dates and nice guy moves, he was approached by a fitness production firm based in the US where couples would compete against one another for that palm patting heartfelt moment American audiences love when a transformation completes from happy-go-lucky losers to my-life-will-never-be-the-same-again-now-that-I've-fucked-carbs-to-the-curve. What appealed about the show for Gwynne was that she knew her competitive spirit could carry her through at least some of the rounds and Damien's newly found confidence was at least good for a giggle or two once the veneer began flaking off and self-doubt crept in. And all live on television too! A big target outlet of Damien's choosing as the post Boyband era career move.

The concept was simple in its complexity, all shot in 4K in the States, hosted by a Sylvester Stallone lookalike and a blonde perfect teethed female so on point a mini stutter would likely result in suicide. Each of the celebrity couples would choose what the other couples ate prior to the high-tech obstacle course. This included a fast meal and portion control which could scale up (not beyond the ridiculous but 5,000 calories remains quite bit for a little Boybander) or scale right down into starvation mode. So the pairs had to adjust working out preparation with the food fuel that provided the energy for maximum performance, then perform a series of high impact strength and agility tasks with the actual smattering of reality immunity, fucking over another pair, sharing your feelings and live maniacal behaviour masked as greater good humanity.

Oh shit! You know when you're whittering on and you suddenly realise you've forgotten to do something or are late for a prior engagement? That's me right now! Kelly's birthday present! Excuse me for a moment while I make a quick call to Bespoke Cakes in West Sussex. I'm dialling; they're talking; they're laughing; I'm reiterating this is for real; they're apologising. Wham, bam thank you cake store. He'll hate it as much as I'll love it then he'll feel he should really love it which will betray his faked post-noughties instinct which will then scream to just relax and go with it just long enough for his guard to be down and another paper cut to destabilise the wonky drunk gymnast. All the girls think the idea is an absolute banger: retro enough to be cool and tacky enough to be retro. Has no one from our generation seen a Steven Seagal film before he did really crap films round about the time Kelly (stunning forever) LeBrock dumped him and he started #MeTooing someone else? When breaking bones actually looked easy, slick martial arts more effective than a hydraulic sledgehammer and garnering more attention than marital arts. Note to self: mention hydraulic sledgehammer creation options to haunted house organiser chap.

After that commercial break, back to Celebrity Beast Your Feast, the contenders licking their chops at making the other contenders not lick their chops. Couples like Chip and Kim, Dan and Jill, Teak and Smith would be up against our very own "allll the waaaaaay from the UUUUUUKKKKKaaayyyyyyy" Damien and Gwynne, Damien clearly letting the side down by not having a one syllable name; supposedly it could have been Dam but then would have to be more how Smith might 'overly praise in exclamation' Teak when a darn good obstacle course got completed: "Damn girl, you did fine!" But Damn! and Gwynne would just be too obscure to explain to predominantly American viewers and the Yanks love those slightly dorky, stuck-up names like Damien, even if his Boyband repute elevated him marginally above that status.

Initially they were doing well: winning or close to winning tasks and managing whatever culinary delights were thrown their way, in the beginning mainly of the measly and low energy variety. They managed to get all the way to the semi-finals when things started going wrong. One of the paired competitors had a theory that due to Damien's lifelong struggles with weight, food and image he'd be less likely to perform on a yuge, kick-ass meal of his favourite close-to-orgasmic delights. One or two visits to Google later their meshuga sugar plan came to fruition when Gwynne found Damien face down in a food coma: pizza boxes, chocolate wrappers, Pringles cans, cheese forks and flakes of pastry adorning his lifeless corpse like a Viking's decorated death canoe. They'd had to consume what was prescribed in separate isolated rooms and what Gwynne gathered from the footage is that Damien started gingerly, picking tentatively at each portion starting with the exotic cheeses. Once momentum gathered, a shepherd gathering his flock and the flocks of countless farms in the area, she saw that crazed look from when she first found him, the sparks at two-thirty of his nostrils twitching, the mouthfuls getting larger, the chewing more infrequent. By the time he was complete, his self-worth was round about inversely proportionate to the distention of his belly.

The task that followed was less disaster movie and more full regime generational genocide. Damien was unable to lift himself past the first climbing wall and fell over on the inclining moving rocks more than a toddler. He would break into tears at each point of failure, further fuelling Gwynne's frustration and resultant performance. They got knocked out at that stage but not before Gwynne won the coveted 'most valuable female performer' award with her individual points tally so far ahead of all the rest, no matter what happened in the final she couldn't be caught. That night, during a night out in Chicago, Damien continued where he left off, eating further into oblivion until Gwynne had to carry him back to the hotel. In the middle of the night, fuelled by enough glycogen, alcohol and saturated fat to light up Willis Tower, Damien had woken with a start and began beating at Gwynne's face. Before she realised what was happening above her consciousness he'd landed three to six lusty blows, splitting her eyebrow and chipping one of her teeth. That boxercise sure was paying off she non-chuckled to herself moving into a defensive position to set for a counterattack. Moments before Damien would realise the implications of his violence, perhaps pulled back to blood sugar normality by the unsightly sights of Gwynne's face oozing thick sticky blood. She didn't smile or cry buy boy did Damien: he sobbed non-stop all the way back to England, momentarily pausing every second to apologise. Gwynne, initially stunned, soon tired of the pathetic excuses, whispering into his sleeping ear on the flight back "For your own good, you really should have finished the job," then pressing on her eyebrow hard enough to make it bleed again and feeling under her shirt where the cracked rib felt like dry uncooked rice beneath her skin. An air hostess looked across and smiled, convinced that Gwynne had smiled back.

She hadn't.

## Chapter 23

# GERSON

"No you cannot eat another human being."

"I'm looking at his cute little pug nose and doey eyes and all that nervous sexual energy and I'm thinking with the right spices and chef he could taste just about decent. Aren't we meant to taste like chicken?"

"There has to be a limit Danny; are we actually okay with being branded cannibals? Actual cannibals like the gorno slasher films or Alive. Where human flesh is consumed. Little Gerson's flesh."

"I'm not saying I want to eat him, I'm just saying sometimes when I'm engulfing him, squashing my body down on his I sometimes think of taking an actual bite out of him. But then because I'm a taste snob I know that raw human flesh will taste so bad, so I imagine prepping him like a plant-based meal."

"Plant-based?"

"Yeah so once meat is out of the equation the veggies

spend months justifying why meat isn't the only thing that tastes great. So the plant-based recipes are so loaded with spices that the lentils get amped, standing up, partying and the eater is downing water for the rest of the day."

"I read plant-based gives you a more consistent and harder erection."

"Well I'd better stop eating plants then!"

"You're funny"

"If Gerson went on that sort of diet he'd expire from relocation of blood flow. It's getting worse. The passing out is more frequent now and any mention of anything sends him cowering off."

"Maybe you should eat him."

Gerson's mother's name was Deloris and father's Reginald. His father had been found murdered in a field just off suburbia in North London. The murderer or murderers, the coroner deemed, had made him suffer to the boundaries of human tolerance before putting him out of his misery. With open issues in the marriage, Deloris has initially been the prime suspect only to skate through with a multiple friend based watertight alibi. The forensics had uncovered nothing of note, the body having been cleaned post-mortem with various strong kitchen cleaning products. Pulp found near the body had included plastic sheeting which had been dissolved in acid and then burnt removing any traces of just about anything. The investigation had then shifted to many of Reg's business dealings, a smattering without the salubrity required by a wink more than the moral police, the starch towards asserting that this indecorous subsection could be linked to organised crime or sour enough to result in killing. There had, however, been no major movement of funds or banking investigation that sparked suggestive alarm, even the central accounting unit of the police task team turning up diddly squat. Just Deloris, pregnant with Gerson at the time and a large life insurance sum to get them through this troubling fatherless time.

Rumour was such that she'd joined some form of commune, rearing Gerson on goats' tears, goodwill and hallucinogenic stimulants. Unsubstantiated and published by some of the less worthy papers, Deloris had funded the commune's locations, sustenance and nocturnal activities until the money ran out. She was always madly in love with Gerson but this was when the funds were flowing; retreating to a traveller community existence meant Deloris began to lose track of responsibility and normal routine, sacrificing Gerson's wellbeing for food, drugs, a warm stranger's bed and the general spiral into some form of disillusioned mid-life capitulation. She'd sold Gerson, luckily to a caring family, for a lifetime supply of weed and a caravan with all the trimmings, as he'd just 'failed to grow up' sources claimed and this was the only real way for him to find his true self, stand up and be a man. To this day, those who knew him stated he never really grew up both physically and emotionally. Post Boyband success Gerson had hired a team of private investigators to track down his mother and reopen the investigation into his father's death. After months and never-ending payments the team turned up a clue that was never looked into: unidentified male DNA found on Reg's clothes in the laundry bin, the amount of which was significant enough to warrant further attention. Gerson purchased the DNA details and was looking to make some headway when the team found what they believed to be his mother, Deloris. Her body had been found in that same caravan she'd traded for Gerson, in a remote wood near Cork, badly decomposed such that the extracting team all passed out and required days not hours to remove the body. No foul play was deemed as she had been found lying on her back holding a blankie and surrounded by field flowers and stems. Gerson was insistent he wanted to see the body and later wished he hadn't, the resemblance more decayed Area 51 alien than long lost vivacious maternal mythical figure. His disappointment turned to anger and he ordered the body burnt and scattered amongst a travelling community party, scenes that made the news for the violent riposte.

Danielle has speculated that due to his mother's decomposed emaciated appearance, he'd been drawn to her curves, always wanting to curl and snuggle up under her bosom, a kind of half-grown suckling Boyband baby chimp. She sometimes had to carry him to bed, standing in squat without even a momentary totter, cogently plopping him in the kids' size bed he'd had designed, turning the mandatory Noddy nightlight on before leaving. To counter the baby of the group métier, Gerson had continually asserted himself to Xtreme Believe in ways that belied his uncertainty. Overuse of the F and C words and large, long, lasting, lamenting screams at nothing into the air, Tarzan of the Boyband Apes, letting off steam that was more like condensation and not at all requiring expulsion. With Danny though, he was hers and she his, he believed. So much so that when she mentioned wanting to eat him alive, he merely came in his pants, giggled shyly and ran off to fetch her a bowl of expensive lentil soup.

*Chapter 24*

# GROUP EXERCISE

When embarking on any exercise as a group one immediately jumps to teamwork or working as one towards a collective goal: the falling backwards 80s corporate away day morphed into the ostentatious 90s PowerPoint graphics into the noughties self-help influencing guru into the tweenies unconscious bias remote training. When girls embark on a group exercise I say it should, at basic fucking below zero minimum, be fun. And diverse. With that diversity embraced like a genuine group hug, pulling each rolling maul participant closer, as many truly become one. Not quite a bunch of hares spreading across the moors, a literal breeding viral covering, but a starting point bound by a collective, structured quest with enough of an incentive to drive out the victim, erm … recipient's true character, nature and beliefs. But not forgetting the fun bitches.

So a literally crude example as a precursor to the actual money shot story I'm skirting around like a teen pregnancy pre parent confession is the date finger. Little known fact: Edward VIII abdicated because Wallis Simpson did more with her middle finger than the caring, conscientious, loyal 30s England would care to imagine. And this historic fork in the road was determined quite simply by the date finger. So tasks (ahem quiet please) ladies are to introduce designated Boyband partner to a one-off date finger, whether or not intimate relations were currently afoot, with extra kudos points for the most outlandish, most shocking intrusion of them all.

It was difficult to topple Debz's kick-off where Sexton, clearly not embarking on any carnal activities with lusty-looking Debz, upon receiving the middle finger up the road less travelled during a band Zoom videocall had headbutted the iMac with such force that it overshadowed the instantaneous mess created below the belt, a cracked screen and invaded crack the unlikely bedfellows for a long-awaited ejaculation in the quiet confines of Sexton's tighty-whities.

Gerson, mouth full of sweet and sour chicken balls, would embrace the more sinister extremes of humour and tragedy when Danielle surprised him on the sofa with a preamble of an innocuous cupped palm reasting casually under his hamstring. At the getting to know you more intimately event Gerson would produce the most unique, yet nervously satisfying fart sound, a kind of cross between a loud sneeze and a coast guard boating siren, the emanation of which would propel Danielle's feet across the lounge floor in spastic hilarity whilst also propelling an oversized deep fried chicken ball neatly into Gerson's gullet. Danielle regaled us with how she watched in shocked awe, fascination and intent while Gerson clambered around his throat, grappling at imaginary air like some sort of magician flinging cards into small spaces, until the complexion palette went way beyond what Word has to offer, through the complete Space Odyssey Star Gate sequence until a possibly weak combination of fear, compassion and knowing that the date finger task was not the answer to the problems – and further knowledge that her bulk could actually do some good – saw Danielle perform a rib-cracking Heimlich to propel the perfectly intact chicken ball Angry Bird style across the room. She'd ended with a sly "That's to prevent any tell-all tales from here on out," to which Gerson could only continue gasping and wondering whether he'd imagined it, tears produced even more festively once he knew he was actually alive.

Renea had to double tap on the date finger to even arouse Kieron from drug induced slumber, the event sounding more commonplace that we cared to imagine, and thus scoring low points overall.

Gwynne, whilst holding Damien in a leg headlock during a martial arts training exercise, had reached down and jab jabbed the date finger until Damien's quizzical pink puppy-like expression wound more into an accepting 'this is just her coaching method' karma.

Maggie's setup with Digby was more traditional: a sensual massage during which the instructed date finger would make an unfortunately welcome appearance: Digby just wanted more and Maggie couldn't explain that, like a Boyband originally written tune reaching number one, it was a limited-edition collector's item.

Tabby Cat would convince Barton to do it to himself after an argument standoff that involved each proclaiming the other was ill equipped for any form of perverse anal intimacy and Jemima would trade Willow in exchange for going fully plant based for a while, not quite sticking to the rules but hey, not only would any fastidious application of rules in 2021 be so off trend it would hurt right down to the tip of Pinocchio's storytelling nose but it would save a few iterations of those one million bottles of water to industrially create one burger patty. And I know you're going there: what about me and why do I get away with not being part of the gang, the experiment, the group exercise? Well it is different for me but yes I did complete the task and the sheer hilarity of Kelly's expression change in the organic deli queue at Waitrose would only be topped by the shame I felt driving home with him, not a word spoken, the elephant squelching into my face, liquid flubber.

There might be a lesson in here somewhere that doing unto others and you would expect your Boyband dating gang rapers to do unto their Boyband rappers and rapers should not be so hypocritical, but a group exercise requires a group. And I. Am. In. The. Band.

Now for the main event, the big kahuna social experiment as administered by the same owners of manicured penetration station elation non-felation date fingers …

"How long before a man resorts to misogynistic one-upmanship to win a fight?"

The nature of this masculine study, like the date finger,

had to be a one-on-one as a group dynamic might skew the results, likely in the more socially acceptable, polite direction which was exactly what we wanted to avoid. We wanted the base, the real, the hardcore, the unadulterated version straight from the spitting red mist peering lips, soon to be racked by guilt and crying for forgiveness. If violence was the end result then so be it: we have to suffer for our craft; suffer and then in turn inflict suffering in a far more persuasive way than being called a Bitch!

So Bitch had to be the first to step onto the crowd encircled podium. Lazy. Uncreative. A starter. But for most of the girls a fighting first. And fighting because it had to be about picking a fight or how else would each Boybander drop the veneer, shunt the pretence into the slow lane and adopt the true nature of a male backtracking at the hands of his female aggressor. This was about scratching beneath the surface so the underlying skin turns a rancid purple-green from being rubbed, then wears away until blood is the least of everyone's worries and the infection and bone and gristle and sinew become exposed like a hundred-year-old aunty flashing from beneath a pink dressing gown in demented confusion.

"You fucking bitch," was the bog standard response from Kieron when Renea had a go about him smoking too much weed. To be fair it only came about after an hour of antagonisation and apparently was delivered in that classic dismissive, comical, breathless realisation that only men can truly pull off as a pseudo affectionate term of endearment. So Renea knew she had to go a bit further which engendered a splatter of androgynous insults. Worth mentioning that to suck out this behaviour, the poison from a rare snake bite, the provocateur had to ensure each didn't stray into the male tit which would receive the female tat; in other words no calling em dicks, cocks, wankers, assholes (as far as I'm aware only men have them as we have buttholes or bottom appendages) or pricks. When provoked further Kieron slank into a lazy acceptance before spouting "Ball buster" which scored highly.

Interestingly enough, Debz achieved the full volley of feminine sexual insults from Sexton including "Slut" "Whore" and even "Prossy" which almost saw Debz give the game away with a chortling snigger as the "Prossy" came across somewhere in the middle of an impressed, desirable and juvenile triangle. But when the mist really descended each of the retorts acquired a menacing "Fucking" or "You really are a" precursor, while Debz feigned reciprocal anger by describing sex acts she'd performed in the past. Seconds later, of course, came the tears swapping the "Slut, Bitch, Whore, Prossy" for "Baby, Baby, Baby, Baby!"

Tabby's conundrum was more profound. The obvious lack of phallic membership on Barton's part was an easy starting point for a fight but not only did that flap into male rule-breaking territory it also risked the very real possibility of actual physical violence from a bulbous source to compliment her latest concoction of accidental self-inflicted injuries. Plus we were better than that shit right? Calling someone a limp dick or small cock was literally and physically beneath us and below where our eyelines normally resided respectively. The bookies had many of us predicting a back handed slap preceding a tone lowering feminist taunt, but who knew he would go all Mel Gibson when provoked. Tabby handled the build up with considerable care and skill too, not even chucking in the roids or spots or size inference for good measure; she really just hinted at a lover that might actually be able to provide the goods, a man able to deliver some form of close to Oh Yeah without having (of all things!) her tits blamed. So somewhere between Oliver Reed and Mad Mel, Tabby's big badass beautiful double Gs were dragged over the coals for being "Lopsided" "Large Areolad" and "Housing a family of asylum seekers beneath each" due to the implied sagginess from the weight. Now because of Tabby's minor celebrity in dating a Boybander, she had her own social media cult following; well her breasts did anyway. She'd never actually exposed them but Twitter usernames such as @TabbysTatatas and @MagnificentAbisGirls existed to directly honour her boobs, with followers in excess of 200k and an array of clothed public photos with wish list responses to please dear God sneak just one peak. A tabloid had offered her £200k to expose the pair, but for Christ's sake this is not 2010 nor Wife Swap so Tabby politely declined and continues to adopt modest sartorial barriers to mask her ridiculously sexy proportions. Barton's retort would prove more blessing than curse, meaning she could wrap them up and not even reveal for Christmas: imagine the Shakespeare In Love scene where young Bill unwraps gushing Oscar Winner Miss Paltrow but over a melting ice cap nature time-lapse that never really ends. That's how tight she wrapped those puppies up after that. Locked away from any prying eyes and perhaps only to be revealed during those final moments. When final Boyband breaths get taken. Funny, Tabby didn't fall down once during this exchange.

Gwynne and Damien was a tread carefully endeavour. And not only because of Damien's two momentary lapses in self-restraint hitherto but because, in reality, the death match was far more likely to result in Boybands crossing themselves than anyone emotionally connected to Gwynne. The kickboxing and, more importantly, the focus meant she could put his nose into his brain with an eye-lid flick of her heel. Effort. Less. With. Out. Trying. It was an unequivocally unfair matchup which made them, as a couple, even more fascinating. Plus Gwynne knew, after using anger as a workout motivation technique, any foray towards baiting Damien into chick shaming would require a more sensitive approach, so she chose to show weakness to elicit the response. Even when he had beaten her in the past she had shown the resolve not to react, not to show the pain inside or out, so for this exercise she chose to show vulnerability to get him to counter motivate and likely throw in her gender to get this point across.

And the manifestation of his bravery with Gwynne wavering … "Cow!" Who said retro farmyard insults were out? It was during another hyped-up gym session, mid-way through Tabata set number six when Gwynne muttered the now immortal words "I can't do anymore," and stopped dead in her tracks, a deer blinded by the faked exhaustion headlights. So thrown, Damien pleaded, then gave up, then one more try spiralling gingerly into "Come on you lazy Cow." That was about where it stopped, a policeperson's raised palm shutting down any further inert displeasure, while Gwynne pondered how best to quell the future riposte from within her bowels. If she had gone on the offensive it felt like Damien would have slunk even further away, always seemingly requiring a Dutch or equivalent courage to reveal his true anger towards women. His true animosity, she knew, lay squarely with his square jawed supermodel mother but this was something, we unanimously agreed, should be savoured for a bigger occasion. Otherwise it would be like rolling out the prize bull for a regional farm-off rather than those award-winning bestial breeders gathered to impregnate Cows for genetically gifted bovine offspring.

Private schooling can uniquely be a double-edged sword. Sure, you theoretically should get the manners, the correct order to cutlery selection at a ball, fold down over cut-away formal attire and a solid ignorance to how real people function and survive but melted into that designer pot is an intuitive maniacal astuteness that should never go unchecked. As we were learning with the Thanos inspired affair (where Jemima has remained more contrite than an AA regular after a wine-tasting event) leading to the long-lost brother and mythical mother mystery, we had to remain like a midget at the urinal: on our toes. Willow was no Callery Pear Tree with enough feigned Woke to keep We Eez Da Treez shimmying up the charts but thankfully was distracted enough not to press the origins story of hidden motive. For now that is. It was coming and it was coming harder than we were anticipating, but at least we were in a state of anticipation, which for us always meant get on the front foot; get ahead. Find Margot. But missing persons don't dwell on a timeline handcrafted by our Craft, so Willow had to show his anti-feminine intent rather than his anti-Jemima intent. So this meant no Thanos speak, mention, blink, think, wink or hint. So Jemima prodded the oldest, most juvenile emotion of them all (and something she knew about more intimately than most): competitiveness. Boys' private schools in this land have a certain pride in past exploits, predominantly on the overtly manicured sports fields. She knew football was a non-starter (Willow wasn't that Woke) and rugby a bit rah-rah obvious so settled on the game which expanded to lower echelons far earlier than most: cricket. Willow had in fact been a decent left arm off-spinner and Jemima herself, as with most forays, had exceled for a time as a teenager playing junior county cricket after not much of an introduction but an eye, an arm and a will to win that none could really counter. So making the bold statement that her girls Grammar would have in fact pummelled his sparkling-white clad helmetless KKK-alikes sent Willow reeling into full stato quote mode and an undeniably impressive 1$^{st}$ XI record. Woodpecking into Da Tree, Jemima kept going, refusing to throw her wicket away and watching the bowling attack's shoulders slump when … Howzat!

"You really are a self-proclaiming old slapper, aren't you?" went swinging wild down the leg side and scored Jemima points on so many levels: new word, the scarce combination the word 'slapper' affords, blending posh chic with chav ownership, bringing the female sexual promiscuity jab into a hooks, punches and swings centring only on sport or sportsmanship (or lack thereof). She'd nailed him: pad planted straight down the track, ball hitting halfway up and going on to hit middle and off. DRS: green, green, green. And not even the excuse of a sticky wicket in sight. At this rate the only stickiness would be Willow's biodegradable recycled tissues being put into correct recycle white bin liner bin.

Maggie knew about Digby's Debz crush of course and the slightly reciprocated attention meant Digby glued on a homeboy straight peaked cap, hiding the temples, dotted pimples and wear-and-tear. With the cap came a lot more bling, a lot more self-hugging leaning black and a lot more Ali G. Maggie asked Debz to have fun with this look, encouraging in spades until obliterating it in one fell let down swoop, sending soaring eagle to his spiralling fashion doom all enshrouded in a scrapyard heap of gold, silver, low trousers and studs. Before that Maggie had to engender her version of an anti-female insult and, with Diggers, this was almost too easy. Silver's green eyes shone when she mentioned Sexton, shone in a way only Digby knew and shining with a presence that required no twitching, pursing, fluttering or other obvious giveaways. We wondered whether Maggie was actually reptilian alien as, after holding an iPhone 12 torch to her eyes, we watched in wonder as the green actually became greener; she could turn it on and off like an optometrist flashing the green cue card over one eye, trailed by the ubiquitous "where is the black blacker?" request. And with Digby becoming blacker by the day, the hope was that his green-eyed monster would kick in to a point where culturally we could understand how pathetic white boys felt the bruthus communicated with their sistahs. Maggie had the foresight to record the tirade when Digby kicked off, channelling Kanye predominantly in how you would imagine a male fearful of any female retort argues, notably stating point on confusing point in a diarrhoea rat-a-tat-tat paroxysm so as to render the female victim unable to respond (not a gap in sight) …

"You, you maaafuckin hoe; you trippin on the Sexton homey – that nigga ain't fine, not so fine as this Diggers dawg, ya feel me?"

"Sexton … he means nothing. He's just a nice guy with a nice smile," cue eyes moving from emerald organic, blended Parshat Tazria.

"Playa hater, you popcorn hoe, hoochie skeevy ho, skank mufucka be-ach, you hoebag, manizer, Benjamin chasin silver sea donkey, yummy diz tail waggin ice queen, heina yak poon twinkie pass around pussy! I gonna fuck yow friend Debz, she fine bitchin tits!"

It would have been impressive, almost Boyz n the Bard rehearsed, had he not whacked his cap off with his forearm, mid soliloquy, pulling the adhesive he was using inside the cap free, the impact ripping some of the latest hair projects in a direction other than intended. The scream was less ghetto and more Bristol, and with shades of a cinematic Wilhelm timbre, Debz couldn't resist recording and using as her ring tone.

Danielle's set up would most certainly involve the three key constituents embodying their relationship: food, sexual suggestion and mummy. Asking Gerson to step up to the male baiting plate was akin to clubbing a baby seal's younger, cuter, more round-eyed infant brother: it felt unjust; unnecessary as one might shovel another mouthful when the distended stomach was screaming "no more" in painful defiance. This pairing had been intentional though, Danny's violent passion for everything teenage Boyband had to be nurtured and replaced by the only thing capable or bitchslapping Boyband worship into silver medal position: food. Enough with the colons already! That's my Anne Brontë breaking the fourth literary wall apology. The only excuse would be that colon is a direct descendant of the digestive tract and something firmly on my mind after a fresh bulimic Wednesday session. Light and fluffy so just imagine the volume consumed. Popcorn. More flavours than even Willy Wonka could have imagined. Let's leave it at when you microwave a whole jar of Biscotti spread … shazam! Back to our friendly puppy Gerson. Dannielle would have to go in hard to elicit a response hitting each pain point in sophisticated succession. It would be subtle made-up bullshit: how she hated her mother and how he would never be invited to a Wednesday gorge session and how sexual prowess was an EL James created fantasy without any foundation, fact or sustainability (the latter point of course being completely bang on but piquing angered arousal in Gerson, this little strange virgin completely convinced that once his cherry was splattered all over the bedroom floor he'd have the potency of an anime brown-purple cocked animal-warrior, impaling maidens and big eyed Japanese schoolgirls wherever he plundered; if he could just make a start it would all fall into place nicely, wouldn't it? This alter ego fantasy).

"You're a bit craggy," would be the start, not sufficiently employing feminine insults to carry more water than we do during the dreaded five-to-seven of the month. So Danny pushed further and resorted to a you-go-girl form of relevant physical violence, but not before warning Gerson she was going to do it. Countless warnings in fact and taunting; how she'd do it, what she'd do it to and the actual compression technique. That's right. She bit him. Square on the bum, so that a few capillaries spouted forth but not to the naked eye. She would explain it felt just right and infused the mummy spanking and foreplay elements succinctly into the masticating mouth on mound. Well. After an abiding exasperation, Gerson finally spouted on both accounts, a darkening continent shape in his pants and an ashamed riposted verbal volley: "You stinky fanny cheese!"

Wait, what? "For real," Danny explained to us. "I can't believe you did that; now look at the state of me. What a nasty woman you are," the first ironically where the actual W word was played, the Ace of Spades as it were. "Where did you learn to behave like that? Did your mother teach you no manners? And no physical boundaries? Are you the maid who is going to clean this mess up? Ladybiter!"

We're on the floor, kicking blurry heels in air cycling hilarity. I've just hit ten kilometres and the other girls are all peddling faster. Is there any way on Eve's Green Earth, that any of us, woman-for-woman, will be able to resist this new pet name for Danny?! Ladybiter.

# Chapter 25

# sexton

It was. Inevitable. Preordained? By the celebrity gods; the celebrity worshipping gods, sitting glued to small rectangular devices awaiting some form of aberrant announcement, watermelons on a firing range waiting to explode from the gifted force of an armour-plated Pistorius-hand-gun-zombie-killer. That whiff of excitement, airport picker uppers sensing the first passengers have disembarked; the watermelons (if they could) looking anxiously yet elatedly anticipatorily, waiting for the propelled metal to slam through their red-pink insides and out the back of the head.

The first Insta shot from Sexton 'Big Changes Afoot' then nothing for weeks, carefully choreographed by the band's publicity team. This was their comeback from mid table toppers; this would get the gossip tongues wagging and Golden Tickle back to opening third on a dry week for music. Fuck the songs. And fuck the girlfriends.

Debz got wind of this early on and put it back to the

council. Initially the reaction was one of invalidation; there was little justification for the purpose if Sexton didn't truly embody the physical, emotional, mental, generational and spiritual traits of a Boyband. And she felt, after overhearing a few WhatsApp calls, that this was perhaps being ignominiously thrust upon Sexton rather than an independent, thought-through decision. Additional letters are all the rage and we would be the last campaigners on the island to deny anyone their true identity or calling but one additional element scuppered our acceptance: selfishness. The physical impact would be minimal as Debz was careering towards an ugly bump burlesque with Digby, and Sexton's bigfoot changes would regrettably remove much of the symbolism of Digby always wanting what someone else had. We were not perfect masterminds after all; some of this was clunky and would require a bit of luck and creative license to pull off but there were a few core principles that each had to follow. And it was too late to sub in and out Boybanders; just too much preparatory water under the take-me-to-the-place-I-know bridge (they were a Boyband at that stage, come on?) to starting trading lipsyncers. Debz took some homage to us academically passing her around the other Boyband Boyfriends, but that one ideal we'd agreed at patient zero had to persist; it had to become the raison d'être every single one of us was tune marching in absolute harmony with.

As a rough working draft we settled on Barton, mainly because Maggie had fastened the erect drawbridge in abstinence after the feminist task, then came brain tsunami to obliterate all brain waves slopping on to shore before Boxing Day 2004: throw twin brother Willow into the mix to create a froth of sibling tension. As it stood, Digby would want what Barton and Willow had; Willow would want more than he was allowed and Barton would mask the dent in his ego at losing out to newly-discovered-bro-twin-Boyband-pal Willow. Now all that remained was not to use Debz as a prostitute in all of this. But as Debz knew better than any of us, suggestion and anticipation can be a significantly more powerful tool than allowing some tool to use his tool and sweat, grind and grumpily grunt until said tool was empty, spent, flaccid and as useful as playing snooker with rope. There was such indignity in allowing a man to orgasm in front of you; each had different quotas but what we all settled on unanimously is that should the Boyband O Face or sound exceed the quota, we'd shrivel up, die, be burnt like a ribbon, then die again whilst in shameful disgust. Next time anyone feels like disagreeing, watch theFace at theMoment. It might change your life forever because when women come it is close to the darn sexiest visual, be it oh gawd blasphemic terrets, screaming, whooping, breathless hyperventilation, moaning, profanity or just a warm loving contentment. It's hot. For any of the straight, LGBTQX or AN Other sexualities. Watch a man blow his load. Cabbage face meets horse eyes after the Grand National followed by a sense of self-congratulations only a woman could recognise. The roll-over, cum avoidance and veiled compliment more directed back in the cock-wearer's direction just to say fuck you after fucking you; the pooh cake balancing on the rotten cherry.

Wait, were we talking about Sexton? Ah yes, apt to the extreme because his O face, historically more prevalent when in his pants faced Debz from across the room, would be no more. Was he attempting to migrate into pillow softened, tussled hair being blown away and back to a pursed mouth, a child's swing that never ends, or was this a publicity ploy?

The best bit (or bits) might just be that Sexton directly requested Debz be involved, her pre-medical degree assessment courses now in full swing (or fully dangling side to side) so a hand holding furrowed pre-med handholding brow would be just the sort of support tonic to get a member (think you get it by now) of a Boyband through to orchiectomy. Her speciality was not quite yet extoling the merits of penectomy versus vaginoplasty but her introductory knowledge of anaesthesiology was becoming a burgeoning specialist field. In a nutshell (or nuts shells).

It goes a little something like this (cue Beastie Boys prefatory riff: underrated and underutilised in explaining a bilateral exchange of parts between Sexton and a medical waste bin), at least as far as had been explained to Debz and from what Uncle could educe – unlike when someone has a crystal understanding and is able to explain with the required brevity, sharpness and definition such that the recipient reciprocates with a genuinely knowing nod, this was bespattered with more of a fingers-crossed, it'll be alright on the night, hope to fuck it is painless and over quickly rap style …

The iconic duo and their leaning over, back stretching across a physio anti-burst gym ball pal get relegated; chucked out.  Snip, snap I was taking a eradication bath.  Then: 'And God created' … both internal and external.  Okay let's get more than PG rated Doogie Howser MD before Gone Girl sliced up his poignantly creepy ass to establish the linen person's worst crime scene nightmare; the creation of the labia, clitoris and vagina.  The full enchilada of removal and creation can be wham bam thank you ma'mmed in one general anaesthetic operation or in stages depending on the emotional and physical disposition of the patient.  Sexton wanted that band aid ripped off in one take.  Despite the surgeon's protestations.  Debz helped counter encourage, "Woman up!" her words, not mine.

Orchiectomy, also known as the surgical removal of the testicles or picking the low hanging fruit in business, happens before placing the pole-vault in the eternity storage cupboard to allow the patient to cut back on the digestion of female hormones.  Drilling Sexton full of oestrogen, an inflated hormonal Boyband balloon, although fun, would likely kill him flat dead no joke.  The wrinkled brain hessian sack, although seemingly flung over the shoulder to travel with nineties coat holding male model to nowhere idyllic, is maintained for the opening clam's shells.  Okay, okay sorry – it's just this is told after a previous retelling with pomegranate, lime and black pepper homemade gin, pink tonic and years of genital female revenge for having ours derided in popular culture!  Translation: some of the scrotum material is left behind to create the labia or to line sections of the vagina during vaginoplasty.  Like when a paid for hessian carrier bag rips and you find another use for it because you paid £3 for it at Waitrose or got it free when spending £20 at Paperchase. But punters, surgery more often than not apparently leads to a shrinking of scrotal skin, think a juicy ripe beef tomato versus last decade's fruit of a generation: sundried tomatoes. This is why some surgeons, earning their £100k a week, do not recommend an orchiectomy as a separate (or unattached) procedure, especially for those who plan to have a vaginoplasty. One last tug Sexton, who wouldn't need anything such as a skin graft from the abdominal region as he was proud to believe that his final tug of the one-stop-plaster-shop would all happen in a crescendo of 'falling asleep a Man and waking up a Woman' AND he could go to bed every night (likely after taking a menagerie of hormone replacement pills to keep the previous regime intact and the new regime fabulous) knowing his ball sack was now the slightly wet flaps stuck to his inner thighs. If you're still upright and not hunched over the toilet or rolling on the floor in your own abdominal pain, let's move onto the penectomy or removal of the penis.

Surgeons again sticking their rich, nosey, meddling noses into all dealings Boyband LGBTQX transformation, advise orchiectomy and/or penectomy without necessarily going onto the vaginoplasty creation. Quite genuinely generously genially geniusly this is called nullification. No one really understood how you did your business in this nullification state but it was a no-fly-zone given Sexton planned the full buffet works. Sexton wanted a vagina more than Veruca Salt wanted a pony on Christmas morning. Why this was atop his wishlist was more of a mystery than how, as can easily be seen in this simple How To Guide: follow this step-by-step manual and, you too, in no time will be living your dream as a confused, post Dracula dating singer songwriter, mimer, dancer fun socialite carb conscious Tweeter extraordinaire. How NOT to Use The Tissue from Your Man Bits to Create your Future Happiness. Penectomy also needs a legacy, so when proceeding to the next stage, some tissue from the penis will be preserved to be fashioned into a vagina and clitoris. That is an actual quote, not quite 'I have a dream' but a singular and informative quote nevertheless. The standalone penectomy involves creating a shallow vaginal dimple and a new urethral opening to allow for urinating in a sitting position. Otherwise you end up like a confused canine, neutered air humping and squatting on haunches when the leg refuses to rise. Without the double plasties (penecto- and vagino-) the opportunity to patchwork your new neo-vagina creation with sentimental previous under-performing dangly bits is lost forever.

Now for the three wise women of the sex change: vaginoplasty, labiaplasty and clitoroplasty; or creation of the … well, I suppose the names are sufficiently exoteric to ensure the end result is not a genital Picasso. As Sexton had gotten semi-proficient at instant orgasms and was fond of the sensation, albeit countered by the humiliation of being clothed, alone and spontaneous, he hoped to repeat with a support package that also looked good, felt good and was able to engulf what he was planning to discard. Surgeons' key selling features and unique techniques included shameless boasts of establishing hairless linings, higher than average moisture production, elastic like a bungee cord, sensitive to the touch months after the procedure, wide and long enough for the most genetically gifted among that 48% of the world and a perfectly horizontal steady downward stream of the urinary tract thus avoiding the 'cheap sprinkler effect' of earlier eras. Sexton was advised, however, that due to his microphallus he would certainly require additional skin grafts to construct a tolerably sized vagina. This did not meld with Sexton's just get it done mantra so he would have to settle for extreme daily dilations following surgery, the undisclosed pumping of a Boeing's tyre, to maintain the vagina's shape.

Raise your hand if you need a bathroom break; or just a complete break, severing the concept you never knew that you now know. Hands thrown up across the nation, readying to drop into vomit worship position. Couldn't Disney develop a saccharine version of a sex change, one where the dashing increasingly flawed Prince vanquishes his ogre-styled demons then, as a reward, the ruling Queen grants him his own Queendom in the form of the most flowy, dazzling, self-affirming ball dress ever seen? Now for penile inversion, Sexton's treat of choice for the vaginoplasty. Without him really acknowledging, Sexton agreed to use a salty sliver of the large intestine as his penis was damaged and he categorically requested all the skin from the scrotal sac be used to make the vagina wider and longer. Debz was of supported consensus that he'd beat himself down there while beating off as a teenager to dispel the odd relationship he'd formed with orgasm, sex and his mother Janine.

Something feels wrong when I say that name. Janine. The woman who claimed she wasn't Janine in that recent exposé about Boybands; the one who claimed she was nameless, had no children and would never consider procreation because of what she had been through and because she liked girls. Her link to convicted Boyband serial killer Manfred Dill, still serving a life sentence in Dartmoor prison, was difficult to deny. With shaky realism and a heartfelt almost-psychotic sadness she'd clearly taken on a financial reward for agreeing to the documentary then either something happened or some realisation but she acquired feet so cold she stepped out of filming never to be seen again; just about the time it all got interesting with her rumoured offspring. Allegations included a girl then a boy and when Celebitchy.com reported the youngest was Sexton, Egotastic.com, PopGrint.com, IDontLikeYouInThatWay.com, PinkIsTheNewBlog.com and Celebrity-Babies.com all managed to produce dubious sources to corroborate the claim.

The clitoris is compiled using a small section of the highly sensitive penis head; this is not a simple Lego exercise. The erectile tissue, which gives (or gave) the penis the ability to become erect, is confiscated in order to prevent the vaginal entrance and the clitoris from becoming overly swollen during sexual arousal. Debz, integrally involved in the medical prep, form filling and general support administration for Sexton would ensure his existing erectile tissue remained in the procedure. The prostate gland, obdurate to the last call, would remain at the neck of the bladder and around the urethra, a bastion of consistency in an ever-evolving world. Emptying the bladder for Sexton would now be a shorter journey and in a separate position, relocating and kerbing the urethra and going some way to explain why us girls always need to pee all the time. With nothing left from Sexton's penis or ball bag he'd have to go off-piste to mould the innermost lips of the vagina or labia minora.

And all this time you thought it was just an eager lumberjack and an artistic clean up team! Both hands for the Disney version being better, cleaner, less real. Actually I'd trust Pixar with this one to bring some more realism and poignancy into a world where the tragedy of extreme surgery to deal with existential transformational ideals is told as it should be, with the danger pitfalls and realisation ideals reality.

We haven't even touched upon the recovery process, breast enhancement, voice alteration, laser hair removal, oestrogen courses and facial reconstruction – all at a cost and a level of unguaranteed complexity. They call it removal of deformities, getting rid of male facial bones. Once the puerile hilarity of boy's bits morphed into first disgust then horror at the physical and mental impact of all this, we as a staunch collective changed tact. We were monsters but not those kinds of monsters. Debz would use every weapon at her disposal to try talk Sexton off the ledge, primarily her lusty promises and the YouTube reality of what could and does go wrong. But as with most things in this little tale, the real drive came from the band, a push to fabricate an elusive exclusivity, for those fifteen minutes, to be a

BoyLGBTQXband and sell more records. We couldn't be held responsible for all Boyband trends, but Debz would hold her hands up high in 'my bad' recognition when she forgot to erase the request to utilise the erectile tissue on the form.

Chapter 26

# FLYSWATTER

There's a mini digression that has to take place, something we've all debated and had to endure through various forms of adulated coercion. Is sodomy a sin? The visual and reverent male of the species will argue why would God put a convivially delicious entry point right next to road more frequently travelled and, of course, our beauticians would attest to creating the most perfect little pink balloon ties in the celebrity world but really is it moral to put something there?

I'm called through to the design studio, the decor impressively understated for what is meant to the most cutting-edge bespoke mechanical studio in the South East. No pictures of fishermanesque triumphs, engineers aside feats of engineering, the felled mane of a lion slumped in disgust near the dental American MAGA conqueror; no historic news articles, exclamations, dated fonts and brown paper headlines bestowing the world's gratitude for progression on the engineering visionary; in fact no self-congratulatory paraphernalia at all. Just faux expensive workshop panel walls and, upon entrance into the working studio, a gasp of activity somewhere between Flashdance's career girl welding in sexy non-submission and hot scientific nerds wandering around with iPads genuinely interested in making, breaking, enhancing and dancing, an almost fluid travel to even the most stoic male hips, gliding between contraptions, the real self-affirming congratulation. Professional to the core but I can't help notice one notice us from behind what looks like a distillery, clear liquid pin-balling past his pale-purply-green bespeckled eyes, likely because I'm with Renea who sports a braless white V-neck t-shirt and tights, the ultimate in 'Fuck you I couldn't give a damn' chic: trying without trying, her dark flawless features in perfect unison with the vibe of the nutty inventors. Instead of being led to a stuffy, corporate office we're led directly to our commission, standing proudly ominous above our heads in unfinished glory.

"We've always strongly followed a design mantra of never asking, never telling, but I have to say of all our commissions this might just have piqued my interest more than any," spilled from the well-spoken lips of our design account manager, tall, lithe, casually well-dressed and with skin that only a plant-based diet could produce.

"It's still in development?" says Renea.

"Yes. We like to show our clients the progress against the original spec, giving each the option to tweak or make any reasonable changes without expense."

"Well I suppose at that cost we would always hope for and expect some form of leeway: the trimmings and toppings phase."

"Indeed. And as your specification was incredibly detailed, we've been able to enhance some of the design criteria and keep all the original features, while adding in some of our own – completely removable of course. For example, we've added a setting on the control panel which is sensor homogenous and can be assigned to a person or persons' genetic footprint. In other words through shape, weight, voice activation and even odour the device will activate if the designated individual or individuals enter the proximity within the target zone. We've also made use of nylon elastic which permits two settings: close and capture."

"This would be a digression from the plastic swatter material between the four sides as per the spec?"

"Yes but the effect will be exactly the same as this nylon can be tightened using that orange dial on the panel over there. At its highest torque or tension the nylon elastic will feel significantly more solid than the original swatter plastic and with the force catapult design the impact will completely nullify whatever is put in the zone: a metal block would have less impact. And the reduction of the tension will enable capture mode where the four geometric angles will collapse around the recipient. A life-size Venus fly trap to accompany the human-size fly-swatter."

"Me likey. A lotty."

"Yes our engineers were rather excited at the prospect of keeping with the *Musca domestica* of family Muscidae theme with an additive twist of nature's own penal repellent."

## Chapter 27

# WILLOW

"So we're brothers. Yeah. Just … just … unbelievable; unfathomable. That we'd end up in the same profession too. If you can call this a profession that is – more like tail whenever we want it, yeah man, yeah! You didn't know? Neither did I. Clearly we're not identical. Watch any of our music videos to know that much. I've always had a calling towards nature; towards the earth. You? Ah, similar. I had hoped so; prayed so; believed so. You're what? Wondering why the size difference? Perhaps you blood sucked all the nutrients from the, what's that thingy called, the umbilical cord. Poor mum trying to feed your big ass. Do you work out? You must do. Pump some iron eh? Amazing. This whole brother I never had thing. Do you think we could attend an earthy midway or protest fracking or shoot the next video at an anaerobic digestion plant or something? I know! How about a joint video? A duet of sorts – We Eez Da Treez with Likely L – brothers in arms cutting some serious shapes baby with lyrics straight from the top-notch songwriters. Who do you think is trendy for songwriting at the moment? Matrix still going? Love those guys. Then could pen out some blasting tunes to come out as brothers. Ooh, ooh we could maybe bring in some Hip Hop Brutha refences then we stare into each other's eyes on stage and belt out a chorus, ending in 'my bruttttaaaa, he ain't heavvvyyyyy' – no wait I think that was done during some war or something. Who knows. But the crowd, and the music video watchers and the downloading fans are left with zip squat nada doubt we're brothers; and tight like brothers should be. You feel me? I feel you. Feel like I've felt you my whole life; felt you were a presence inside me, deep inside and only you knew it. Our little secret. Until we unleash it on the world, our brotherly love gift of love to show our love and love one another while everyone loves buying the tune. Love you brother of mine. Always. And forever. How was that?"

"Comprehensive," Jemima commented, glancing up from a tanking share graph while juggling another legal conundrum. "Could you do it with more feeling next time? Practice always makes perfect. If you are able to deliver it from the heart but supported by the script, Barton will feel you all the way inside him as your true, bound at the hips and soul, brother."

"My soul brother. I like it. Soul brothers. Boyband Soul Brothers. Apart for a time, now together forever. Let me find a pen to write that down."

*Chapter 28*

# Renea

According to an unnamed British doctor just prior to the start of the twentieth century, when supporting the president of the Royal College of Surgeons of England, circumcision was deemed a cure or efficacious prevention of masturbatory insanity. Upon removing the 'vestigial' prepuce, additional benefits included curing nocturnal incontinence, epilepsy, hysteria and, most significantly, an irritation that might give rise erotic stimulation and, consequently, masturbation. The poor old, useless, bacterial-laden foreskin had a bad rep in those days and these, apparently with a 48% increase in the chance of acquiring a nasty STD for the ruinous recipient. None of us girls liked them in any way, shape or form, in particular Renea. As another physician, P.C. Remondino, so eloquently added 'circumcision is like a substantial and well-secured life annuity … it insures better health, greater capacity for labour, longer life, less nervousness, sickness, loss of time, and less doctor's bills'. Renea had kept hers in a small jar of formaldehyde to remind her how much she hated it and how much she hated being a man. It sat there, a pickled relic, mangled in preservatory defiance, a rotted piece of jellyfish washing ashore. Renea often pondered whether she'd gone through with the full procedure just to get rid of the tapered appendage so, in her honour, we decided all Boyband Boyfriends should be relieved of theirs, preferably through nonelective persuasion but not excluding any and all means …

A flatchested flatbottomed television on its side in a pool of adequately spilled beer separates coupled clumps of human bodies. The crusted lips bobble hopelessly at moisture in the air and most are too afraid to raise an eyelid and allow destroying light beneath a lid. The television splutters no static, the cracked screen refracting dim light into the sunken black, unable to move to a channel, the tangled cords immersed with the remote control in the golden froth that collects in pockets of sunken carpet.

The first stir emerges from the host, clothed in flattering underwear, alone and hotdogged in a cream duvet bunched into three of the corners leaving a foreskin inserted between the heels of her feet. She doesn't know what century she's in, surrounded by her guests in her own apartment, the ceiling weak from repeated bashing from the upstairs neighbour. Her tongue, plastered to the roof of her mouth, wrestles free to touch the tips of her teeth and pulls back from the sensitive sensational shock. At first her head is numb until her eyes find a spread apart packet of cigarettes containing broken soldier sticks, half-eaten and unused. Then her head is alive, pushing ephemeral signals to all corners of her cranial globe, forcing her to wince in pain and make sure she hands her purse over to the hangover in gentle and uncompromising union.

There is a man three feet from her asleep on his back with an inverted empty punch bowl covering his groin. Both his hands are clasped over the decorated bowl as if he were a dead body pushed into a mid-price range casket being wheeled down the tunnel of doom for a quick singe, scatter, tear and forget. Renea's head is not ready for a soldier with a big glass hat on nor the memory of what Kieron performed on his soldier's big floppy hat.

Inside her bathroom are two women locked in an embrace kept prisoner by the high Victorian ceramics. They are bone dry. In the kitchen most of the cupboards have been ripped free to form a makeshift fort on the floor, housing a naked couple asleep with their curved spines arching fiercely at one another. A crusty condom has somehow become wrapped around the man's toe and in his slumbered state he is unable to shake it free. The kicking, first toe then heel, almost unsettles the angular fort but does nothing to deter the sleeping pair.

Swallowing water fast. The cold filtered liquid escaping down her gullet to ease the suffering on her liver and recreate the cells that scorn her in every corner of her body. She wraps a gown around herself, not visibly cold but nevertheless naked around all of Kieron's friends. His musician friends. The ones she met at the weed parties. The ones who knew him. The ones who could explain who he was. The ones who have become scattered around her awkward apartment as she searches for the crime scene.

The remnants of scattered pot adorn the top of her kitchen counter amidst more shades of marijuana, black coffee granules and sugar: a garbled edition of the Vinland flag, mottled with abandoned beer spills, scuppering her morning brew. An ill-conceived and now abandoned serving lightly lathers, brewing on the stove top, the tiny filaments of green herb sliding up and then down the brown bubbles of caffeine, ending discarded at the foot of each mound, abruptly motionless. Soaked and unsmoked.

A clothesline of underwear, male and female, has been joined from the bookcase to the desk. Renea doesn't recognise any of her own in there and is even more surprised to find no one inhabiting the worn-out room, now reluctantly receiving slats of sunlight through the window. In the main bedroom a human pyramid spills over all sides of her double bed, faces buried in armpits, hands slipping between legs and round bottoms peeking from among the human remains like spotlights. Amongst the mayhem, immaculately preserved, almost enshrined by an inanimate glory, rests Kieron's Lord of the Rings sword and knife collection. Sting is missing.

Inside Renea's cupboard is a choir of empty beer tins. Forty-four bottles of beer on the wall! She pulls on a pair of old jeans underneath her dressing gown, somehow failing to upset the tins. She abandons her stained Sunday top for a new tighter fitting one; one that she recently purchased and didn't fancy too much yet wears for the sake of wasted income. In the hallway she is forced to hopscotch another chapter of partly clothed bodies. Who are these people? Did they cheer Kieron on in his drug-fuelled state, antics to show bodyhorror bravado with a subconscious request for cleaner intercourse swirling around a tangle of apathy, barbiturates, alcohol and desire? Were they unaware and it just happened? Did anything actually happen and did Renea's hangover mean she cared less to find out?

Outside is warm. Renea's hands are warm and shaky and it takes her a few attempts to submerge her keys in her jeans pocket. The key ring cumbersomely juts into the solid part of her thigh muscle. The blur of the day is annoying. Everyone is already at work. A truck driver passes and whistles, sticking his tongue out at her and allowing his head to follow her form until the taillights have disappeared below the ridge of tar. She tucks her hair behind her ears and slumps onto a bench circled by tall trees and bus stops. An old woman waves and boards a bus. Renea tries to smoke a three-quarter cigarette. She coughs hard, the mucus from the previous evening's activities collecting below her chin, but persists, as if completion will lead to some sort of unnatural redemption.

Her face feels smeared everywhere. Her fury teeth drip sweat and her jaw hurts from maybe laughing or smoking or talking. She's forgotten what it's like to be outdoors on a weekday, the reality of her only excuse to enjoy it being searching for Kieron's foreskin. The one-woman Bobbitt search team. This is not her; this inactivity; this waiting for some kind of healing. Infusing an urgency into the search would not only betray her core chillaxing disposition but sledgefuck her unabating hangover in a way that might mean her head actually rolls off her shoulders, lawn bowling away from her feet then exploding under another truck. Or a white van, the tyre swatting her abandoned watermelon in a cruelly ironic twist. No longer a man, her life was profoundly different.

Back at her apartment the guests are still all comatosed. The man with the glass bowl has rolled into a pocket of beer and the wall mirror has now fallen from the wall without shattering. Renea changes clothes and washes her face. The application of a quick respectable amount of makeup and a haphazard teeth clean is all that will suffice in her attempts to cull the torpidity. She calls Kieron's phone and hears a buzzing towards the back of the house. There's a trail of blood at the back door, punctuated by the closed door. Renea takes a moment to open the door. Kieron is lying face up in the lavender hedge, his dusty-white underpants soaked in desiccated blood. He wakes up momentarily and finds an old joint, insentiently lighting it before rolling to one side to further congest the blue-purple flowers. Renea checks her hands, not a Lady Macbeth moment in sight, yet her smoking hand's two 'fuck you' fingers remain yellow from filter stain.

# Chapter 29

# KELLY

Upon entering a room where everyone knows something or anticipates something bar the entrant, there is that involuntary side-to-side hunt for reassurance. Attempting to answer the question "I am the only one who thinks this is a bad idea?" or "Am I the only one feeling a tepid tear drop of sweat entering in between my butt cheeks like those 300 ripped, buffed Spartans being ambushed in the gorge?" This is what I (completely understandable; understandably unavoidable) await from the faces still peering into these pages, still enduring the fantastical nightmare, still awaiting the dénouement on How NOT to Murder a Boyband.

Here goes: Kelly wants me to meet his mother.

Maybe this is the twist; setting everything up so we show some empathy, some kindness when confronted with a middle England old lady who loves her son, wants the best for her son and will miss her son. Hoping for a cheap-brandy-swilling, profanity-laden, still-skirt-wearing, Bingo-fiend megalomaniac is a tall order I accept but where mothers are concerned, other than the incredibly rarefied Smug Dad scenarios, they tend not to vindicate homicidal or body disfiguration pastimes. Mothers embody either the soul of what the child should have become or shine a blinding light on the unaccounted-for constituents that maketh man; especially man. Little boys and their mummies, so eager not to impress in direct contrast to the patriarch, fortuitously become the worst bits of their mothers. So making Kelly's mother out to be some sort of shapeshifting, Boyband moulding monster, I knew, was putain irréalisable. Cowardice suffices if branded something more than running away, so making excuses until my quiver was forlorn of any arrows was a short-term fix and the handbook on How NOT to Meet a Boyband Partner's Parents advised fight or flight including breaking-up, asking for a slow in pace or diminishing the relationship through claims of not being ready. Emotionally. But Kelly, although with his flaws, was no mug, so could see through the feigned lack of confidence and understood the social curiosity personage, so could only take to heart refusing to meet his mum. Perhaps consciously he never gave any of her personage away, piquing my interest but also embracing the true meaning of the word so I was piqued with interest but also without, pointedly angry or annoyed. He never bestowed her virtues as a mother or hinted at past resentment; he never referenced genetics against what she might embody, positive or negative; he didn't have any pictures or video clips. A mythical and potentially fascinating creature I could never meet.

## How NOT to Murder a Boyband | by Jason Roche

When you are stuck with a person for an extended period, their inability to own or control anything can have the desired effect you are striving for. In other words when you glance across at someone you are beginning to resent, exclusively for who they are rather than what they represent, you attach these character weaknesses to physical peculiarities, mannerisms and idiosyncrasies. Feels like I need to whisper now as, at this very second, I'm sitting with my legs tucked under my bum in one of Kelly's XXL shirts on the sofa watching him watch TV. Hashtag Boyband Gogglebox. He is downright oblivious to my stalking, my eyes ransacking his features but a nose can only point more upwards if the person is doing fuck all to avoid this. He's eating raw peppers. Jesus … cue nose becoming a fully-fledged ski-slope and little murderous teddy bear button-like! Okay breathe and keep it down or else he'll know; he'll glance up, considerately put The Crown on mute and ask me if I'm okay. So his niceness fucks me back both now and futuristically, a time travelling dick of polite niceties waiting to surprise me when I drop my futuristic keys! I know you're asking where does this come from; how do the nose and healthy snacking morph to exacerbate this transference? Well you get attached God dammit and he's letting the rest of Boyband shunt him to the back and, as a whole, they haven't had a top 10 hit in months and all this makes me want to grow my own pair and shove them down his mouth along with those carefully sliced red, green, yellow and even orange peppers. He glances at me so I quickly marvel at how much I miss Claire Foy, now being forced to watch national treasure Olivia's sulky expression, weak chin and emoted tearing to remove dialogue. Can't Olivia Coleman just play Olivia Coleman? The crunching ensues, spilling that fresh veg flavour into my nostrils and making me want to sprint to the fridge, fling it open in triumph, slam my face directly down on to the salted caramel and biscotti quadruple decker cake I've just baked in my head, lick like a possessed lesbian, come up for air, back down to devour, then finally raise my head in calorific glory shouting "I ate my cake!" and beating my breasts for goodwill. But I don't. He puts a reassuring hand on my knee without taking his eyes off Josh O'Connor's exaggerated stoop.

*Chapter 30*

# GWYNNe

Persuading Damien to take on intermittent fasting wasn't difficult as he was already firmly on the body dysmorphic self-improvement that might or might not last until you're forty. Gwynne was never one for passive acceptance so the entry level, training-wheels 16:8 would never do – Damien had to jump firmly with both feet into OMAD. This did wonders for his physique but not his mood, outbursts of anger and organic-roided-rage becoming more commonplace that his now obsessive daily press-ups. What worked well was that Gwynne was able to redefine her self-defence zen, forcing herself not to kick his arse and just defend his hapless and uncoordinated lunges, thrusts and mafioso downward angled kicks. She could deal with this as Damien was starting to institute this level of aggression as commonplace in an active relationship. When Gwynne found out Damien had been paying prostitutes, not for sex, but just to beat them up, we all knew the timeline had shifted, urgency infused into our game like in Cluedo when a player has the murder weapon and murderer and just needs to get to the room (family rules). He would pay the pimp extra in exchange for no warning: the girl had to be unaware, grappling with fighting back versus calling for non-existent help in a lone apartment detached from societal support. There was a new one each week until the pimp grew tired of the complaints and Damien's beatings became more severe. It was either change Damien, change his behaviour or change his existence. Three was endgame, so Gwynne settled on stopgap one through inculcating excessive bad calories into his one meal a day, in the hope that his fasted state would facilitate a huge insulin spike then sedentary emotions for the other 23 hours; this coupled with the inherent failure of putting on weight despite best efforts and a return to affable Porky Pig from psycho hairless woman beating wrathful Piglet.

*Chapter 31*

# MAGGIE

Aristocratic ruffian has a certain charmless irony; a paradoxical carrot dangling in the blustering kingdom of united girls hunting down the ideal boy. Girls not only want their cake and to shovel it down in grotesque gooey handfuls, but we want to stay slim doing it, get the bustard to cook another while we watch from a safe following distance. Wanting a non-preening-opposite-of-metrosexual man is on trend, someone a bit rough around the edges, clean of course but that drizzle of unrefined: able to flip you over or cogently lift you up should the passion of the embrace dictate. But we also want breeding, manners and some level of historic greatness far above gutter, council flat or middle England.

The most easterly tribes of the Haudenosaunee or Iroquois Confederacy were known as Mohawks, Iroquoian-speaking North American natives, more famous for the enduring hairstyle than the population decimation from European smallpox in the mid 1600s with no defensive immunity.

Fashion surviving over human suffering: who knew. Urban legend, mythical scary bedtime story or early Boyband, the Mohocks, for some inexplicably irrelevant reason, adopted a version of the name and began raping women. Oh, and doing other stuff too like disfiguring male victims, putting an old woman into a hogshead to roll down a hill and severing useful body parts such as noses and hands during the early 18th century. The Mohocks were reportedly well-born Londoners intent on unprovoked terror, lawlessness, impunity and luridly violent acts. So as with the time's primary social media: word-of-mouth, the notoriety of the Mohocks took on larger than life proportions, facilitating transferal credit for anti-social public displays and the first real identification of a posh psycho, shamefully adopted by Bret Easton Ellis' eighties banker Patrick Bateman, then Kubrick's Droogs and, more recently, the protracted dig at the BoJo SamCam's bloke Bullingdon Eton gathering gratuitously shrouded in yobbing blowjob requests throughout The Riot Club. Remember it is no happenstance that the Mohocks put an old woman into the head of a pig and rolled her down a hill. None would ever match up to the notoriety of The Mohocks, such brazen displays of visceral violent disassociation, with many an envious street brawling London bunch only really grappling for the pretender's crown, most boringly notably the Hectors, the Scourers, the Muns and the Nickers.

When Maggie shunned an advance from Stubzy and surveyed the gang of white boys trying to be black, she didn't even see any remnants of Hectors, Scourers, Muns or Nickers. DeliverU2Me was the worst of both worlds: trying to be rough but with no breeding or sophistication to speak of. Maggie, forlorn at being dragged to a publicity book signing event, surveyed the little dabs of dried blood beneath Digby's straight peaked ironlak ghetto blaster cap and wondered whether she could fit him into a hogshead. Fleetingly though because Debz, now the welcomed ubiquitous third magnificently-titted wheel being snapped at every flattering angle by the publicity hounds, was in tow to put a reassuring hand on Maggie's bottom when those eyes went green. Silver directed her gaze, green beams tippy-toeing all over Debz's punted plump lips and she raised a hand out to touch her mouth. A sudden flurry of digital cameras erupted, flapping seagulls morphing in an ascending helicopter. Debz, as is Debz's way, would take the soft pressing of fingers to her lips in the most sensual, posed way, pressing her lips back against Silver's neat nails, pursing in sisterhood ardour. DeliverU2Me would all stop for a moment, aware that not a single camera remained fixated on them, the glare of flashes dethatched from their book signing table like a searchlight missing escaping East German prisoners. Digby though, would further mind-rape Debz, right there whilst bestowing the literary merits of dressing like a rapper on a suspecting public. The self-help novel had been ghostwritten by a black American ghetto chic fashion designer known as Braidz; he'd helped the Boyband understand how best to transition from saccharine sweet to menacing African American street which specifically dealt with sartorial tips for white adopters. So "Dressing Faaaan If Yow White" was destined to become a bestseller, especially when the human live guineapigs for low pants, baggy baseball jackets, flat caps and bling were none other than Britain's very own redefined Boyband DeliverU2Me.

This was a situation where the collective would always prove stronger than the individuals, where sisterhood and support would prevail without pre-judgement on perceived weakness or stamina for the fight or disappointment. This was not a Boyband sprint after all, a flailing skinny jeans arms and legs waving gorilla scaring charge down the lanes but rather a 'she ain't heavy she's my brother' endurance relay, with a consummate understanding that batons do get dropped even at key moments but that there is always more than one Boyband-dating superstar chick to casually bend down, pick it up and place it back in the palm. That said no one dropped the baton, it just changed hands so many times we decided to help out with the wobble. Maggie, although possessing a character more solid than most army veterans, was, after all, human and, more importantly, she carried scars unable to be eradicated with a simple 'Expelliarmus'. Always the bridesmaid and always a close second it seemed unfair to use Debz's genetically bestowed expressive virtues to make Digby swap Maggie for Debz; we had to replace Digby's physical petition for Debz with an envy of Maggie herself. So, in theory it was like this: dick-fuck-wit Digby wants perma-pout-perkytits Debz, who in turn wants nothing other than emerald-eyes-poised-to-rule-the-world Silver, thus making dick-fuck-wit Digby want emerald-eyes-poised-to-rule-the-world Silver when he realises all perma-pout-perkytits Debz wants is Maggie. Consciously Maggie would pull her hand away from Debz's mouth and Debz would leave a lingering, longing hold long enough for Digby to notice. Flash forward some weeks and, after Digby had engineered a drinking session with Debz and plied her with enough white wine to halt a bucketful of charging Karens, his Dutch courage lurched forward to plant his now augmented lips on Debz, two swollen caterpillars boxing well below their league weight category if way above the actual Newton pound-force equivalence. Debz would traffic warden her palm into his chest, an unnerving sternum click halting proceedings more suddenly than a pigeon flying into a reflective window.

"I'm in love with someone else," she would protest.

"That Nancy boy muthafucka Sexpest don't deserve yow fine ass," would be his rap-battle riposte.

"It's your girlfriend. Every time I close my eyes or brush my teeth or let my mind wonder in any way, it always comes back to her. I don't want anyone else in this world but her and I know I can't have her because her passion knows no boundaries and I know I can't handle that. If I brought all my love, sex, filthiness, passion and smut to her I just know from hanging out with her that I will never measure up."

"Well you could try?"

"It would never work. She deals at another level to me. She'd destroy me. And I'd be destroying what a beautiful union you both have had in the past."

"In the past?"

# Chapter 32

# LADYBITER

"The shipment's arrived early. I don't know where we are going to stash it all!" yells Danielle, ex-Boyband superfan, likely chewing some of the shipment. The background noise on the other end of the WiFi call line beams with workers working: loading, shifting, 'allo mate-ing. Then the unmistakable pour.

"Did they get your ratios right?"

"Looks that way although difficult to tell with the incredible volume. That's them pouring into a few old one cubic metre log bags I cleaned out. Moving them from here will be the logistical challenge – we'll have to get more 'no questions asked' movers. Looks mainly red from what I can gather." Munch munch, another handful.

"You're denting the stash, aren't you?"

"Overcatering, as you said, would serve us all in the end. If I lay face down on the top and kept chewing until they put a person on Mars I wouldn't even Harvey Dent it!"

"Leave the red ones alone. Just in case."

"They are unmistakably multicoloured, a rainbow nation of anaphylaxis, but I do believe the one red to every other colour ratio persists. It says so on the form. So visceral!"

"Indeed. The core of any contemporary statement. Plain Jane nothing doesn't grab attention. It's the food, celebrity, plasma mix tape – gotta love your vision."

"Actually coming to fruition as I see them load the final bag. I'll have to cling wrap and seal somehow as this could be a neighbourhood advert for the entire street's rodent population."

"And hide from Gerson."

"That's not a problem, although his little moon face might explode if he came across all this. And he'd likely sneak a few what with me fattening him up for the slaughter."

"Maybe he'd do that badly-behaved disorderly thing he does in his pants."

"I'd bend over, sprinkle a few all over my back and wait. That would work."

"Patience girl. The house of sweets is almost complete and the witch is hungry."

Munch munch. More masticated messy mani multi-coloured M&Ms.

*Chapter 33*

# OCCUPATIONAL HAZARD

There was always going to be one or more of these popping up to counter our productivity. The key was to not treat each female occupational hazard with the same level of prophetic disdain but rather eradicate any threat and (if at all God damn possible) weave the poor girl's misguided intent into the Boyband narrative. There was always room for more but the emotional baggage vetting, deep personal shared trauma relationship and overarching intellectual integrity couldn't just be magicked up with a 'welcome to the club' slap of the heinie.

The first would target Maggie and be more of an ominous watching begrudging presence than anything malevolent. She'd send weirdly obsessive badly written poetry to Silver until a rookie error of quoting the Quran meant we could pass the letters onto Scotland Yard who opened a special terrorist prevention case against the stalker; poor girl probably just got a bit too liberal with Google rather than plotting to behead Digby's girlfriend. Gwynne's stalker was clearly more maniacal and careful, initially that is; she received pictures of deformed and decomposing animals, mainly pets but also wild animals. This was deemed non-threatening by the authorities until a human corpse was included, a vile half head axe wound showing a dirty brown cross-section of a man's frontal cranium. Gwynne being Gwynne, defiant to the last high kick, wanted the sender to sign it so she could get it framed and hung pride of place in Damien's gym palace. As a group we decided to visit the incarcerated girls and both visits threw back the inimitable truth that bog standard middle-class celebrity-worshiping folk were the true victims here and that perhaps the sequel (if we ever got there) should involve publicists, media, marketers, band managers and / or anyone bestowing the virtues of a person who gyrates and melodises for a living into becoming pop gods. Both girls, sweet girls Angelica and Patricia, were so in love with the Boyband boys they'd been duped to believe were a certain way, they had no other outlet or orifice than to eradicate the better half, the arm candy propping up the emotionally impotent imposter. We'd regularly send them care packages with nothing sharp of course and articles on music theory.

The most shocking occupational hazard would involve Tabby Cat but luckily enough not physically. Whilst Barton was on tour he'd invited a silicone pretender Abigail lookalike from one of the backstage pass wearers. Being of general male weak disposition, the sight of the necklaced backstage VIP pass dangling between the oval borders like an indecisive railway switch turnout made Barton feel that old adage of 'while on tour' seep into his dick; plus he was still pissed with Tabby about something or other he'd forgotten about. Upon exiting the Miami concert arena via the back where little security loitered because of its anonymity, an ardent fan flung a jar of acid on Barton's date for the night, running off screaming "In the name of love, in the name of love!" The intended target was her face but with the enhanced hemispherical protection resting beneath her chin like two knees, the groupie would acquire the sickly concoction of fluoroantimonic acid, Piranha solution, aqua regia, $(R_2SiO)_n$, polydimethylsiloxane, skin, blood, tissue and fake tan, the PDMS increasing in viscosity as the molecular weight increased, tangibly producing an oily, sticky volcano. Paparazzi, first on the scene and unable to help what with the snapping digital cameras greedily embedded in their hands, would capture the moment each silicon pouch exploded, the plastic surgeon's 911: the second more spectacularly gawked at than the first. Barton would deny any responsibility as he claimed 'nothing had actually happened yet' and the victim would sue for new boobs and win, forcing Barton to shell out for (you guessed it) double Gs moulded almost exclusively on Tabby Cat's real trend setters. So every time Barton would change the channel to reveal his date's daytime tour explaining dealing with hysterical stalkers and recovering from trauma, he'd be reminded that she wore Tabby's assets with an imposter's pride.

*Chapter 34*

# ORIGINS STORY

Long held beliefs proved lazy, in that there was no real reference point for the inventive brutality but that the weakest sex of the time was always the victim. We were determined to solve the former by ensuring each could link back to something germane and, regarding the latter, we had to hurry because it was fast emerging that there really was no other conclusion than men, so negated by their own draconian beliefs, had neutered themselves into servitudinal weakness, not only in the workplace but in the bedroom, the household, society, social media, popular culture and general mental fortitude. Would a Boyband float? Did it matter? Even if we tied their air guitar strumming thumbs to their opposite pedicured big toes and flung them into a river, as per Mary Sutton of Bedform, the result was blatant win-win. Sink and drown; float and guilty. But what relevance for thumbs, toes, swimming and rivers? Sinning, though against a popularist understanding of the mutually exclusive subset misinterpreted from Dante's real journey, was not only perfectly aligned to the victims and butts, but sufficiently macabre to irritate the sensibilities of even the most ardently worthy tabloid writer.

But what of the beginning station; the actual origins story pre having seen Hugh's mid-forties abs enough times to feel queasy; did we actually have to know the superheroes before we discovered where they had started? This topsy-turvy psychological citation comfort was too mechanically mercurial for our predispositions: knowing where we'd come from should be influenced by the evil dealings of evil men but not wholly defined by it; the core existential pat on the back was not exclusively a retaliation but a celebration of the origins story, pre the viewer asking the question "How did she get that way?"

Christians get the credit for many an evil woman origins story but about 800 years before celebrating a virgin procreating through a huge immaculate cock from the sky shooting seminal seminal holy water up the fallopian tube to fuse with the untouched ovary, Homer gave us Circe who had the power to turn men into animals; not beer ... doh! Early laws against female sorcery centred on outlawing special skills, tools and words; the BC equivalent of telling a woman to shut up when the calm science of her options fucks a man's bloated argumentative shouting in the ass. By getting too far ahead, women were punished and outlawed, made to be burnt and drowned and raped and tortured – just like what's happening in 2021. Black Lives Do Matter, but heck Women's Lives More So, gender injustice a significantly eviler evil. And more prevalent. And more impactful. One of the earliest carnations of fabulous fierce female heretics included Bertha or Perchta or Befuna, a female embodiment of winter who punished social disobedience and rewarded good deeds, an early pioneer of empathetic baby carriers. The association with the coldest season of the year, synonymous with cold, mush, misery and frowning against the elements would be another classic betrayal of origins and assigning a convenient seasonally prejudiced caricature, manifesting in intellectuals portraying Bertha as an old hag. Her good deeds and general stand for rooting out bad behaviour and celebrating goodness were rewarded with a cold, desolate old witch's depiction. Hag becomes hat and broomstick becomes marred, lopsided, infertile, hating like the dead – all attributes designed to taint origins, hide kindness and sensationally glamorise the only real threat: a woman.

*Chapter 35*

# VIDEO EXPOSE

We gather. There could be a charity involved or it could be a glitzy post pandemic celebration ruse, gerrymandering our voting of the best Boyband videos of late. It is one of an incredibly rare opportunity for all of us to be in the same vicinity: Boybands, Boyband Boyfriends and Boyband Boyfriend Lasses. As the evening progresses we vote using button display panels not dissimilar to your experience at airport security except there is no unhappy red face, only a less smiley Boyband emoji, not crying just a sadness behind those withered cartoon eyes; the top 10 results are revealed in Mockingjay-tribute-falling-like announcements, a district replaced with a Boyband. But there never are any real losers are there, because even when the lower places are announced we all suspect some level of gratuitous 'add-on' reward to compensate for not finishing top. This is for charity.

One of the O2 halls has been booked for the event. A Covid coming out party, Boybands all vaccinated well before the eighty-year-olds anyway through overzealous agents and a bigger than standard bank balance. Covid wiping out Boybands: that would be a cruel yet satisfying twist on what those clever Chinese scientists were trying to effect in Wuhan, a bit too efficient at controlling on those shores whilst the competing major economies floundered with strict governance, accurate reporting, service-based economies and viral fatigue. Ballgowns and black-tie adorn the video displays, the playful motif of shooting music videos ably supported by vintage cameras, director chairs and set lighting. Spotting a few of my crew from across the hall, enshrouded by the Boyband music video lights emanating from the display screens like some angels of death, I'm breathless from the core, unashamed beauty of each – and instantly drawn towards challenging whether this is all folly. The sophistication and glamour of these girls is unbecoming of a Boybander; they deserve porn tits, fitness blogging, surgically strangled faces to match their images. My girls are just plain stunning, inside and out, which begs "Are we being duped?" Is this ploy so conscious it dispels the Boybands of old, pedestals the new breed and renders each accompanying womanly side act the main attraction?

Debz emerges from a pocket of babbling, champagne swilling, hysterical chin jutters – a royal red velvet rose amongst the thorns – her bare feet trailing into the luscious carpet, toes scrunching in sensual reciprocation. Her dark honey complexion and deep coagulated blood red dress merge, making the delineation between strapless shoulder and top of the garment undiscernible, a pulsing hot beacon of odorous carnality. Not a living soul notices when I send her the tiniest twitch of an approving wink, flicking the imaginary booger all the way across the room while she decides to vote. Sexton, being heedlessly dragged in her slipstream like some underperforming, inadequate younger sibling tries to guide closer towards the music video as he spots a brief cameo of himself gazing into the camera, a "Look at me mum," moment, only for Debz to randomly hit the nearest worst rating button and push back against his palm, then lazily give in and vote again on the other side of the board, failing to notice the rejection notice of 'You've already voted!'. The words My Love Is All True and All For You performed by Lone Survivors ticker tape across the screen on a continual loop as the sketchy narrative unfolds. There are no multi-coloured, multidimensional Boybanders, no stage, no screaming model-like fantasies, no Day-Glo suits but rather a brokeh blur of brown, grey, white, beige and black J.Crew, middle America taken care of in one humdrum ejaculation of safe wardrobe design. Lone Survivors are not even as short as their predecessors either, not really tipping the six foot two glorious mark but within safe following distance of five eight. The narrative is almost something to do with road safety, the boys each helping an old lady across to road to the geriatric equivalent of a tumult, teary eyes and nodding in made it to the other side appreciation. There are still the dreamy looks, slow-mo fades and hands on hearts but clearly young dumb bimbos no longer represent the downloading heartless, wife swapping the silver pound firmly in. But what is this video saying? To society? Look before you cross? Be nice to old people? Old people have Boyband friends too? The lollypop man is out somewhere lollygagging?

Method of Execution: that Cronenberg film Crash (not the overrated Oscar winning racial tension fare) but with real outtakes. That or YouTube footage of drivers dozing off and ploughing through pedestrians like a cricket bat through a watermelon. Note: no old people were harmed in the making of this video.

"Excuse me," says a shoulder into the arch between my shoulder blades. "My bad," comes bouncing from the tonsils of one of Xtreme Believe, caked in man make-up, batting weirdly curly lashes and supposedly genuinely sorry for almost shifting my person into another physical realm. He faces me for a millisecond and I give the game away, slamming the heel of my hand into his solar plexus so his dinner jacket engulfs his meagre Boyband frame in a crumpled ball of masculine suffering, his pink cornbraids creaking at the seams. Kelly, spotting the look he really should not be familiar with, heads off at the pass muttering "Really sorry mate, terrets," before shuttling us both off to the masked pomegranate gin bar, where I compliment "Dodgy oyster," the only other patron who has noticed the retaliatory assault bolt upright incredulous, while Xtreme Belieber self-hugs a few coughing convulses longer. Must be stronger than I thought.

The gin's the wrong colour and the wrong flavour, tasting peachier than anything else and embodying a dark rum orange hue rather than the on-trend pink. The masked

barperson has asymmetrical abs, a throwback to the Abercrombie retail support staff days, one line of dominoes all at least an inch higher than the other parallel line making him look sawed in half by a Sci-Fi film. He smiles at me so I gag back at him looking down into the gin glass yet insisting on another. He might have been smiling at Kelly. Snapping back from social boredom through antisocial random acts of violence is fun, yes, but not the right way forward here as the general pulsation of the room seems increasingly directed at me. I take a Debz moment and remove my shoes, curling my toes into the fabric of the carpet and breathing in while wonky-abbed barperson is replaced with wonky-lipped gin mixing proxy, this one with a more appealing midriff: aligned and probably hairier. She smiles at me so I smile at my toes.

It is raining: hard, fake, cum white computer bowels rain, angling across the shiny road background to wet the faces of our latest nominee Boyband. I'm staring at Willow who is staring at himself on the screen, before quickly voting the highest then fly fucking off faster than anyone could notice, drawn back to Jemima, a yoyo on a string. We Eez Da Treez eez all wearing rain jackets; I mean who in the world of non-believing bejezus wears an actual rainproof coat in a rainstorm in a Boyband music video? And they're staying dry like a wily street cat cowering beneath a drain or snuck into a fallen book obstacle, considerately tented up. If you swung the cat you wouldn't hit a single shaved moist armpit and you certainly wouldn't hit a V-neck white t-shirt and, even if the cat was four foot long and shaped like a barrel, you wouldn't hit a hip thrusting dance move; they're just

standing. Staying sheltered while trees fall in black and white noir flashbacks, as though the illogical irony of global warming is that trees fell back when temperatures were mild and now rain floods the poor little cowering sheltering covered up tree friends, not cooling the revolution but fuelling that they care. One of Willow's chums does a double footed kiddie plunge into a puddle, venturing to decimate Willow's dry pants, only to splat-splot the most pathetically benignant spray a centimetre away from Willow's foot. Jemima struts over to me pocketing what looks like money, kisses me on the cheek and slams the highest rating. I look at her quizzically approvingly and she mouths back "I want more," before excusing herself to take a call. She thinks, taking that actual moment intertwined with the increasingly frenetic drone of celebrities agreeing to calculate something brilliant. Angels in driven intellectual heaven hear the cogs churning in her brain, playing harps in tune along with the industry until she gets to her achievable end goal; she gets there before she gets there if you know what I mean, then turns back to devote some attention back to me, her dark yellow ball gown depth charging those around her to ordinariness.

"Sorry," she says to me.

"You never need to; it is what makes you exceptional."

We perform a mutual Covid-hug in symmetrical harmony, the germane nod to Willow's willow. The Boyband's social positioning kicks in at the end of the video like a white glove across the face, not dissimilar to that early nose morphing Boybander's Earth Song, except the

relatability to the planet dying unintelligibly includes baby seals dying, a dude from an E-list gorno with a flame thrower clad in dull leather and an eclipse of the sun. Then back to the rain, ah there it is – at least some homage to the past – teenage heart soaring gaze up towards the studio lights with perfectly placed Jenga hair across the forehead, except the finale is quite different.

"Willow told me if you're not making a statement, you're not making a difference," Jem smirks, popping a caviar roll then another into her mouth before a third just to get through the next scene. We Eez Da Treez begin melting, the effects not half bad as the acid rains drains eyeballs to the ground and renders skin a discarded accessory. They all melt in sequential harmony, Willow fittingly last, raising a final hand to the sky with the words 'Da Treez Eez Safe' above a clothes pile of masticated skin, hair, shininess and recognisable bodily appendages.

"Seems a contradictory message: if the trees are safe why do they need saving from the acid rain?" I ask Jemima, clearly horrified at remembering she'd agreed to a cameo in the video and had not appeared.

"Something like the Boyband is the reason the trees are safe; buy this shit take of a tune and you'll save a tree. Think I negotiated some kickback from each towards real tree pioneers. And us."

"Just a sliver?"

"Just a sliver."

Cue tree death hug.

A sense on loneliness can envelop one when surrounded

by excessive people; people all milling and being seen and looking but not seeing, mesmerizingly bobbling towards one another like a skimmed ten pin skittle. Wanting to fall but failing to. Wandering in isolation and wondering in isolation as I can't see anyone familiar, against the grain like I'm heading anti-clockwise at IKEA, each disapproving stare a notch on my belt buckle. Boyband video screens greet me chronically, replaying – a cow's muddy dropping fuelled by the ever-green endless supply of English countryside. I'm playing that game we all played as kids on family journeys, even though I never had one, where the passing cars are categorised and scored by colour, make or whatever creative fancy tickled the ubiquitous middle class driving to a destination holiday – except I'm doing it with cover versions. Somehow even if I block the sound, the way the video is shot and even the gyration of hips and sordidness of emulating mouthed words is apparent. Station fifteen and it's a love ballad because they're each nodding in slow motion and looking sad, not really sad like if someone skinned you with a cutthroat razor, but sad like you think you should feel at the dawn of a shocking human tragedy on BBC that, in reality, means nothing to you. Love ballad because each has a beard, trimmed and shaped so precisely it could be Lego.

Boyband Lego Beards
Attached, smooth and feared
Real but for the shears

This beardy Boyband I've seen around on the usual chat shows, morning crappy psychedelic fodder and MTV Hits but they never really cranked up enough to appear as a target for us and the video vindicates this decision. It's not enough to all have beards but they need to be stroked, extended pointy faux phalluses, pointing the wrong way. The disjointed cuts of scenes tells even the amateur eye that, between strokes, each beard had to be restyled, the beard comber no better than a fluffer because if you are feeling man enough to sport a beard, by gawd, you'd better have the hair density and thick testosteroneness to keep it all together. Shout out to Old Amish beard oil, yeehay. Voting complete and low for so many reasons including one blatantly hypocritical: by making our Boybands the biggest we make the pedestal for our Boys the highest and hence the longest fall to the ceramic floor where the legs break, the patella shatters and the shin bones come spearing through the skin to leave a bloody Hacksaw Ridge scene on the lounge floor. To make something disappear, you don't slowly and gently eradicate the concept like Nokia phones, you raise it up – Simba held to the cutesy deadly African animal groupies – then let it fall so far, the shattering explosion of baby lion brains at the bottom of the ravine making even the most ardent supporter question why we blindly followed from the beginning.

In my head Elton is busting out the Circle of Life when, like a Japanese retailer of stationary quickly appearing in front yelling 'Supplies!', a man stands directly in front of me smiling, causing the record scratch back to wanked beards ejaculating all over the floor, a hair salon's 'little off the bottom's' worst nightmare. Time to start sweeping as his stare is uncharacteristically calm and coy, so he's not a

Boybander and likely not a manager or supporter.

"Can I help you?" I offer, angling to move past.

"I'm not sure if anyone can help me, Miss …"

"… I don't engage with strangers unless they play their card early. That's the end of the Mrs in case you were struggling with that."

"At an event like this we're all strangers really, aren't we?"

"So poetic. A relation of Simon Armitage?"

"The only poet laureate in my family tree is likely distant cousin Marshall Mathers."

"Cute. One more time: can I help you?"

"Just hoping to understand what you're really up to; you and your girls."

The slightest flicker of recognition I, like an amateur numbskull, give this man. Does he notice because he doesn't show it, pa-pa-pa poker face prick. There has to be an honest honour to all this: embrace the provocation like sticking your hand into a cow to help with the calf delivery, or else what is it all for, what's the meaning? Hiding your agenda in plain, blatant sight. Plus what's really happened yet and what part of the escape plan is flawed?

"If that's your question, the answer is simple. Humiliation most foul. Until every last one of you is reeling, cowering in the foetal position, covered in your own shame while the world takes a whazz on you from the top of a frozen mountain, the golden icicles stinging every masticated mess of man as you try to get up. Too vivid? I'm just a sucker for Elsa's exploits perhaps."

"I want in."

"This is not the BA Executive Club. You don't just approach some chick at an event and ask to enter; once you've spoken the secret password the door doesn't magically ajar."

"Just because I'm a man?"

"Being a boy dog doesn't help but this is not some game for a wannabe soldier to doff his cap at *my sweet little feminine disposition*," I add in pinpoint pitch perfect southern drawl because this man is either American or some weird South African American hybrid. Batting an eyelid and sticking my arse out to the side seems the only sensible thing to do and it does seem to deter him, a speckle of disappointment at (I hope) the rejection but more likely the patent sexism I'm hoping he'll gulp down until I can find out the source of the sharing, the leak in the movement pipe. If it is that big I worry it becomes bigger than all of us but sometimes these idealistic games can become a life of their own.

The first, second and third rule of How Not to Murder a Boyband is you do not talk about How NOT to Murder a Boyband. Tyler said it but by fuck no one stuck to it or else who were those sweaty slabs of man meat pounding each other in the basement?

A small gap in an evening where I imagine I imagined the application. The lights above don't flicker but the pulse of heat rays rat-a-tat-tat on the top of my head. The background score has been amped up beyond Boyband instrumental to a deeper drum-base, the throbbing reverberation a teeth-chattering unwelcome head-cloud of shittier tunes. I see Denim, and not how Ed Sheeran saw a city burn, but offensive spots like those raindrops on your windshield just after you've turned off the wipers. Blues, deep indigo to apple white to faded, torn, tapered skinny. On large fat arses … record scratch with a serrated blade across the inside of your cranium. Barton looms, inactive African hill tribe derrière wrapped in a non-descript blue, bulging way far away from any wet sidewalk, the felled eight more like two loaves of bread tipped onto their smaller axes but the strain apparent, toothpaste wanting out. Then a screen and bluer than an Attenborough sea scape, Boybanders embracing diversity through not having one ounce of taught buttocks between them.

Tabby glances over, of course in blue but a resplendent, shimmering blue – an anti-Denim placed like a fallen soldier in between the spunked denim surrounding her, Custer's last blue note. She almost twists her ankle, going over then rebalancing before Barton instinctively catches her then seemingly lets her fall in indignant protest. He looks down at her skull resentfully then she loosens herself from his gorilla grip. When jeans were fitted – cowboys generally embodying how to wear them, well Brad in and out of Thelma perhaps – Boybands of yester suffocated their privates in a quest for recognition that they wore them well, even if they were too short and the waistline too high. But now the replacement video sees Levi laundrette replaced with big baggy dad-jeans and tucked in white shirts, not a button fly or brand in sight. The chairs remain though but it's as though they're trying to be ironic, even satirical as they wait in a testicular cancer waiting room, mocking the Moonsnaps of old with the only hunting down their buddy's pants taking place from the cool soft embrace of a doctor's palm. The video even includes an inference towards a prostate check, the doctor coyly placing both hands on Barton's shoulders before smiling and Barton making the crinkled new emoji face. At the end of the video a helpline appears as if to validate the tasteless flippancy of male-orientated disease.

Tabby votes, a reluctant press of the button, her traditional obdurate deportment absent. Moving swiftly towards her, jinking through Boybanders like a seventies Welsh rugby wizard, I acquire whiffs of varied aromas – faint notes of weed, high-glucose spirits, perfumes matching that sickly sweetness and dirty faecal-sweaty-BO that holds open the back of my throat and horse-kicks my uvula like a Rocky training montage. I arrive at Tabby, the first responder on the scene, touching her arm with all my fingers splayed, a benevolent gesture of sorts but more laced with the disquiet I might be instituting.

"I'm not sure I can go on much longer," she tells me without looking up.

"Tabby Cat, we know the toll this is taking. You've drawn the stubborn bully-boy of the group."

"It's not because I'm bottling it either; it's that I want to move faster – make this happen quicker so we can move on; so I can move on. And fall over somewhere else."

"You've looked after us as a group for so long now I knew you'd be sharing this burden. But I also knew you'd never throw in the towel."

She raises her chin like a cartoon hero, stiffening the back of her neck so soft contours of her inner back muscles sandwiched between the V of the back of the blue dress flutter to insinuate proud defiance.

"I'm not built to ever let go of the towel; I'll hold onto the towel and watch the world burn until that happens."

"We are almost there."

"I can wait. I just want to know my next trip and fall is into something softer than a Boyband's belly."

"We all want to find the right life with the right people – not a male crutch – but a sense of relationship that supports who we are, what we are and where we want to be. But things will never be the same again."

"I know that and I'm ready for that."

Barton glances over then reinserts himself into a Boyband conversation, a cut-and-paste of Times New Roman into an otherwise Garamond conversation. Tabby stares back and a mini staring competition ensues, neither blinking, neither flinching until an announcer somewhere hits the lights and the darkness momentarily wins until a few strobe lasers dance across the incredulous dummies waiting for something to happen. The anticipation is palpable, a Boybander alongside me shouting "What's going to happen next?" as the lights morph into a medley of classic Boyband tracks, remixed in a Run DMC style with popping, overbeats and mixing seldomly heard since the towers fell. A sudden paranoia washes over me, cool at first then sickly warm, a sweaty hand holding session, imbedded by years of deep inexplicable phobias. They're coming towards me, boxing clever Drago, Rocky's Apollo death lamenting driving flashbacks, closer with each strobe, hiding just in front of my vision and choreographing dancing closer with each blackout.

Virtually any object can become a fear object. Assumption is that even the most obscure noun, take the flakes of Gummi Bear beard dandruff, should have an associated phobia. Foe Be A Girl.

Ataxophobia ... the fear of disorder or untidiness.

Atelophobia ... the fear of imperfection.

Catagelophobia ... the fear of being ridiculed.

People laughing, mocking, pointing. Boybands, stopping in their darkened tracks, no longer fearing the indiscreet laser, pointing, mocking, laughing. Spitting, shouting, hurling, humiliating. A male gaggle, bleeding aloud in the dark until their one common enemy is beside them, dating their kind, holding their hands, teasing their pricks, gatecrashing their adulation. Me. Us.

The light reappears, a welcome respite from the jagged uncertainty, followed by a loud blast and an attack of what looks like a street dancing mob, somersaulting leather-trousered male dancers and camo-clad alpha-women. Some twirl fire, others move their torsos in shocking quakes as though they are being riddled with bullets or pecked by crows. A small dancer chap grabs me by the arms and twirls me twice then subsumes into an increasingly clammy orange-taupe slushpile of mushroom sprouting hands, hairless armpits and those antelope-horn muscles appearing above the trousers. And cynic or not, they were all pretty darn good and the spectacle was one of the highlights of the evening in that it took the attention away, albeit momentarily, from the Boybands and their music exposés. And then, as any flash mob should epitomise, they were gone; imagined or real, disappearing like drain water and onto another gig.

Famous flickers drag us all back to the reason we are in attendance. A video, recognisable, but one where the recognition is not definitive. Like when you get a flash of a film and you don't know where you remember it from but you've seen it – Leatherface wielding a chainsaw on a desolate road – it has memory capital, value, which means it was either a former number 1 (even though the charts mean less than the daily Covid death toll at this stage) or the band were a reality hundreds of hopefuls show, remade for a generation more interested in blowing a realistic zombie's head off than watching 'musicians' hugging each other and loving each other and forgiving each other. There is one enduring theme: tedium and togetherness can only truly be encapsulated and bestowed when laced with a big score, an emotive soundbite so cinematically grand, sometimes your tear ducts act out of their own accord, refusing to protest, bowed by the TV watching Smug Dad system. This narrative quick-cuts between when the pre-band-boys tried out and their miraculous transformation into 'best-friends' with 'the world in front of them'. The audition shots are, in a home movie sort of way, quite endearing as they've yet to be styled, carved, blown, mashed, disfigured and contorted into a stylist and publicity manager's wet dream, almost as though their fame redemption is their surrender of any humility or anything satisfyingly boringly normal. Gone are the jeans, spikes and spots and in are the cropped trousers, corn braids and airbrushing akin to sandpapering David's dick off in Florence. Another enduring theme is the selection and, admission of guilty research-based viewing, the evident omission of notable hidden gems, hoofing out the one that might have actually been able to belt out a proper tune and the one that might have been good-looking in an understated Van Wilder way. Keeping the dregs is a national pastime, just look at the politicians, breakfast TV hosts and corporate leaders; endurance and lack of endeavour shunts potential as a rule of both thumbs.

Kelly brings me a drink looking sheepish; like he feels he shouldn't have left me for so long whereas in reality I don't give a monkey's. I grab the drink – a 'better be good' single malt – too forcefully to play along. The pissed-off-at-a-party-girlfriend is so from an era when women needed petting like fuckable pets that it's perhaps back on trend. Perhaps. But Gone Girl Cool Girl while Ben fondles a quite frankly odd-shaped pair of boobs, rat noses peering up from the toilet bowl, cannot be now or useful either – it has to go further. Being pissed or cool needs a third dimension – being disruptive or aggressively provocative. While Kelly glances away from my ignoring stare, I deftly flick the helmet of his penis, his Jewish ridge calling to me through the fabric of his trousers, with all my might. The tough centre of the nail catches the curve between the fish's mouth and the bell end's ridge just about idyllically, Kelly thrusts his hips back in incredulous shock but not enough to give away the public poise he's practiced for years. The real give away is his eyes filling with water, that middle finger of mine so deft at flicking to attention, the recipient of the volley might actually take note. The tears forming in bantam painful pools under his eyeballs betray his cooperative acceptance of my 'way', although to be fair the initial shock-horror jolt was more real; anger and disdain placed deftly away into the top pocket as only Kelly knows how.

Pink is a previously-mainly-masculine colour that somehow seeks to stand out – a beacon of alluring hue, spiking pretenders which surround, the welcoming entrance nestled into the hindering pubes. And speaking of ... Renea wears pink and Uncle glows in the increasing dimly lit oval arched space, the dark heaviness of her curls bouncing on her copper shoulders. She has every man enraptured, everyone except ... and I see those pouty pinks, disassociated and clashing with Renea's dress, two swollen worms levitating towards a sea of sheer pink fabric perfection. Aside the group the band's video is playing, only glimpses afforded to me, a rush hour scene obscuring an invading tank cruising up the high street. Kieron's lips make regular cameos, big close ups of the contrast between his pink and almost grey coloured skin. His eyes are almost always droopy-cool-tired and I see the make-up artist has given him a squid tattoo up both sides of his neck, the purple-yellow tentacles lashing up towards his ear lobes. Fleeting glances within fleeting glances. Then the video's theme assaults the viewer, more socially conscious crusades that actually mean very little. All the five boys are sitting in various forms of undress in a row, some shirts off, some trousers, some facing down. While a gorgeous nurse (it had to be really – some habits you just can't kill, but not edgy-porn-when-it-was-cool-and-not-rapey hot like Janine Lindemulder on the cover of Blink-182's Enema of the State; rather cutesy-helpful-NHS-might-actually-employ-her-but-not-on-the-Covid-ward     helpful with a half a zipper length of cleavage and her own pink pout to boot) lasers them. That's right, their fake tattoos are all being removed while they giggle and squirm and high five each other, Kieron still to be bothered by anything activity based, staring straight ahead in a weed haze as the octopus is John Wayne Bobbitted and badaboombadabing there is no hint of Blue Planet left on any of them. A guitar's shaft soaring up the lower back, sprouting from the middle of the butt, is the last to go, the nurse clipping Kieron's wimpish, prepubescent, toothed fairy band-boyfriend in a giggle crescendo finale, not an African desert or vulture in sight. Hardcore becomes softcore becomes the most flaccidcore such that if there was an actual real needle near one might consider actually jotting down a tramp stamp in protest, the soothing buzz to discolour a person's outer dermal protective layer and provide a fashion statement that can never be returned to the retailer, an actual protest option. Kieron trudges off, fiddling with something in his lap, no doubt a joint, then gives up and sits down in a corner.

There is a newly discovered urgency to proceedings somehow; the air has altered forcing everyone to frantically vote and find another terminal to either cup their Boyband friend's balls or cut that prima donna down to size. A sale, patrons grappling with merchandise, the last Xbox going going gone. The flurry subsides at a terminal and I notice Digby throwing some mathematically inaccurate shapes back at me, straight rimmed cap down low and pants even lower. Without the sound he looks like he's chewing toffee wrapped in molten tar. Unbelievably they've painted him black – not quite Trudeau's blackface – but not a million slave ship leagues away. The offence this is likely to cause is on show when I notice all of the band are made up to be black. They reveal their Black Lives Matter t-shirts is relative unison while one of them unsuccessfully spins on his head out of shot, the spinning top that crashed and didn't make the cut. And then the babies; oh thank God when singing love songs men still believe the highest form of affection for a woman is to be called baby (and even higher elevation when that baby is at the end of a sexualised sentence and spread over nineteen syllables!). "You are my moon, my world, my sunshine and I     want     to     fuck     you     in     the     ass     oh baaaaaaaaaaaaaaaayyyyyyyyyyyyyyyyyyyyyybbbbbbbbbeeeee eeeeeeeeeeeeeee," mouths out of the screen, a silent verbal assault shielding us all from the imposing lyrical assault. But then suddenly the video shifts gear as I see Maggie appear, resplendent in Springbok rugby green, the trail of her dress kicked aside by her purposeful stride. The video has a clip of Kanye, now gleefully single, then back to the band holding what can only be a black Jesus. Five white guys dressed as blacks anointing a little baby black Jesus.

"I want one of those," says Maggie.

"Jesus – the brother version?"

"Just because I don't have one."

"Would everyone know it was the actual son of God or are we talking more Madonna adoption accessory?"

"Well because the latter is so unfashionable and woke yet really anti-woke because of the accessory connotation it makes me want to … have one. Not have one as in belt one out whist huffing into a blue curtain but have one … at my disposal. From the loin of God would just be a bonus … for the kid and me."

"How is the wigger?"

"See for yourself – Boybandhandling the black Jesus," she mutters, watching Digby place the poor child into a floating basket made of iPhones. "Getting faux-blacker by the day. He starts every sentence with 'Hey Bee-utch' nowadays."

"Oh Lord; I mean oh Jesus."

"More apt."

"Any further mulling on Invidia?"

"Even more apt as we'd be making him whiter and the apple would bring in the biblical reference. Still uncertain as to whether his forked tongue would be able to catch the apple or if we'd just have to allow his hand-eye coordination to save him. He doesn't have any so either way he's going whiter and the itching will become unbearable."

"You raise a good point though: do we allow any redemption? Do we set a redemptive counter which absolves Boybander of any wrongdoing? In your case the simple skill of catching an apple doesn't seem significant enough to absolve beyond punishment. Jezuz I sound like a satanic priestess!"

"I'm the mythological sister in this fable! Magik! Practising magik in a reincarnation of Lovers 4 Lucifer, old flaming bearded Lurid reincarnated to exact revenge on Christian Boybands."

"And Christian Rock. It's only fair. And Just."

"We will avenge the deaths of our brothers in the middle ages, hunted down and slaughtered like pigs. We will avenge the deaths of our sisters: the witches and pagans of the middle ages. O hail."

"We're no virgins lest we forget. Well I am but that's another matter."

"In Greek it is Nemesis. And it couldn't be more apropos because not only have they wrapped an additional goddess trait of retribution but Invidia was closely associated with occasions where justice was offended and the sight of undeserved wealth and shamelessly exercised authority caused grief."

"Didn't she have pale skin and discoloured teeth?"

"And a lean body!"

In a whisper of shadowy green she's gone or I'm gone, moving backwards like a POV horror film, Maggie's hankering eyes losing grip as Kelly floats me into another socially repellent jamboree. En route to rediscovering my charm, smile and nodding teeth I spot another video, this one shot as a cartoon. And it looks like He-Man fucked Lion-O and the baby they made came out more ripped, more tanned, more bulbous crotched and more suave than if James Bond,

Phil Heath, Danny D and anyone from TOWIE added their genetic weight into the spawning concoction. It's worse that the old Bruce Lee double bicep cartoon too because these caricatures have twelve abs! There's almost no space for their junk which udders beneath them, the illustrator intent to have them sway, weave and duck with each pow, kick and high five, the undercarriage a character all on its own. The Boyband watching are enthralled seeing themselves in this form, yet I'm unable to match any to the onscreen heroes. Kelly just shakes his head and keeps dragging but, when I notice they're battling huge breasted, purple eyed, equally ripped evil women I have to pull my arm away to see who wins. The battle is intense to be fair, the tottering of bodily appendages giving the mêlée a Newton's cradle impression; one of the ballbags actually swats a boob clean to the side of hot female henchman number green fangs, peering around the corner past the middle of her lower back then back to nip the other boob the other way but with enough distraction and power to render her dead. Purple-brown blood everywhere and the boys win. Or do they.

Snacking in a corner, Danielle and Gerson, facing away from each other. Danielle wears orange, making the orange dots in her eyes prominent, spessartite garnet stones on some discarded beach, companions with the sun's rays alone. Danny drops a crumb and Gerson instantly drops in prayer pose to retrieve, retrieving, then unsure what to do with it; place it in her mouth (slowly, sensually, shoving), place it in his mouth (bit gross, might not like the taste) or throw it away (litterbug, careless)? He ends up running across to a hidden bin to discard then notices his own video playing. We all know Dannielle has given it a massive thumbs up but that's who she is ... hungry superfan to the blast-off end.

The video beams and there isn't a scantily clad pulchritudinous female in sight, not an adoring pulse-igniting hot extra stare in da house. They're at an Xtreme Believe funeral, mourning the departure of a Boyband member for a solo career. Gerson tearily looks up at the crucifix and crosses himself, undoubtedly unaware of the Catholic implications, his pre-pubescent features holding his tears like pockets of rockpool seawater. They start singing and swaying in unity, linking elbows in solidarity a flashback to some of Dim or Sum or Fum or Dick or Nick or Spic or Knip or whatever his name was then drop to their knees pray-singing as a light shines from (let's call him) Dim Sum's anus onto their faces, the warm gooeyness an instant transcendent aphrodisiac. Unmistakably Gerson mouths "Thank You Jesus" before fading to white doves flapping in slow motion above a deserted tour area, four microphones upright and one fallen. Our mighty Sum Dim, stood for nothing, created nothing, meant nothing. Now gone. R.I.P.D.S.

My mouth is as dry as my throat and there's a break in Kelly's drag so I hop off to find and suck on the germ-infested stainless-steel water fountain or order from a welcoming slobbering barman. As I'm chewing on dry air and motley flavours of saliva an announcement booms stating the highest ranked winning video will be shown on all the monitors proximately. I look around, a child who has lost her mother in a crowd. There are no free video screens left.

Everyone is loving the top Boyband videos of the moment. I'm panicking. They're not allowed to steal my spots. This isn't junior school. Number one is about to start. I can't miss it. Not now. No matter how flat the screen is. I wipe my brow with the bottom of my dress because now I'm really sweating at the prospect of missing the favourite video. I want to cry. I want to yell to everyone at the O2 how I plan to murder these narcissistic fakers on the screen and that this research is crucial to my quest but realise that everyone's gone over to the dark side when they start gyrating from side to side and clicking fingers as the best ever Boyband video hurtles onto the screen like the H bomb. I'm frantic now. Looking backwards and forwards. Everything's busy. Even the tucked away monitors down stink cologne alley. Thank God a big gaping gap opens up in the far corner and, like a polecat, I'm off towards it, determined to beat the steroid freak lumbering from a shorter distance. I'm almost there. I jump. And make it. Sort of. The apology is complemented by the fumbling of the dials to shut the volume down to zero and popping ear plugs in after storing them unpleasantly the whole evening. He mutters something and marches off to shoot up in the toilet. Suddenly everything is clear. I have purpose. He hath spoken. I own the space tensing my core and putting a forcefield around me avoiding any tension reduction and preventing eye aversion in any direction from the champions of the known Boyband world. The bestest everest Boyband song; the number one; the song. #1 She's From City Love – Coastal Love.

Really? Nah. Times have altered significantly from

trying too hard to admitting any form of trying is trying too hard. More of a homage really because it was such a moment. For my dad. From his memoirs. Really? Put it this way, would I be able to admit that a person who let a Top 10 countdown of Boyband videos in a gym then went on a violent, clumsy retributionally disassociated killing spree influence my tombstone, my ethos, my mantra? Playing the victim, as Paton did, where his life forced him to do the degenerated stuff the whole of Twitter knew he did seemed a soupçon pathetic to me and perhaps a) why I don't have daddy issues and b) highlights the key difference between men and women: men only do historically monumental things when there is a sense of purpose or justice whereas girls just wanna have fuh-un (or at least want to be capable of making the choice, not being chosen). Sprinkle in morbid fascination, psychotic tendencies, infamy hunger, a sisterhood for the ages and a general acknowledgement that no matter what you do, how you do it, who you do it to … it won't really matter. Lessening attention spans, news stories that last for like … wait … there: gone! that long, don't change lives, they just shape an overarching slow painful sense of societal and humanity degradation: the proverbial itch that gets scratched so hard you forget you're bleeding out. And plus. I love Boybands. This ruse is my therapist's recommended indulgent remedy – have a fantasy while your boyfriend invites his friends to fuck you and the pain of a childhood bounced between people who never cared clingfilm wraps your head, face and neck until making it all up is the only way to get through the day without too many pills, too high a building or believing your bikini line trimmer could actually make an incision along your wrist.

Really? Of course not. Here comes Gwynne, not smiling like Alice's pussy but intently happy. Or unhappy. For once I cannot tell. I remain rooted in the middle of the O2, void of any screen proximity when the video begins. Gwynne, ridiculously strong, manoeuvrers me towards something.

"Okay brace yourself," says Gwynne strutting alongside me, arm in my arm, her black dress fashionably dull enough not to look blue. I spot some of the other girls proceeding to a secluded screen all looking reasonably concerned; anticipatory yet anguished. The flicker of the screen lights their faces as a million heads turn to face the best Boyband video.

"What's going on?" I spout, nearing a familiar scene.

"I didn't know," says Gwynne spotting Damien journeying towards us who mouths "Surprise!"

The screen is Gwynne jump squatting then me in all my glory, my face staring back at me in mini judgement. Then cut to Debz walking in the street then Jemima laughing. Our collegiate, scheming, plotting faces, all outed for the world to see. Renea flicks a smoke while Danielle drinks an iced smoothie – shot on iPhone, an intimate portrayal, showing a little more than anything intended. Maggie and Tabby, together, holding hands then back to me, head on Kelly's shoulder. It's a cover – has to be – a remake of Julio Iglesias's *To All The Girls I've Loved Before*, modernised to make it about monogamous loyalty, a castle siege slingshot distance from Spanish crooners cading, wooing, serenading and ejaculating in a host of women, each one loved in turn in a different way disguised as a vessel for man juice. We are no longer secret. Tabby falls. Debz pouts. Gwynne runs. The boys belt out the obligatory anguished note but this is a genuine love letter centring on the strong women supporting (erm making) the Boyband. I close my eyes and we're all bending over shining actual rays of sunshine from our behinds, melting each Boybander seriatim until I open and there we all are again, the devoted strength to ward off teenage fans and show that with true dedication, love and commitment, Boybands can change; they can be a publicly one-woman Boyband. So many rules begin tumbling around us, the dream a waterfall of colostomy bag filling, sealed in plastic and placed in the hazardous waste bin. There will be new declarations; there will be proposals; there will be parental introductions – rules sixteen, forty-six and three all dissolved in an award-winning mess of a setback.

I bite down so hard on my lip that I feel the warm blood seep down into my throat and from my peripheral vision I sense the unease from the troop, shifting awkwardly in uneasy unison so bared shoulder muscles harden and adoring glances are paid back with a blenched counterfeit benevolence. Travelled in and out their doors, but mainly in as the words have been altered to show we're permanent fixtures. Cameos from each of the other boyfriend Boybands, the unity between rival groups so sickeningly palpable, the upcoming backslaps clamping my teeth shut to grind and pumping bile from my gallbladder to my throat. We are the ones with the raised eyebrows, the longing pained expressions deep into the phone camera's soul. It's us. And we're shorter in real life. And more arrogant. And more stupid. And fatter. And they love us even more than they do in the video. The greatest Boyband song of all time. We will die. And suffer. For our portrayal misleads the youth of today and taints the youth of tomorrow. No famous cameo money shot, just a dashboard of female sitting ducks, splattered within heart graphics and the reveal of each of us in tattoo form on an array of body parts from pectoral to thigh to back of neck to bicep. Unnervingly real and likely real in most cases, the follow-on surprise in the bedroom in an hour, the ultimate sacrifice to enter the pants, some for the first time. My thighs are now cramping and I've bitten through most of the end of my tongue. It's time to go home.

Chapter 36

# TaBBY CaT

Transcript of telephone conversation between design engineer and Abigail:

"Would the ledge be manual?"

"No completely automated. There would be no levers, just a height-adjustable platform keyed in from a wireless hand-held device."

"Down to what level of accuracy?"

"Centimetres as the first decimal point. So point zero one would be the first height above zero, at a height of one centimetre."

"I see. And how high would the platform be able to go?"

"Theoretically to the moon as the column folds out as the platform rises. It's more dependent on the size of the room or are you planning outdoors?"

"Indoors. Having checked with the property there is a room allocated which has been designed almost like an entrance hall, encompassing the full height of the property but tucked away in a corner of the house. I believe there was a dumb waiter design that was modernised."

"The design of the shortening length of the platform and the base has also been tweaked a bit but I believe you'll approve. The platform disappearance speed was initially variable and random but there was always somewhere to hold onto so the new design is a trapdoor where the entire floor of the platform drops away, either from the middle vertically or horizontally. It should be impossible for whatever is on the platform to remain on the platform. The base has been extended to a wider area so as not to allow any spillage with small angular undulations randomly changing with each new height."

"So the spillage will never land the same way, a new angle greeting each drop?"

"Precisely. And for fun the measurement of the load will be fully simulated before the drop, recording the actual drop and measuring all physics as a result of the drop."

"Recorded in 4K?"

"5K ma'am, using the new GoPro Hero 9, with six cameras – two placed at the base, two on the platform and two tracking the drop. There will not be one moment of whatever you have planned not captured in exhaustive detail. If you are after the sweat's sweat, there will be enough of a close up to taste the salt."

"I can hardly wait. What comes before a fall?"

"Whatever you specify."

*Chapter 37*

# WILLOW & BARTON

Momentary distraction from the shame, the glory, the ignominy, the reveal. The uncertainty more than anything: mugs roll over and wait to be kicked in the ribs whereas real mugs could be playing a double bluff game. I refused to either show the girls my feet scarred with eggshells or open my blinds for days so would hear this story third hand. In fairness it was likely the fishhook that yanked me from gloomy recession and back into the solving world, slapping a red pull the trigger sooner rather than later against a black suss out the implication of appearing emotionally naked in a Boyband video, a worse shame that performing the eagle for Dogfart Productions.

How Tabby and Jemima pulled this off is beyond a guess – perhaps Barton and Willow's veiled apology for giving up their romantic video selfie collection – but happen it did. The brothers in arms could not be kept under wraps forever so on a Zoom back in lockdown sibling coming out party, Margot's boys were convinced to speak to each other in a rap battle. Barton got convinced it was for charity, any transgression another twenty pence denied to an Alaskan seal and Willow, nervous to the point of hysterical nausea working through the expressive cathartic art of rap battle as the tonic to find your brother, deemed him 'not heavy' (even if he was nineteen stone of permawobbled pocked possum-nosed moobs and swollen thighed sausage-dog distension) then 'really back-snapping heavy but still ultimately my twin brother'. Nothing would get him down, or Barton for that matter as each rapped God dammit, run rabbit run. It went a little something like this …

The Zoom call and each smiled, supportive brides loitering off camera, cheerleading their men towards touch cloth glory. Willow could taste the air, the nerves, his brother's disdainful frame filling the screen.

"It goes a little something like this," started Willow bopping from side to side and throwing a shape to signify battle commencement, inviting Barton to retort as this was a tit-for-tat-bounce-off style rather than each-MC-gets-a-minute-yawll.

Barton bopping his melon head – for the seals – spouting "You motherfucker substandard Boyband; why yous giving me all this nightly shit when alls I is wanting to do is (pause) stick to my own land?"

"You see my brother, I wanna call you my brutha cos there is more than mother to our muthafucker smother."

"You trippin dawg, you a stinky substandard Boyband log."

"What does a log have to do with what I'm bout to say, other than this is some important shit and if I may, a log a delicate and beautiful foray."

"I'd heard you Willow were a bit of a weeper, hugging logs and holding out for deeper; the penetration a hard knock life for any dick from the midlands, wishing he was someone with a logger's fiddler."

"Now hear me now you big ball of earth hating loaf, I got more big shit to spout than what you ate on your toast."

"If you done any proper research you would know, I haven't touched a carb bouncing a stone to show."

"If a camera adds a few pounds, I'd say what I'm looking at needs a few rounds; with Rocky or that big Russian, I hope you wouldn't rush him?"

"Now back to the story——"

"That's Will Smith's glory."

"Fuck you you little annoying piece of leftover shit, you're worse than a kid brother so please just split."

"Okay relax, take a moment, because now we're getting to why we are here; I'm sitting here staring at an heir. When have something multi-big in common and it begins with being a woman."

Tabby and Jemima, almost in unison, departed the room cupping hands to mouth, imaginary laughter-sick spewing between their fingers.

"Women, now weez takin, cos I is a big fella stalkin."

"This woman ain't no ordinary woman, holding a boy and a boy insider her——"

"What kinda ho-bitch be takin two boys in her, she be

rubbed so raw there be no fur."

   "She yow mama."

   "She yow mama!"

*Chapter 38*

# DEBZ

Wherever in the world Debz ventured, men became producers. Some fake, some real, all instantly spellbound by her front-teeth-baring open-lipped non-pout pout, offering part after part after fame after role after come back to my hotel suite first and massage my fat, hairy Weinstein wiener. The way Debz dealt with the attention was the truly admiral part, never alienating a would-be adorer yet with enough disassociated ease to slip herself from their sweaty grasp like a live eel in the back kitchen of an amateur sushi chef. Throughout our time together she had never wanted the additional adulation, comfortable in her own skin, Buffalo Bill nowhere to be seen, so that every encounter instead of watering the ego just washed over it: the golden slope of her alluring decolletage subbing in as the proverbial duck's back. But a girl has needs and, what with Sexton in the midst of an action-orientated gender crisis, the attention was getting more pushy, more forceful and more expectant.

**How NOT to Murder a Boyband** | by Jason Roche

Men seem to have this sense of divine right which bestows whatever they want but not whenever they want; as though they can take the rejection and the ensuing mouse-chase but underwritten by the strict man-code legalities that it will at some point happen. If there is genuine realisation that the happening is at risk of not transpiring, the modern man gives up and convinces himself that he never really wanted it in the first place whereas the Boybander tries many dirty tricks to take what his 'rightfully' his. And familiarity also breeds a kind of entitlement – person at work gets hotter the more you sip chai lattes across from them – until the conversant starts dropping clothes in one's mind at two in the morning. The danger triangle, let's call it OTR or Open To Rape, is fully completed by a man's ability to adopt violence whilst self-professing that it wasn't really that violent – a scratch, a bruise, a broken something. Entitlement. Familiarity. Violence. With Debz the Giza in magnificence, looking and sounding and smelling and tasting and holding herself the way she does, like OJ didn't really believe he murdered his ex-wife and some nice chap returning her mother's reading glasses, Digby believed he didn't rape Debz.

*Chapter 39*

# Renea

"I didn't get out of bed for like … a week maybe. Just couldn't be bothered. Not counting trips to the lav and the fridge. Didn't shower of course. Made everything even riper than the usual ripeness. Kieron complained. Said down there it was furrier than a goose down pillow and more rancid than his mate Gaz's bathroom. Bothered face; this is my bothered face. And he joined me for most of the lethargic week, slopping around, bringing me food, trying to get me to fuck him or play with him. Lazy fucker wouldn't even try feeding the pony, although to be fair feeding this pony at the current moment would make Livingston presumably easier to find. But then having someone drain your laziness is disconcerting: I'm the only one who should be allowed this level of slovenly filth. And I know this is the pairing of choice but I guess I just blurted it out. Spat it at the lazy git and I'm not sure he even blinked any acknowledgment my way, his droopy eyelids closing intermittently throughout the day. I probably blurted because he blurted – a disassociated double finger fuck you to his measly bird proposal. 'So do you wanna?' he followed up, no knee, no father's permission, just scratching in between his shaggy arse cheeks not even making eye contact. If I did actually love him I'd have burst out crying, but replying with 'You wanna marry a man?' didn't quite resonate at first, perhaps at all. I didn't get to scar showing point as, by then, he'd either dozed off or gone for a dump, I can't remember which, but when he did emerge he was higher than he'd ever been before, retching convulsive laughter at me previously being a dude. He jumped on the bed and waved it in front of me shouting 'You miss this; playing with yours' and then slumped back down, staring panickily straight ahead at the stain on the ceiling, breathing deeply, each exhale emitting a little hoarse wheeze. It was one of those big-small moments where everything around you exaggerates: the still windless air becomes a ringing deafening smog, the flickering light butt-fucks your eyes with luminescent spears and the broken floorboard presents a chasmous crater ready to engorge, swallow, digest and crap you out somewhere in the middle of the Pacific. It was happening. Not as exactly planned but there was never going to be perfect union right? We all want different things from our adventures, rectifying wounds and being fabulous while doing both until someone gets hurt. And maybe I did it not to hurt him but to avoid him being really hurt, because by hurting him in this way he might actually save himself from being flattened. But then I remembered his response, dragging me firmly back to why this all matters and should happen the way we want it to; his having a go then finding any way to adulterate the truth from his own selfish reality. He'd never understand the hurt he'd caused, and not that you'd expect someone to just be okay with it but rather that having shared at least a modicum of affection you'd hope for some level of enquiring why you would put yourself through such trauma to change, whether you were happy with your decision and what it meant for the future. Those breathless nervous acceptance chortles: base and Boyband all the way. Whether the ramifications of the press getting hold of this wandered through his drug-laden brain beats me, but there was more me in this than her ... erm him.  And after proposing too – the ultimate betrayal shattering an always fragile relationship, built on maiming ideals, arm candy, weed and taking a different smelling, sounding, looking man-girl to the prom."

## Chapter 40

# @BOYBaNDMURDeR

Losing faith is normal. Isn't it? Didn't all the greats, all the conflicted television series protagonists have that one questioning moment of morality, of convenience, of stature, that wobbled the bridge before stiffening the resolve to cross and cut the whole God damn thing down Indiana Jones style. What provides hope is clearly that the wobble was temporary, a self-imposed glitch in the perfect line of code, the rat poison in Walter White's blue meth. And the dragging back redemption? You fuckers. The baying masses, calling for heads, demanding a neat bowed ribbon where the sick fallacy is dispelled and the flawed heroine triumphs, standing legs akimbo atop a body mountain of Boybands. She should be enjoying it so much it doesn't matter that she wobbles; it is just a knight to bishop four of a multi-faceted play. Buy what if it really isn't? This narrative is more about telling everything how it actually happened and a couple of heart opening moments of celebrity culture, life, love, dreams, aspirations and perversions.  But what if we played an extended game of literary cat-and-mouse, me crapping on about the virtues of going straight, going decent, going non-murder; would you ever forgive me?  Or more to the logistical point how long could you last while I bit my bloody lip and portrayed each against the backdrop of complete unchecked Boyband behaviour.  Or, even better, ditched the Boybands completely and went a Simpsons tangential route, only I didn't actually write how this was going to be – license to be clever and unify the narrative – I just set it up such that (for once) girls could attempt to have the last laugh while our all-conquering male counterparts sit in a pool of their own fearful shit and fear and loathing.  The truth is when the shit got real we laughed in the face of that challenge, pissing upwind and bearing our chests in Viking defiance, but now with the advent of actual suspicion, groupies, forensics, flawed exit plans and something so theme park elaborate the risk of any element failing is peak, the shit went past real hit scary tedious and settled on life ruining.  And fanatical.  And and fantastical.

So there's this big fat arse blocking my path and making me so nervous that I need one of you, one brave reassuring leader amongst you, to put down this book, check your phone and Tweet me on @BoybandMurder saying everything is going to be okay; saying we back you despite the flaws, the suspension of disbelief and the subconscious rooting for the male of the story irrespective of height, demeanour and general decency towards women and broader society.  Go on, I'll give you a minute …

Thanks. Much and greatly appreciated like a big fart during a debilitating bout of gastritis or an ulcer that never quits … love that saying and apologies for the repetition but when a woman's arse never quits the uncertainty of its perfection and endurance stamina being wholly synonymous with shape, bulge and tautness is near the most genius play from the man's how to objectify women's body parts playbook. My arse won't quit and I suppose I shouldn't really even if I want to; even if I sit awake staring at the faces of each of the girls whose lives will never be the same again, who I convince myself I've helped rather than brainwashed towards manumission. Getting through a bout of selfish discrimination never sets aside your true self-reflection of knowing whatever way you want it to happen normally does. So if I now don't want any of this to happen and we all walk away relatively unscathed, will you ever forgive me? No Tweets have popped up so …

The End.

*Chapter 41*

# KeLLY

The wind blew on the dusty plain, harsh yet fulfilling. No really. We walked in slow motion, each a lost soul among lost souls, hoping to find that one true love, that one man capable of truly loving us for who we were, what we were and how we opened jars with our minds. The countertop stood alone, cupping a million fossilised unopen jars, the Boybander incapable of opening any. Some had expired even before the great plague beset our world, our society, our freedom, turning a generation of screen hoggers into a generation of screen integrators. WiFis across the nation, across the world would pay in service juggling a smorgasbord of Zoom calls, Xbox and pornography, household yells of bad WiFi ringing out of terraces, detacheds and flats like the wailing beside a wall. The isolation would destroy some, marriages capitulating and divorce lawyers getting rich in their pyjamas, but for most the unity and solidarity of family would replace the effervescent frivolity of peripheral friendships. Clamping down on all of us meant we had to revaluate what was really important once all the menial admin had been ticked or crossed off and marked as non-essential; when being organised took on such a high level of pride of place, the obsessive compulsive reaction of a misplaced task or spontaneous request would send most of us reeling for the list book then slumping in front of the TV to find a lesser known series after watching all the greats.

Kelly couldn't open jars and I loved him for it. He had big tentative strong hands but no grip, a golfer rather than a baseballer. With the advent of food stockpilings and my general disdain for anything not fresh, he'd amassed a triple-layer eight row deep library of jarred goods, from pesto to ginger cubes to artichokes to damson jam. All in the name of preventing starvation or, as I put it, keeping the consumer bandwagon rolling on into mouths, upsetting systems and all ending in the same nonrecycled place. Lucky for mankind and Kelly in particular my hands were stronger than the world champion male masturbator who, according to legend, had whacked off on an impressive ninety-thousand separate occasions, leading to overdeveloped wrist and lower forearm muscles that would propel him into folklore and Guinness stardom. Incidentally he remained single all his life.

Kelly would ask for a few to be opened – the ones he wanted to actually ingest that week, but old antagonistic habits die hard so I would force open enough to know that he would cave in the 'I'm unable to waste food' mantra and eat even the jars he detested so as to beat the going off date. He was looking a tad emaciated in my defence though and I certainly wasn't going to eat that slop as we settled into couples heaven: slow walks in the woods, staring at our phones together in bed and a general noncommunicative tedium that, if it weren't prevalent in just about every other long tenure couple out there, would have made one of both parties flip out, freak out, grappling the electronic turkey slicer and cutting the whole house up until each and every strand of normal equals monotonous was gouged out of existence. One such party was me but I smiled and met his mother on WhatsApp – liked her – felt guilty about plotting to maim her child and then emptied the bins. Kelly was heading for a momentous life decision I sensed what with my newfound harmony, stability and togetherness – he was either plotting to leave the Boyband thing behind or marry me, both of which would have been disastrous a few months ago but which now, as I forced myself to accept mundane normality, appealed. Little cliff top detached in Cornwall, walk to the beach, wrap up tight against the stinging wind. Not a dusty plain for miles. Just me and my contentment. Told you. Now put away the bird slicing sheers madam.

*Chapter 42*

# Danielle

"Sick of justifying," Danielle over for a 'talk me off the ledge' visit. "Making excuses for everything as though we're sorry or not sorry but regretting and seconding guessing every fucking move, morsel in the mouth and like or dislike. If you love Trump you're a racist; if you love sugar you're an out-of-control lardass; if you love Boybands you're so last season. Why don't we just be? Just do what we want, to whom we want irrespective of the calories."

"Thank God it's Wednesday because I'm also in the mood for a blowout. And to answer your question, doffing my rarely seen sensible cap ... because true human emotion is designed to be suppressed or else we'd all be killing each other every five seconds and spending time in jail. That's not what I want. For us."

"We all knew the risks and bought into it from the outset. Some more quickly than others – my loving penchant for everything Boyband rode deep up my arse – like those claiming to be medium M&S thongs!"

"Ha – got you! You don't shop at M&S you pillock!"

"I don't want to end babe. Not now and not like this. Once the first break-up happens we'll crumble all in sequential unison – quicksand into nothingness. We could scale back? Or shore up some of the defences?"

"There is an actual social media trend on us – someone, somewhere has clocked what we're up to and they want part of it; or they're morbidly curious how far we'll go. Like that flapper in Oz who said he'd name his kid Spiderpig if he got over a hundred thousand likes or retweets or some shit and, when he got to a million, he reneged."

"You're reneging now."

"I don't think we got far enough to renege. No real damage has been done, no lives ruined, no jail sentences, no actual blood on our hands."

"But we all want the blood, we want the meaning, the next big meal. I want to stop thinking about doing it and just do it. I've thought of the million different ways I might cook him and can barely be in a room with him anymore without leaving bite marks. He gets this look teetering between dejected, pissed and fearful – gets me hot!"

"Speaking of … let's stuff. Faces. Full. Of. Shit."

We set new boundaries, new lows some might say, shovelling two deep pan full topping pizzas each as an adequate sodium-coma inducing starter. We collapsed in each other's arms, me getting the raw deal with Danielle flopping over onto me for me to Sherpa her mislocated centre of gravity, pins and needles deadening my right forearm and fingers. When we woke we disagreed into a key lime pie before throwing up a few times and cracking on, powering through the uncertainty, Danielle hoping this would be the cathartic slap on my tits to wake me from my self-doubt laden cautious slumber. I did need something else, almost wishing some level of misfortune upon myself to stiffen the resolve, sharpen the senses, strap and unleash rubber intrusion fury on whoever felt like being dominated on haunches in front of me: the world perhaps. But eating to extinction was not going to be enough, no matter how good the food, how Wednesday the Wednesday and how much Danielle really needed a binge so pageantly enormous there were likely a few liver surgeons licking their scalpels.

"You'll be holding my hair this time," I said, tucking into a number somewhere past the dozens range of double chocolate, chocolate death, death by chocolate, more chocolate than you could shake a chocolate stick at chocolaty chocolate infused chocolate cake.

*Chapter* 43

# DEBZ & MAGGIE

When they walked in, when they entered the room side-by-side, or more specifically the hotel lobby, there was a collective gasp. And by gasp I mean me, my tonsils, the last seven percent of oxygen left in the lungs when exhaling, my sphincter, my sense of purpose, shame, my partridge, the solid gold dancers high kicking directly into the wall of my stomach and my tear ducts. Maggie nodded, content for once to be second or more specifically not the centre of attention for all the wrong reasons. A female hotel waitress approached, involuntarily reeling back then back to the day job: a tick tock bounce from female solidarity to the paycheck. I imagine her sticking an arm out to touch Debz's arm who feigns nothing being wrong, no golden-purple bruise swimming between her cheekbone and her eye, parenthesis with her eyebrow where the hairs looks like they've been ripped off. At the top of her breast is a long scratch running down into her cleavage then a pause and back to the golden advert-smooth skin, continuing down the other breast obscured beneath her top. She notices her concealing scarf has accidentally shifted and coolly readjusts, walking over to me, Maggie in tow even now marvelling at how she'd never pull off broken victim quite as glamorously as Debz. When she sits down the other physical abrasions list themselves, jumping in uniform erection to form an orderly queue of hurt and the miracle of colourful body recovery: blues, green and yellows all merging into ice cream swirls of red, black and orange. Her wrist is bruised, bent even and possibly broken. Her tooth looks wobbly like a fake Lord of the Rings stalactite wobbling when a clutzy extra couldn't get by in the hiding chambers of Helm's Deep. The back of her neck has an arced bruise, clutched gratuitous by a grotesque gorilla's guerrilla grip, pressing the dark horrible containment into a skin destined only for … well … no bruises. She is unable to rest her hands on her thighs, keeping them at her sides and sits down with an unease more familiar with old people.

This is that moment. I can't help but sob and we end up in a triangular embrace as my crying puts all the lobby loiterers off their pre-wrapped snacks and morning alcohol free cocktails, off the disassociation, off their novelty travelling now that Covid is imagined past. There is no holding, no containing, no wishing it weren't there – just loud, hysterical, convulsive retch-sobbing … all the rage. Even Maggie is unable to watch, drawn into the outpouring, her green eyes the murky fountain of milky tears. Then we all calm down, the slow tightening of a garden tap so the sprinklers don't just suddenly feed the drought but rather leave the earth moist and affected and fertile.  The breathing slows too, in perfect inverse proportion to the tuning up of patrons checking into a hotel and milling in societal freedom; our crowd ungathers and arbitraries around us gather.  And then bam I see him, the guy from the video event, dressed in camo gear with new recruits and then just as bam he's gone, replaced by a chandelier and an old gentleman stiffening the quaff of his pocket-handkerchief, limply flopping forward over the pocket for a millisecond.  The elderly lady beside him shakes her head, accustomed to years of this fussing, something both sweet and impatiently familiar in equal measure.  The porter whisks their luggage away as the gentleman greedily eyes the bar.

This is what a couple should be, a lapping of respect and care, waves onto an appreciative shore, tough love and frustration the necessary seashell and pebble accessories.  Romantic love, the jam in the seasoned couple sandwich, of a higher metaphysical and ethical status than sexual or physical attractiveness; and not because that's all the remains when the hips give in and kneeling becomes tedious.  Love (or translated conscious coupling before the antithesis has its own social identity) stems from the platonic tradition that it represents a desire, not to be consummated in any way, stimulated by a mutual respect, actively pursued in chivalric deeds rather than the endemic imagining or pornographic sensual pursuits.  Conquest used to mean holding onto solidarity rather than a doused tissue or expired OnlyFans subscription.  Modern romantic love should return to the special love two people find in each other's virtues … one soul and two bodies, as Aristotle beautifully states. Love deserves to be of a higher status, ethically, aesthetically and even metaphysically, than the love we've all been indoctrinated to believe exists in modern society, one-upmanship and beneficial selfishness the eternally heart-breaking replacements.

Leaves only one-upwomanship as the door number two solution.

# Chapter 44

# DON'T NEED a REaR HOE

Normally opening one's curtains or blinds you're greeted with the prospect of immediate hope or impending hope, dictated by the all-conquering, omnipotent British weather; the very same weather that ginger royal and his shock-inducing father-alienating publicity-seeking Wallis-sequel disregarded in substitution for Oprah's sunny disposition. Upon opening my blind, there he is. Not the weather, or Prince Harry, but the guy from the video event. Smiling: not ominously but reassuringly. Wearing dark green, almost army attire. I shrug, my politer version of the bird and lower the blind. An hour later I look again and he's still there so I motion I'll fuck him up, desperate not to seem intimidated, symbolised by calling the nines. He doesn't budge but he also doesn't volley any maniacal animosity back. This would all be fine if his one-way street wasn't staring through the bay window of my sanctimonious abode. Like a watered plant I decide to leave him for a while, hoping he'll wither, but in a teeny dark corner of my being somewhere on the highway between brain and soul, my curiosity is piqued, no not piqued but rather embalmed. Morning routines, mine in particular, will be the end of him I'm sure.

Saying the name Suomen Naisyhdistys correctly whilst brushing my teeth is a satisfying second act of the day, like that morning reaching bed-laden stretch once you've woken, a hitting the finish line victory pose. And Finnish she was although given the shallow attention span of our generation she's more famous for the sounding of her name that her actual exploits. In 1884 the worlds political, social and educational were reserved for the high-flying men-folk, us lucks gals possibly (if we were super obedient, cooked a belly-warming feast and posted our derriere in the air for landing) would get to hear about these developments even in a comparatively progressive Scandi culture.

Now the point is not to berate past generations for not doing enough but rather laud them for providing those first steppingstones towards real gender equality. Now, granted our pinnacle represents a lofty level of retribution and playful feminist dominance but the 'Association for the Improvement of the Status of Women' (later dumbed down to the 'Finnish Women's Association' for those slow to cotton on, hard-working, blonde-bearded Lars-mother-fucker mother-fuckers) established an unprecedented level of organisation, order and expansion never seen before. The association never rested, publishing newspaper articles and booklets, organising presentations and discussions, cooking and craft courses, gardening, counselling, beginners' courses for out-of-school children, summer settlements, distribution of scholarships and awards. The founders mainly belonged to the highest social classes which, let's be fair, even today is where most of the progressive shit gets done and where we all swan around in subservient gratitude. Working to elevate a woman in an informational and moral relationship and to improve her economic and social situation, first in Helsinki then globally, proved that a measured approach can work but throwing one's self in front of a horse tends to make more gory headlines and spawn more cinematic interpretations. Play the Google game and compare Suomen Naisyhdistys with the Suffragettes and … well … that fucker is still outside my house! Crikey his quads must be dense.

I mouth "What the fuck do you want now?" and he mouths back with a one syllable nod which could be 'in' but I couldn't be certain. Clearly old habits encircle me, wisping me into random ostentatious action like when a cat smells catnip so I turn and moon him out the window. He laughs and bows, arms raised above his head. Blinds back down, arsehole tucked back neatly into my G-string.

Covid has fucked with many a worthy soul but none so more than Helène Aylon, the first ecofeminist, who the Chinavirus recently took at the age of eighty-nine. Now I'm not normally one for listing a string of grandiose yet inherently useless achievements but what Helène did to take this cause in a far more funky, progressive direction was groundbreakingly gobsmacking. Expressing her views mainly through art she took the seventies and eighties and pimped up their bitchin art rides with process art and anti-nuclear art respectively. She even took on the Bible. Striving for Helène's level of symbolically depicting change through running oil on paper is literally one of my favourite examples of protesting without protesting, shocking without shocking, simplifying a message and cause without following the baying, madding Karens intent on making everything about race. Excuse me, small adjustment to the thong, having gained a fair level of excitement after puckering up my sphincter for another man, the adjustment is necessary. Helène's series called *Paintings That Change* included groovy names such as *Tar Pouring*, *Drifting Boundaries*, *Receding Beige* and *Oval on Left Edge* – all part of the transformational process art relying to a large degree on chance. Think Boyband torture warehouse as feigned horror house immersive experience … what could go wrong? Which way would the oil coagulate and form? Her sequel series was called *The Breakings*, pouring any self-respecting cricket willow's finest tonic – linseed oil – onto large panels placed flat on a studio floor. The ensuing physiology would permit the oil to form a thick skin, like when you were a kid and your milk warmed. Tilting the panels at the right point and tempo in inventive evolution would cause the oil to form a sac underneath the surface, a beautiful boil ready to burst and bursting in turn discharging a spunked climax she would refer to as 'very wet, orgasmic process art'. What a chick!

Laser beaming down, this time from the upstairs bay

widow and, like a bloodhound, his snout is pointing up towards me, aware of my every move up and down the non-decked halls. I do the other fake stair descent across the window then, realising the familiarity folly, follow up with a flounce and an imaginary flair gun aim at his forehead. He takes the flair, stumbles forward then back to subservient upright, awaiting instruction pose. I can play stranger danger flirty-fuck-off with this fellow all friggin flood.

Then came Earth Ambulance, a permanent foray into eco-activism or eco-terrorism as we like to place it, igniting with a converted U-Haul van as the saviour delivering elucidation from nuclear catastrophe. Filling pillowcases with mustered dirt from Strategic Air Command nuclear bases, uranium mines and nuclear reactors, Helène had orchestrated carrying the 'patients' on stretchers at a demonstration at the United Nations during a session on Nuclear Disarmament. The pillow imagery would persist into the nineties manifesting in a seed-filled ambulance sequel and chains of knotted pillowcases, inscribed with dreams and nightmares about nuclear war. There's scoffing in the rafters I know but take a moment to reflect on how a vivid visceral visual representation can sometimes be more powerful than any verbosity of written word and, more significantly, during a pre-camera-phone-intrusion era where this sort of out-there associated symbolic protest was akin to Emily Davison painting the horse purple, white and green before handstanding, vaulting and landing at the hoofs on that iconic day in Surrey. Or maybe it just means we have license to be grotesquely creative, but really, who would notice or give a monkey's if a throat or two was slashed or someone hanged from their bollocks? Eco-feminism needs a gory makeover for the celebrity-hugging tree-stroking woke-awoken generation.

He'll never see me from the dollhouse-window of the downstairs loo; and it's always open so I'll be able to sneak up – all stealth like – and peep at the peeping-tom. Maybe that's the next play: a little suggestive wandering holding something phallic in my pants, gown trailing in disgust. One of Helène's (don't you love how we interplay between birth and family name: me all familiar and shit with eco-non-bitch-slapping warrior terror-princess Mrs Aylon [née Greenfield]) most admirable trait, not worth, in worth overt solitude like the art, was her patience. Once widowed, her wings unfastened from an obeying sort who likely did say that back to her in the vows, she took on Moses, his patriarchal God complex and spanned two decades. What she put out there with the G-d Project is so farking bang-in-there street; inspired; so far from the box it's criminally progressive. There really should be a queue of rotund Hollywood Jewish movie executives bestowing wads of cash on anyone with half a scriptwriter's ability immersed in a 'this shit writes itself' narrative: five books of Moses resting atop velvet covered stands, nonrelocating toupees in their wrongful spots … each page wrapped in translucent parchment, the infant wrapped in a Moses basket analogy surely not escaping even the most limited critic. The sound of turning parchment pages is played in a loop, fifty-four sections of the Torah on glass shelves along a wall adjacent to the five books of

Moses, a pink highlighter underscore – denoting our most beloved stereotypical feminine pigment – stressing, bringing our plight to the fore …

Cruelty.

Deception.

Misogyny.

Vengeance.

False attribution to God.

Sorry, forgot, is God depicted as a man? Remind me. Not here to shove that down any dutiful reader's cheerleading throat but take a moment to look at the first four … really look and study. Tell me what pops into your head.

Man on woman.

Man to woman.

Everyone to woman.

Woman to man … 2021

All that falsely attributed to God … or accurately attributable to Man.

It's too relevant and too hilariously destructive (and likely the only way I am able to quell this Braveheart sensation I feel building up to go and wipe out the English institution of male). At the big bay window upstairs again, a lighter, harder to find in a household where the gas BBQ's ignition switch has long since failed than you might imagine. Plastic bin beneath both my hands, his attention more at attention than his attention, no sign of any tiring. I must have subconsciously picked the oldest with the most bulbous, pronounced cup size, the light blue lace lipping around the pony pink cotton. I'm burning my bra, praying a stray dog-

walking biddy doesn't wander by with her limited brown
Lab, a pyro-porno for the neighbourhood book club's next
romance novel rendezvous. He's still and I'm holding on
while the flames amplify, reaching up towards my fingers,
desperate not to look like a nonce and drop the supportive
icon, shaking my hands like I've missed the wall nail. The
mic-bra-drop is about as coolly timed as I could have hoped,
the bin, thank Christ, not full of tissues but some worn
Amazon packaging. He pulls a pack of smokes – so toking
last century – from his breast pocket, pulls a golden filtered
cancer stick from the almost crumpled box, places it between
his increasingly magnetic lips, looks above his eye line
without raising his head and flicks the smoke up towards his
mouth. Now in any badass badboy performance gesture of
this magnitude we really should have him fumbling around
on the dog mess free lawn while the cigarette cartwheels into
a dirty puddly road scar; lung cancer's ultimate diatribe. But
no, this dude lands it perfectly, wanting my light to jack that
stick up and really light his way. I am frozen, impressed
frozen no matter how hard I try not to be, the remnants of bra
fumes standing-wall-fucking my nostrils in turn, first the left
then the right, then back again, the ultimate bacterial taboo.
The smoke sits in between his open exposed lips having not
uttered an inch of delineation from where it landed, a
gymnast holding a perfect landing, the tens rolling up on the
scoreboard in direct defiance of winter Olympic paltry figure
skating sixes. He probably deserves an invite. The question
is where to.

All this bullshit about a man and his castle, well what

about a woman and her kingdom. Like an NFL double chest slapping halfwit chanting 'You don't come to my house!' I slap on a pair of jeans wondering if I've accidentally selected my sexiest pair or if my hand searched through the layers of mangled denim to find the butt hugging arc that only Diesel knows how to do for a woman with long legs, small hips, heavy up top and an actual waist to speak of. They slip on, the smell of bra fumes still offensive in the room, and I lie on my back to pull them up, old teenage habits tough to shake except not requiring girlfriend application help for this venture. A non-burnt bra is twisted around me then I pause to wonder if putting on a bra defeats the initial object of burning one, my heavily teenage indecision now grating the sides of my jaw and forming a slow cool headache at the sides of my temples. The fact that I'm actually foraging into every girl's fashion life mantra for a smoke toting stalker is not good – the 'I just threw this on' deliberation of looking good without trying but actually trying harder than you would ever if you were dressing up for an 18th century Russian ball is betraying Suomen and Helène' more than taking a man's juice on the forehead. The jeans are on so they'll stay there; the bra is fastened so too in the interests of efficiency (nee laziness) it will stay too … no sorry, it's coming off. Now the top is going to be random – I'm going to reach in and whatever is clutched first is toppling over my head and adorning my sitty uppy adorables no matter how cold it is or how much glass needs cutting in the vicinity. Fishing, feeling, floating, fingering, found one! Oh. My. Gawd.

Strutting outside my front door, he's instantly nervous I

can tell, my breasts swaying more freely that they should. He doesn't look, doesn't cast a glance even as I hold out the light. He retrieves the smoke from behind his ear and takes what appears to be the most satisfying drag in the history of mankind; ah to be a habitual smoker. Mid second suck I rip it from him, take my own faked pull, trying harder than a Chinese gymnast fearing execution not to cough, and flick it back in his face, the spray of red-yellow technicolour mini-fireworks bouncing off his cheeks and setting fire to one of his eyelashes. He doesn't blink, letting the dynamite fuse burn to the core of his eyelid, not even a pain-tear appearing in physiological protest.

"You can put that thing out on me wherever you want," he says.

"What the actual," I spit, playing the impatience card a bit early, perhaps betraying my true curiosity.

"I'm in," he says. "I want to be in. I can help. I have people. You need people for this."

"I need your people to tell me where to get my hair done, my bikini line lasered and my eyebrows threaded."

"Come on. Do you even know what eyebrow threading is?"

"Do you?"

"Not really but I have had my balls and anus lasered."

"Ah okay. To each his and his own."

"I'm not gay."

On cue a full chateaubriand prime beef non-minced fillet breeze sweeps across the street, blowing the remnants of the cigarette embers into a puddle surrounded by yellow leaves and moving said warming to (am I?) weirdo's fringe to the side he'd not intended, a cow lick gust flipping the fifty-two hairs to the left of the dealer Vegas style. I look at it and laugh; purposefully at him, the tone so mockingly finger pointing he knows instantly I don't really buy into the slapstick routine funniness. Instead of putting it back, the dabbed hanky equivalent of a seagull shit on the face, he leaves it flapping incongruously like the T-1000 in Terminator 2; and if it's not his judgement day yet I'm about to make it so. He butts into my abuse engine lock and loading.

"Since I was a boy ... no really, all my life everything has come easy. Grades, chicks, jobs, money. So when crusades run out or your efforts become squandered the time comes to acknowledge following a higher power. And not God. But women. Or woman. And not because you're drooling all over yourself in awe of said woman or trying to get in said woman's pants ..."

Now he looks at my tits, chilling under my 'Boybands Do It With a Smile' t-shirt present from Kelly, cut into a skimpy crop top with the 'a Sm' region scissor-mangled into what I hoped looked like 'Dn', the rainbow joining the 'b' and 'd' unspoilt.

"... but because you understand your true calling is to support and make it happen; you're best when you're not winging it but rather putting all the grimy, dirty, unfashionable pieces into place so the tapestry can be realised. And you'll know you were a part of it – a small big part."

"Then you'll get in my pants?"

"What's the opposite of collateral damage?"

"I don't know what you think I'm doing here or which crusade you think I'm championing or how you might have gathered this false rumour – Twitter probably – but you're mistaken. I get up in the morning – take a dump – put my face on – go to work – come home to a Boybander – go to sleep. About as mundane an inspiration you were hoping for right?"

"I don't really care how I know or how it emerged," the fringe still on the wrong side. "But I know something is afoot. And I want to be a part of it."

"Okay Hercule, what do you know?"

"There's a haunted mansion being fitted out with bespoke devices. I have people who can help get rid of the audit trail here as every item that gets made is generating questions. I know key members of Scotland Yard if this shit gets real, and by know I mean have influence over. I know some of the Boys are talking about your unity; they're aware so the facade can't go on much longer."

"This is a game we're playing with them. The Haunted Mansion is an immersive experience where we're all going to scare the shit out of each other – it is part of the deal. And the cops, gawd what do you think we're planning? We're little girls who dutifully touch our toes when a Boyband hollers – groupies who pretend we're in control and loved for anything more than how good we look in the mirror or in front of a paparazzi's lens."

"Also I know," he pauses, the flopped hair returning to

normal. "What you've all been through."

"That is beautiful. You know what we've been through."

I can quote it in my head, the words rattling around, fossilised – what do Americans call them – gumballs, shaken in a plastic cage. Julie Bindel, when baited about whether heterosexuality would survive women's liberation, stepped off the soap box and onto the mantlepiece, rejoindering 'It won't, not unless men get their act together, have their power taken from them and behave themselves. I mean, I would actually put them all in some kind of camp where they can all drive around in quad bikes, or bicycles, or white vans. I would give them a choice of vehicles to drive around with, give them no porn, they wouldn't be able to fight – we would have wardens, of course! Women who want to see their sons or male loved ones would be able to go and visit, or take them out like a library book, and then bring them back. I hope heterosexuality doesn't survive, actually. I would like to see a truce on heterosexuality. I would like an amnesty on heterosexuality until we have sorted ourselves out. Because under patriarchy it's shit'. Defending women who had been prosecuted for the less intelligent of the gender, those beaten without the typical subtlety of psychologically eating away at a woman's self-esteem or using power and influence to do coercive sex stuff, leading to a celebrated, timely self-defence retorted death would land her squaring up to transgenders in her Guardian column 'Gender Benders, beware'. Called, scum, filth and the ubiquitous cunt, she was attacked by a trans activist after her call to end gender entirely, arguing that gender-reassignment surgery fortifies gender stereotypes and that the diagnosis of gender identity disorder is fostered on archaic views about how females and males should behave. If the attacker had only taken a moment not to take it so literally and look at the real goodness of conquest of supporting violent females who hit back, slapped back, kicked back, spat back, shot back. She fought to change the law so that nagging was no longer a defence for husbands who killed their wives and injected some retributional fear back into men that if they crossed the line, their wives, girlfriends and bitches just might break every exposed bone protruding over said line, grinding them into powder for the little lady's hot fresh loaf being baked in the kitchen then posting it back over the line to force feed him the carbs while he drools from the holes in his cheeks and looks longingly upon the missing appendages.

"It's okay to receive help even if you haven't asked for it; it's okay if others around you are the silent support to get your stuff done."

"I'm the one with the platitudes."

"I'm just saying, resourcefulness is not a crime."

"It could very well be. The resourcefulness will be avoiding the implications of the crime without disregarding the criminal intent."

I'm suddenly cold and showing it: opening up is a bit unnatural, trusting even more so.

"From the periphery there are too many flaws with this and this is where I can help."

"There is not one single flaw; just not enough time to get everything wrapped in a sweet pink ribbon for consumption.

It has to be a now or never regurgitation, using what we have even if the risks are too high."

"This is what I do: take away the risks," going for his hair he smooths the fringe but not in a way a Boybander might be messin with his stylist's creation; rather his version of an outreached tactile reassuring gesture which he'd lose his arm at the elbow for if he had the audacity to try. I will not cry or else that tear will end up smudged like a midway stubborn next-day-curry loo excursion. "Let me at least try to prove my worth?"

"I've chucked in the towel anyway; said farewell to what was really a lot of old nonsense and just stirred up by the PR folk really," I backtrack seeing the disappointed colour drain from his face. Colour reforms, the filling of an ecoprinter.

"And after what happened to Debz?"

"What happened to Debz?"

"She was raped and beaten and they filmed it."

"Do you know what Catagelophobia is?"

"No."

"It's the fear of being ridiculed. It's what revenge porn is founded on. It takes the concept that a woman is ashamed of her body and the things men do to it as a form of public consumption. When you've been through what Debz has been through you don't have the time, the luxury of Catagelophobia."

"What about Atelophobia?"

"Fear of imperfection."

"That's your great fear."

"Oh I suppose if we're swimming in these waters, what's

yours? Rectophobia? Fear of rectum or rectal diseases?"

"Catagelophobia, actually. People, humans laughing, mocking, pointing. Isn't this normally when you laugh, mock and point at me to lessen the severity of the situation?"

"I'd prefer raise the frivolity as I'm a glass full-full atelophobe remember? My trajectory needs to go up not down. I'm getting colder now; I'm going to return inside and get on with my overdue chores."

"I'll let you leave with the last snappy-wisecracking line but know this – I'm in this for real so when something in the background nudges you closer and you marvel at your good fortune, know I have your back."

"I have nothing."

# Chapter 45

# DANIELLE

*'Whether therefore ye eat, or drink, or whatsoever ye do, do
all to the glory of God.'*
*1 Corinthians 10:31*

"Why would you start with the third circle of hell?" asks
Danielle snacking.

"We're not starting, I just happened to be speaking to you
first."

"Worms and three mouths. Got it."

"I'm not poo-poohing your original idea, just making it
more relevant and more funky. Not designed to offend. And
leaving the details to you. Your expression."

"Is it about me or him?"

Gerson, once sold by his mother, took on guardianship in
the wrong sort of way. When Danielle met him, he'd been
fronting many CBBC young kids' television shows with
unfettered access to the droves of aspiring child actors,

bouncing conditioned curls and all, normally only granted the privilege of blowing up a balloon in the background, consigned as a featured extra. Gerson hunted in threes, his equivalent babyface looks instantly dropping not only the parents' guard but the kids too, and his infamy also helped put him closer to the action that some of his dark web compatriots would be travelling to Cambodia and Malaysia for, putting themselves opportunistically as the harm in the way of impoverished children. Gerson would require oral concession in threes, demanding each of his students physically feed his 'three mouths' habitually with fizzy jelly worms with flavours ranging from Apple Sour to Cola to the more traditional Wild Cherry, Pink Grapefruit, Watermelon, Lime, Grape, Pineapple and Lemon fruit flavours. As familiarity improved, bubbles slowly forming in a home aquarium, so the manner of consumption would border on oddly emphatic: biting of little fingers, knocking the worm from the hand then demanding the child pick it up with his mouth, slow licking of the digits once swallowed. Danielle had seen it first-hand and to remind is sometimes to embrace as she recalled one of the disassociated mothers never comprehending why her daughter had fitful nightmares at three in the morning and never chose pick and mix at the cinema. The backdrops in these gregariously colourful sets did perhaps depict a gateway computer CGI scene: landscapes of living organs, violent storms, mud, piles of human waste complete with sprinkled worms torpedoing through the glutenous excrement, the concession for each mouth a Gerson being with three accessed anuses. The

Damned would be forced to burble forever in the foul product that made most of the circle up, with Danielle now having to face the three worm-like heads protruding from an open maw, Gerson's gape feasting on the souls trapped in kids' TV feigned euphoria. The Gerson Worm: kingly custodian of filth, with worm-like features to cannibalistically consume his sugary offspring, spending alone time ripping carcasses and tainted unsullied corpses apart, any unwary victim refusing to enter onto the worm feeding ladder instantly devoured in other ways such as removal from the show or celebrity blacklisting until puberty. Danielle had to lure him from the ground out of the dusty area and try to snap him. Or a more fittingly modern twist: eat him alive.

# Chapter 46

# Renea

*'Go to the ant, thou sluggard; consider her ways, and be
wise.'*
*Proverbs 6:6*

Waking suddenly typically means something has woken you
up. A loud noise or something external, intruding on your
rest, thieving your subconscious epiphanies and adding to
your cortisol. I was standing on the edge of the deepest
abyss, the dark air immovable at my toes but almost thick
enough to step onto. The loud noise that wakes me is sharp
like thunder, emanating from those depths and, just prior,
Kelly had asked me to follow him down and I felt trepidatious
but not out of fear, rather a refusal to pander to his pale,
desperate whims. I need to get back to sleep to see what
happens next so I start counting sheep, until the sheep start
looking lost, infidels in a world where everyone believes in
something. Entry into the darkness is not cartoon pit or

slasher horror but rather airport waiting lounge with no prospect of travel. The inhabitants, all Boybands, wander aimlessly through a crepuscular wood, innocuous campfires the jagged runway path, saluting me as I pass: one of their own in excluded solidarity. They're all talking at me, some singing, some whipping out some dance shapes – gibberish as I can't understand the appeal or the plea or the sanctimonious rationale. In the distance is a castle with seven walls, a banner sigil resting limply down each of the walls, the faces of Sexton, Gerson, Digby, Kieron, Damien, Willow and Barton. For the first time it feels like I know I'm in a dream, transposing something I know onto my life for justification, hoping for someone to talk me off the ledge or push me from it. The limbo dream gets literal as I wander over the stream, through the seven gates, a meadow and then onto a small knob of a hill for my sermon, the protuberance lumpy beneath my toes as I spout the names of all authority figures in my life who've not quite been there for me, regretting to name them all. The souls in this dream counterintuitively appear innocent and righteous yet punishable, but not by me; the punishment is self-inflicted, their disassociated celebration and selection of who they've become the ultimate purgatory.

I think I'm awake again staring at the ceiling, Renea's ceiling because I can smell her next to me. She's lightly snoring, pancake flat on her back, our post-horror-film sleepover a mess of screeches, tears, laughter and laziness. Kieron had been around earlier than me and I could tell because the loo roll shone dull brown carboard instead of brilliant double-ply-white, always waiting for others to lift their hands. He'd used three drinking glasses, leaving all of them dotted around the house, a dishwasher hunger treasure hunt. Above the sofa is a Northern Irish poop-art-protest of his boogers, neatly wiped in ever-expanding circles above his head until running out of room and spilling the now crusty globules onto the top of the sofa and down behind the cushion. So fossilised is the trail, one of those (again) Northern Ireland police water cannons likely would fail to remove the barnacled mustard-snot seeds. The toilet he uses is perpetually stained, both the back top edge of the bowl and the under-rim of the seat, indelible splatter and a coated tan crust respectively. His clothes in the wash basket, inactive for far too many lunar cycles, smell deflatingly heavy, a heavyweight boxing presence of rancid coconut to uppercut your jaw to broken if brave enough to square up. Renea once asked him to pop his dirty laundry in the washing machine and it ended up in the dryer; she asked him to put his curry takeaway plate away and it ended up in the bin; asked him to clean his teeth and he swished with mouthwash.

That feeling. When you want to rip a plaster off because the corner, a flapping appendage that's lost its stickiness, catches on your clothes or your nails, the reminder of a hurt and the lack of proper props to fix it. That feeling if you don't do it right away it will live there in perpetuity, dangling off your skin, a constant irritation, always there, smelling after showers, going blackened-burnt-orange from the non-living waste particles floating in the air sticking to the non-sticky previously-velvety side, tarnishing the strip, a bungling runway. I know why I'm obsessing about plasters. Kieron's discarded, forgotten about covering; previously confining the kept not-so-secret formulation of a pus-pressing to get out like a gangster victim under the ice, infected boil, the plaster placed so haphazardly it digs into the side I imagine, coating not only the small letter-shape gauze perfectly in the rectangle middle, but spilling along the edge and onto the sacred furry top. I shouldn't know this because it was dark, I shouldn't know this because no one really should know this level of fetid detail. I imagine it dislodged from his being without Kieron being any the wiser; that or he peeled it forth as casually as opening a Müllerlight and dropped it, without even flicking, right there next to the bed, gravity finding a home face up next to the side of the bed where my foot would choose to aim and hit. In the dark. And when that happens of course your darkest, most hygienic fears shriek, a million plastered miles from OCD, basic hygiene figuring out in the midst of a genocide while normal obsessive cleanliness figuring is gang raped by a platoon of bacterial soldiers. When that gap between your middle toe and the arbitrary one flanking the pinkie (the carb clean piggie deprived of the roast beef) acquires the still moist warmth of a squirted mayonnaise sachet expulsion, tickling both inner toe flanks until there is no other choice but to allow a lamp to reveal the horror and extricate the beast without letting your soul get within a mile of the thing. The calm set in when I laid eyes upon his discharged boil cap, worn down low. Disregarding all reason, all traditional behaviour, all regard for self-preservation in an infection-savvy Corona-laden world, I plucked it from between my toes and studied it close to my face, the drip concealing itself long enough until that warm splash of coagulated brown blood and yellow dead cells found the inner groove of my bottom lip.

Testpattern. Static. The mayhem of the worst most gratuitous battle you could ever imagine, limbless soldiers screaming in agony while explosions and further limbs are ripped off. Tom Hanks finding his neighbour's bones in The Burbs. Entering the first circle of Hell, taking your boarding ticket and thanking the attendant for the cramped, claustrophobic, ear-blocked experience you haven't even had yet – the place where virtuous pagans hang in da crib. Seated passengers born without the benefit of Christianity, only the lucky ones travelling with the Mighty One to Heaven, prior to me tasting Boyband boil product. No cliché like hunched over the toilet a moment later or a marathon teethbrushing session rivalling a zookeeper removing a chimp's gingivitis, just deep hurt down the jawline into the neck out the throat into the dark stink of Renea's room, back in without journeying through any air or window, back to the sternum shooting straight down the gut into the base part of where I believe my appendix resides then fairy dust rising back to the top of my migraine. Dizziness. Ogh fuck the inescapable dizziness.

*Chapter 47*

# sexton

*'But I say unto you, That whosoever looketh on a woman to lust after her hath committed adultery with her already in his heart.'*
*Matthew 5:28*

Sexton was a girl. The party to celebrate the world's first Boyband with a gender embracing convert was a public relations dream, garnering acceptance of acceptance speeches as physical revelations of Sexton's new curves, body parts and sartorial stance. With Debz's wounds heavily covered up and Digby at the party there was an element of caution we all had to commit to exercise: letting this pussy out of the sack would waterfall a never-ending series of suspicion and attention so, even though sternly against what should be every woman's code of tell it as it was just after it happened, we chose the assault as the reinsertion onto the bandwagon; well I did anyway. Strengthening resolve is easier when you are still tracking the escarpment, but when you've fallen off the mountain and are lying in a snowy bloody mangle of snapped limbs, the healing bind back to full strength is seeing a friend suffer; more so because of you. The result is attacking a bigger mountain with more Sherpas and more va va voom (and equipment and planning).

Sexton chose to parade with Debz, his jeans tight enough to show he no longer had a cock, and his new tits gloriously lopsided with one nipple pointing up off a sideways slope and the other downward cast from the middle-inner curvature. He still walked a bit like a man except every now and again would catwalk a pronounced hip strut to show he was trying to come off his training wheels. With a woman of Debz's aesthetic he wanted to show the world that it didn't matter your sex, your preference, your standing in the Boyband or your race – what mattered was that those around you stood by you through your chameleon body horror episode translated as 'Boyband's Life-Affirming Change'; they were there for you. For other Boybanders to rape while the lumberjack sawed away on the operating table. Debz's eternal poise would get her through most things, her raised chin always aligned to her upwards facing top lip and top of her real breasts, the ham in the parallel gluten free bread parenthesis. Photos incessantly blinded her, aiming mainly at her new girlfriend as the happy couple swanned between other celebrity guests like a Beauty and the Beast same sex pinball, until Digby sent a seemingly innocuous wink Debz's way from across a tray of fizzing champagne and regurgitated-looking canapés. Something changed just for that moment in Debz's effervescent blue eyes like an aerial shot of the ocean when a cloud darkens the surface, the shimmer confused at first then helpless to betray the girl behind the radiance. He followed with a flick of his jaw upwards then continued to talk Boyband shop to whoever was near, Debz's presence now fleeting and no longer fully required either due to having secured the ultimate possessive humiliation or that it might acknowledge his crime. Thing about wanting what you can't have is when you take it you realise you're further away from it than ever; cue denial. When Sexton pulled at Debz's arm one too many times, a toddler's attention needing massaging, she instantly snapped out of it then our eyes met, me mouthing "He'll be hurting soon" hoping she made it out. Debz would then avert her gaze to her girlfriend, adoring the limelight, knowing she had to focus on the extrication of this creature, the now 'one of us' mantra scrawled across her neoteric chest, Adam's appleless throat and crotch not able to even get close to cutting the Apple into equal slices or shimmy across the room yelling the Boots jingle "Here come the gur-urls." Élan focused and pinpointed for the greater good then onto the self-gratifying retribution with Maggie ... there was always room for one more and, in Digby's case, particularly room for one less.

A female photographer, in desperation to get closer to Sexton the bridezilla, ended up blowing Debz viciously back, the doors forced open by an obnoxious wind in unspoiled harmony, not the rest and recuperate remedy we'd all prescribed, re-enflaming her wounds in prevention of eternal rest and peace. Debz as the fleshy pleasure and Sexton now having more of his flesh altered in adulterous displeasure, wrapping his non-existent phallic tail around himself to shelter from the intrusive wind. Debz looked as though she was going to faint then brought herself back from the brink, recklessly underwritten by becoming abjectly aware of the incessant noise of the party, the increasing darkness amplifying the moaning, shrieking and lamenting; then Sexton gets audible, more audible than he was when he was a man, desperate to show woman has a louder, moaning, shrieking, lamenting voice than man. Sexton's weave bounces as she puffs out her chest to reveal:

"Call me Francesca."

From now on. Sexton's lack of carnal knowledge of Debz's carnal curves will expectantly create something of a Blue is the Warmest Colour re-enactment, Sexton now the pushy director and the oppressed star. Sexton's sweet thoughts and desires appear the eponymous victim, lured into the sin of impious desire to be something different, something complete, something feminine. Is this the antithesis of downfall or should we pity the mauled figure, parading in equestrian triumph, lifting those hooves higher with each prance as adoring media slap, snap, snack, package and parcel tomorrow's (scrap that: this is the instant gratification millennial generation of today-right-now) salacious droll-fest copy blotted for fifteen minutes; a glance at the transformation then back to life's other tediums.

Sexton and Debz stand in the middle of the room's architectural circle, the structural ends of a balcony bridge residing on each side. Atop, looking down in desire are the event's gold statues including Cleopatra, Tristan and Helen of Troy, separated at the left and right of the bridge with purple lightning arching between them. A fake rocky chasm further enshrines the smiling couple, massive pointed towers rising from the earth beneath them, substitutes for what neither now possess, juxtaposed against the surrounding welcoming labia arches and single life-creating womb: Sexton's due to Debz's irreversible injuries sustained. Her seven existing would never become eight. Catching a couple in a compromising position normally denotes they aren't actually a couple, the illicit depravity now a Hugh Grant Divine Brown badge of honour rather than the devil forcing his way onto a slave girl's innards to ruin them forever; forcing peccadillo came from unrestrained desire, manifesting in self alteration and leaving a void for others to commit the ultimate penalty. I weep. I faint.

Coming to, it's just me and Sexton, Debz knocking on the door from the outside, the hum of the celebration showing no signs of abating.

"She's fine; she's awake," yells Sexton without rising to unlock the door. "We'll be out in a sec."

Flat on my back starting at the ceiling I get a rare moment to study what remains of his old features. When Sexton bonded onto Debz and we all followed the Meet The Friends routine, the accustomed consensus was that Sexton was a beautiful man, his features more classically feminine that overtly angular male; not to say he had a podge moon face but that the contours of his jaw and nose ridge were distinct without being harsh, moulded clay rather than folded paper. His eyes and hair, being the same colour as my own, had instantly drawn comparisons and the boon resemblances had been more in jest than belief. But when Debz told me of a small birthmark on his upper thigh in the shape of a foetus dangling by a wavy umbilical cord, identical to mine in both size, shade, stature and positioning (just straddling the jutty out bulge of the top portion of the sartorius) my late night sweaty evolved into a gleeful abjuration disposition to the point where any mention of the name Sexton got as close to conjuring a shared foetal birthmark as … well … there is nothing to compare that to. Looking at him now though, he's even further from sharing anything with me, his eyes permanently discoloured from the pain of surgery and the hair covered by a fabricated creation akin to Shaggy from Scooby Doo. His skin too, once close to flawless porcelain, is now a teenager's wet nightmare, the hormones face fucking him into adolescent girl purgatory, the calm sea landscape adorned with jutted, meddling rocks at every tone. It is as though he was always destined to make a gorgeous woman only to not become one, his feminine traits tucking tail and retreating to be replaced by those relatives you wish you never had … and their friends … and their distortions. On show for ridicule. Is this the moment to joke he looks like an ugly person's arse hole bust in on itself and erupted in a beige-gold lesser-known Picasso that is his actual face?

Momentarily, studying his features while he talks in mime to me, I've lost the nebulously concerning notion of why we are alone together in a tucked away room after my episode.

Where's Kelly and why had Debz stopped banging?

"I believe we could be related."

Oh my actual … I'm related to Caitlyn Jenner two point zero.

"Can I call you Franny? Short for Francesca," my feigned concern not even denting his stride, the sound of my booze-laden croaky voice even shocking me more awake, Frankenstein's monster's bedside friend rising from a similar dead.

"Does the name Janine mean anything to you?"

Now he … she has my genuine attention, the words spewing forth from Forbidden Fuchsia lips, pinching each syllable as though she owned them.

"You see I've hired someone to find out about my family and it seems that this Janine person connected to those Boyband murders in the noughties could be my actual birth mother. And you could be connected to her as well, which means connected to me."

Does that make us soul sisters?

"How do you know I'm involved?"

"He found adoption papers prior to my birth and some evidence she had a girl with a man named Paton Stipps then a little bouncing baby girl … just kidding, boy … that is me; erm was me, with a man named Douglas Perfors."

Now there is a proper ringing in my ears. She knows too much, this new to the bitch-code bitch. If I strangle her now, would it look obvious … intended?

"My name is pretty darn, bog standard common. Is there anything else linking us?"

"Not yet but my man is on the case. He's looking into everything."

Which means we have to look deep into his soul, stop his shenanigans or at least send him down a rabbit hole deep enough the bury the very real past and its implications for what we have started, where I have come from, and the embarrassing link into all of this mayhem.

"I guess this means we're sisters," she says crying a perfectly choreographed separation of immobile cheek makeup, the tear wavering at the end of the now battered clay jaw line and landing flat bang bull's eye where Kieron's expelled pus chose to rest, the salty sentiment in some ways more unhygienic, more wasteful and more offensive than a truckload of forgotten gunge. She hugs me, her frozen boobs upper cutting into my ribs such that I'm actually winded, grappling for air above her back, remnants of male back hair peeping through the top, unsolicited onlookers at my discomfort, while her man hands grip me tight, an adjacent sisterly bond that couldn't be reproduced. There's no way anyone in my gene pool would have actual back hair.

Or would they?

*Chapter 48*

# JEMIMA

*'He that loveth silver shall not be satisfied with silver; nor he that loveth abundance with increase: this is also vanity.'*
*Ecclesiastes 5:10*

Cryptic texts: they're a fraudulently foreboding forewarning of what happens if curiosity rolls in front of the puss-puss, the woollen ball trundling across both traffic lanes. This one's a little too personal for some phishing exercise and I'm acutely aware of the source, my interest more cruxed on the cause and effect, validation and continued disassociation, attempting no return gratitude no matter how significant the gesture.

*Went to work like I said – two*
*boys paying unnecessary*
*attention, both dealt with* 😎

*Some info for you on your past though. Without being intrusive thought you should know about it ...*

*You know who this is right, your friendly neighbourhood spidersupportersolver. Gee predictive . texting almost fucked me up on that word*

He is a bit funny and maybe maybe (not really) maybe deserves more than a Simpsons-coloured fuck you bird emoji. But this is supersicksensitive danger territory. Treading with extreme caution ...

*What have you done son?*

*Your Willow problem with the genetics documents solved – relieved from his possession so unable to make a case. Sexton's PI has been sent down a hole where he'll fine a boring resolution of Sexton's council parents as deceased and no connection to you, Paton or Janine*

> *Feel wrong leaving the obligatory emoji on the magnitude of the last one?*

My heart butt-fuck-pounding, kicking me both hooves underneath my sternum from the inside until Alien 1979 burst from me … phone buzzes with a lone emoji …

😐

> *Not sure I want to talk to you.*

*I'm not trying to force you to do anything. Just want to assure you these two loose strands are sorted but there is some information on your birth I thought you and only you should have but it is none of my business and I'll shut up and leave you alone. I'm going to keep doing what I'm doing though* 🔨

Oh he's good, because now I'm on the ropes and the ball

is so squarely in my court that if I'm not careful I'll step on it and crack my head on the court. If I reply, I'm desperate to know; if I don't, I don't find out. But he knows I won't because any admission is what the tin says: an admission. He's an inside man but for the life of me I can't figure out how he is inside. The only possibility is one of the girls blabbed outside the circle and it has somehow made it into a resourceful, good-looking groupie's stern hands. But to get on the Sexton case so quickly and steal from Willow requires reconnaissance at a level that is military, not dissimilar to us before the distractions. His anonymity is a crazy asset though, operating in the shadows so we don't have to, hiding in not so plain sight but with what recriminations, what expectant favour does he require as a reciprocal thank-you? It is me and me alone?

I'm en route to a protest with Jemima, not even sure Jemima knows the cause but promised she'd appear in solidarity with Willow then peel away to walk with me. Upon arriving the gathering is sparse, even with Willow as the token celebrity to raise the profile. It might or might not be anti-policing; it might or might not be anti-animal cruelty, Jemima's snakeskin shoes twinkling in the beige sunlight in between the stomping high-top Converses; it is likely some form of anti-capitalist rally wrapped up by individuals wearing designer clothes and from privileged backgrounds. There seem to be two distinct groups chanting "Down with the rich pigs" pushing through each other with their outstretched chests: hoarders and spenders. At the front of the march is man dressed as Mickey's loyal pall Pluto who looks agitated, so Jemima and I decide not to pat him or tickle him under his tummy. The two groups to the naked eye are the same yet we're all over which is which, the hoarders sporting last season's designer kit and the spenders this season's. The rival factions joust with looks of disdain, the hoarders on the left volleying spat looks from the spenders on the right.

"I want to turn him into what he's protesting against so he can understand the do-gooding is a side-bar when true belief is absent," says Jemima accidentally on purpose tripping a hoarder with 'Black Lives Really Do Matter Mother F*cker' written on his headband, apologising gingerly then heaving forward. "These gatherers, these hypocrites, these greedy fucks all wanting statements over conviction killed my granddad."

"Lovely old Mr Styx, I miss him too," I respond, putting a limp reassuring hand in Jemima's pocket inadvertently fondling a large wad of cash as punishment for my gesture. "Somehow we need mud, but I'm sure you're all over this like a fat Karen on a black policeman."

"I am: all under control and all in hand. Just desperate to get going. How much longer do we have to wait?"

"A few snags which I need to check have actually been dealt with and the Covid situ which needs to evaporate at some level before we can all gather at the house; the excursion is officially off limits without any follow up booking date available."

"That doesn't sound much like you."

"What do you mean?"

"Checking something has been dealt with, without sorting yourself? Accepting a rule when getting someone to secure the venue should be your bread and butter?"

The wind whips up stuff, a sickly concoction of expensive scents from the spenders, freshly ordered online in glass bottles complete with illogical, ornate designs and an overly eager spray applicator.

"You're right. I've not quite been on the ball lately."

"Because of Debz?"

"Amongst other things."

"You need to tell me what is going on. So I can help. Don't take this all on your own shoulders; we're all part of this. I'm not having a go at you, just honest observations from a friend to improve the situation."

When I told Jemima about the mystery man and Sexton she was genuinely thrown back, tackled onto her heinie but with an expression of hunger. Jemima would always hanker for acquisition, be it the solving of a conundrum or supporting a friend and not as trophies either but as simply building upon another part of her being. This made the protesters, in her mind, even more like her but afraid to admit their true intentions – wanting change in the world when your day to day revealed you were quite content with the status quo was an economical waste of resource that more truly represented materialism and spat in the face of generosity of spirit. Being surprised by Jemima's go-to solution was always something I garnered delectation from and her mention of helping out, I must admit, injected the element gallingly vacant from proceedings of late: fun.

*Chapter 49*

# GWYNNE & DAMIEN

*'But now ye also put off all these; anger, wrath, malice,
blasphemy, filthy communication out of your mouth.'*
*Colossians 3:8*

Hopscotching between friends like this makes it all seem make-believe. Really though, life is a busy old exploit – just the menial survival part. Daily ablutions, systematic feeding regime, metronomic oblivion to all the world's evil barricading into your psyche through news, media et al, attending to long-standing medical afflictions, plotting vindicatory avowals, flipping through mindless posts, perusing lists of 'never will happen' chores, checking your name on fan sites, flicking out the proverbial quirky, getting the heart rate up through some form of self-inflicted vanity-driven human-suffering pain, meaningful booger post to keep up appearances, day job for actual income, staying grounded through something worthy and that mindless addiction tele

Netflix binge vision.

Backtracking back into that list and no, not stopping at the obvious clue where this is all going, but rather bee pollen seeking settling on human suffering. Gwynne is forcing me into a one-on-one personal training camp of boots in the park, forcing me to actually go out in public in active wear and join the millions of mummies country wide completing all that list and more (mainly in the retail realm) bunched into black, grey and sometimes even burnt orange lycra. Racing Gwynne is like a Rocky III moment except Rocky never actually beats Apollo, those little Italian legs really no match for Action Jackson. Now my legs are a fair bit longer than Gwynne's but more resembling a baby giraffe than a triathlete although, to be fair with no Gwynne around, I'd back a poll of 100 to go at least 80-20 triathlete-giraffe if filling a stadium to watch me line up against the Blade Runner striking a cautionary note to not go pee-pee and risk getting shot. Spotting Gwynne across the Green, warming up without a smile, head tucked in between her ankles like an elephant's dick, swaying forward and back, perhaps this could be a Rocky moment. I'm feeling strong, lithe, alive and Gwynne looks distracted so this could be my moment.

Alas not. The gap was less than last time though. Putting me through my paces is brutal, to the extent that it feels like masochism, though it is publicly Gwynne doing this to me so officially I guess it's sadism. Shuttle runs, burpees, knuckle press-ups, deep squats with our butts stamping the tallest fronds of grass, planks for days, side and back lunges, even pulls-ups on the abandoned football post until we're both staring at the greying sky, my breastbone continuing the press-ups while Gwynne, with a sweat on I must add, finds a normal heart rate a little more seamlessly.

"Everyone is ready you know," she says without looking at me.

"I know. It's just that I'm not."

"You feel like you've got us all into this and that you're responsible for Debz. But you're not."

Turning to look at her she's forcing the tears back, angry water bursting to bust forth but Gwynne holding the control reigns in utter defiance.

"He hits me almost daily now," she continues. "Like it's a game. I've created him now his is the degradation of me. And knowing I can kick his arse so hard at any point makes it strangely better. The waiting is making me enjoy the beatings. Afterwards he stares at himself in the mirror, tensing his abs, then punches himself in the stomach then the face. He's replaced a dozen mirrors when it spirals."

"Feels like I've been preaching, cajoling, manipulating. The anger I felt attacking the repressed anger you all felt, drowning beneath the marsh of society's veil of female resilience and suffering for the sins of men."

"Whatever came before, during or since, you are our Queen and not a self-appointed one either. We are your Fallen Angels ready for the ferry ride into the city, escaping from the rage but embracing it too. Harnessing. Moulding. Taking each drop of rage to set fire to the temple because we've all been seduced. We're your daughters. Human reason failed to overcome our obstacles so this is the divine feminine intervention we're re-enacting on the lost souls Boyband to bear witness to the Great One opening their gates."

I force out a high-pitched girly fart averring "Great One indeed," as the moistness of my cheeks convenes with the grass's secretion.

Gwynne doesn't smile.

*Chapter 50*

# MAGGIE & TABBY CAT

Cheating, it could be argued in some circles, is making a truth fit the reality you choose to believe in, a reality that if bent for the right, logical reasons, gets the limited locals nodding in revelatory consonance. Close Enough. This has to be the epitome of a Close Enough generation, each youthful optimist full of promise, self-worth and vicarious value achieving absolutely zap squat but crediting the cachet more with the unbridled attempt than the end result. A trapeze artist finally acquires the stones to ditch the training wheel safety net, but didn't practise quite as hard as his rival Sergey, stopping short at ten thousand grip, rip and flips only to crash and burn upon re-entry into the circus universe; the snapped limb tragedy is never put down to good effort – this only applies to failure when the consequences aren't dire and by not dire this applies to the entire wider United Kingdom mollycoddled baby state, sitting on fat public sector cushioning not scrabbling around in the food is scare life dumpster of say Africa or any other leader-ravaged tearjerker of a nation. In our case though, it has to be deemed Close Enough; we know we're cheating but literary parallels are all the rage I'm told, especially clever ones, which instantly disqualifies the How Not To guide I know, but c'mon, wading through a Tom Clancy snore fest this isn't, the intention far prosaically superior and obvious than any Goodreads critic will provide credit for. Heresy, violence, fraud and treachery ... the remaining circles so obviously not uniformly ascending in severity but equally close enough to Maggie and Tabby.

*'Fret not thyself because of evil men, neither be thou envious at the wicked: for there shall be no reward to the evil man; the candle of the wicked shall be put out.'*
*Proverbs 24:19-20*

*'Charity suffereth long, and is kind; charity envieth not; charity vaunteth not itself, is not puffed up.'*
*1 Corinthians 13:4*

We're forced to meet in a supermarket, Sainsbury's off Market Road, garbed in undercover mummy shopping wear, conscious not to overstock on loo roll or loiter too frequently near a fellow zombie apocalypse survivor, beating off the Karens for the extant organic peach. Masks help too, although with Maggie's eyes, revivifying the mask to the extent that she could have had a pig's snout beneath it and it wouldn't have mattered, and Tabby's bookshelf chest, even though modestly wrapped in seven sports bras, appearing around the corner of the special offers like each one the most special of offers, bouncing just enough on each stride to tame even the highest decorum of gentleman, made sneaking around under cover of fluorescent light incredibly difficult.

"I should get a mask for each one of my boobs," whispers Tabby almost tumbling over in the toddlers' big boy pants aisle. "Because no one actually looks at the mask."

"On you babe, you alone," quips Maggie, pointing the evergreens unrequitedly at the pair then the Pampers. "I believe we are fully back on, eh Capitan?"

Now I'm stung. Confirm and I'm reaccepting the responsibility that made me regret the consequences I was fostering for these girls; waiver and the momentum deflates, ferment replaced once again by pedestrian indifference.

"I want us to tread more carefully and with a heavier heart," I mutter eventually, nodding at a smiling old lady with mismatched English teeth and a basket full of bathroom air fresheners. "I can't handle the burden of thinking this was all for my selfish agenda."

"It wasn't," says Maggie.

"Isn't," chimes Tabby.

"If we do this, whatever each of you choose to do is for you, and details and decisions become your expression. If it is flaming tomb sinking into a river of boiling blood and fire or a coerced suicide or a hound chase to the flesh ripping end, that is your choice. You are not sorcerers or false prophets but expressing your hurt and suffering through this tapestry. Or not, should the will to go through all remaining circles depart at the crunch moment, frozen beneath your icy lake of squeamishness or contrition. Be they panderers, seducers or flatterers; corrupt politicians, hypocrites or thieves; I cannot and will not betray our love as Judas did to Jesus with a smiling kiss. I stand by your actions or inactions whatever they may be, as deep within the ice as you wish their sin to be shown. Did I just say that out loud?"

"Hail Satan!" shouts Tabby, her left bosom knocking an entire row of Pringles down a dominoes line towards an angry shelf stacker. We run towards the fresh fruit section, Maggie now yelping "Hail Satan's Bride!" in my ear, until Tabby falls down, polypiling into a display of AAA batteries, forward rolling through the metallic creatures and out again like a cartoon dog bursting through a drum.

"Everyone wants you to know the same thing babe," says Maggie once we're all back on our feet and careering down the confectionary aisle in sugar-crazed delirium. "This is not because of you or for you; this is with you, alongside you, arms linked in solidarity, glued together at the elbow not letting one Red Rover Boyband through. Ever."

# Chapter 51

# KELLY

Kelly's behaviour has been super odd lately, perhaps influenced by mine but I severely hope my masking skills remain sturdy throughout the wobbles. We had a takeaway dinner last night and he anxiously fidgeted around his chicken achari without touching his dahl makhini. Of old days I might have pandered, stoked the "what's wrong baby?" fires to further bow down towards the nonexpresser bottle it up strong and silent male bullshit mentality, but you know, I just felt like eating curry. The rocket sparks pre lift off beneath his chair told me we were in for a dénouement; as much as men pretend to keep in all under wraps, their baby boy mummy wiping nose fetish always comes out when a soft, cool complexion looks on with genuine concern. I wanted to see just how far he would sulk before springing it on me, just how sullen those droopy eyes and hangdog hair would sink before screaming 'Okay! Okay! Something is bothering me!'.

Jiffies before diffident lift-off number three, the sun setting deftly outside the kitchen window, splatting the sparse clouds with upward rays of pink and yellow, I quickly got overly excited, spouting "My God look at the sun setting deftly outside the kitchen window, splatting the sparse clouds with upward rays of pink and yellow!"

Deterred he backed down, returned to safety check double figures then started the courage regeneration process, me finding something even more arbitrary to scupper his efforts, my Jerry mouse not even a match for his hapless Tom.

"There's a new Netflix doco on the US University basketballs." Not a hint of let's Netflix and Chill anywhere near the TV, fridge or rug next to the fire.

"Do these things actually work?" I ponder over a red wine infuser Kelly bought for my birthday.

"I'm thinking shocking pink. In the hallway. And even more shocking pink above the picture rail. Maybe even the ceiling too."

When he trudged off to bed I knew I had to try hack his phone; get a head start on his moody blues. But would that be admitting I cared and ruin the surprise? I'd have to wait for him to actually be snoring, his phone neatly tucked an inch away from his pillow as an alarm clock in his bedside drawer. Luckily, in this situation though, he is a habitual snorer, belting out chafing tunes, his tongue, throat, nose and bubbling saliva a mistimed orchestra of insomnia dealing displeasure. Being a bad sleeper all the time doesn't help though but in the early unsuspecting days it was fun. I'd store up dead moths and niftily place them up his nostril, quickly rolling over to portray my own light snoring tune. He'd wake up with a flurry of hand slapping, clawing his face – bam! light goes on and all hell breaks loose when he discovered the now mangled moth on his boxers.

"Do we have a moth problem?" I'd say stretching for effect.

"That thing actually flew up my nose would you believe? Could have near lodged itself in my brain."

"Lots of room up there babe. Maybe it crawled?"

Moths would evolve to praying mantises and spiders and orifice locations changed based on the severity of the dying warthog sound emanation: ear for two spears in the warthog and mouth for more. I even tried up the old road less travelled when, quite unbelievably, he was snoring on his stomach, his butt raised on a pillow for his lower back spasms. The first attempt was woefully unsuccessful so I froze one of the moths, moistening it with hand cream and bamn! a moth was seen to actually fly up his arsehole. Might have been where the game got given away, who knows. After a period of calm and earplugs he began sleeping with that one eye closed again which is exactly what I need tonight.

Tippy toeing in an Edwardian floor-boarded detached is not easier than it looks, an almost full moon intruding on my intrusion, catwalk lighting my tortuous path, the slight shadow following and judging in equal measure. You think about the darndest things when trying not to make a mouse sound and your own breathing sounds like a reverse gang bang porno scene, castings strictly straight lesbians. At this moment I reveal the big twist, the smart alec film viewer's version of 'I knew Bruce was dead all along' or 'Kevin is actually Keyser Söze' but to a lesser degree because if you've followed the original not-made-in-China-how-to-manual: How to Murder a Boyband, you'll know I came from the loins of a fellow Boyband hating paternal lineage, hell bent on a small fry lone Boyband rather than the whole institution. Paton and my mother were just living together and, although the press would fill their boots with the Manfred done it motif, it became pretty darn apparent that the real underworld cult hero or villain was Paton Stipps. Paton Stipps the Boyband murdering psychopath, another dumb male – my father – led into believing his accidental foray into celebrity and a single figure body count would result in little more than self-redemption and cracking the life meaning egg so far open you'd be able to actually look inside. But he never did. He just died at the scapegoat's hands while I sucked on my mother's umbilical cord and his genetics coarsely coursed through my tiny little veins, likely not even hair diameter by the time he took his last breath. My mother, having given me up for adoption almost the second I took an actual breath, never held much appeal, chiefly because her choice was to abandon me to abusive adoption and a life where you know you'll never belong to anyone or anything. So her name would be Janine and she would clearly procreate once again and, this being one of those neat full circle fables, he would become a she and then become disabled at the hands of another she I truly care about linked to a bunch more shes of the same ilk, all dating those spawned from the so-called ultimate male. The procreator and chief. Used for his little soldiers to march forth and make boys. The Boys from BraBoyband.

Kelly's dark outline sets against the lit blind, an African watering hole after dusk, serene yet ominous. As a member of a Boyband and supposedly in the prime of his life, Kelly had this uncanny ability to look like an old man in poses of a standard, menial nature. His back glued to the mattress, his non-existent tummy distended, likely mainly duvet accordion, but nevertheless Churchill he has become. And his relaxed muscles in his face, drooping in pissed off bass pose and drawing his skin into unnatural lines, an aged youngster, moonlit but without the soothing hands of Mahershala Ali to almost drown him in the waves. His hands too, placed linked on his fake belly, mature and sausage-worm like, conducting the bellowing noise beneath, proud of his acquired bump as I go bump in the night. I'm pretty sure he's deep into a dream wank with one of my girls when he smiles and takes his hands from his duvet-foetus and places them both in his boxer shorts. Perhaps I'm getting sloppy or I've not read the signs correctly but, as I make it to the bedside table, my hand outstretched to fish for the drawer handle, he opens his eyes and stares vacantly at the blind, now shimmering from the obstructive moon. In a deft bootcamp inspired move I drop horizontally, softly hitting the floor in push-up position, thank Kerist landing on the excessive pillows I've forced Kelly to keep on his side of the bed. He's in La La Land because he mutters something about Cadbury's, accidentally belches then rolls over to face away from the scene of the crime, the arch of his back consistent with the old man routine. It is apparent to me now I've also got to get the darn thing back in its cosy resting place between the saccharine bookmark love poem I gave him for Valentine's Day and the pile of unused glasses cleaning wipes.

I'm downstairs in the study, door slightly ajar for any suspicious movement upstairs, going ape shit crazy as to why face recognition isn't working when I'd previously intruded on his phone for this very eventuality. He would never have changed this or deleted my profile, would he? Would he even know where to begin? I'm forced to try a few model poses and even scrunch my hair up in desperation to hack this rectangular piece of California-assembled Chinese-made necessity-laden frustration. Let's go old school: keypad pin … his birthday … nope … his mum's birthday … nope. Let's fast forward a few minutes, say eight, by which time I've ripped a few of my teeth out, killed the neighbour's dog, screamed internally until I vomited internally then threw the phone so hard at the wall it woke Steve Jobs in his plush coffin. Not really, but let's just say restraint is exercised in the face of a plan gone bad, manifesting in a new plan but one which let's just say had an added element of danger. I knew what I had to do. I had to get back to the sleeping mass and hold the phone to his sleeping old man face.

Déjà vu: moon, creak, sneak, repressed memory. My birthday, supposedly a day of joy and cakes and kissing relatives but mine with foster person's saturated paw squashing my voice shut, attempting to perform an act beyond what I was willing to entertain. Losing my tooth completely that day, embedded in said person's jawline would be the first pinball of many between families, behavioural issues the standard rationale, even including when I was framed by a genuine mental issues contender who used an overzealous pooping session to decorate the halls of the home. Kelly hasn't budged an inch which might make this easier as he's facing me. I've turned the screen lighting down as far as it will go or weez talkin brutha in the five-oh spotlight, drugs tucked in da rear. Feeling the buzz of success in my palm is a relief, especially given the angle I had to get me and phone into to align to Kelly's now almost horse like appearance. Old horse probably requiring putting down.

Scrolling like a mad person once back to relative safety, noting how inane all his WhatsApps really are: more emojis than exist and frankly incorrectly used. I can't resist so send a fuck you to Digby. A familiar number I don't recognise bites into my being when I hear Kelly's voice from upstairs, another distraction from his mum, clearly dissuading him … from something … what … what … scrolling down … oh my farking Jezus no. I'm heading back upstairs unable to tear my gaze away from a big fuck off Africa-looking blood diamond, handsomely atop a platinum band. Now this is that moment when all that is cheesy and clichéd and female bride in need Hollywood should make me retch with disgust, but I am (sort of) human after all and the thing is quite simply magnificent. Emerald cut, each angle complementing the other, a full rainbow on each surface surrounded by that brilliant clear only diamonds possess. I am really that pathetic and Kelly is directly catechising where his phone is, light on, bolt awake, the old man having toddled down the street into oblivion.  He goes storming out the room in search so I zap around to his side of the bed, ensure the WhatsApp message is closed and back to the Chats screen and insert in between bed and bedside table, a fallen bookmark comrade. An hour and full waste of my fake searching and ringing the darn thing later he's relieved, stroking his device in solidarity and none the wiser that I'm about to be asked to be Mrs Boyband for ever and ever after, to love, honour and obey.

# Chapter 52

# RUBICON

"We're losing some of the control, some of the unity," says Maggie. "So this is the only way to get them all together."

"The haunted house excursion isn't enough?" says Debz.

"Well, it might be," says Tabby. "But there is some potential wavering."

"So we needed this as an extra carrot?" says Renea.

"Exactly," says Jemima. "This guarantees it."

"Okay, cards on the table," I say. "Who wants what?"

The rule of six gathering in a garden has just been allowed so we're gathered at Jemima's pad on a gorgeous spring trying to embed itself day, the daffodils moistly underfoot and the first stinging rays of the season curling around our dusty shades. Although not necessarily sticking to the rule of six, what we're about to embark on would likely render this gathering the drop in the conniving ocean and, upon being bust by an eager police unit or Covid SWAT team, we could always lower our esteem and revert to shameless flirtiness to get off this infringement, especially what with the talent on show around this metal table, all sipping a mighty concoction of Pimm's.

"Gang wank," says Tabby Cat.

"Same," says Danielle. "Except only voyeuristic."

"Blow bang," says Jemima.

"Full on," says Maggie. "All involved. Gang bang. No survivors. What all his 'mates' have been up to supposedly, he wants too."

"I've not raised it," I sheepishly chip in. "It's not really his thing … he's so nauseatingly into me, any more of you stunning bitches would just be too much. Plus he'll be there if I tell him to."

"I've got oily gang bang with camera phones," says Gwynne, frowning without changing a piece of her face. "Feels his new body is a shame to be wasted and he has an industrial supply of baby oil for all the posing in front of the mirror and at the gym."

"Could be an awesome slip and slide then?" says Debz, remembering her hardship and backing down back into her shell from the frivolous fun of old. "Francesca's all in too though. Boys and girls all lined up."

"Not much committal my end," says Renea. "But there was reference to smoking something 'real' before any group activity. What's a gang wank, anyway?"

"I've refused to touch him for moons now," says Tabby. "So this is likely the only way he knows how. Plus he's big in all the places he shouldn't be and small in the place he really shouldn't be so I think he's been perfecting a technique of squeezing at the base of his balls so it appears bigger."

"I'll bring rear-view mirrors," says Renea.

"When I bust him in front of the mirror the other day," continues Tabby. "He'd grabbed it so tight it looked like a deformed pigeon awkwardly lying across brain matter."

"And this is the only way we entice?" says Jemima. "Through the promise of perverse group sexual forays?"

"I can't even begin to tell you what Francesca is envisioning," says Debz straightening her top.

"This will have to be dangled," I add. "Not as a starter or this will quickly digress into something where we are the ones being forced. If we lose the control but keep the promise of promiscuity apparent then we have a chance. But too overt and flirty the whole thing goes up in flames. They can't just have what they think they're getting on a platter."

"Is this actually going to work; for real?" asks Debz.

"The booking is back on," I say. "And because of the celebrity element I got the firm to all sign NDAs with only two people really aware of the full picture. They won't be around that day either."

"Post that day?" asks Jemima.

"Still shoring up all eventualities but suffice to say it's the old carrot and stick – bribery and compromising elements of their lives they won't want in the public domain. And deniability too with no record of the interactions. The device manufacturers all following the same mantra with both our escape plan plus the 'instructions' we received from our partners undeniable."

"This is actually going to happen," says Renea. "It has to

be out there for the world to see: a backfiring escapade gone horribly wrong."

"For those unlucky enough to be in the firing line," says Gwynne.

"It always has to be about sex doesn't it," says Debz. "The enticing I mean. Even though the gentleman veneer was dropped some time ago, the next level of copying pornos to get off, gets on."

"It's control," says Maggie, her eyes dulling to still represent a magnificent deep-sea green.

"And humiliation," says Danielle.

"When men are enabled to commit horrendous social crimes against women," Maggie continues. "They will and do as a collective, their individual impotence suddenly spurred on by a flanking buddy holding his own dick."

"The funniest thing," says Renea. "Is that if we actually did this group sex thing, in whatever guise our holy high rollers have dreamt about, come the big occasions, I'm willing to wager the anti-climactic let-down cock-up each would act out would put them further from the fantasy that when the screen flickers and they watch a man bolt all over some poor chick surrounded by willies: branches surrounding Brer Fox."

"That's where the violence happens," says Debz. "When the frustration of unrealised ideals becomes too much for a fragile ego."

"We've got a lot of this nth level planned," I interject. "But let's be on guard for the unknowns. There will be situations where all of this follows the path and some subplots which we can manage. We've said all along we'll do what is within our boundaries and, if it feels wrong, it is wrong. We don't need to follow through with anything if our squeamish dispositions kick in. Call on a friend if in need; call on a sister."

"When we set out on this reckoning we swore we'd make it look good," says Tabby Cat. "It has to be not only cool but fun; I want to get off on this for years afterwards wherever or whatever we are. It's about stating the bleeding obvious and bleeding the stated obvious."

"Nice," says Maggie wishing she was also a white female rapper.

"We might have strayed from the initial brief," continues Gwynne. "But at least we know who we are, what we represent. If we get to that point where we allow choice for the repenting soul, we should let them take it. Allow the redemption if it presents itself."

"I had assumed the time for redemption had passed," says Jemima. "That we've allowed sufficient opportunity and not once has it presented itself."

"Or have we not allowed it to present itself because of our preconceptions?" stammers Danielle. "And our pasts?"

"Maybe I'm the only one there," I choke out. "Kelly is not really of that ... ilk."

There is a small silence but enough to feel I'm being ganged up on; or at least questioned.

"You're bottling," says Renea.

"I don't want this to be about mine versus yours which is why each must do what is right for each sin," I come back with. "Perhaps I just have to look harder for an overarching flaw. But if it means letting you all down I will never not follow through. I just want it to feel right. Maybe it is bottling but I'm just trying to be straight."

"Straight is for lesbian girlfriends who used to be Boyband boyfriends," says Debz instantly lightening the mood. "Take it from me."

This is not one of those groups where a prolonged silence bothers; and there is no Pulp Fiction need to address the perceived awkwardness by acknowledging its very existence. No wind blows through, no metaphoric cloud to shield the rays, no monster earthworm bellowing through the grassy lawned earth and onto our laps in Dune Sci-Fi horror unmoment of the year. No one even farts for comedic effect although that would be classic fodder, the ultimate fig puckering ice breaker for ice that doesn't need breaking. We just breathe each other in, gentle glances at the inner and outer beauty on show, a smorgasbord of pristine shade complexions, each characteristic of some hidden trauma and the ability to shake it off decorating every feature, the eyes no longer swollen but charged, the lips no longer bleeding but drawn back to fire arrows, the necks no longer gripped in submission but possessing the arch of untold poise, propping up the faces of angels. We're not going to get soppy either, no words of final encouragement or sisterhood rhetoric, even as a tear drops down Danielle's cheek and Renea wipes her nose with her fist. Gwynne, stone faced as always, displays a hint of benevolence only those who ever knew her would recognise, achieved without the customary human being curling sides of the mouth. Tabby Cat, maternal presence checking everyone's face that they're really okay, and Debz, leaving the incident behind to focus on fixing it, not a temporary plaster for show, but a permanent surgical replacement to make her memory nothing more than an imagined nightmare. Maggie, looking on in admiration but with enough of a self-belief smattering that we know there is no longing and Jemima, wanting more but knowing there might for once be no further acquisition after this masterpiece is hung, drawn and quartered, up on the wall, the proverbial Boyband Moosehead staring vacantly at the opposite wall in frozen solitude.

"Why is sex humiliating for a woman?" says Maggie, breaking the silence with something real. "It shouldn't be."

"Seeing a woman's body has become a man's power tool," says Gwynne. "Like the shame of having it put like this together in this way is shameful."

"Add a cock," adds Jemima. "And the whole thing becomes getting one over on us, them all big hero courageous hiding behind the lens and pointing down at the one-eyed appendage."

"Has anyone ever felt," begins Danielle. "That if we actually saw James Bond's hard-on it would take it down a notch?"

"Yeah! Yeah!" yelps Renea. "Like when he enters a shower scene, all pretend hunk and there below him is a weird standy uppy boner, taking the scene from debonaire all-inclusive superhunk to pointing, laughing, Peter Sellers comedy!"

"I'm pretty sure," I interject my two pennies worth. "I saw a dodgy Pink Panther cartoon in Amsterdam where he dead anted a whole raft of cherished childhood favourites … Snow White, Bathsheba, The Queen. And I remember thinking why have they coloured his penis more pink than his body, his smug expression betraying what Blake Edwards had really intended? Why couldn't he have rodeoed Clouseau? At least he would have deserved it."

"You're all right though," continues Tabby. "We need to find a way to stop women shaming their bodies through revealing them and interject a bit of male humiliation."

"And not just for those who happen to have been born with large willies either," splutters Debz. "This statement has to be about what sex means to women, men and those observing the act of sex. There should be no shame in the visible portrayal of a woman's body who doesn't want to be visible … only recriminations."

"Does anyone ever get scared?" asks Danielle. "That all this will be for nothing; that the likely outcome the morning after is that men wake up, jack off, get up, abuse women, joke about abusing women, have misogynistic thoughts throughout day, go home, pay for sex and then go to sleep?"

"That is the reality isn't it," I answer. "And the most likely outcome. But maybe just maybe there will be enough fear in the heart of the next Joe Abuser to think twice before coercing his way into a girl's pants."

"This makes me surer than ever," says Jemima. "That we need to make this big; so cataclysmic that the reverberations are felt long, hard and forever. Not only the deep-seated hurt being spilled into the expression but the visceral pain. We need GoPros."

"What and film it?" says Renea. "Shame them like they always shame us."

"Exactly," says Jemima. "The wet pants expression of immortality should ring true for any girl seeing her boob flop reveal on Insta. Our job is to create a final hurrah of these moments for the Boys, promising only further acts and revealing what it feels like to be shamed; creating our version of revenge porn."

"I love it!" says Debz. "It is our way to turn the tables. Once they see this it stays forever. The demise – as with some poor girls being put on show involuntarily for the world to witness – is our version."

"And it'll stay longer," says Gwynne. "These will stand out, not like the commoditised – thankfully – fodder getting placed on incessant media around the planet."

"Hero 9," says Jemima.

"Ex-squeeze me?" says Maggie.

"The latest GoPro," says Jemima. "I'm buying, but we all need to get sick familiar with the workings quickly. Take away action task."

"Always the structured planner," I say chuckling. "Think I've completely handed that baton now."

"The worst thing is we'll be branded a bunch of lefty woke men-hating Karen Millennials," splutters Renea. "Who hate porn and its misrepresentation of women."

"We don't hate porn," interjects Debz. "It's kind of funny, isn't it?"

"It's a business," says Jemima, making a strange gesture with her thumb as though she's counting imaginary air money. "It's preying on desperate losers, all convinced they've formed a real connection with some Czech bimbo on OnlyFans. Although sometimes rapey and undoubtedly exploitative at the lower echelons, those top-level women know exactly what they're doing and how much money is ejaculating into their bank accounts."

"You seem to know a lot about this," says Tabby Cat. "All I know is that I've had way too many offers. Why are big breasts still such a draw card? Why are spherical bags of fat drooping from a woman's chest so appealing? And why is showing a nipple the hallowed ground of full topless exposure? Does it track back to boys who weren't breastfed?"

"Or those that were overfed," says Danielle accidentally making a sucking pouty noise. "Mammary glands define mammals and the procreation associated with survival and enjoyment are linked."

"Ah the old 'why did God give us a clitoris if he didn't want us to enjoy it?'," says Maggie.

"But then why do men want it more if we enjoy it more?" says Tabby.

"Do they want it more or are they more content spunking into a tissue hunched over melonstube dot com?" says Gwynne.

"In the wild," Danielle giggles, realising she's about to give us an Attenborough speech with us actually paying attention. "A couple of primate species have been seen stimulating their own nipples while masturbating."

"What's that got to do with the price of eggs?" tuts Jemima. "Or more specifically the price of an OnlyFans account?"

"I'm still on the theme of why boobs and, in particular, nipples represent the incarnation of sexuality, reproduction and self-administered pleasure," says Danielle.

"This is where everything is going," says Gwynne. "Or should be going. Moving men to just be suppliers of sperm to fertilise and leaving the enjoyment factor to women alone."

"I have to confess," says Debz. "I've come every time I've been impregnated. And I've enjoyed every one of them in their own special way."

"Perhaps because each represents a being you now love," I say, realising I've been a bit silent for a while, drawn into the examination.

"Perhaps," says Renea. "But take it from someone who has gone from owning one of those floppy hatted alien looking soldiers to really having owned one – if you get me – there is no comparison in enjoyment: girls dig it more."

"Then why do they have their tits slapped, faces spat into, anuses rammed in front of the camera?" asks Tabby Cat.

"There's a theory in nature," says Danielle closing one eye to emulate Sir David. "Few mammals other than humans mate face-to-face; and isn't porn anything but boring missionary face-to-face?"

"And here's one to add to your collection Danny," I add proud of being able to provide an actual numerical stat.

"Ninety-seven percent of mammals do not form monogamous relationships, yet society tells us we should or we're sluts or failures or lonely aged aunts about to be eaten by our own cats."

"We've all got to admit loving porn," Jemima sneaks in. "It's important we love it as a medium for empowered females to make stack loads of cash using their bodies as hot assets."

"But what about when that aggressive bedroom manner slips into the real world?" says Danielle. "As it is in our little incentivised promises. How do we stop this culture of one gender feeling entitled to take and abuse the aesthetical creature in front of them because of an oversupply of testosterone and an oversupply of images purporting women being dominated in the act of faux procreation, whilst also showing that we, the other gender, want to enjoy the act without being labelled as frigid, boring or unadventurous? What do we actually want to achieve in bed, with men in general and whilst watching simulated sex?"

"I watched a dominatrix strap on something bigger than anyone anatomically possible," says Gwynne. "And educate a line of about twenty submissive men, touching their toes. Now she wasn't getting any actual pleasure from this physically but it was a spectacle: a gender switching visual to highlight which side of the dominating fence watchers were fascinated with. In bed we want what we want at the time – I might want what I just described more often than I'd admit but I also have moments where just soft love and affection gets me off. The only thing porn shapes is the visual in the memory bank; and the barrage normalises this."

"For me it is about pushing the boundaries," says Renea. "In life, sex and even, say, gardening. Knowing individuals who are always pushing their version of what represents the uncrossable line of taboo is what makes true diversity in society. A relationship between two, three, n members of two, three, n genders – check out that poetry – should be about exploring boundaries together. Compatibility is defined by how much and how far (if at all for that matter) connected beings want to go to cross them."

"Like us," says Debz once again being the reality check of the group chinwag before frivolity completely blanketed us on that pristine patio, that day in the sun while the world slowly came out of hibernation. "We're never actually going back from this. For us our boundaries of speaking out against past abuse and society's disdain and normalisation of letting young girls be dragged through the self-loathing when they've done nothing wrong are too lean, too near. So we're about to push those to a place where society will have no choice but to take notice."

"And be fearful," admits Gwynne. "Knowledge that celebrity and power and personality tedium and personas of the nice guy who still date rapes and takes his sexual chances whenever he can – can no longer continue. This will make not only Boybands but Boys keep a close eye over their shoulder when dealing with a woman."

"If we pull it off," says Tabby Cat. "Just right."

"Getting to this level of inner sanctum collusion, control and outlandish demise is exactly where we want to be," I say.

"If it makes fuck all different then by Gawd we'd better enjoy getting it done. Sorry I went away for a time ladies. But let me assure you, I'm back and more invested in making this happen than before. Whatever the result – even us smiling, shaved headed Manson comparisons, in the dock – or sitting on an island far away from all this reminiscing about what we achieved; it is going to be worth it. Worth the planning; worth the pain; worth the insufferable girlfriending to these limited – dare I call them – musicians."

"Is this shit about to get real?" says Renea. "I've always wanted to say that and actually mean it. Cue cheesy lines; your turn Debz."

"There's no going back now," says Debz. "Tabby?"

"Let's turn up the volume," Tabby stifling a laugh. "Danny, yours?"

"Hoes before bros," Dannielle's inspiration breaking the seal of hilarity. "Gwynnie?"

"Digging deep … digging deep to not dig them deep," says Gwynne hesitating. "No wait, does it have to be made up, or must it be established cliché?"

"Whatever tickles your fancy," says Renea. "As soon as there's a rule, a restriction, a prescription, it gets boring. Mags?"

"Let's get outta here," says Maggie. "Film buff, couldn't resist. Jem?"

"Everybody has a plan," cautions Jemima. "Until they get punched in the face. If anyone slates the poet Iron Mike, they too get a punch in the face. Right Gwynnie?"

It's at me now for the real sucker punch; the moment

when it all comes together in a sweeping statement; the end of the trailer call to arms when the hero has absolutely no fucking other alterative than to be the hero. And no one says my name; needs to say my name, the small nod to the nameless mother until she outed herself with an actual personification boring ass name in the sequel. She was nameless when she was the villain, named when the hero – is that the same treatment for me? Or is my life's work the other way around. Taking a moment to catch the eye rays of each woman, a bilateral joining of their diverse sins to my cardinal sin, an umbilical joining, woman to woman, sufferer to sufferer, punisher to punisher, prescient to prescient. The transfer of their patent transgression now being plotted to splatter across the likely recipient, suffering as individuals for the collective portrayal, acquiring the sins as penance to each woman for ... for ... what? I see Danielle, goumandising her hapless repast, so deliciously arbitrary it might not even warrant a satiating burp; Jemima's avaricious acquisition amplified by a sense of worthy sustainability disposition; Abigail's superbia, standing firm in the ultimate stand-off then falling down between the sexes. I see Maggie's greens, burning in the sunlight, wanting more and deserving more, latched onto the one who took more; Debz, the fertile epitome of that want, the smitten smoting goddess; Gwynne, storing the ire behind a smileless face, birthing today's mirror vanity of chemically enhanced body dysmorphic rage; and Renea turned female from indolence with society's lethargy, the sickly-sweet smell surpassed. It is my turn to scoop all this up and act and not only for the solidarity, pinkie linked in this abnormality but equally driven by the historical significance, unable to roll over in usual marching, protesting, ineffective servitude but holding onto the ideal that world could, should and is a better place.

Because of us. Because of this. Because of how. It will be done.

"It's not whether you fall or whether you get back up. It is how you dust yourself off and shoot the fucking horse that has ridden you and your kind for far too long. It is how you look deep into the horse's eyes as it lies slumped in a mess of its broken legs and, before the colour drains from those adoring, betrayed eyes, you turn the beast into a gelding. But not before the eyes show that they understand that their suffering will prevent the future of your kind's suffering."

A natural follow-on silence ensues that irritates me because I can't be all about the big Armageddon moment speech before the world implodes but I have to symbolise a certain eloquent closure to the pre-raid estrogenic outdoor picnic party. I'm also about as against one-liners as say Christopher Walken in BOTH Pulp Fiction and True Romance, preferring enriched prose to make subtle, poignant and hilarious moments indelible so that once you've shat out a Reece Witherspoon dissolution on busy-body neurotic females, you're ready to embrace that gender – like race – should just not be so much spoken about as to create the 'thing' behind it … the first woman in space; the first black person to, fuck knows, take a shit unaided. When all these emotions well up inside you like a lifetime supply of Berocca, unleashing cute, fizzy Hiroshima bubbles in a thimble, you have to betray those around you, those that believe in you and most of all, what you believe in. Like I said there shouldn't be a one-liner but heck, here we are, sitting poised on the cusp of something a bit more special than the first of anything, classic funny-racist dialogue and / or whoring to be a slave to the punchline.

"We are not the bad guys."

# Chapter 53

# KELLY

Let's call it a trial run. A test of female physicality (more specifically my physicality) over my male coinhibitory proposing likable buffoon. Let's check out if all those hours of thinking about boot camp and toe press-ups and secreting in a gym have paid off. Every person wants to believe they've been blessed with natural strength and, because I have no baby pictures to verify, I cannot say for certain I was born a she-hulk, but I know I have strong muscles; not in a stick me on the cover of Fitness Hotties way or anything but my abs show, they stick out like piano keys all contained between two jagged flank lines, prisoners facing east and west. My arms feel dense too – I can lift shit like Jean Valjean or maybe I've convinced myself as a dare before I take the plunge, and I say I because I have no other choice but to betray my sisters, an economical hypocritical decision of sorts but one which would take too long to justify and likely scupper the whole deal. Stare closer to the page, look me in the eye and tell me Kelly deserves to die. Now. Knowing that I wouldn't follow through with it if push came to shove, mixing squeamishness with guilt lasered onto Kelly – I can't even watch him dig out an ingrown hair from his neck without wincing in pain, rocking in the corner sucking my foetal finger. My blind hope is that this applies only to Kelly as following through on true offenders should – theoretically – be easier, like Arnold administering true justice right? But having Kelly at the haunted house venue – all rickety and ready to go as we speak – would set in motion a fear of follow through and, although no one is judging anyone's safe word boundary point 'I'm no doing this anymore' my real wussy fear is that my inability would set off a stone thrown into a raging sea as opposed to a platelet shifting to spur on a continent changing coastline. This is why I have to subdue Kelly and leave him behind.

First action item, get that classic best friend involved who always steps up to the occasion no matter what shit is going down where … alcohol. Unlike most men who acquire that ever-welcoming aggressive drunk streak, Kelly traditionally goes the other way, sobbing like a little bitch and getting so emotional with his undying love for me that he's actually cried on me in the past, drops of tears making me feel like a shower as they smell like his urine. But if he does go minority agro and swipe out, I have a theory worth testing: you know in films when a girl gets hit she is so incredulous, so shocked at being struck she treats it as a pause moment allowing the attacker to gain an advantage? What about, like a boxing match, before the pain receptors have grasped they're in distress or the ubiquitous female mouth blood (we always get hit in the fucking mouth for God's sake!) trickles from the corner, lopsided vampire style, why not swing back then? Bam .. bam back atcha rather than bam ... bam – note the one dot missing to denote less time. Those who skim read might have missed that. Please pay serious attention from here on in as I can't be responsible if you miss something or if a key element of this case is thrust upon you when asked to testify.

Kelly gets home, walking through the front door looking around as though something is genuinely wrong. Am I that obvious as I bound over and hand him a Penfolds Grange Shiraz, filled more generously than I'd ever admit, well ... might admit later. I've got to drink as well or it will seem suspicious so I take a sip and kiss him on the cheek. He blushes of course. Unashamedly I'm wearing a crop top and my tight jeans, channelling Uma perhaps but subconsciously revealing a physical show of strength when, as Renea so eloquently put it, this shit gets real. Festivities start in twenty-four hours so I won't get another opportunity to incapacitate Kelly for his own good. In a rare show of confident assertion, he puts his hand on my midriff and runs his fingers over my stomach grooves and across the top of my jeans, stopping short of titillating across what would have been the top portion of my pubes if I had anything more than a neat Superman triangle a few inches below. His sip of wine is bigger than mine, a courage slump of the same urgency, which tells me something is wrong. Approach with caution.

Too nice and the rat makes me put my hands on top of my head; too casual and it's just killing another evening before we die or humanity ends.

He takes his suede jacket off and dutifully hangs it in the hallway, me noticing his small domestic gestures so uncharacteristic it's like a politician telling the truth and passing a lie detector test.

"Everything okay? With you?" he says.

"Everyone okay … with you," I mimic trying desperately to get back to whatever quirky, unmannerly version of me he thinks he lives with. "Feels like you rushed that jacket hanging that's all … and should perhaps have another go. Looks like the pocket is turned inside out. If you go to prison that might be the sign for all the hardcore brothers and right-wing Hitler lovers to butt fuck you in a long line one by one."

"Very funny," he says, seemingly returning to normal. "Why the wine?"

"Why your whine? Give it back I'll drink it on my own if you're not in the mood."

"It's not that, it's just that this is good stuff, right? Could smell it as I walked in."

Hope to Kerist he can't smell the low-density polyethylene that now seems overpowering, echoes of me practising the art of subduing a man around a chair without fumbling the rope or inadvertently waxing his eyebrows off, pealing up my nostrils and behind my eyes, moistening my gaze. I forgot about his bloodhound sense of smell; thankfully I've accidentally put too much toilet spray on because I was too lazy to reach for my scent earlier.

"Are you wearing the Tom Ford Private Blend Tobacco I bought you?"

"Exactly."

"Love it. Smells so assured yet cleansing."

Thankfully Febreze Heavy Duty Odour Eliminator combined with a nerve-settling smoke whilst expelling a day's worth of anxious digested provender equals the butt-plug lidded Tom Ford scent from Selfridges online.

There's a feeling of cowboy slow-mo as we walk down the entrance hall corridor, the moon's light blushing over the Mayan art at the other end, an inanimate snowfall encrusting the metallic baby elephant, hanging monkey and gaudy rikshaw. We're walking together, shoulder to (almost) shoulder, our tannin-stained teeth covered by tense lips above our drawn bulbous-glasses red wine pistolas, pointing upright so as not to spill but no less portentous. Acutely crunching imaginary lost bones, I hear his footsteps echo down into the foundations through the floorboards and he hears mine, my overt, fitfully worn Sophia Webster heels perhaps the final disclosure. As we reach the entrance to the kitchen, the unbroken intrusion of incorrectly calibrated lightbulbs hanging above the island bending through the door's slit only marred by the hinges, Kelly reaches for his pocket and drops beneath me, ostensibly readying for a tackle. This is one of those moment if you instinctively or fretfully hesitate, you are likely toast, smeared with a topping you haven't chosen or are unwilling to admit you enjoy.

Yet I do. Hesitate. Feeling myself hesitate renders me even more deer-like, Kelly's raising hand headlights and faltering knee freezeframing into double hand fanning isolated numbness. Arching his hamstring he drops, lifting his head slowly up, a small black box – open – beneath his chin. The moonlight, pissed to be wasting time on the Mayan tackathon art, averts its gaze, finding a rock square in the middle of the box, blinding me so I shield my eyes with my forearm and fall back all the way through the kitchen and into a pile of laundry in the utility.

"Will you?" his voice calls out as I smell a cleanish brewed amalgam of both of our semi-used garments, my face buried likely in his ManSize jocks. Shooing the assortment from my face, breathing like a horror film victim coming out of a bloody bath, then falling back beneath the Fairtrade cottons, scrabbling for stability and only finding Kelly's outstretched hand. It's still there when my focus refocuses: a big fuck-off engagement ring, away from the moon so duller yet no less apocalyptic.

"I can't imagine any moment without you," he says pulling me back to my feet but with enough of my resistance to sit cross-legged back down in the washing pile. Full circle, mum dropping the pile at dad's feet, opening scene. "And if you say no – which of course you can – I'll change whatever part of me needs changing, as long as that changing is happening with you. I know you don't approve of my career and that is about to change forever."

Throating lumping bouncing in my neck, intruding towards my chin. I almost go blind for a moment, this innocuous face staring over me, wanting all of me, forever and always, richer or poorer, obeying me while I try desperately to love and honour him. This. Was. Not. Part. Of. The. Plan. And bullshit: time doesn't stand still in these moments, it speeds up, the pressure of an acknowledgement, response, blink if you're being held hostage tick amplifies such that you actually hear time screaming at you, the deafening soar of wind rushing through an hourglass putting your temples on high alert and making your lips sweat. Every second I see the colour drain from his eyes, his hope and credence in the romance novel truism of me screaming "Yahessss" somersaulting up, flinging my arms around him like I'm catching an oversized beachball and lifting one leg just for comic effect dissipating. Did he genuinely expect an affirmative answer – have I been that good – or is this some form of test, a fraught lunge at the cliff's edge with only a smidgeon's chance of clinging on? His grip loosens on me as I feel my face flush with blood. Still in focus quest mode I think I try put a loving stare through my eyes without changing my expression, but likely this hops forth as a sympathy quiet before the rejection storm or perhaps even a semi-constipated look of wanting to get something out but having trouble. Just before the world ends and Kelly's head explodes, I reassuringly jump up and smile saying "Wait here," as I skip out the room, momentarily channelling Julia Roberts when she figured out she'd no longer have to splatter lube on a dry jonny with strangers for a living. Outside the kitchen I breathe for the first time in, like, forever, allowing appreciated oxygen to my brain, senses, motor functions and sensibility. Returning into the utility he's still hunched over the pile of laundry, the back wedge of his dark hair resting on his collar like a book on a bookshelf. His hunched demeanour is not resigned though, even optimistic from my exit strategy. When you know someone you just know their hunches and yours are not hunches but certainties.

The quack of the tape being pulled jolts his hunch into taut shoulders – having pre-folded the edge (picture me picking at the tape with a nail while my fiancée inadvertently consigns himself to a lifetime of humiliation) just right so I could extend a length of tape long enough to do the business with – and he begins to turn around, slowly enough thankfully for me to wrap his mouth and face once, twice, thrice. Covering his eyes gives me a slight advantage but his strength will count for something if I'm not quick. I think he voices an ever-polite phrase of "What the f——" before the lined grey tape turns the murmur down to nothing more than a veiled bark. This is the bit I was dreading but knew was an absolutely necessity as Kelly stands up and stumbles around, bumping into the clothes horse and kicking over a wellington boot or seven, a man with a concealed face on fire. Swinging through a person is not as easy as it looks in action films because following through for maximum effect is met squarely by a rigid skull. Now I didn't want to kill him with the blow – that was kind of the point – but he needed to be fly swat stunned so, at minimum, you do what you like to the fly without popping his or her tiny body. The nearest extended swinging device, let's call it, was the antique guitar Kelly had collected from a Korean designer, displayed in all its glory in the entrance hall. Wasteful, yes, as I did quite like the guitar, but poignant as Kelly had never really even played a chord – absolutely. Upon entry the guitar followed through quite nicely putting his stumbling back onto his arse with a nice soft landing into the now ever-present laundry pile. As he was still lucid and upright I swung again, supported by a mid-swipe apology, sending most of the guitar to the four corners of the room and Kelly L-shaped, falling sideways into a part of the laundry pile dominated by socks. Time to wrap this up. Time to wrap him up. Binding the hands and feet with the duct tape was standard really as there was no mule kicking or struggle. I could see one of his nostrils, distended beneath the tape in a felled oval, lifting up and down for air, so we were all peachy on that front. Once bound with sufficient precision and care I had to get him to the designated holding point I'd designed for this very capture and explain this was for his own good; try to explain.

Using the vast majority of a roll of duct tape is easier than you think, binding his hands and feet in an eight shaped loop to the sturdiest radiator in existence as well as through oak floorboards where I'd made enough of a gap to feed the ends through. I felt bad – I'll be honest – not only for the girls but Kelly, looking like a fetish game gone horribly wrong, more tape binding his appendages to immovable parts of the house than … well, there is nothing. My binding needed to last for at least twenty-four hours so it couldn't be tight and I'd left him within no reach of anything able to support an escape yet with enough water and food to survive until either I returned or police blasted through the door and informed him of my death or disappearance. I felt underhand, which is why I made a conscious decision to stay and make sure his head was okay – no blood or swelling to speak of ... yet – and try to explain what was going on. It was against my instinct and liable to cock up the whole venture but there was this small sympathetic non-sociopathic side of me that felt he deserved to know that I was being cruel to be kind; or being selfish to be selfless ... perhaps a bit noble for a person after these pursuits so scrap that and stick to the cruel-kind neater justifying-to-myself-really platitude.

It didn't take long for him to come to after I'd fully adjusted all the tape to allow easier breathing, access to the water bottles and M&S party food packs. Without even seeing his eyes I knew he was crying.

"It's like this Kelly," I began forcing myself to keep it as brief as possible. "I'm doing something that is bigger than us."

Through the tape it sounds like he screams "I know!" but I can't be sure and I can't risk him speaking or engaging in dialogue.

"Probably best for your own good you don't know anything."

Again he screams "I know everything" and perhaps "They all know." This is proving harder than I thought; never quite imaged he'd object like this.

"You've got to stay here so you are not part of what has been planned. It is quite simply for your own good. Not only am I uncertain what would happen to you, I'm more uncertain as to what I would do to you when in a situation of righting so many wrongs."

Again he mumbles something, can't make it out, but it is

either prohibitive or desperate. "I only wanted to fuck you," but the 'fuck' is two syllables so who the fuck knows.

"Please don't make this harder than it needs to be; you're a decent guy who probably deserves to be happier. When I chose you I wasn't sure you were ever right for this but you provided enough innocuous cover and freedom for me to scheme in the background. Without detection."

With that Kelly goes into convulsing meltdown almost breaking his arm and screaming at me, shaking his head well-nigh Exorcist style. There is nothing left to say or do here: Kelly is safe and that was the primary betrayal here, a necessary evil for a necessitous evil. Standing up I retrieve the engagement ring and place it on my finger as I walk out, closing the door gently behind me and locking forcefully as the night swallows me whole.

*

## Chapter 54

# TIME TO GO

It's go time.

Not a well-worn garden path in sight, this is actually happening. And despite what anyone says or prophesises from a sheltered soapbox, when fruition – or the beginnings of fruition – unleashes in that unwell-worn path towards the ever-elusive multiple Oh, you feel it. All the way down there. And perhaps because it is below the acid high-tiding in your stomach like a scientist swilling a beaker in front of his eyes or perhaps the collective (no, we don't all have our period together but women do feel a queenship when properly together) but, as I look at each of the girls' faces, there is a clasping effect, legs squeezed together across one another like a twisted murdering rope knot.

We're travelling in a plush minivan of sorts with each couple paired on blue-maroon sofa-like seats as we bomb down a deserted country lane, the power of the lights from the vehicle mismatched with the country landscape and sporadic banks of mud and growth appearing suddenly to sometimes deter the driver. A few of the boys, more prone to a city existence, marvel at the remoteness and creepy darkness, spotty teenagers riding a horror rollercoaster. Despite the anticipatory frivolity or sexual madness there is that sense, that pounding, that leg squeeze cork to keep everything at bay: we're in one of those air raid war films where we're about to jump from a plane to rescue some hostages, only we're also going to betray some of the other jumpers. Debz is on the far end to Digby, with Sexton/Francesca still fawning over her, their feminine hands grabbier than when they had black hairs above the knuckles, the proximal's shine now more effervescent than their forehead. Kieron is asleep and Tabby's boobs bounce almost in unison with the potholed road, the silent thunder after counterintuitive noisy lightning; Digby watches from afar never missing a flutter. Danielle nervously nibbles on fresh air whilst Renea vapes against the rules. Barton anchors the van, in the corner and appearing jammed into said corner, the van likely to float away without his intervention. Gwynne looks like she's seething next to Damien but I believe is likely going through the plans in her head, astride Damien with a t-shirt that would have looked tight on a weedy 12-14-year-old boy. Gerson, bug-eyed, staring out the window, momentarily landing on Danielle's lap every now and again; and Willow points his nose at the open window to absorb the fresh country air. Jemima doesn't have time to even roll eyes and looks even more calculating than Maggie, running scenarios through her head, voracious at the outcome. I sit alone, no

Kelly, but near enough to the hired driver to appear coupled up. Thankfully the topic has not been obsessed over, the can far down the road in a gutter pool, as I've said he'll be arriving later because of something to do with his mum and, without any real alone time with the girls, my word has been accepted. I am hopeful the evening's festivities will shy any attention away from my obvious (even if well intentioned) perfidy. But the girls have their hands full, each Boyband boyfriend sufficiently needy and engaged to require constant monitoring, pandering and remaining in character. The journey is longer than anticipated which serves only to rachet the tension up for me, the dial love pumping way past eleven, with each axle-bending bounce along the now dirt abandoned road splashing more acid along the digestive tract, unearthing places I didn't know existed. At a point we all know is about halfway, an abandoned chicken battery warehouse jutting almost into the turbid track, I see Jemima's concern at the transport of some of the heavier machinery along this path. She smiles and rubs her thumb and forefinger together which I know to mean we should have spent more on logistics to ensure the designs arrived as they should have, on time and on spec. We'd previously been under far more relaxed circumstances during the day to test drive the episodes but, what with the urgency of getting this set up and booked, we'd not had full access to the set up and some of the devices had not arrived when we visited. So we'd had to put faith – backed by above market fees to incentivise – in the event orchestrator in conjunction with the machine designers. At these moments there is always a sense of expectations not being fully met but the hard relationship work done at the outset and the belief in the capitalist repeat business model told us that we should pull this trigger and let the Boybands fall where they may.

Upon drifting into a reminiscent place, replaying many of the events that have led each of us to this point, the couple murmur hum now only a dribble of comments, words and niceties, the mood is sickly sweet pancake flipped, a light switch going beyond on to 'awn' when the gravelly road unexpectedly ends, replaced by a smooth wooden bridge, shutting even the chattiest Kathy of the boys up. The slats of wood resemble a train, the intermittent clackety-clack signalling we are nearing the venue. The bridge dissects a lake of sorts, lit dimly by some purposefully broken lights to only reveal slightly more than the moonlit sky. Across the body of water, in the distance, is a clump of trees obscuring the tips of the Gothic-looking towers and turrets, haphazardly peering above to tallest trees at varying points of depth upon the spoilt oncoming thrill-seekers.

"We're here," mutters the driver, slowing to a canter to respect the age of the bridge and add to the immersive experience. His brief of not engaging with any of the guests has thus far been on script.

"Ooooooooooowwwwwwww," Barton chides in response, a clear indication of trying to hide fear by demeaning the experience.

"We're all super scared," tuts Damien flexing his outer shield for protection.

"Come on guys," interjects Tabby. "This'll be fun."

"Remember what we promised," says Debz, the girl taking the cause to another level by sprinkling the unsaid taboo, all eyes now undressing her as we approach the hatted archway of natural growth.

After a brief interlude, intense darkness, the van's light no real match for nature's canopy, we enter a lawn fronted clearing eliciting an undeniable collective gasp from the travelling unwitting party. Lit in all the wrong disturbing places stands the haunted mansion, resplendently Victorian horror, steep angles, dark grey, decaying woodwork compiled across more wings, towers, rooms and turrets than any of us have ever seen, the lopsided and mismatched heights of each tower and the extended back girth of the property all held together in menacing fragility.

"Wow, you girls fucking nailed this," says Kieron, now more awake than he had been in years.

"Do people actually live here?" asks Willow. "In the off season?"

"This is bookable only four times a year," says Jemima. "The rest of the time it is restored, added to and enhanced for little adventures such as ours. Don't think you get more top notch in the haunted mansion immersive experience really, like the Masters … keeping the course pristine for only the best experience. So if you dickheads aren't scared shitless, then they've failed. Then we've failed."

"How long are we here for?" asks Gerson.

"As long as you live," says Gwynne. "Or as long as you are able to survive."

A large genial groan meets Gwynne's declaration.

"And we really needed to bring nothing; nothing whatsoever?" asks Digby.

"It has all been provided for you," I say. "Your other halves equipping the experience to a level where you will lack for nothing. Top notch everything. No visitors. And despite the living crap being scared out of each of us, there will be time to luxuriate in unparalleled decadence: this firm sets a new barrrrrrrr."

The word bar is interrupted by the minivan coming to a shuddering halt, careering for a few seconds on the laid gravel, shy enough of the property to hint at a foreboding approach walk to marvel at the ominous grandeur of the looming estate. With our footsteps crunching the buff stone Cotswolds chippings, the steep roofs become more obscured by the jutting balconies, adorned with carved shapes and spindles, painted iron railings chipped and scuffed, containing enclaves of moss and darkness. The round and cone shaped towers together with carved gables, now out of sight, give way to irregular sash windows as our herd transgresses towards the large front porch, each dormer its own unique protective skin from the outside world. Rain distorted demonic carved stone creatures flank the porch as we enter, eight imposing bay windows each surrounded with an inimitable stained glass ornate design, jutting out from the house, peering at us and following our reluctant footsteps up onto the porch, the darkness from within almost shimmering.

A large blast of noise likely from a well-hidden set of speakers sets us all reeling backwards, Gerson almost tumbling back down the porch stairs but for Danielle's catcher's mitt reflexes. The sound, an unnerving blend of animal screech, breaking glass thud and nails across a blackboard, is timed to split the front door a crack ajar, just enough to welcome us into the feigned madness. A light appears from inside, rays dissecting between door and side panel, an alien ship's light from above sucking us in rather than up for the ubiquitous anal probe. Entrance granted.

A dimly lit behemoth of a room awaits, likely the largest reception any of us has ever seen, columns stretching, endless high ceilings somewhere in the rafters above, held unfirmly by two straight and two jagged lines of columns, some starting from atop a few wide intricate, dark wood staircases. Large, arched fireplaces crackle in the dark, spitting intrusive embers out like sprinkled dust onto worn hearths, the authenticity becoming difficult to deny. No tacky skeletons popping out of a coffin or goggle-eyed witch dropping from above; no big fake furry spiders or flickering energy inefficient bulbs. Just an atmosphere, thick with intent, the air sticky sludge escorting the stale smell as authentic as the dusty old curtains ruined around the bay and across internal balconies, littered above double doors and ornate furniture. The hardwood floor creaks beneath our feet, tilted mini hallways disappearing in ten different directions, expensive oriental rugs from cornice to cornice dotting the path into further darkness. Subtle enough to be noticed if not studied in detail, a stationary carving with its head missing and the unmistakable appearance of moving severed limbs, a Paralympic sprinter of sorts, joined by other unexampled stone beings, cast unnatural, perverted shadows across the floors, walls, door and drapes. No one says a word or screams the childish 'Helllloooooooo' to hear the echo, such is the genuine apprehensive ambiance. The Haunted House delivers. The door slams shut behind, causing a ripple wave heart buffet flinch across the group, pursued closely by an old-fashioned locking sequence. Then the lights go off and everyone starts screaming, especially the Boybanders, drowning their legitimate fear through that old trick of pretending to act like you feel to show everyone you're feeling the opposite. But something is a bit different, perhaps the setting or the fact that it is becoming hazardously real what we are about to try and where the sign marked 'Point of No Return' is going to sit up, the uninvited skeleton in the box on one of those middle-lower fairground rides. Us girls all have that sense we are now fully in control; I feel it and Debz and Renea's warm palms reciprocate the sentiment in the dark. That is until the lights go back on.

All the boys are standing together, somehow separated a few feet away from us, their heads looking anxiously around but almost a different kind of fear, a prophylactic nub. Each of the girls looks uneasy, separated from their targets, momentarily placed swimming motionless in a demoralised barrel. Then they started walking away from us, a military march with the synchronicity of a well drilled army, think North Korea over the Kingdom of Eswatini, each of us now groupies peering above one another to see where they are headed. A table of sorts with smoke billowing forth, cascading over something upright and uncharacteristically colourful, out of place amongst the gloomy greys, brunet browns and dusk blacks. Two tables in fact as my eyes zero in on both; two tables of pulchritudinous cocktails billowing dry ice between candy-stripped straws, long gaudy exotic fruit and plastic toothpicks. En masse they all veer left, anchovies steering away from an approaching shark as we collectively gather our wits and attempt to re-join the class.

"Cocktails for all!" shouts Barton turning on his heels and heading us all off at the pass, picking at least four of us up in exuberance. Digby and Kieron, startlingly deft lieutenants for one, flank Barton's already thick thickness, causing an impenetrable puppy-dog-excited viscosity, the mere possibility of any form of alcohol sucking the frat boy nature into action in true brewsky chugging readiness. We're held up by three Boybanders, our physical space invaded once again involuntarily as a man shows off his supposed ability to dominate materially. If there ever was a time for a unified knee to the groin or palm to the nostrils, this was it, but it might just jump the gun and floor the experience before it has even begun. Lifted high above my colleagues in crime as I squirm up and over Barton's hairy, sweat-laden forearm, I notice that there is pink smoke erupting from the table the boys are at and blue smoke from the one where no one is. I see Jemima and Danielle notice the same thing and shoot a quizzical glare over at the remainder of us cheerleaders, raised aloft like a starting to kick and shout ragdoll.

"Time to put the ladies down now," says Tabby glaring at Barton.

"I will not," says Barton in defiance, Tabby falling over in desperation to get at him.

"Cocktails for boys and girls," yelps Francesca. "Oh my gawd, I wonder which I qualify for now." They immediately snatch a blue glass to toast and down.

"You don't deserve one really," says Willow also angling away from the increasingly dispersive group as the ruckus subsides when Barton, Kieron and Digby adapt their tight end duties from blocking to receiving the blue cocktail, unbelievably not high-fiving for hindering us from joining the party. Obstruction is replaced by chivalry as each retrieves a smoky pink glass for his partner, leaving me to annex my own, the last remaining cocktail complete with broken pineapple piece and bent straw atop a crumpled tablecloth. I look across and all the blue bubbles are already being tucked into, the boys obviously eager to take that edge off prior to the evening's festivities.

"What if I want the blue pill?" asks Maggie reaching a hand towards Digby.

"Well then you can have it," says Digby downing the hefty volumed beverage in a few violent gulps then handing Maggie the glass. "It's all yours."

"Can I get another one of these?" says Damien. "They're so good and even taste low-cal."

"I wonder what happens next?" says Gerson.

"Bottoms up ladies," says Danielle. "I suppose."

We all take a sip and the taste is sophisticatedly sweet, moreish sweet which denotes another sip then another, the peanut gallery looking on in dumbstruck support. Danielle takes a bite of her kiwi shaped like a pentacle and Debz spills a bit down the side of her mouth and into the caverns of her cleavage, an explorer lost to the light of the world until shower time. Tabby necks all of hers after an inaudible taunt from Barton suggesting she can't do it and Renea chews all her ice before settling into quenching a thirsty palate. I'm near to being one of the last to finish mine, a slight tingly burn at the unknown concoction of expensive booze on show in the most untheatrically unGothic moment of the evening thus far. The drinks had obviously been thrown in as a little welcoming extra, a precursor to the eat all you can in the dark haunted medieval buffet feast planned purportedly for the next few hours. Tabby stumbles backwards, but I think nothing of it; then Maggie follows suit. The concern becomes real. Danielle is the first to fully collapse, a lone bowling pin falling flat and sending her held glass into innumerable shattered pieces at the feet of the Boybands. Then Debz falls forward, Digby catching her before she lands on her front teeth, only to neglect Maggie long enough to allow her fall's crack to splinter a tooth. The lunging forwards first to help her, then sideways to steady it. All. Goes. Black.

Nothing but darkness, pessimistic murky darkness, my cheek flush against the wooden floor and someone pulling at my heels. Was this all part of the act, the experience, the deal? Or more sinister than even a haunted house. Girls screaming and shadows pushing over my eyelids but unable to open my eyes. A sense of joyless motion sickness. Then that darkness you'll never remember.

# Chapter 55

# VIRGIN'S VI®GIL

Waking up to tied up tits is different. Looking around seeing seven other sets of tied up tits, perfectly round and sprouting from a double-looped rope knot is only marginally more distracting that discovering you are hog-tied on your knees and there are seven Boybands wearing Jemima's GoPros on their heads.

Seriously, where were the tits planning to escape to?

A few groans derive from either side of me, groans muffled by rope; realistic groans succinctly intermingling emotional failure, cerebral ache and realisation shock. I hear Debz belt out a helpless scream, a sea creature flopped onto land for no apparent reason (and not in the evolutionary sense either). I can smell oil too and my skin is wet with this oil, baby likely, buckets of the stuff dripping from every nook, cranny and pore, the golden surface reflecting still candlelight in milky waves. We're in a different room, a ballroom looking place with a long table, food exposed and irresponsibly eaten, carcasses of pre-prepared delicacies bitten once and discarded in decadence, wasteful, neglectful Boyband appetites on show. The rope is wound tight around at the back, where my wrists are joined to my feet in close proximity. A riata of two strands extends up my naked back and around my neck then crossing down across my chest to encircle my breasts, sparklingly drenched, the rope digging into the groove underneath where erogenous gravity has started to show its worth. From the corner of my eye I sense a kerfuffle as Willow, ostensibly drunk on a jungle juice herbal beer perhaps, urinates on Jemima then – relishing such control, confidence literally gushing in a yellow-brown spout from his horrible withered bent stick-looking cock, the foreskin longer than the actual hose – moves onto the line of bound prisoners including lucky old me. Lucidity is further apprehended when Damien spends a few minutes reminding us with the flat palm of his hand just how precarious our situation is against his power, his shirt off and enough of the stash of oil used on himself, channelling anyone from WWF. But this isn't set-up, contrived or rehearsed; this is real with peril, unpredictability and a true sense of what the actual fuck have we got ourselves into here. I hear Gwynne crying which I don't think any of us have ever heard before.

Digby leans down closer to me, the stink of his face skin up close against my pulsating nostrils, his head clasped by the action-cam head strap camera mount, the GroPro channelling Hal 9000 in red blinking menace, my face likely a cow-looking, bedraggled, oiled up porn princess in fisheye 4K.

"Doesn't feel too good to be on the receiving end, does it?" he says leering forward to lick my clavicle then my chin then my ear in a strange sequence of maltreated body parts. I can smell the coke from his nostrils and the Dutch courage barrel of wussy alcohol-lite fruit-flavoured martinis and Jell-O shots. I politely indicate for him to loosen my rope gag to talk, my eyebrows the primary translation mechanism.

"Your silver fork tongue ain't coming out bitch. Well maybe for something else. Everyone here knows what the fuck you bitches have been plotting."

Some more disorderly turmoil to my left, Danielle I suspect, Gerson feeding off his brothers' intent and no longer forced to play the onlooking orbicular-eyed support act. He's feeding her and she doesn't want to be fed, interrupted by Kieron, joint in hand vaulting onto the dining table sending seven trays of beef wellington, couscous salad, boerewors, quail eggs, orange caviar truffles, baked Alaska and mini breaded plaice goujons tumbling to the floor, the shattering of ceramic bowls now another hazard to avoid against our naked flesh.

Taking a long toke of his cone shaped doobie he begins: "Oh you girls almost had it; had us; by the short and curlies," unable to resist picking his nose and eating it. "But all this talk of gang bangs, blow bangs, sharing, swinging, watching, all just seemed a little too intent to get us to this place of haunted repute. It broke your characters of always the best for yourselves – suddenly we were in the pound seats and it all just felt wrong."

He kicks forth another bowl of perhaps skinny fries,

landing on Renea's lap in pieces. Francesca has lined up beside us, wanting to be part of the gang, their twisted roadmapped body causing more averted queasy frowns adjudicating that their only weapon remained girl-on-girl somatic avowal, the carnal desire not in any way diminished by being overlooked. Sexton begins eating the skinny fries from Renea's lap.

"And all this just so you could make a buck. Greedy bitches syphoning off our celebrity just for a laugh. All these contraptions just to make us look silly on social media and for you to sell to the highest bidder. Laugh at the Boybands. That's what everyone loves doing! And what everyone is willing to pay for."

An ephemeral silence descends as the oil starts to sting my eyes. I blink a few times and gather eye contact across the room for those still kneeling: Tabby, Gwynne and Jemima.

They don't know.

They actually don't know.

Which might just provide the smallest possible modicum of hope as to what might happen to us from here on in. Had they known our limitless true intentions this could be far worse … debatable whether a forced rape gang bang is preferable to life imprisonment or death but still … there's hope. I see the same flicker along the line of captives. The only way they'll follow through is as a collective, their performance failures bound to come to the fore and be replaced by vindictive violence. The real chance is appealing bilaterally where I am at a loss without anyone to appeal to, yet I can help I'm sure. Debz flops back to kneeling from under Digby and Barton, screaming.

"Let's let the bitch speak," says Barton taking his saddlebags of lard from her person. They lower the rope from her mouth, letting it rest gracelessly between her chin and bottom lip. She speaks, her kind voice a kind of tonic for us all.

"How can we partake in any of this in the right way if our mouths are bound?" submits Debz (ah, you good girl) getting the bilateral communication lines back online. "It will improve significantly if we can use our mouths. Some of you prefer that I understand?"

The boys look anxiously first at one another which swiftly turns into triumphalism, high-fiving, whoop-whooping each other but no one taking the reins just yet, a swarm of flies circling Debz, the heroine guinea pig. When, backslapping each other forward as a communal throng, they descend on Debz, she yells again, "We have to be able to use our mouths!" hopefully freeing some further persuasive rationale. This works as each Boybander pairs off to remove the mouth rope leaving me unattended and thus still voiceless. This is hopefully that moment men regret giving a woman any sort of voice in this world because it is our last true hope to salvage this situation and add the 'un' to scathed. I'm shoved down onto my side, the angles of my contorted bound body preventing any real observation but undeniably this is working. I see each most of the boys agitatedly turning the girls' faces away from them, unable to shift the cowardly lions in the room but female lips moving – fast and furious even if facing the opposite wall. Then the undeniable effect, they're all kneading in agitated desperation with not a single possessing the intended snooker cue, turning to make the tricky three-ball corner shot with only a rope. A line of small, ugly, dangly depressed worm heads hanging in shame, protesting at the moment of truth. Invariably and expectedly this leads to further vicious acts, the coercive dominance a flawed tactic to ensure the mini soldiers pay and stand to attention for the battle. No. Such. Joy. The girls, my girls' mouths lifting the tone of the room, I hear words preventing rape, words leading to violence but keeping intact that most sacred cherished ideal not many men understand.

Consent.

You know that moment in film when all hope is lost and the heroines are staring down the barrel of too many shotguns and the door gets kicked in with the saviour on a white horse? Or let's get more relevant, say End Game when all the ashen, floaty, start-of-their-careers actors come back to help those saying farewell to a tired character arc through those flaming circular portals; or to embrace DC-equality and involve the woeful Justice League, when Supe, realising he's been dicking around too long pitches up to shatter Steppenwolf's horn and dreams by making it the unfairest fight on screen? I hear the door shaking behind me, clearly someone trying to get in while the boys fiddle inoperably with their malfunctioning apparatus, pulling furiously along the full inch and a half from base to end, squirting more oil while swapping to beat other Boyband partners, many reattaching the stifling ropes to stem the flow of reason. The doors are shaking! This I know but no one else does so without any viable way to succour this outcome all I can do is lie like a beached whale on my side, hoping the cavalry is literally at the door. Willow notices the commotion so I draw his attention to me, convulsing forward on my side, all parts of me moving in different directions: multiple worms for Willow's bass mouth to feed upon. When he arrives he hits me with the back of his hand and takes hold of the knot between my feet and hands, his puny strength unable to lift me towards a presentable angle, so he stumbles over me face planting into the wood and breaking his nose, the scream drawing more flies, helplessly throwing in the towel they've seen on fuq.com a billion times. But I'm now the centre of attention as each of the unmunificent seven surround me, planning to take whatever inadequacies remain on the self-appointed leader of the gang, the one with no claim to Boyband in the room. My darkness is established, each blocking out the remaining shards of candlelight, a flabby, pared, putty oil spill of pasty skin, swollen fists and bad teeth. I imagine I'm Hulk, turning green underneath the swathe of uninvited, unsought, unsolicited Boyband, exploding out of my ropes sending them aeronautical, winged quadruped gnomes that they are landing as far away from each of us as possible, distorted neck, knee and skull breaking the fall. Something does happen though because although my skin remains oily-copper, I feel the pressure relieve, the re-emergence of light onto my tightly shut lids, even warmth from the candles' flames. It might be time to sneak a circumspect peek as the noise surrounding me is different:

female anxiety replaced by a lower timbre's angst. There's a gun in Barton's mouth and Digby's temple is bleeding, slumped against the bulbous dining table leg, touching his temple with intermittent care. I see a baseball bat being wielded above my eyes, spraying Boybands like popcorn at a horror screening and a shiny black gun removing persons through applied pressure to the cranium. I am completely free of Boybands now and snap and wriggle back to my knees to witness the destruction. It's him. My mystery man. My stalker. Our saviour. Oh gawd ... saved by a man, us damsels in pulsating distress. Beggars and choosers though. And grateful, more grateful than he'll ever know, although ending up in trouble when Francesca slams a bowl of roasted lamb on his head. Collapsing onto one knee he drops the gun and the metallic bat, stunned just long enough for Kieron to charge towards him. Renea, having spent the better part of this episode sawing at her ropes with the shards of the skinny fries bowl, frees her hands and lunges at Kieron, taking him completely off his stride into a fallen purple drape. Dazed, not confused, our man reacquires his gladiatorial munitions but clocking that the real artillery would come from collective solidarity in us free to fight as fit fisting females, flinging as many sharp knives from the dining table towards us, in particular Renea, now slicing damp ropes on the hoof. Completely unnecessarily and creating more danger than dealing with the Boyband threat directly, unnamed 'I'm holding out for a hero' attends to me, sweeping my hair from my forehead, covering my body with a loose cushion cover and wedging a knife between my hands and feet. Ah the freedom when the rope breaks, my muscles no longer taut in servitude and free to free my neck, boobs, ankles and wrists. His eyes, lustrously shiny, burnish in front of mine, a slightly endearing mix of sympathy and splendid adoration. Until they go dead.

# Chapter 56

# DANIELLE

Danielle would require the kitchen and the bathroom. But first the self-styled Medi-Tent, dabbing the side of her temple while the aftereffects of the drugs wore off. We'd discovered the concoction was good old, solid, ever reliable, lacking a bit of originality Rohypnol, but a quantity worthy of killing the average human. For good measure and to ensure a quick felling of a formerly coherent Boyband girlfriend, they'd played immature chemistry set experiment armed only with scant concern for welfare, drug documentaries and Google, mixing a potentially fatal assemblage augmenting DateRape101 with beta blockers, bee sting antihistamines, benzodiazepine and diazepam. Varying degrees of lethargy, drowsiness, fatigue, impaired motor coordination, staggering, hurling, cramps, induced periods, blurred vision, slurred speech, bipolar mood swings somewhere between depression and euphoria, confusion, skin rashes, diarrhoea, constipation, anxiety, headaches, blackened stools, dry mouth, lesions, migraines and swollen throat glands had presented in all of us, the recovery to a semblance of functioning normality more difficult than fancied. Moreover, sprinkling in the physical blunt force trauma, emotional fatalistic mental health impact and general disquiet as to the perceived failure of the venture, fox force eight were waylaid into inactive recovery for far too long. And the whole end thing, attempting to regain control and how badly some of that went – well … a clusterfuck of hindering giant skyscraper hurdles with only a small pole-vault to hand.

Danielle's dent on the front of her nose had reopened in the fracas, which provided a steady stream of blood in perfect vertical symmetry to the scar: an upside-down exclamation mark of sorts, dribbling down the tear drop shaped hole above her top lip, slicing downhill across both lips and stopping only to drip at the point of her chin furthermost from her face, meaning she left an indelible breadcrumb trail of blood drops wherever she went. I could tell we'd been in the bathroom for some time deliberating how to get the party started because our feet were wet with her blood, all dots meshed together in circular heel and toe swipes across the blue and white bathroom tiles.

Gerson lay face up in the bath, his body bound with tape and rope then secured again taut as a guitar string along the pipes at each side of the Victorian bath. His eyes, saucers of unease and deceit, pinballed along as he followed our movements. The huge metal tube pipe, embellished rings at intermittent points, stood pointing down menacingly towards him, a giant metallic downward pointing canon, the fuse contained somewhere in this beautiful woman called Danielle.

"I'm not sure I was ready to go through with it," began Danielle. "Before ... um ... but now there is no other path. This has to be the way. He's got to get got for what he did and it has to be special. Then, as he's consumed he's consumed again. Mainly so I can shit you out!" she says, shouting at Gerson, so that he shook a few times more than he had been doing, a quivering child's toy.

"This was meant to be fun," I interjected. "But that might be out the window now."

"This is going to be just like one of our Wednesdays. You'll see. It will be fun. This is about us after all. Not him. Not them. Us and M&Ms."

Both of us in unanimity turn to face the lever, two chess knights with duplicative profiles, our cheeks facing Gerson to signal that we might be ready for lift off. He shifts nervously then has another furious attempt at unrestraining himself, pulling at the ropes looped back beneath the feet of the bath so only really serving to pull against his and the bath's own weight. Insensitive perhaps, but we let out a little involuntary chortle, not laughing at him per se but that feeling when something funny happens and you can't help yourself, even if you're not biting the sides of your cheeks. The reason for the reluctant mirth is that with every fish at the end of a hook struggling convulsion, the tap drips, hitting him squarely on his monobrow, flush between the eyes; and with every drip his swirling swollen pupils angle inwards to check out the unpleasant spatter. And come on, who doesn't laugh when someone makes themselves go squint? Old fashioned body contortion humour, but this one ever the more poignant and waggish. It's the tonic because it sets us both off until we are clutching our sides, sliding around in Danielle's blood until Gerson gives up the vain escape conquest and thus quells the squinty-eyed aerobics session under the dripping tap.

It's time and I'm so content to be around for this one, not only for its outlandish experimental nature but the obvious choccy-woccy benefits that should be available for a sneaky back of the palm extrication, even if the debilitating nausea lingers like piles. The lever is placed high up on the metal cylinder, particularly flimsy looking when juxtaposed against the magnificent sturdiness of the tube, as though it might snap off, especially when Danielle, not much above five foot (cough cough) will likely have to either stand on something (nothing readily in sight) or jump starfish style to pull the darn thing down, a tepid snap the worst likely outcome. I bend down to check that the flame heaters are positioned correctly beneath the bath, soldered segments of small metal pipes running the length of the tub, each with a dozen or so hole lines, uniform as a crow flies. Gratefully the ignition and dial are low down, behind the singular hot and cold mixing tap and thus behind Gerson's small brain. I walk over slowly and remove the tape across his mouth and, in desperation, he tries to bite my hand then resorts to spitting then pleading. The rope job is superb, placing him squarely facing the hole of the empty pipe, his high-pitched howls echoing up the hollow chamber then back down again. I look

at Danielle, then she looks back at me – both of us oblivious
to the Boyband hitting octaves previously unrecorded, and
we go in for the hug; a real proper woman hug bruv. I'm not
sure she wants to let go so I do so first and kiss the tip of her
nose, tasting her blood and stopping the bleeding. When our
eyes meet again I lick the remaining blood from my lips and
her eyes tear up but not an afraid tear or sad tear but a ready
tear; a go time tear.

"You don't have to do any of this," I say joining in the
waterworks. "You can walk away now and probably not get
into any trouble. It's not too late. But pulling the lever and
then some starts something——"

"Something I want to start. And not just because of
tonight. This is for all of us suffering at their hands. And I
still want to eat him."

In possibly the deftest 'embrace the moment' swoop I've
ever seen, Danielle – without being unkind or inaccurate to
describe as having a less than coordinated disposition track
record – skipped on one leg then pivoted, twisting mid-air to
grab the wooden-handled level down, pointing to exactly six
o'clock.

Then?

Nothing.

For an uncomfortably long time; so long that Gerson
began to acquire a newfound sense of entitled one-upmanship
privilege, a condescending exultation at our first failure.
Then something stirring from the bowels of the metallic
beast's belly chamber, a deep hum and shake then a bigger
shake and silence. Close silence until it kicked into

systematic gear, the clickety-clack of beads falling into compartments higher up the supply chain, the gun loading for lift-off. Then something unnatural, unplanned and unexpected: nothing came up but clearly not for lack of intent, the contraption pushing with the might of seven women going into labour, the build-up so intense, the agitation looking as though it might fly from the ceiling and spin around the room like a balloon being released. Then it happened. Oh my farking gawd, did it happen. The first one, expelled forth with such rancorous force – a red one at that! – it tore clean through his front tooth, the ten-pin ball sliding down the side at a straight controlling angle while missing the gutter and sending the outer pin cartwheeling into the darkness at the back. The red M&M lodges in his throat and we notice that the tooth has in fact been snapped rather than clipped at the gum, a serrated cartoon cat's smile decorating the end of the quarter remaining. Now imagine Kubrick's hallway blood scene married to the world cup of fireworks both on steroids, but with M&Ms! A kaleidoscope of M&M bullets fired in a metre diameter stream at Gerson's head, thwack smack jacking off in a myriad of directions after first impact, the ceramic bath's smooth angles pinballing the entire room with peanut (always peanut!) coated multi-colour (privately-owned Mars I doff my knickers to you) best-ever chocolates so that we're two small girls playing in a water fountain catching discards in our mouths while the GoPros on our heads take a brutal pounding which would undeniably be super cool in slow-mo especially as we've set them to one hundred and twenty frames per second! And insisting on topping up the supply seems the right call in the end because it just never seemed to end.  Long after the hefty bath was completely filled – Gerson's little body and previously pocked beehive face completely submerged inside an M&M prison, the countless shrapnel cast-offs forming a thick snow layer to mask the tiles and Danielle's blood with predominantly red M&Ms – it refused to quit, like an American fitness competitor's ass.  So much so that we exchanged nervous glances at the increasingly real hazard of drowning ourselves and Danielle even looked up with the intention of jamming the lever back to its starting position. Before this all began.  Before we learnt How NOT to Murder a Boyband.

*Chapter 57*

# DeBZ

Cross-pollination was to run deep, a revision of one-on-one personal retribution, but the new design had subplots like Digby, always wanting something he couldn't have, until he forcibly took it, a spoilt kid in a toy store shoving the pack of collectable cards down his pants when his mother said no. In Debz the first of likely many conundrums arose: with her vitriol directed away from the woman previously known as Sexton, did she have the conviction to take out the woman now affectionately known as Francesca? During the recent dining room averted rape and brawl, Francesca had clearly not been equipped to champion the aggressor status but there was little doubt she was a cheering from the side-line willing participant. Putting it bluntly: she hadn't attempted in any way, shape, form or protestation to stand up for her newly discovered gender and say 'Boys please don't rape anyone tonight or any other night. Respect someone when they say no and clearly don't provide consent and please don't tie their tits up like that.'

By now Digby was likely stewing in a metallic tub of bleach and Debz, reluctantly on squawking Francesca watch duty, representing the right woman in the wrong place at the right time, a litter of clown attire having erupted from the suitcase tucked behind the dark wood Aima Moucharabieh bedroom screen while Francesca lay bound face down on the cute four poster bed, was not in the correct headspace. Intimating that I might try sent my stomach into fluttering tremors with a steady reminder that half of our genetic code was likely from the same human. Debz, being allowed a definitive stance after a more horrendous ordeal than most, would be afforded the valid inquiry of killing a relative being more common than sleeping with one, the retort swift and clear in referring back to Debz's vision of a dual demise based on both! But we had to stick to instinct and what felt right – if it wasn't right for one or two of any of us then we shouldn't follow through and I certainly didn't want to be the coercive force behind future regrets. So all I did was persuade Debz to put on one single sexy clown costume, jump out of an imaginary box and see what happened.

Waiting outside the panel, tapping my bloodied foot with some level of needing to be somewhere else in another girl's fantasy just to make sure they were safe, out of view behind Francesca sobbing into a pillow, it would be fair to say at that point that nothing in this house of full-on repute could or would surprise me. But when it comes to Debz and the visual control she has over anyone with eyes I should be careful to be so assured. After scrabbling around behind the screen, bumping the apexed panel join every now and again for good measure, picking what she felt to be the best combination, Debz emerged as a sexy, scary clown. And it wouldn't be a stretch to say I stopped breathing; at least for an hour or two. Now I'm as straight as is considered normal nowadays but Jeez H. Christ did she look delectable. If a normal woman – no a supermodel – donned a bright pink afro wig, a blue and yellow boob tube, thigh-high green leather boots with laces all the way from the ankle to the starting ridge of the thigh muscle, white face paint, fangs, real blood splatters on the face from the previous attempted rape, a G-string patterned with recurring candy-floss pictures, angel-wings, nipple clamps on the outside, a strap-on and a big, red, fluffy nose, a normal person would likely marvel at the mash of motifs, tilt the mouth in semi-nodding approval and move onto the next Halloween disaster. With Debz though, you just wanted to jump her; in any way you were permitted … with consent of course. She never should have looked hot but I'm not sure she ever looked hotter, her body's proportions allowing for each fucked-up-clown apparel addition. Even the nipple clamps, so perfectly clinging on to her perfectly erect nipples like rock climbers with a last gasp survivalist instinct; the lumps of breasts hugged by the crop-top below a satin décolletage and sloping in mathematically impossible flawless proportions, two Labradors sitting in symmetrical obedient attention. My mouth opened slowly, my lips parting to ape her perma-pout, an expression you'd think she'd be used to. Then without warning, nudging or anything of the persuasion ilk, my expression perhaps indication enough of something magically 'the circus is in town' relevant, she ran to the front of the bed where Francesca lay, grabbing her weave and lifting her face to witness the concocted creation.

Hypothesis: does a sex change alter phobias, hang-ups or general fears, notably Coulrophobia.    Result: No. Francesca's scream, when confronted with this horror, aided by the dimly lit room, dark blue blinds and black night sky visible through small prisoner windows, rivalled the Exorcist girl's, both tied up on a bed for relevance's sake. She seized oxygen where she could, the sight of Debz's odd clown clamping down her lung capacity and involuntary ability to draw air into the cavity of the chest. Her face changed colour a few times, her body relatively still, while Debz screamed a reciprocating horrible scream back in her face, completely betraying her usual beauteous poise.

I stood by, helpful to the last breath, watching my half-brother sister take his her last breath.

*Chapter 58*

# MaGGIe

Trekking between rooms proved baffling, even psychedelically mesmerising. You'd get distracted by an old oil portrait down one of the countless corridors, usually an austere woman clothed in a dull grey ball gown staring down at your little soul, your little eyes judged, the sticky lines of brush strokes failing to mask her disdain. Apart from the lines of various heighted pictures, most of the corridors appeared the same which made remembering where we'd set up the seven plus one base camps incredibly demanding, an elaborate game of homicidal hide-and-seek. Sprinkle in the woozy, plastered nature of detaining and restraining prisoners not wanting to be either detained or restrained and the whole affair required more directional, organisational and wits-based savvy than ever your worst ever physics teacher could imagine.

Coming to a corridor T-junction, hearing a commotion on the left side, I could be forgiven for widening my stance in anticipation should what sounded more exigent than I was hoping to hear outside the torture chambers come tearing into vision and hang a swift right into my face. What went past my vision not only made me question my current consciousness and resultant sanity but also whether the girls had, after all, decided to add an additional element of gameplay to proceedings. A white naked apparition spat by, knees powering high and handsome, hands in pointed homage to Daniel Craig, discharging a continental pattern of blood from the mouth, landing squarely on a Napoleonic-looking chap with unreasonable sideburns too nonplussed to even face the oil painter. A moment late tore Maggie, equally fast, equally blurry, equally bloody but a fair few shades darker and clothed. Without wanting to distract the cop showdown chase, I joined the pursuit, giving Maggie a reassuring tone behind her so as not to disrupt her progress or startle her such that what must be Digby, fresh from his toasty bleach bath, escaped. Conscious that I caught up to Maggie quickly I didn't want to ruin her prize of prey so used my speed and ability to step off both feet depending on the corner to urge her forward. When Digby ran out of runway, appearing trapped in an extended cul-de-sac, he turned to face us and that's when I knew lacing the heroin with ephedrine to really heighten the solution urgency of catching the apple with his forked tongue was a bad idea. Facing us both, an animal trapped in the headlights he chose to go the other way and took a Superman dive at the small window at the end of the corridor rather than bust through our defensive line. On his back the words carved 'Invidia' would appear faded under his burnt skin, then flatten as he went for it, only really making it as far as his knuckles, the fortification of the window's frame not even reciprocating a polite wobble in return. Nothing gave. Digby stopped, full throttle dive, parallel to the floor a meter or two above it, then crumpled into a body-hugging ball, his fingers all shattered in diverse dreadlocked directions.

Debz needed a piece of that broken rapist.

# Chapter 59

# Danielle

Maggie and I had hardly dragged Digby two feet when another flying figure, this one brown and drippy, came flying at us, sending us both clattering into opposite sides of the corridor, Maggie the one to wear one of the frame's corners on the top of her skull. Gerson, eyes more swollen than usual, honied in chocolate giving off the most pleasant mellifluous saccharine odour, runs on the spot a couple of times upon seeing me before one swipe from the appearing Danielle puts him quickly at unconscious ease.

"Slippery little motherfuckers, aren't they?" I say snapping back to my feet.

"Who knew a Boybander could run so fast when confronted with a horrible relevant death," says Danielle wiping the rolling pin free from all chocolate residue.

"Please may I borrow that?" says Maggie politely securing the pin then lashing Digby until he quietened down to below church mouse but above cadaver.

"What happened?"

"Well," they both began in annoying unison, Maggie giving the conciliatory opening of the palm to habitually allow someone else to go first. Danielle duly obliged, eager to get back to whatever phase of the undertaking had been interrupted.

"When you left just after the M&Ms were all unloaded, I lit the heaters under the bath, eager to see how long it would take to cook him in a vat of chocolate. A girl wonders you know. It was a sight; I cannot wait to review the footage because it was unclear whether he would boil first or drown first and, as the colours melted above him, it was this like final impressive survival act to shake hard enough in the bath to spill the liquid chocolate and get his head above the level. And all the gooey heaven must have meant he was able to slip his small, masturbating hands from the ropes because, just as the bubbles were really going for it, he got free and bolted. But check out the parts of his body that were touching the bath."

Danielle flips his limp carcass over and dusts away some more of the chocolate from his behind. We all reel back in impressive veneration, as most of the skin from his bony butt is missing. If you're getting squeamish think of the kids okay! And think of this complicit fool ready to rape.

And failing all that, think of the music he's made.

# Chapter 60

# GWYNNE

Peering around a door, palpably petrified about what I'm about to see. I courteously knock, letting out a little old lady "Heeee-lllooooo-hooooo" in the process. The room is dark; well it is the actual dungeon, the designated torture chamber which might have never seen this sort of perverse filth before, a Boyband that is. An exclusive retreat, the imagination runs wild in a room like this: DiCaprio and his chums Brad and George all cavorting around, shielded away from the prying eyes of the world; the eyes this amount of money buys to keep shielded; the same amount we've shelled to secure all … this. The apparatus in the room is diverse, angular and intrusive – let's just leave it at that. The only light is from a spotlight that is fixed on two figures, one sitting on top of the other, a face smugger than any American dentist having felled a helpless Rhodesian leopard.

Teeth showing. Gwynneth. Not bared; showing. Unadulterated joy. The eyes giving it all away, twinkling gold in the spotlight's glare. Tears down each cheek. The lines of her veins pumping heartily from the exertion.

Smiling.

What's below her surely ain't. Smiling that is. Still alive though.

Remember it was going to be violent.

Recall it was going to be sadistic.

Recount it was going to be energetic.

More so than any of the others was the brag, the night the Discovery Channel led us from outlandish fantastical feminist revenge to slumber. To this. Come along way.

Chapter 61

# SINGLE FAULT
# COTERIE

"I am for rhe-ahl. Never meant to make your dawda cry, you should have apologised a septillion times, I'm sorry Ms Jack-it-in-Son …"

Is there a better chick sing-along on the planet? Not our genre, our taste or our disposition but, by Jove, so catchy we'll all challenge you not to be humming that in your mind right this moment.

Give it a sec. There you go. If you hummed it, take your palm (do it!) and put a rotund, thick-bottomed whiskey glass in it, fill that empty space with golden-tan hope (single malt bitches), lean back in your chair marvelling at the spreadsheet you might have concocted earlier in the day or the action items list you fucked right outta the town's meeting, and feel satisfied; content, even virtuous.

Because you deserve it!

Sing along. We're all doing it, calves flopped over the single sofas in utterly extremely comfort, comfortable in the knowledge that at least two of us have checked the binds that binds.

Between 'Ms' and 'Jackson' in an impossible space, Uncle lets off a rotten sounding, exertion singing fart that sounded like it stung. Too farking funny: so puerile it is actually laugh out uproarious which sees Gwynne get sick over the side of the patterned chair, a debated causal determinant between date rape cocktail, exertion of date raping armed with apparatus and pant pissing girlie sing-alongs. We're all plonked in a study of sorts, haunted and spookier than your auntie's cellar with an impressive collection of jammed bookshelves, not one book written before about 1700. We took a collective executive decision to take a break and smell the roses, understand where we were, why we were and reconnect (no this is not a punt for mindfulness) with the true reason we were all here: one another. And a complete state we were, the aftereffects of subduing males – albeit less courageous and buff males than say the World Cup winning rainbow nation of the year credited with the Beta variant but that really deserves to be more synonymous with that come-back fairy tale from seventh in the world to actual top of the Fuji-world – scribbled across most parts of our exposed bodies. Everyone always craps on about how much cleaner women are than men but, when not cursed with the foul stench of body hair and fat stinky pits, we girls have the luxury of smelling like blossoms while looking and feeling like we've been dragged backwards through the worst, most dense, injurious hedge on the planet then rolled in our own blood, a baker, butcher and candlemaker's wet dream.

Debz is still in her sexy clown outfit, the blood from her nose finally having dried up into an arid riverbed and the missing tip of her ear less noticeable. Gwynne, still smiling, looks marathon spent, most of her camouflage dry-blood attire not her own. Danielle looks queasy, a classic girls' night out gone wrong with a happy ending of too much God damn sugar. Uncle has bits of probably bone in her hair, lazily picking one or two out every now and again while sipping on the St George's virgin cask single malt. Maggie's blood to bleach proportions make her look like a red and white leopard and Tabby's unavoidable chest is completely soaked in blood, making those volleyballs in a sock look like they've beaten the entire volleyball team to death, double handed. Jemima defiantly smokes an actual cigarette, pushing the smoke from her lungs out into the world to purposefully hurt the planet in protest and me, well, would you believe I have an actual live male next to me. Resting. An honouree male, deserving of all that come his way. Our mystery hero dude with more explaining to do than Bill Clinton when the dress's DNA report came back cum stained positive. He's resting. We think. We hope. But we couldn't leave him alone. And part of the mantra has to be goodness, gender agnostic goodness: it doesn't matter if you're dicked, dickless, black, green or orange – your actions define what comes next.

We all take a substantially slaking slurp of whiskey, savouring the smack. The whodunnit man stirs, a babe in the wood of babes.

# Chapter 62

# Renea

Renea had to renege; Uncle had to undo. The turbine spinner remained in production, but in hindsight getting overly elaborate with this sort of vengeance-based murderous intent, can be, well, needlessly baroque. The industrial size fly swatter went through like a dream, Renea's cool charm meaning not only did we get a whack discount but a bevy of likely completely unnecessary, yet likely sick dope features that would have to be test-driven. Yet Uncle was determined to honour the turbine idea by at least gluing Kieron to the sofa before swatting him. This meant getting him naked: a challenge when we'd wound him tighter than Piers Morgan in the face of the Megan-induced Oprah gasp, at Philip's pondering of hue, likely a small talk replacement for eye or hair colour when that was more of a certainty.

The set of the room appeared almost warehouse-like, the clearing of an oversized bedroom to accommodate the swatter device. Kieron lay bound, gagged and bleeding in the middle of the floor, his odour apparent even from the doorway. To support Uncle we tooled up as best we could, bringing in some additional muscle in Maggie, Gwynne and Jemima. What we'd discovered to our general dismay when restraining Kieron the first time is that years of dope smoking can lead to superhuman bursts of power. Couple this with a general disposition of none of us wanting to get at all close to him due to his general hygiene and ability to transmit something onto us even more harmful that full-viral-load Covid, it was a team-effort, kid-gloves, maybe-have-to-each-adopt-a-stinky-limb-to-allow-Renea-some-quality-workshop-time exercise. The carpet in the room had been removed to reveal a patchwork of some wooded floorboards and concrete panels. The device loomed above us all, the criss-cross of the plastic net filtering light to pock mark us with black squares as our faces moved into functional get the job done mode.

His breathing was a faint shallow flutter when we got to him, so Renea began to untie his feet first. Once each leg was free, she unfastened his grimy jeans and pulled them off with the skill of a bullfighter. Maggie and Jemima each secured a leg, gripping the scrawny pipes close to their chests with both arms. An overbalance witnessed Jemima face plant forcefully into his crusty arse crack, a moment that would have to be cackled over at some later point. He didn't stir so Uncle started on his t-shirt before Gwynne and I each secured an arm, my hand regrettably slipping up the underside of his tricep, lodging in the moist, dank, black waves of his underarm hairs. Jemima didn't miss that either, her warning glance a foreboding 'See it's not that fun after all' reciprocation. At that moment Kieron went berserk, even before Renea could point the glue gun and begin applying superglue to his body (the sofa was already moist with about four buckets full), so we were forced to wrestle the alligator. And the sinewy, disgusting motherfucker was about as strong as an alligator but five very driven, carpe diem bitches really made it an unfair fight, this alligator destined for designer shoes before any real possibility of escape. Plus, after the earlier scenes, both Renea and Gwynne were in no mood to negotiate or leave anything to chance, so a combination of back hand punches to the face and another shot of the sedative we were starting to run low on soon calmed everything down so that we could flip him back over and Renea could draw snail tails of globby glue in mesmerising patters around his pinboard boils in various stages of ripe maturity. When we were afforded the opportunity to slap him onto the sofa, we took it, but the job was not really done because Renea wanted to ensure attachment was permanent, so she sprayed the remainder of the glue all over his front to bind as much of his exposed flesh as possible to the pre-fasted immovable cushions. With this much glue Renea knew she'd have to hang around for a while before it dried but this didn't seem problematic as a joint had dislodged from his jeans and, old habits yippee ki yay motherfucker, so Uncle had fired that bad boy up before Jemima had even doused her nose with my hand sanitiser.

Chapter 63

# UNCLE

"You didn't?"

"I couldn't resist. Him lying there, all squishy, it just made sense."

"That is wrong!"

"And removing his filth from the planet is less wrong?"

"Maybe I'm just sad I missed it; we missed it."

"It's there, all there; captured."

"You kept in on … for that!?"

"Look he did the same thing to me."

"I remember you saying, so wacked out, he just went … on you."

"He'd actually requested it previously, the filthy beast. So the uncontrollable staggering dope mixed with Malawian Gold routine might have been a ruse."

"Well, the, I suppose——"

"Okay so we've established that it happened, impulse of sorts, but fuck I enjoyed it. Because the glue was hard enough to hold him and, squatting low above his face, it stung him first, woke him, then watching him writhe to get out of the way of the golden split stream was cinematic gold, as you'll see."

"Water sports might be a bit too niche for our audience, plus isn't it only Germans who love that shit?"

"Sometimes girlfriend, you've got to get more with the times. This is so common practice: teenagers are adding this as third-and-a-half base! It's the power thing, control. I already had that so simply unloaded because I needed to go. And his smell couldn't get any worse so thankfully I'd not eaten asparagus for a few hours."

"People ask why a dog licks his balls——"

"Because she can. Precisely. And I told him. Figured it might be the last opportunity. Kept the diction clear and concise for the edits."

"And?"

"If you think being pissed on whilst glued to a sofa messed him up, you should have seen his eyelids when I reached around for pictures of when I was an Uncle Fester. Roly-poly then the other, then a few coughing spews and a thorough realisation that his macho 'I only bang birds' babe mantra was tarnished for eternity."

"Special. Not a long eternity remaining though. I mean, if that's the path you choose, the destiny you deem."

"I'm leaving it to the insect exterminating gods. That and physics. A fly's resilience is tested when wounded, when a wing remains. Even a fat, lazy fly has survival instincts."

"All that hiding up cow's arses and all. Country chic on

show for all to drive past, even the most ardent Gary Larson detractors unable to frown at that one."

*Chapter 64*

# Me

The timers on all the pre-set ovens and warming devices worked quite spectacularly, what those in the customer services trade would call a five-star experience. The house had been rigged with hidden mini speakers that sounded various spooky soundbites every time a gourmet meal was ready to be consumed. The first had been laid out in accordance with the initial dining experience, hot trays a little higher tech that those cute tea candle lit individual dishes you crave at Indian restaurants, with the remainder a combination of self-service from industrial sized ovens and rooms arranged to come to life as and when someone entered, a marvellous buffet take-away for on-the-gals intent on murderous maiming. With the initial scary sounds we jumped but after a period of acclimatisation we became nicely accustomed, tootling down to the kitchen, not out of place in a period drama depicting the inner workings of a Regency household, eager to feed some increasingly famished mouths, what with an appetite eagerly established in enacting vacuous celebrity retribution, the likes of which the world had never seen but which was shaping sweetly to sneak into that top spot, a hidden gem climbing the charts without any sane person's sentience. And as time floated by, and we reloaded the GoPro memory sticks for more keepsake moments, the implications of the acts didn't start to resonate, not one bit. Yet, perhaps. This was truly an immersive experience and the calling it provided to each and every girl on set was apparent: we were born to do this.

At times I felt like a sexy school head mistress, sticking my head around corners to watch the other smoking hot wet-dream teachers torture and sermon the unruliest, most brutally ignorant, unashamedly naughty schoolboy in the class. Admonish the little fucker, pontificating in rave spasms while administering puhn-eesh-meant again and again until it actually meant something; and there was something utterly cathartic about the experience, in complete contrast to the anticipatory guilt or squeamishness or gag reflex or fear. The Colonel Mustards with their floppy lead pipes had done it in the dining room to Miss Scarlet and this meant pulling their names from the worn pack; holding the cards aloft in triumph was a dish best served cooler than pissing ice cubes and from a place of moral elevation. Well, apart from the GBH, intent to harm, bodily violation and possibly the murder thing. At this faithful juncture, no one was dead and this seemed okay, a nice 'middle-ground' for now but potentially when the first glassy eyes stared back we could have a gal-pal-gaggle of wet shoulders replacing the 'I wish I'd never slept with him' with 'I wish I hadn't killed him' but aiming to end on a high with the Oscar acceptance speech of 'I wish I hadn't killed him … so fast.'

# Chapter 65

# Jemima

Girlfriend got vitriol, like she hungry faw it, wanting more. Acquisition not merger. Filling one's boots so they overflow and then the excess is cupped into new boots, not yet bought, but owned like a trade future or call option. With vitriol and the hunger for it came an unnerving efficiency, the likes of which neither Haunted House nor Boybander had even seen. Of all the girls, the champion of fierce independence was undoubtedly Jemima. Everything she touched turned to gold and that gold didn't sit in a vault gathering dust but got put to good use somehow, the sequel to Rumpelstiltskin more Wall Street with a heart of actual gold than say Die Hard with a Vengeance.

We were outside for this one, a chilly wind nipping in that gap between your collar and neck, left exposed by our now matted hair wrangling in clumps on top of the collar. From this vantage point the marsh was visible, thick mats of sedges and rushes interloping upon the moonlit surface, a tortoise shell missing some teeth. Willow was bound and gagged, blood tears rolling down from beneath the green bandana where Jemima has stuck her fingers in the dining room after the assault. She felt proud having accidentally started Mammon's disfigured tapestry, crying blood to expel the ecowarrior hypocrisy and embrace using it for selfish, greedy promises of future wealth. This season's Sustainability Funds still making copious amounts of money for the fund managers who then drive home, fucking carbon emissions as they whistle dixie in the Range Rover, drunk on all the light at home to allow their privately schooled kids illumination, eat a big fillet even though a million bottles of water have gone into the cattle production line not to mention acres of land decimated to feed the damn bovines before slaughtering the beasts for our orgasmic meaty pleasure, but all the while investing – putting the stain in sustainability. Willow's trousers were on the moist wood earth beside him and he was bound akimbo, each of his ankles stretched towards a neighbouring tree to make him look like he was in mid-bootcamp star jump. I discovered that Jemima had spent the better part of the evening rolling up fivers ('Fifties would have had more impact,' she'd said, 'But I'm not a fucking wasting money moron am I.'), dipping one half in petrol, placing the wet half into Willow's anus, pressing just past the irrigated line (all the while keeping the note rigid), letting go so that the note unfurled a bit (not much at first but he began to relax into it a bit more apparently, that or the money started making real inroads) and lighting the dry end: the fuse. She'd set up a spotlight and removed the blindfold in anticipation (classic Jemima), leaving the 90fps, 5k resolution pointed at the real impact of wasting money, watching it burn up his arse. She told me at first nothing happened and that he just looked a bit uncomfortable as the note died, a toddler who'd outgrown nappies still wearing them and going pooh-pooh in public when he really should know better. But then she pulled a few of the notes back to allow the petrol infused bit to stick out a bit, the path of rectal decimation nicely figured out by the thirstiest of our knowledge seeking princesses. The second this remedied enterprise took effect, exploding a little and setting the remaining hair Willow had down there alight, it was captured in micro lens detail as Jemima knelt, going all method handheld indie director on us for those Wayne's World inspired extreme closeups. And let's just say that any fears of Barton's little brother being an evil genius capable of exposing our exposition were quickly dispelled when he tried to fart the rolled notes out, the methane burst serving to further fuel the fuse, burning deeper, with more doggerel and satisfyingly longer. As Willow had focussed his raping attention on this part of Jemima, she felt it was only capitalist to return the favour: economic arbitrage at work, in the wood, that very night. On the floor at his feet there was likely over one thousand pounds of rolled fivers in various states of disrepair, some cigarette like, smoked to the filter and some malcontentedly half burnt, a disappointing semi with no one to grab a handful of liquid soap to help out.

As I put my arm around her, a congratulatory gesture of sorts, she shook free in a direction away from Willow after my one-armed hug had nudged her forward. She looked at me with annoyed concern.

"It could go at any minute," she said looking up. "Nature is unpredictable."

# Chapter 66

# GRATUITOUS

There are mercifully two meanings for the word 'gratuitous'
– two primary meanings anyway. And this is not for one
second defensive! When some busybody who hasn't been
through a modicum of the trauma we've been through utters
the woefully unnecessary phrase 'It's getting a bit gratuitous,
don't you think?' I'm standing, hips thrust forward in
combative defiance.

Loaded.

With the facts.

**Gratuitous**

1.   *done without good reason; uncalled for.*

The actual example provided is 'gratuitous violence', a

classic association, the obvious paradox of self-contradictory absurdity misplaced and actually more suited as an oxymoron, the subtlety of the enduring true contradiction always consigning violence to the unnecessary, unreasonable and uncalled for scrap heap. But ladies and gentlemen, and by 'gentlemen' I'm also hinting more directly at the moron in oxy, this is called for, shouted for, bellowed for. From every dark, isolated corner where a woman is taken from safety and put in the clutches of power or bullies or testosterone or selfish wilful rapey horniness, this is called or. How many gentle-men are there really in the world, forced to do the right thing if there are no recriminations? If Georgie Porgie, pudding and pie had no fear of the others coming out to play, would he kiss the girls, would he make them cry? Would he run away, the cowardly little shit?

Concession, yes, violence is just about gratuitous all the time. But the girls know this and, do me a favour and make it happen for me in case things go a bit awry, put on my gravestone in some idyllic English village down East Sussex way ...

**Done with good reason.**

Now I don't want to be one of those obnoxious win the argument at all costs know it alls, I'm always right bitches, but the second meaning is:

> 2.   *given or done free of charge.*

There's no numeric gain for any of us. Just a statement, a stop the madness plea in shameful, shocking, bright, 3D technicolour.

**Given to the world free of charge.**

# Chapter 67

# TABBY CAT

What happened next was an unlucky fuckup.

No one had had much sleep, combined with Tabby's general clutzy falling phenomenon, the hand-held wireless device was bound to have some early teething issues. And who knew Barton would emulate his ex-girlfriend's nickname and actually land on his feet? Luckily, I suppose, he charged in the opposite direction to us, his overriding fear – having seen the front middle portion of Digby's tongue, after a rather nifty piece of fork-tongue styling on Maggie and Debz's part – not ratcheted up to beyond where his bulk could have steamrolled us into an old fireplace or, say, jail, he chose to bestow a sneak peek of the device, a trailer of sorts, and barrel out of the window onto a neglected rock-bejewelled rose garden below. In those action films like when little Tom jumps between buildings, the arms and legs normally flail, like they're clawing the air to make extra yards. In reality, when hurtling towards an uneven, broken paved earth in a desperate quest for freedom, the subject stiffens up, so landing on both straight legs is, well, painful and very bad planning. Mainly due to both the legs snapping in two, the knees hyperextending back in symphonic puppetry. Blaming us is harsh and it's also worth noting his orthopaedic surgeon did recommend he lose a few stone to take the surplus excessive weight off the patella and ACL, both now some way off the large crawling, whimpering ton of Bart.

Perhaps pride would come after a fall in this case.

Getting him across the rocky decimated rose garden, through the front door, back up the countless flights of stairs, down never-ending corridors and back onto the device, upon Tabby's insistence, was no mean feat. Tabby's first foray into operating the converted dumb waiter had simply been premature, and he'd been quick to react, land and run. But this time, looking at the state of the malfunctioning Boybander, he wasn't likely skipping off anywhere, let alone towards the broken window, now an ominous reminder behind him of what could go wrong if you're a spoil sport and refuse to play with the lady and her remote control.

Slumped over, a resigned tramp, up motioned Barton. As he rose, the platform pretending not to notice the behemoth of man lard, ascending at scarily precise pace, the angular undulation of the base began to adapt. In Tabby's eyes, the tittle of kicking a man while he was down was absent, years of his cheating abuse front and centre, like Barton's chin, nailed onto his chest in abject dejection. Was this his ploy, play the sympathy card? Was Tabby's pride too proud to actually follow through, his wilful egging of her intent a constant stand-off contention? And one of the most contentious items, there in her hand being pushed and jabbed and deployed. She'd never been allowed to handle the precious penile extension that is the sacred remote control, as though being female and just changing the channel she'd alter all the mechanics and software in the device such that not a single new boytoy appliance would respond to the user until a padded and greased, hairy paw was back wanking the channels into boring docohorror submission.

She aimed. She fired. The platform gave way. Trapdoor. Horizontal release. Quickly Barton's surprise was palpable. And funny, like, YouTube funny.

*Chapter 68*

# DANIELLE

This was somewhere between Willy Wonka's wet dream and a mildly erotic bath oil commercial. Gerson was back in his spiritual spot, reattached after his momentary dash for freedom. The cooking had begun and clearly what they don't tell you on these cooking shows is that human is a dish best served sweet. Sick voyeurism aside, most of the girls really gathered to stick their fingers in the hefty chocolate fondue. Debz, still adorned as a mash up clown stripper seducer, brought marshmallows and Renea collected pokers from the abundance of period fireplaces scattered around the house. Together we were able to dip, lift above our mouths to catch the dripping residue then shove the mallow or dozen down our collective gullets.

Getting us all to the dunking mallow point, Danielle had re-established Gerson in the bath, immersing him back up to his eyeballs in a new stash of M&Ms. Gerson's eyes had in a strange way resembled the globular treats, she regaled those arriving late, lost in amongst the red-centric, muddy colour explosion. Danielle had proceeded to light each of the heaters below the bath, growing increasingly impatient at the lack of progress, before firing the whole lot of those bad boys up. The effect appeared lacklustre but for Gerson's wailing, as the underlayer apparently melted quickly without impacting the outer weight of nutty balls. As the slushy bubble pot homage to witches where we could spout Shakespeare and dance around the cauldron with our breasts out didn't really materialise, Danielle decided to turn most of the heaters off and slow cook Gerson. Make an evening of it, event if you like, immersing ourselves in the frivolous decadence of too much chocolate while Gerson's extremities immersed themselves in a new fusion cooking that was bound to catch on eventually.

Beelzebub chillin then heatin the tub.

# Chapter 69

# Me

Have you ever wanted to smooth away a man's hair while he sleeps? Does this tippy-toe ever so carelessly into fetish territory or is this, as parents might blissfully describe a problem child, 'normal'? I'm sitting beside my so-called saviour as he recovers, breathing slow, deliberate heaves of breath, his chest raising the old-fashioned sheets and blankets then lowering like a duvet settling. We're tucked away – missing the madness if truth be told but craving some recharge to maim time – a little corner room with an ornate fireplace, single bed, maroon single seater (with my sweet ass parked it in, doting in some way) and a red patterned rug not dissimilar to those psychiatrist charts always popping up rudimentarily in dated, clunky films, the symmetry overdone. The room is still, peaceful, like the only sane island in an Armageddon state where the zombie bitches chase after the lip-syncing good guys: the Boybanders.

Man X, or Man A perhaps, snoozes in front of me (the

lazy fuck) after his heroics. We've – or I've – tended to his wounds as best was possible given the situation so now, slightly sedated, he rests to regather his strength or whatever. So I plait his hair. Somewhere between boredom, adulation, an obsessive-compulsive fiddling disorder and the brow clearing fetish mentioned a few dozen inhale-exhales ago, I braid my gal-pal-who's-actually-a-cock-wielding-dude-maybe-hero's hair. Just the front bit, the fringe, so his dreads begin to look like the back of a peacock, a confused Rasta. My kingdom for some beads right now!

It looks funny so I turn the GoPro on momentarily, popping it on the mantle to capture the moment, a video selfie showing hair braiding gratitude for averting impotent rape-induced beatings, well … further beatings anyway. He did save us, I can't live in that denial bubble any longer, none of us can – a man saved our asses and paid some level of price, securing a pack beating with various cutlery before we were able to mobilise sufficiently to join in the fracas. He was jabbed a few times, blunt knife puncture wounds the Boybands would claim were self-defence but what do you call it if their original self-defence then led to offensive offence and ultimately our transferred self-defence through captain knight in shining armour here, still kipping with a plaited fringe?

For no apparent logical reason I get into the single bed beside him, spooning behind his back and adding my warmth to his angled shape. I'm probably not that good at affection, which is why it comes more naturally when the person is passed out like a cadaver in front of me, rendered useless by recovery rest and unable to either try mount me (as would have been the likely response of any red blood should that hint of affection be sacrificed forward) or quizzically stare deep into my eyes and soul, thus inducing a pukey, try-not-to-giggle soap moment where jacking someone off is easier than elucidating you have lesser feelings for them, the involuted door number two.

He stirs and I'm pathetic teenage girl nervous suddenly, behind him, easing my breasts away from his jutting shoulder blades. I'm almost kind of hopeful he'll let off a morning catarrhesque fart to decimate the moment but he doesn't, turning gracefully over and facing me in the bed. No confusion, no doey eyes. Just there. Right in the moment. Ball in my court to play cooler than I feel, my insides tightening, a banjo knot thumping down my ribs into the sploshy gastrics.

"I'm feeling good now," he says feeling his braids and laughing, a small laugh so as not to reinjure anything.

"I'm not really one for big grandiose gestures," I say. "But thanks are in order. Big thanks. Solemn thanks. Heartfelt thanks. From all of us. How did you know? We were here? Doing this ... thing?"

"Kelly."

"My Kelly?"

He takes on a reserved look, retracting like I've said something wrong. So to correct ...

"Kelly who I hang out with sometimes, live with and always make fun of? And never sleep with."

"He hired me. Initially. To find out what you were doing,

what you were about as there was nothing he was getting from you. He wanted to know what was behind the eyes of the woman he wanted to … marry."

"God, we've had that little moment. It sparked a – shall we say – incident."

"Did you say yes?"

"Did I shit, no! I bound him, gagged him, tied him up and left him to survive on some basic food and water while we all came here."

"Did you keep the ring?"

"Do you see it?"

"I saw it earlier. On your finger."

I shift more away from him now, trying not to accidentally drop off the side of the bed.

"So let me get this right: you walk in on a mass attempted rape, me bloody, constrained and naked on the floor and you notice the rock on my finger?"

"I'm sorry. It's all just worked out a bit different to what I expected. With you."

I can feel his stale breath now, uniquely stale blowing on my forehead, like he'd probably have sweet smelling morning breath if we were a normal couple and I woke him after a night of excessive drinking to kick him out of bed for a Nespresso or, even better, Sage barista coffee. He jumps back in, replacing what might be his strange unfulfilling quest with functional information dissemination, the first overtly male thing he's done all evening.

"In the beginning I gave Kelly everything I found. On you. All the historic links to each of the girls and the connection between each of them and their Boybands. The blackmail attempts with Deborah were the easiest and, once the first domino fell, it became quite easy to uncover what you and your gang of merry women were up no, just the why remaining elusive."

"Do you want me to perform the answer in mime? Didn't you see enough earlier? What happens when men assert power over women? Normal fucking societal behaviour."

"You don't have to explain. I get it. Think I got it a while back and wanted to be a part of it. Wanted to be a part of you."

Feeling the cold line of a tear slip past your usual defences down a cheek is not natural and, for once, I'm not afraid to leave it there, evidence that suffering is your own. He doesn't wipe it away either, wanting it out as much as me, pulling for more if they exist. He's still, not dead frozen still, just understanding still. Like he wants to tell me, confess to me, but is allowing me this moment so as never to be accused of coercive tactics in a vulnerable compromise.

"Kelly, despite my growing resentment, always did have your best interests at heart. He knew you were planning something big, something that was going to get you into a shit ton of trouble, so he wanted to stop it, talk you off the ledge. We were due to meet prior to this excursion but when he didn't show, I figured I had to follow through without him."

"I didn't want him to be a part of this. He's my one selection mistake. He didn't deserve what these pretenders are getting. And not that he was too good for it, just that he was too boring for it, not hiding his menial behaviour like the rest of them, just void of it. I wanted him spared."

"I think he knew because of who your father was there was this destiny quest with the whole thing, which is why I never told him. I wanted you to go through with it, be who you are and be here if something went down."

"Never told him what?"

He hesitates, his brain reaching out a reassuring hand as if to calm me.

"This might not be the best moment of moments to give——"

"There's no other option now sailor. Now that the chicken pox has set in, we have no other option but to get scratching."

"Paton is not your dad."

I feel the world flip a bit and suddenly he's on the other side of the room, a hallucinogenic swat to beyond the fireplace, splattered against the door in protest. He's far away now, gone almost. Gone Boy.

"I know that you harboured real feelings for the man you never knew and died before you were born but he wasn't your biological father. Your mother, Janine, had an affair while they were dating and fell pregnant then tried to pass it off as Paton's. This was what finally drove him to murder Floyd and Bryan K, their fate sealed in his despair of finding out. Janine was his redemption as he hadn't killed yet, but this took away his final hope. So he murdered a Boyband. And pinned the entire thing on his boss, probably more revenge than cowardice. He left Janine with a baby inside of her, a girl: you."

# Chapter 70

# ME AGAIN

I've always found the concept of alone time bullshit. The presence of oneself is not a one-off, girls-spa, give-me-this-shielding-moment treat. It's forever. You're in your skin perpetually so essentially you're always alone, passing wobbles of skin, bone, gristle, babbling lips and pixelated brains filling the spaces around your person, unwanted buzzing flies that make you not want to run but stay and squash their brains in, between the balloon fissures of their arse pipes, so they never start buzzing near your alone time again. But alone time, as per American cinema, is a more solemn, sombre exploit, a reflective moment when, instead of your life flashing before, it meanders, a journey of gastric pulp slippy-sloppy-slappy-sliding in slow motion down the large intestine. I don't need alone time because I am the embodiment of alone time, but I do need a clearer picture now that my eyes hurt, are crusted over so I can only see through milky clouds and my dad is actually not my dad but a folk hero idol who failed at the moment it mattered most: being part of my genetic destiny, only to be replaced but some substandard generic office fling, his tie slung over his shoulder while he likely fucked my slutty mum after a drunken white wine spritzer or seven. Paton, no longer my spiritual Sherpa, now only connected to me in spirit, is no more than a faux pedestal straddling mythical criminal, and I worshipped him like some other fans you might have thought about (or not, don't care) for the past few chapters. I'm a Boyband Murdering groupie trying to Murder Boybands in the name of some Boyband Murderer whose seed got pipped at the post by someone as connected to Boyband Murders as that woman who nicked the original idea and wrote some fucking useless YA help a Boyband nonsense.

Finding a stream, a real stream not a stream of consciousness or a stream of pee, a literal babbling brook outside the house, down past the footpath entrance to the right beyond a small mound and a clump of wet hedges. I must have wandered, subconsciously heard the soothing dolphin-flap of water on other water and been drawn towards this hypnotic problem-solving real mirage. I can see myself in the moonlit water, my face a smorgasbord of purple and black and shimmering grey. I look funny like a distorted, disabled, comedian – or someone you might see on the electronic poster of The Undateables. I'm laughing out loud at myself and the laughter further exacerbates my facial distortion, so much so that I want to swan dive into the shallow depths (another paradox in the same paragraph! Shut the fuck up you worthy boasting so-and-so), swallowed up from this all becoming inane. Worthless. Worse yet: meaningless. And no knight or girlfriend in shiny amour to rescue this rescue mongrel (literally a mongrel – what kind of father did I actually have? Perhaps an ill one with three legs, but not Paton Stipps) and take me from the shelter to those rooms where they gas the canines, unwanted and unloved to the extent that being kind to be cruel is the only way humanity justifies removing the soul forever.

Settling for toes is scant reward … I lie, minor reward, the spaghetti tails of tepid liquid worming over my foot knuckles, a sheen reflecting from toenail to eyeball. Trying to 'think' is pointless, just like alone time, because you force yourself to adopt a resolutory stance on something that just might – like religious wars around the world – have no actual way of proving one higher being with zero scientific evidence of existence (EVER) better than other, the mere forcing of neurons to solve the dilemma making them sluggish and revolting in nature, preferring to insert sordid images of sick shit and sexy shit and weird shit that might never enter anywhere near your cranium, except in situations such as this. And yes, sicker, sexier and weirder than all this sickness, sexiness and weirdness we've – or I've – thrust upon a bunch of witless, unwitting celebrities, so confused at doing right that they end up feigning wrong. All the damn time. We are creatures, unable to control desires to dominate and force and prey upon our fellow man with woman, historically an easier target given our perceived lack of physical defence in a predominantly solved by violence end game. Which should make this all the sweeter, but somehow it just lacks the final punch, the final ribbon, the money shot that would have justified what stating a purpose meant, a true statement. The water doesn't even tickle anymore, my feet nature clean and exfoliated, the obligatory calluses layer the last bastion of protection against club feet concubine subservience.

I want to get sick, force this feeling out of me like the tequila worm in one of the Poltergeists. And it is not the moment of morality wanting me to about turn from my sisters-in-shame but, without the true perseverance, I'm irritated I might just go along with rape, body disfigurements and perhaps murder just because I can't really be arsed to turn this tanker around – really just too much of a schlep to talk each and every one of the seven off the ledge, so I'll smile and wave, the ultimate apathetic response, a go-along crowd pleaser too numb to say NO. Would no mean no to the girls or would no mean now? Who exactly am I saving by losing that final will, myself, my dead not-dad, a Boybander or seven or the ones holding the knives – the real reason I'm here? Solidarity is perhaps what steers a woman with water hydrated toes stewing in a one-way pot, taking one for the team, going above and beyond even if you've dropped your knife and the blade sinks down the river, comingled with your toe jam remnants and other general bacteria associated with the most overrated of body parts … feet.

*Chapter 71*

# Me Again Again

Is blacking out a thing? I mean not BBC or anything so
overtly anti-racist that Black Lives Matter so much that they
need to be paraded in front of gratuitous porn producers like
Donkey Kongs showing those well-raised US white girls just
how falsely loud they can make their fakegasms pitch should
the right brutha be ploughing away looking as interested as if
he were actually playing Donkey Kong. Is this still
shocking? Even though now our senses are so programmed
to boring IR sex that if we actually ever saw a white guy
involved we'd faint? But back to the actual blacking out, not
the blacking out of the scarce single-race act, advertising and
general lower-class act of fuck-you-father rebellion by a say
Ferrari, Candice, Chantelle, Cheryl, Chloe or Mercedes, but
a non-metaphysical losing consciousness for reasons other
than physiology. I think it happened. Time seemed to pass.
My head seemed to be still for an extended period. And when
I woke up I felt actual anger at society; yes it's that obvious

suddenly: chuck in a film rape or female abuse slash fear scene just to chew up time and pages and further tell every little girl and boy out there it is okay to abuse women. Like it is so frequent and so far removed from the narrative that, when it happens, most viewers actually switch off, more shocked when it doesn't happen. The screaming, writhing, struggling, distressed female under a male body or running from a weapon wielding fellow, chap, dickhead, baddie. And maybe this is what is irritating me so much and creating so much uncertainty about the next monumental step: merely switching places – making the Boybander as representative male the screaming, writhing, struggling, distressed victim is not enough; it's lazy. It needs to be more. Bigger. So that when any sweaty palmed 'celebrated' Hollywood scriptwriter sits down, dabbing the sweat from his brow and cupping under his dinky pinky thinking of how a female's fear of her body being somehow hurt by afore mentioned male character (even if the fucking antagonist!), a little red dot should appear at the side of his temple, followed by lots of reds dots on the keyboard then a splatter onto the iMac, because

IT
JUST
FUELS
THE
SYSTEMIC
HABITUAL
MALTREATMENT
Whoa! Using CAPS like that all on their own line is

seriously freaking liberating.  As I suppose is watching a bunch of Boybanders fight for survival in a bear pit.  Not the worst way to come to from a blackout – disorientating yes, but likely not as much as for the Boys when they realise the only way out, the only way to survive, is to remove the life from the fellow hip pulsator beside you.  Much debate preceded, surrounding shall we arm them, à la Mad Max Thunderdome style, and I'm sure you know where Gwynne stood on this one!  The design of the pit was quite special and lucky too, an outdoor area tucked behind the mansion near the vineyard – a too deep to climb out of metal bowl used for stomping on grapes.  With the ladders removed and the slippery nature of the metal there was lots of fun watching the blinking, semi-injured Boybands try to leap to safety as we circled the tank, laughing, baying and flicking cigarettes at them.  When they started the teamwork and formed a human tower to try get out, it got even funnier because a Boyband on another Boyband's shoulders is all very well but the height of the ground level was just out of reach and higher than a two-person job meaning they had to attempt the trio, the three-man pyramid with severe reluctance to be at the bottom.  So, even though we were armed with rowing paddles and cricket bats, we hardly had to employ any sort of 'back you devils' as the Boys, like the Middle East when fighting Israel in the 70s, could never unify long enough to mount a credible challenge.  And the wipe outs were truly spectacular with enough of their own body fluids to make it Total Wipeout, the bloody teared Boyband edition.  And remember the GoPros?  Still running.  God bless technology.

# Chapter 72

# THey want IT THaT way

Getting the band back together. Ah the relevance! The now of it all! Reforming the group after years of squabbles, estrangement and sulky fighting so that all Boybanders can link arms, sing We Are The World and not let go of each other EVER AGAIN like little Jacko number 5 with the discarded mudpie nose holding onto those trees in Earth Song. Watching all the Boys scrabbling around in a huge metal vat, nursing injuries and adopting the other's terror glances of what happens if hell's fury is scorned to the point of jovial psychopathy … so much God damn fun. As fun as say watching little kids spot their relatives at the airport and run to embrace, the sheer will of missing someone cherished, a more than equivalent match for any flimsy bureaucratic metal barrier. And this is the big misconception about blatant retributive psychopathy: you are allowed soft, touching moments that have an altogether different warming of your soul; as though watching the kids jump n' hug is that stewing all over chicken pot from your mum warmth and torturing a Boyband is more of a flame grilled double touch blue fillet mignon.  Each with its own merits of warmth and neither absolute as no one feels like a chicken soup when you've got a hard-on and equally no one feels like chateaubriand when you've just watched Marriage Story.

They're drunk toddlers, slipping and falling over one another as we unfurl our industrial strength sling shots (what do the South Africans call them – ketties?  We're marking them in the same way those robust Afrikaans kids would tally their bird kills or the lone Boer sniper picking off the vulnerable X marks the spot outnumbering red-necked Brit; notches on the handle).  But more on that later.  We're all – us girls – just standing watching the pathetic lack of fightback, Gwynne willing at least one of them to escape and make a break for it.  As though survival has become so removed from their pampered, social media, back-slapping, you're awesome Jonny culture that the actual fight or flight gene has been extinguished, stomped out by celebrity.  No lawyer or manager or publicist or tour manager or wardrobe designer or girlfriend to get you out of this one, with the significantly real threat of death whistling through the air past their ears, temples and eyeballs, clattering into the metal human boiling pot like hail.  Hapless Gerson and Digby run into each other, the inverse contrast almost poetic with Gerson's chocolatey brown covered skin high-fiving Digby's bleached white, a slap of bare chests echoing between the sides of the basin. Barton is crumbled in an imaginary corner, away from the confusion, having dragged his impotent legs behind him, a kind of adorning superhero cape that forms no useful function any longer. Damien looks the most disorientated, blinking in the harsh light, glass shards sticking from the side of his temple, cheek and hamstrings. He can't walk properly either with his torso wrapped in enough duct tape to cover the continents in darkness from moons and those two words confirm my worst (or at least medium) fears when I glance over at Gwynne smirking as she fires another snooker ball (pink this time) connecting with Damien's butt, dropping him instantly. He has an unwelcomed intrusion inside him, taped in prison confinement making both the continent and moon comments earlier sickly and gleefully relevant: his kingdom to be able to moon and the resultant incontinence viscerally visible. Some of the other Boys, although sporting their own afflictions, afford the time to twitch an eyebrow up and move away from the scene of Damien's crime. Francesca might be the odd one out, not visibly injured but walking in small circles muttering to herself dressed in Debz's clown garb, the fright enough to have perhaps persuaded Debz that her version of honouring her sons might stop at scaring to death. Sexton does though, in fitful bursts, keep grabbing at what is no longer there, likely conscious that even a world that rotates around the dastardly appendage can't be fixed by one. Kieron, holding up the rear, is covered in curtains of dried glue, a cushion or two permanently attached to his backside, complete with square pattered lines of blunt force trauma all over his chest and thighs, the blood capillaries fighting towards the surface, making his front look like the racing grids in Tron (the original). He finds Willow and they embrace pithily before realising they're still quite literally in the firing line, and we see each sidestep the other, roll and weave straight flat bang into a stone and a pinecone respectively. Willow has that crazy hair, dragged through a hedge backwards look going on but really because he has actually been dragged through a hedge backwards, his hair a nest of twigs, brambles, thorns and stubborn leaves. He's also lost his pants and capitalism's burning motif manifests in a circle of charred butt and upper hamstring body hair: the waterbuck hunkering on the white wet painted loo of the Boyband species.

We'd almost forgotten about the ketties too: beautifully and robustly designed in equal measure, Hannes the wizard building a bespoke leather strap for a smaller female forearm, for stabilising when aiming. The V part of the Y design was also custom-made, the arches wider and curving, the elastic made from graphene and the leather pouch to clasp the slug bigger than normal and coarser on the outside to allow grip. Hannes had insisted that with slightly less tightness in the elastic and a softer grip, the missiles would fly 'hard and true' and you know what – "Woah!" we all scream as Renea finds joy felling the muttering clown with an oversized marble – he was right. The weaponry had to suit the symbolism of the event so Jemima shot coins of various denominations, Danielle M&Ms and Tabby stones. Gwynne was launching snooker balls and Renea marbles with Maggie the godmother of the frozen green vegetables, in particular clumps of peas, and Debz an array of carefully carved wooden paraphernalia. But there are some occupational hazards with playing Boyband paintball-fish-in-a-barrel, notably that the competitive streak among us girls tends to spill over into hysterical, infantile 'I'm not playing anymore' territory and the boys can fire back, albeit with weedy arms and not much power but still, getting clonked by a wooden cock-shaped bullet is not much fun. Fuck me the hypocrisy!

Space invaders as men are our space invaders.

"Dance, monkey, dance!" shouts Jemima mic dropping another handful of one pound nuggets, Maggie enviously glancing across, adopting a foundational stability stance with one foot slightly in front of the other and spiralling a frozen chunk of broccoli into the back of Digby's peroxided neck. The black eight snooker ball whistles past my nose followed by a volley of red M&Ms (the surplus stash) with the fifth through ninth all melting into Gerson's person, a cartoonish Vietnam low budget death scene as his brown arms flail into the air, one either re-chipping his chipped tooth or blinding him in one eye. The girls channel an older, more sophisticated, nubile Lord of the Flies collective, the Boyband their metaphorical fire, dancing in slow motion between shots, screaming, jaw-frothing, spitting, celebrating, competing and – as a hopefully incarcerated R Kelly once muttered to his hapless Toine: 'There will be a lot of fine bitches with their hands all up in the air' – fixating on each other, scooping barrels of ammunitions from the surrounding bins and firing indiscriminately, a guided fetish on oneupwomanship to locate target, hit target, ruin target just like their victims' celebratory WhatsApps might have bragged to other males bout ruining her. The Boys, dazed flies in a closed jar, suddenly got full pelt frenetic as Tabby unleashed a fireman's hose onto Barton who might be dead – oh, wait he's not because the power of the hose pushes his into the side of the drum so that he sits up, blinking as the forceful spray blinds him and those around him. With the hose now just comes hurling – everything – furniture, stone gargoyles, broken cement slabs which allows enough distraction time for Digby to exit stage top of the pit, three slumped bodies his trampette, and make a desperate run for it. All heads enviously turn towards Maggie and she's on it like a flash, hopping on the ride-on mower and tearing after the ghost in the darkness, his white butt cheeks bobbling further into the distance, the daubed with green veg chlorophyll acne subterfuging him into the night's murk. Without being fully confident of what happened, it seemed that she managed to quite spectacularly mow him down just short of the lake because shortly afterwards she drove back up to the house with his white body draped over the mower like an antelope trophy. Without so much as a fling, she lifted him off the mower and dumped his flatulent body back into the pit, his ankles charred and sliced into shredded pieces of paper.

"Fatherfucker shouldn't have run," mutters Maggie, reassuringly restrapping the sling shot while stroking the cooling mower, her transportation cohort in vengeance.

"Is it time for a group sing-off?" says Tabby, turning off

the hose much to the Boys' relief, all seven slumped at uniform distances in the slushy, orange, debris-laden pool that's formed almost ankle deep.

"Or we could just fill it up and drown them?" says Danielle.

"Decisions, decisions," says Renea. "Like there isn't really a bad option here."

"My vote is sing-off," says Jemima.

"With the worst X-Factor contestant getting one of these," says Gwynne revealing a small crossbow from the treasure trove of toys behind us.

"Listen up!" yells Jemima, as the first hint of daylight sprinkles light spikes above the lake's horizon, turning the darkness a murky grey. "Calling all singers or supposed singers. This is your chance to impress; your one chance to avoid the penalty of being the worst singer of the worst singers."

As Gwynne loads a sturdy metallic arrow with a green, gold and orange marking at the base, the Boybanders shift nervously in the pit, reminding each other of the gym class student asked to volunteer for the cross-country race.

"If you sing well enough, you live," shouts Danielle. "Simple as pie. Ah, I could go for a bit of pie," she sheds to our reciprocating nods. "All this exertion has got me peckish."

"Think they've got some partridge and apple pies in the larder here," says a helpful Debz.

"Great shout after we've judged," says Renea.

"The song you'll be singing is *I Believe I Can Fly*," pipes

Debz.

"And if it sounds anything like the horrendous original, you get the prick ... of the cross," announces Maggie.

"Right so who goes first?" concludes Jemima, as the quickly infiltrating light reveals more of the broken horror in the pool below.

From the out of nowhere Barton, very much alive, belts out a growled death metal version from his inanimate body, the only giveaway of the origins his moving mouth and protruding vein in his forehead, earthworm like in width. His eyes remain closed yet the verve with which he belts out the "night and day" is admirable so we nod in unison and Gwynne points the crossbow elsewhere. Then Francesca's turn in falsetto defiance of Barton's death metal, commencing on a different verse so as to draw the poison-like attention elsewhere, the quiver of the high-notes so offensively off key we all tilt our ears to our necks in contempt. Then Digby raps a verse, throwing some shapes against the "keep me runnin – Usain Bolt ain't got nothing on this nigga – through that maofuckin dow" and it's all just too much for Gwynne so she shoots him straight through his thigh with the arrow, sitting him down with a scream and ending the R Kelly nightmare fow fucking eva!

It's light. We're hungry. And a bit tired. Knowing the crossroads is upon each of us, Digby's wound pump-pumping spurts of thick blood down his leg, the writhing rolling so authentically representing the searing pain, it's not at all overdone, unlike any Boyband performance preceding ... all this.

Sometimes just believing you can fly is not enough. No Lord of the Rings eagles to jettison any Boyband off to safety. This time.

*Chapter 73*

# MANTERRUPTING

Enough with the preaching. Enough with the self-doubt. A hard deadline was approaching and we all knew, departing from the Boyband stew, that it was go-time, equivalent lady part on the block time. Decisions, decisions! And no, I didn't just run to Kelly's Hero to escape the coercive push; my work was done in a way and yes, I did want to absolve myself of guilt and take no responsibility for what happened next but not because I'm a coward rather because what each woman did next would live with her for the rest of her life. And that memory, the feeling, that closure needed to be of each's own volition. Some I knew their fate, others not so much. The correlation of past abuse, hurt and perceived injustice at the gender imbalance played a part of course but in this final go round the Monopoly board this was that sexy lethal mix of impulse, victim's latest attempt at redemption and deep-seated psychological introspection. With Kelly not there my decision was avoided and the girls noticed I'd likely gone a tad mute for a while but with the baton firmly handed on as each dragged their counterpart back to the respective chambers of perturbational relevance, some kicking, most screaming, there was sense of finality in the air.

The fun was done.

Now Lucifer, Mammon, Asmodeus, Leviathan, Beelzebub, Satan and Belphegor all had to face judgement. The demons had approached the gate, each disarmed of his deadly sin and now stood in emblematic solidarity as the killer blow would or wouldn't be dealt. Me speaking in the affirmative or the deleterious would have no bearing on the inescapable outcome.

Even if I did have a few 'favourites' who were emerging from the suffering Boyband pile, I couldn't let my selective softness get in the way of the girls' tapestry.

Back along the corridor, the vapid stench of a dated, carpeted enclosed space apparent, making my way towards … just to see how he's doing. Moths could eat him you know, in his steadfast state. Around the corner Jemima, Renea and Gwynne are waiting for me, expectant, and I know this discussion even before it has taken place. Arms crossed, all three, bouncers, instructors, pupils no longer. My turn to take a turn.

"He must go," says Jemima.

"Heez gatz ta," chimes Renea.

"From this world we mean," concludes Gwynne.

"He saved us," your honour, I begin.

"He knows too much," says Jemima.

"He knew before. About everything."

"You won't have time to remove Kelly from the equation."

"He's tied tight. Plus this guy can help with that."

"When we started this," says Gwynne. "Yours was the biggest piece of the puzzle and now you don't even hold a piece."

"So you have to end him," says Renea. "To be a part of all this."

"I'm the one who never prescribed!" I find myself yelling. "This is your choice and my choice is not to end the person who helped us get to this point."

"The man."

"Irrelevant. Could have been a they."

"Either you're going to or we are," says Jemima. "This is your choice."

"He's fair game now that he stepped between you and a raping Boyband dick?"

"He's holding you hostage … emotionally. The real damsel in distress. Him being here kind of defeats the purpose don't you think?" asks Gwynne.

"What is the purpose then? Is it what I taught each of you or is it what you learnt yourself from your relationship? This was a targeted exercise where every chance was given to the other party to prove the stereotype wrong. But each failed."

"Except Kelly?" says Renea.

"And Old Spice on his white horse, resting his weary head while his princess debates the merits of him making it through this," says Jemima.

"What does that picture look like? Boyband slain plus

one? Oh and the plus one is a stand-up decent chap who happens to deplore masochistic behaviour and saved each of your ungrateful arses. How does the 'message' sit where an innocent dies?"

"C'mon bitch," says Renea. "They're all really innocent aren't they? We're the guilty ones. So guilty we don't even know why we're doing this anymore."

"I know exactly why."

"Daddy issues?" says Gwynne.

That bites. If there was an imaginary line somewhere in all this it has been crossed, been slaughtered beyond repair now.

"We've got four alphas at a crossroads here. We don't do the bravado, the low blow insults – this is not who we are. This is who THEY are, and not THEY as in every dangler funboy effing and blinding down the street carrying two point four kids in feigned daddy hell, but THEY that hurry, THEY that fake, THEY that only take what THEY believe is due. I don't want to have to stop any of you but if it means standing firm for what we believe in then I might. But you are all closer to me than sisters, closer than any bond and I want us to be united in this, but not in this way. If it means you all feel I'm not part of this because I'm victimless then tell me where and when and I'll dive in face first until I'm all in. We are all in this together but everything from now on has to be of free volition. It is too late for all of us to go back but there are levels of severity from here on in. The pain of the assault has subsided and not watching these Boys hop about in terrified solidarity is becoming tiring so we finish this. We focus our vitriol on the target we've been grooming for years, allowing inside us, letting them feel us – but we don't start a rampage against a person who helped us and supports the cause to the extent I do believe he's willing to die for it."

"Let's make him kill one of them then," says Jemima.

"To fully join the gang," says Renea.

"Or we have to end him," says Gwynne.

# Chapter 74

# FRancesca

According to Debz, Francesca hasn't moved for over an hour and her eyes are wide open staring at the ceiling. Is this the first actual red line through the name on the kill list? Post pool party, Francesca proved the most malleable, cast under hot Debz's spell and led back to the circus tent of a room now filled with an exotic assortment of the latest, most ground-breaking sex toys. The catalogue list Debz ordered from read like a foreign language, the assumption that we knew what, for example, a tenga or STU were either highlighted the commercial extent of the populous bored of old-fashioned missionary or our extreme naivety vis-à-vis the accessories now mandatory to ensure sharp outtakes of breath. This, according to Debz, was where it moved out of her control with Francesca, literally a bitch on heat, attempting to command each and every apparatus in a frenzy of trial and error. Mainly error though looking at her diluted pupils, bone dry and pointing slightly to the left like trees in the wind.

# How NOT to Murder a Boyband | by Jason Roche

Debz might have become a believer in fate as a result, never sure what the outcome would be but with an equal intent to follow through, to provide an outlet for Francesca's obvious hormonal overload both as Sexton naturally pre-procedure and then as the butterfly he hoped to become in Francesca, the latter likely through an overdose of progesterone and spironolactone to speed up the transformation, plus failing to block the androgen receptors. The passionate agitation had seen Francesca adorn a vibrating nappy-like contraption with a bolted lock, meaning when turned on and locked, the device would not stop until the power ran out. Debz was keen to point out that not much happened in the beginning but then, when the rodeo went full postal, her orgasms took on an exorcism motif, as though Sexton had been waiting his whole life to cum this hard. And it just might have killed her, Debz feeling absolved of any true responsibility yet equally satisfied at the result, the soothing buzz of the prison y-fronts reminding us in the background that sex toys should be operated with care, consideration and most importantly, concern.

## Chapter 75

# Danielle

A flurry of activity whilst the kitchen approaches: one of those Dolly Zoom effects where it feels like I'm face-still and the gaunt corridor in the lead up to the kitchen is morphing in unnatural movement towards me, the lit door of the kitchen the end square on a board game. The odour, wafting through, peeping around the corner then strapping on before Alien-out-of-the-chesting my nostrils, a familiar spiced cream with nutmeg and lime. And chocolate. But detached, not dissimilar to how a restaurant's bathroom smells different to the restaurant itself, the culinary expression betrayed by the intruding citrus chemicals, all holding pooh particles in workwomanlike solidarity.

"Someone's cooking good looking," I say before reaching the entrance as there's an innocuous shuffle of pepper grinder but no response. Danielle appears, to me at least, as I enter, her tired back facing me, sandwiched between me and the hob's brew. She's convulsing, ever so slightly, little hip-hop jerks of stomach into rib cage that I can tell (even from the back) shake her breasts like maracas. I go to her incisively and hold her from the back, her sobs bouncing me around in rodeo as the human contact sets the emotion hares felling to all parts.

"My baby girl. This is not something you have to do."

"It's not that," she responds.

"Let's raid the larder and rekindle Wednesdays by cranking open a few B&J brewskies; sure they have some of the old and news faves clattering about."

"Put mine on ice."

She wriggles free, not in a way indicating wanting free of me but one where I might just be that small hindrance that pulls her away from something.

"It's that I want this. And more. I've never wanted to go through with something more in my entire life. And the tears are because I cannot wait any longer."

As she moves to the side, two coarsely filleted pieces of raw rosy meat peer around her flank: two reluctant swimmers about to be thrown into the pan. With no lifeguard about. Unable to swim. The deep large diameter pan bubbles the creamy sauce into a froth, the lozenge black pepper flakes losing their heads below the surface.

*Chapter 76*

# UNCLE

Gluing to glue – or old glue – is harder than it appears. Harder to make everything stick.   Uncle's approach: fireman's hose volume until almost submerged into position, the slob-couch-cushions combo an antheap of glue, teeth, skin and furniture but perfectly positioned.  The first swat should have broken his neck given the ferocity of the connection but only succeeded in denting the target into the floorboards, a baseball hiding in a catcher's mitt.  So Renea ratcheted up the torque using the orange dial and adjusted the angle to swat at each limb in succession until the screaming stopped.  Not so ice cool, pissing ice cubes now are we Mr Jeans always too low?

*Chapter 77*

# GWYNNE

It's the cover of a nineties' album cover: smoking, wounded, bandaged, bejeaned antihero sweeps up rose petals. Well, he had to start somewhere and helping Gwynne's energetic tableau remain tidy, orderly and almost hygienic seemed just about the right place – a graduate placement programme for homicidal zealots. And the disguised subtlety of my approach after dragging (let's call him) Dougfred from his restbed onto a stage of torture, raised eyebrows not even allowed in the building through lowly inadequacy, then assigning him to Queen Wrath knowing that there could be only one dealer of the final pain blow in this corporate, and it wadn't gonna be no myan.

But fuck me this guy is helpful. Like if Fifty Shades was not only a master at getting us secreting flower petals 'wet' (try just not finishing the drying cycle on your pants), but was also a cleaner upper extraordinaire, as though him wearing only an apron and a toilet brush got me wetter than India in the monsoon season, all 390 inches per year of it. Swoon; he missed a petal and leans down to pick it up, flirting a glance my way. Need to piss.

Gwynne is wearing a spiked mask leaning over Damien, pushing the longest spikes protruding from the cheek regions into his regions. He looks unconscious, spewing a clutch of rose petals that have been 'forcefully placed' in his mouth. Some similar looking spikes have been forced through all his major muscle groups, his biceps, pecs, quads, lats, calves, traps, hammies and tris all skewered in likely protest against excessive steroidal gym work. Gwynne had instructed Dougfred to remove the duct tape container – his own personalised ManSize garment – from his torso and he'd dutifully obliged until they both agreed it was folly (God bless those product engineers) and whatever was trapped should remain *ad infinitum*. The unspoken elephant between the pair was what else had actually been going on underneath the tape but, really, God bless those product engineers for keeping it all under wraps.

Chapter 78

# Maggie

"I want what's she's having," says Maggie throwing something into Danielle's pan. Grooved in the middle, pink and dotty and pointed at both ends, the polar north not crusted in blood like the south. Danielle, whipping her head around as one might if your child was being snatched, retrieves the item and flings it across the kitchen back at Maggie.

"Whatever you do with your tongue, keep it to yourself!" yells Danny, Maggie simultaneously taking a low left-handed catch, clutching the item close to her chest.

"All I ever wanted was some of yours. How about adding an apple? I'll go get it."

Following Maggie up four flights of stairs to a now indelible room tucked somewhere in the south wing, Digby is rebound, whiter than before ... well, those bits of skin hiding amongst the burn marks anyway, a red and white giraffe pelt. His leg still has the arrow protruding from it and, true to form, the palette epicentre, a red apple hammered onto his remaining teeth. Maggie tweaks his nose shut, tightening both her fore and middle flexor digitorum profundus tendons aside his proboscis, until his flailing reaches crescendo then dropping the catch back in the water. His forked tongue is hopefully caressing the swollen apple in his mouth, Adam's true envy of Eve's plentiful supplies, and the marks on his skin where the bleach has irately reacted have sunken, making him wish he was one of the other Boybanders.

Gerson perhaps, all sickly-sweet smelling, covered in chocolate and in that key moment where certain parts have marinaded just impeccably and are ripe for cooking.

*Chapter 79*

# Jemima

The night air once again pinching at my nips. The lights lighting the crime scene flickering and Jemima's agitated perfectionism on display, lifting the arms, placing them around the tree only for each to flop back in wilting protest. Small droplets of sweat decorate her brow, so tiny that only someone who knows her well would be aware of their presence, hidden patterns, clues even in an intricate puzzle. Jemima's physical exertion has betrayed her usual poise, another attempt at each arm, pulling the fingers towards each other, the click of knuckles ignored but the same end result: Jesus pose on the ground beneath the tree rather than I will never let you go love song. Burnt currency flutters around him, Willow the money magnet, separating from his person then back again as though the wind is reluctant to separate the debris too far from its host. With his clothes burnt too it looks as though Jemima made him a sort of greedy treasure chest, stuffing his shirt, pants and orifices full of money then blazing up to watch the EcoGreed burn, watch the hypocrisy melt and erode, capitalism's next true victim: those believing that sustainability is anything more than a money-making scheme for those that will really benefit. It's unclear whether this was before or after she dropped the tree on him or perhaps even during. Frustrated, she departs, leaving me alone with the tree that refuses to be hugged: We Eez definitely Da Treez now. A twenty pound note oscillates past my tangential vision, distracting me sufficiently from the Ophelia scene below, the artificial light catching the remaining plastic sheen of an unburnt section of the note, Adam Smith's distorted half-eaten face giving me a raised chin 'what's up babe'.

Jemima returns, calmer, less apparent exudation, and nail guns each of Willow's hands to the tree, his palms lingering on the bark, fingers splayed in comely symmetry. Two loud, decisive shots in the lit dark, the hands' backs inversely first-Alien-film-male-rape-invaded. He doesn't flinch. There. Perfect.

*Chapter 80*

# TABBY CAT

The falling contraption is spent. Not necessarily through malfunction, just excessive use. Up, drop, down, reload. Up, drop, down, reload. Repeat. Again. Dougfred, swapping sins to support once again, gets a repeatedly descending Barton onto the platform – no mean feat, given his heft. Lifting a hessian sack of disjointed parts is likely even more troublesome than when they were attached, each part hopping over the edge of a straining forearm like an escaping jelly bowling ball. Tabby looks satisfied, content almost, and Dougfred nods my way when quizzically enquiring whether each and every setting has been explored. He stopped bouncing after the first two dozen or so which lessened the spectacle and, of course, made the wingman's job considerably more difficult, herding connected feline body parts. He looks tired too, as though the last few were really for procession rather than any actual upshot. Classic Tabby though, unwavering until the end, arms folded across her colossal chest, sending them face bound for one final excursion as she trips over the lifeless nineteen stone lump in distorted angles on the floor, his neck resting on the slant so than his swollen face appears to have twisted around to face his backside.

He threw down the gauntlet so Tabby threw him down, the plummeting, bullying, bulbous dewdrop seeping within his own skin, likely no longer comfortable in it and surely wondering whether it was too late to reach towards the humility circle of light.

*Chapter 81*

# THE DEADLY

"The death pact."

We all react, laughing, controllably. That feeling where you've agreed to something and now you're so far into it there is no turning back; the seal broken on the good, no matter how out of date or spoilt. Then to remorse, flicking the switch to cricopharyngeal spasms, hidden beneath a still intact exterior but fluttering in the austere comprehension that this was it; this was the end.

"So let's get the order right: Danny does Jem, then Jem to Tabby. Cat, Debz, Gwynnie, Mags, Uncle and lastly to finish off … Alura. Last woman standing."

"Not the first time you've finished yourself off."

Some stand-up chuckles at the back of the auditorium, late to the punchline, the reality more sodden than the quip. No one is equipped for this. Yet it must be.

"Dark Knight opening, bank robbery style, until Heath is left holding the gun and the loot. Everyone is whacked."

"Birtha takes out Saphira then onto Lucia who in turn takes Delilah. Then Jezebel blitzes Elvira and penultimately Aergia. Aditi, the mother of the Goddesses."

"So this is the last time."

*Chapter 82*

# GERSON

**Temperance** cures the excessive, relentless consumption of organic and inorganic matter by implanting the desire to be healthy, therefore making one fit to serve others.

The slight gap between fork and knife upon completion was the edifying irrevocable betrayal of etiquette and affront upon excess. As was leaving some of Gerson on the plate.

*Chapter 83*

# WILLOW

**Charity** cures the excessive pursuit of material possessions by placing the desire to help others storing up treasure for one's self.

No more trees died in the filming. Only two. Willow atop Willow. Jemima left the remainder of the unburned cash in the staff storage boxes.

# Chapter 84

# BARTON

**Humility** cures an undue view of one's self without regard for others by removing one's ego, pertinacious obstinance and boastfulness, therefore allowing the attitude of service.

Tabby vowed only to cum before a fall or never fall again. Barton, now a string puppet without the strings, could find service making a Geppetto somewhere happy that he was no longer a real boy, his nose, although in a new position, liable to never grow again. An unreal Boybander, wooden once again but this time malleable in putty-like service.

*Chapter 85*

# sexton

**Chastity** or self-control cures the uncontrollable sexual craving or desire by controlling passion and leverages that energy for the good of others.

Wanting one's self counted and Debz, harnessing the way Sexton would have come into this world, left him warming his hands down his pants, the stereotypical male pose so much more than anodyne hand warmth. Without their best reassuring weapon to provide clammy solidarity, Sexton was just another lost fiddler without a working violin to bow.

*Chapter 86*

# Damien

**Patience** cures uncontrollable anger and hate towards another person by taking time to understand the needs and desires of others before acting or speaking.

He looked peaceful, all intrusions painstakingly removed, the serenity of the extractions and considerate collaboration with the clean-up team of one completed in complete soothing silence. Gwynne left the corners of Damien's mouth nattily stapled to his cheeks, no longer glowering.

*Chapter 87*

# DIGBY

**Kindness** cures the intense desire to have an item or experience that someone else possesses by placing the yearning to help others above the need to supersede them.

A moose's head on a wall – even when slating the woke generation – is just too much, too cruel, too bullying. Maggie left a mounted Digby's splayed arse on a board for the trophy hunters to envy, above the need to light a wet wood fire in the fireplace, incredible how the bleach superseded the tension piles.

*Chapter 88*

# KIERON

**Zeal** or diligence cures excessive laziness or the failure to act and utilise one's talents by placing the interests of others above a life of ease and relaxation.

Those fat, lazy horse flies that never cared would never come in through the back sliding doors again. Washing the swatter, freeing the debris of bloodied, creamy, arse-through-brain mangled insect wasn't necessary; neither was wrapping the little pointless creature in three squares of loo roll and flushing it, cautiously not getting any of the shit-sitting residue anywhere near … anybody. The spray of arms, legs and wings could be left detached until the inclination rose above the festering, or so Uncle yawned.

Chapter 89

# DOUGFRED

**Preservation** or protection helps structure the forces of chaos such that when an inside king is required to step up in the aftermath at the end of all things, he will. Again.

He was made to run – in symbol more than threat – flee from the scene to save himself. He could have walked. Marduk, the hero preserving the order of the goddesses, presiding over justice, compassion, healing, regeneration, magic, fairness and – more important than all of that – the primordial chaos brought by my Tiamat, making clear the necessity of a protector deity.

Monotheism … we all hoped not, believing the Boyband debris would inspire a generation to be better, treat better, act better. Belief that there was more than one good man out there had supposed that the ringing in the ears was from the starter's pistol.

The women wanted him to run in his pants, so he threw on a pair of ManSize and disappeared into the sea of prodigious blackness, the matriarchal paradigm left baying and wolf-whistling.

# BREAKING NEWS

Transcript

Clive this story has been building on social media for some time but, until now, we were not permitted to report on it due to certain legalities and consideration for the victims' families, agents and image rights. But it has just become too large, too significant and too ingrained in what will likely be society's consciousness for many years to come.

The widely reported 'Haunted House of Actual Horrors' in Berkshire, where the grisly murders of members of multiple Boybands took place during a themed weekend excursion that got out of hand, is now the subject of a film anthology. And not an adaptation or documentary series either. Footage of the murders had been sensationally put into the public domain — professionally edited using the independent filmmaker's favourite software suite DaVinci Resolve — in the form of a seven-part trailer-series, originally released on social media. Given the graphic nature of the scenes captured mainly on the latest high resolution GoPro cameras, social media platforms banded together to censor and ban the teasers. But the damage had been done with both the excerpts and the hype generated from the news stories when the murders were discovered.

We interviewed a cross section of the population with resounding evidence that even those disassociated from the consequences were readily willing to jump aboard the growing bandwagon as some of the increasing swathe who have already downloaded the first two films ...

"I just absolutely had to see it, even though I knew it was probably illegal," stated a builder and independent property developer from Putney.

"It was just too magnificently shot, coloured and edited," said an indie filmmaker from Twickenham. "The narrative was amazingly captivating for what should have really just been a gorno," he continued.

"The graphic real violence aside, it spoke to me on so many levels," quoted a city banker and previously self-professed Boyband fan.

"Entertainment publications and institutions are calling this the 'day we saw real' and the day 'movies changed forever' — a 'new reality of reality'," from our entertainment correspondent Lizo Mzimba.

Distribution and access for the first film's release moved onto the Dark Web, with payment for downloading encrypted such that viewers could safely ensure anonymity but were required to fund through a new cryptocurrency that has now become a market watch item with MI6, the FBI and other world security bodies expressing concern at the sudden rise. The success of the downloads initially was picked up by entertainment trackers who charted the rise of the film, entering the Top 100 grossing films of all time across all mediums within a week of release. Once the second film was released there was no way to control the commercial success of the streaming with all major content providers such as Sky, Netflix, Amazon Prime and Apple TV as well as streaming services Hulu, Shudder, Sling, Peacock and Fubo moving swiftly to buy the commercial package and offer a sanitised, censored version of the films. Spokespeople for each platform would defend the decision against those claiming the footage glamorised violence against male musicians — Boybands specifically — potentially leading to copycat initiatives and a normalising of this type of reckless behaviour with impunity, by saying their public had a right to see what everyone else around the globe was queuing up to see.

## How NOT to Murder a Boyband | by Jason Roche

It had gone fully mainstream, and a quirk devised in the cryptocurrency model — likely by the perpetrators — meant the media provider purchase would push the revenue from the first two films way above the collective take of both Titanic and Avatar as well as, more recently, Avengers Infinity War and End Game, at an impressive £4.5 billion and counting, as the downloads continue and anticipation mounts for the third instalment of the franchise, simply entitled 'Manners Maketh Man'.

The end destination of the proceeds has come squarely under the spotlight, especially as the finest forensic and technological criminal investigators around the world grapple not only with who is directly benefitting but more pertinently towards the elephant in the haunted house — what became of the perpetrators, the women responsible for these acts of brazen savagery and destruction? The primary beneficiaries of the eye-watering sums generated from the distribution of the underground movie cult have been charities, most specifically women's charities specialising in not only remedying domestic and related violence but organisations which go one step further towards retributional consequences as opposed to merely throwing cash at abused females. The funds, likely cleaned through layers of illegal laundering, regularly arrive in each non-profit organisation's account, completely revolutionising the scope, scale and method or funding these types of crusades, making many some of the wealthiest charities in the developing world. The circulation to these women's charities has represented approximately 99% of the films' online and streaming takings, leaving the burning question of the remaining 1% with many certain that those accounts, narrowed down to either the Bahamas in the Sampson Cay vicinity or hidden somewhere between the Ronde and Caille Islands near the Kick 'em Jenny underwater volcano near Grenada, will lead to the whereabouts of the increasingly cultish, self-proclaimed heroines dubbed 'FeMANinisMAAMs'. Until then, viewers in their droves will likely continue to watch from the edge of their sets in horror, failing to sit back and failing to relax as a Boyband was murdered.

BV - #0098 - 061022 - C0 - 197/132/25 - PB - 9781803780986 - Matt Lamination